"Delany's forte has always been the creation of complex, bizarre, yet highly believable future societies; this book may top anything he's done in that line."
—*Newsday*

_____

"In its combination of imaginative reach and dazzling clarity of vision, this is surely Delany's best novel to date."
—*New York Daily News*

_____

"The novel marks a return to science fiction—to the galaxy-busting universes with which Delany first made his name. . . . This is an astonishing new Delany, more richly textured, smoother, more colorful than ever before. It is terse and muscular and explosive, and its author more in control than ever. It is Delany's first true masterpiece."
—*The Washington Post*

Books by Samuel R. Delany

FICTION

The Jewels of Aptor
The Fall of the Towers Trilogy:
   Out of the Dead City
   City of a Thousand Suns
   The Towers of Toron
The Ballad of Beta 2
Babel-17
Empire Star
The Einstein Intersection
Nova
Driftglass
Dhalgren
Triton
Distant Stars
Tales of Nevèrÿon
Neveryóna
Flight from Nevèrÿon

NONFICTION

Heavenly Breakfast
The Jewel-Hinged Jaw
The American Shore
Starboard Wine

SAMUEL R. DELANY

Stars in My Pocket like Grains of Sand

BANTAM BOOKS
TORONTO • NEW YORK • LONDON • SYDNEY • AUCKLAND

For
Frank Romeo

I planned and worked on early drafts of this book during a most pleasant term as a fellow of the Center for Twentieth Century Studies at the University of Wisconsin. It is a great pleasure to be able to acknowledge their generosity here, at the book's completion, many drafts later.

STARS IN MY POCKET LIKE GRAINS OF SAND

A Bantam Hardcover Book / December 1984
Bantam Spectra paperback edition / September 1985

Library of Congress Cataloging in Publication Data

Delany, Samuel R.
    Stars in my pocket like grains of sand.

    I. Title.
PS3554.E437S7 1984   813'.54   84-41580
             ISBN 0-553-25149-X

Published simultaneously in the United States and Canada

PRINTED IN THE UNITED STATES OF AMERICA

O   0 9 8 7 6 5 4 3 2 1

CONTENTS

WRITER'S NOTE

Stars in My Pocket like Grains of Sand is the first novel in an SF diptych. The second novel in the diptych is *The Splendor and Misery of Bodies, of Cities*.

—Samuel R. Delany

PROLOGUE

A World Apart

"Of course," they told him in all honesty, "you will be a slave."

His big-pored forehead wrinkled, his heavy lips opened (the flesh around his green, green eyes stayed exactly the same), the ideogram of incomprehension among whose radicals you could read ignorance's determinant past, information's present impossibility, speculation's denied future.

"But you will be happy," the man in the wire-filament mask went on from the well in the circle desk. "Certainly you will be happier than you are." The features moved behind pink and green plastic lozenges a-shake on shaking wires. "I mean, look at you, boy. You're ugly as mud and tall enough to scare children in the street. The prenatal brain damage, small as it is, we still can't correct. You've been in trouble of one sort or another for as long as there are records on you: orphanages, foster homes, youth rehabilitation camps, adult detention units—and *you* haven't gotten along in any of them. Sexually . . . ?" Lozenge tinkled against lozenge: the man's head shook. "In this part of the world your preferences in that area can't have done you any good. You're a burden to yourself, to your city, to your geosector." Lozenges lowered, just a bit: the man moved forward in his seat. "But we can change all that."

3

He pushed back in the sling that was uncomfortable and costly. A blank and intricate absence on his face, he raised one big-knuckled hand to point with a finger thick as a broom-handle—for the technology of that world still made lathes, lasers, bombs, and brooms: the nail was gnawed almost off it, as were the nails on his other fingers and thumbs. Crowding his wide palms' edge, whether flailing before him or loose in his lap, those fingers seemed not only too rough and too heavy for any gentle gesture, but also—though, if you counted, there were only ten— too many. The finger (not the fore- but the middle) jabbed brutally, futilely. "You can change me?" The voice in his nineteen-year-old throat was harsh as some fifty-year-old derelict's. "You can make me like you? Go on! Make me so I can understand things and numbers and reading and stuff!" As brutally, the finger came back against the horse-boned jaw: a mutated herpes virus, along with some sex-linked genetic anomaly, had, until three years ago when the proper phage was developed, rendered the ordinary adolescent acne in the urban males of that world's lower latitudes a red, pitted disaster. "All right, change me! Make me like you!"

Either side of a plastic diamond, the mouth's corners rose. "We could." The plastic swung with breath. "But if we did, then you wouldn't really *be* you anymore, now, would you?" From the black ceiling, through the orrery of masking bits, a hanging lamp dappled the man's naked arms. "We're going to make a change in your mind—a change in your brain—a very small change, a change much smaller than the one you just asked for. We're going to take that little knot of anger you just waved at me on the end of your finger, that anger you just threw back at your own face—we're going to take that knot, and we're going to untie it. Maybe thirty brain cells will die by the time we're finished. Maybe six thousand synapses will be shorted open and left that way. Maybe another thousand will be permanently closed. The illegal drugs we know you've put in your belly and your lungs and your veins over the past twelve months, not to mention the past twelve years, have already wreaked more biological havoc among your basic ten billion than we will, by a factor of several hundred thousand. Indeed, a side effect of what we intend to do is that you simply won't *want* any more drugs. You'll be happy with who you are and with the tasks the world sets you. And you must admit that, as worlds go, this is a pretty beneficent one."

He didn't know what "beneficent" meant. And though he'd heard that there were other cities (other than the three in whose slums and institutions he'd grown up), other counties, other geosectors, even other worlds with beings who were just not human, it all struck him as only dubiously credible.

Behind the mask with its plastic shapes a-bob, the man was saying: "It's a decision many men, not to say women, make. . . . Indeed, I read a report last week that said almost three times as many women as men on our world make this decision, though it doesn't seem my experience. The men—and women—who've made the decision we're asking of you include some fine folks, too: artists, scientists, politicians, well-respected philosophical thinkers. Some very rich and powerful people have decided to abandon their worldly acquisitions and come to the Institute here. They feel, I suppose, we have something to teach them. And though we certainly would never claim such a thing—our method is much too simple—perhaps we do."

"I can learn things," he suggested hoarsely, pulling back in the sling and looking down; for the tests he'd been given over the years suggested strongly that he couldn't. And the few times he'd hung around the places that were a confusion of books and tapes and films, they'd asked him to leave, or put him out, saying much what this masked man was saying now and saying it much more angrily. "I could learn if you taught me . . ."

"You've learned to beg. You've learned to steal. And I gather in the last year or two you've learned that, for you, begging is better than stealing because you haven't learned to steal well enough to keep from getting caught. That stands you in good stead here." The mouth's corners rose again.

Deciding it must be a smile, he tried a small smile back—an expression he seldom let hold his long, rough face for any time.

"As I said, we're not out to change the fact of who you are. We only want to change that small bit of you grossly unhappy *with* that fact. All right. Do you choose happiness? You have only to say 'yes.' "

He said: "Will it—?"

"Destroy your will? Oh, we don't do anything so simple or unsubtle. If you can make fine, fast, and fertile decisions now, you'll be able to make them afterward. You simply won't be inclined to make new *kinds* of decisions, at least without instructions."

He said: "Will it *hurt* . . . ?"

"Say 'yes.' There's no pain, I assure you—either physical or emotional. After all, what did you come here for?"

He said: "Well, yeah. Sure. That's why I—"

"Say 'yes.' We need a voiceprint of the actual word; this is being recorded. Otherwise it isn't legal."

Which confused him. " 'Yes . . . '? Yeah, but that's what I—" and felt something terrible in him pull away or something gigantic in him vanquished; and its departure or defeat was a relief or a release, which, because he had never felt *any*thing before to such an extent, seemed more something that hadn't, rather than something that had, happened: not an overwhelming occurrence to him so much as a total surround revealed—or removed. He asked, because the question had been struggling with the back of his tongue and came out through momentum rather than desire: "When you gonna do it?"

"We just did." (He really didn't want to know . . .) "You, of course—" The man laughed— "expected lightning to whip down from electrodes in the ceiling and crackle about your beleaguered skull—really, we *must* do something with that ringworm! I mean, on a young man *your* age? Actually, we use midrange gamma-ray lasers . . . but you wouldn't understand. Put your thumbprint here." From beneath the desk the man took out a yellow cube, extended it.

He reached forward to press the great sausage of his thumb on the transparent face.

"There. That gives the RAT Institute license to sell you to a labor project that, in our estimation, will be both profitable and humane. Let's see . . ." The man's other hand came up to scatter more cubes, clicking, across the desk. Lozenges dipped to study the inscribed marks: turquoise, orange, lavender. "You had a vasectomy in the orphanage back when you were—" he turned one to another face—"thirteen . . . apparently a reversible one, should you or anyone else want to bother. Well, though you're not likely to initiate anything in that department now, it's astonishing how many people still try to use slaves for sex. And we haven't done anything that'll stop you from responding—if your accustomed stimuli are applied. But that's no longer our concern." Lozenges lifted. Those over the eyes (purple left and green right) were transparent enough to see through to blinking lids. "You're as happy now as you can be, aren't you?" (The silence welling in him obliterated any need to deny; and, anyway, he had never been much for denying what was told him with sufficient authority.) "But I don't have to say that to you. You know it. If you'll just go through there . . . ?"

He stood.

On the arched door were the three hieroglyphs: *Radical Anxiety Termination.* In his search for the Institute, he had finally come to recognize them, though he still could not really read them, if only because—as a number of people had explained, patiently or impatiently, while he'd been searching—he could pronounce none of the three correctly, even after they'd been repeated to him many, many times.

He did not think this as he pushed through the flap, where, after waiting nine hours, he was given a shower with some fifteen or twenty others in a hall set up to wash hundreds.

Three hours later he was given a shirt too loose over his shoulders and pants too tight under his crotch, both of them as usual ridiculously short for his long, long legs and arms—he was just shy of seven-feet-four; and though on that world six-foot-eight or six-foot-ten was not unusual for a man or a woman, still all of that world's beautiful people (and the vast majority of its famous ones) were under five-foot-five.

An hour after that, in a narrow room, he ate a meal standing elbow to elbow with a number of others it did not occur to him to count at a chest-high trough—on him, to his ribs' bottom. They ladled up metal cups of lukewarm broth, drank, then ladled up more, drank those, ladled up still more. Some wiped where the broth ran down their chins with the backs of their sleeves. He didn't—because they hadn't changed who he was, and he certainly wouldn't have otherwise.

For five hours he slept in a blue dormitory with green plastic sleeping pads fixed permanently to the floor: in better condition than those at the detention house he'd been in three months ago, which was the last time he'd slept indoors. There the edges had been split, the stuffing soiled and lumpy. He looked at these, remembered the others, and was aware of no contrast.

For three days he was transported in a freight car through underground tunnels, during which time he was not fed at all—an oversight, apparently, from the resigned humor of the supervisor at the other end who discovered it: "Look, if you don't feed the rats, they ain't gonna scurry."

"It was an accident, man! Besides, I hear you can let 'em go thirty, forty days without food and they'll still—"

"Just do your job and feed 'em?"

For six years he labored among the dozen porters at a polar desert research station where, at the printed orders of the computer console in the research station vestibule, he carried small machines strapped on his side to an information relay outpost fourteen kilometers away; and carried papers and tapes back to the research station in a dark yellow canvas sack with a dim picture of a lizard in brown and gold above the self-sealing flap.

At the orders of the men and women who worked there, he dollied medium-sized machines up and down from the station's underground refrigeration crypts, where his bare feet left wet prints on the frosted metal walks, where the thrum of some machine down one of the storage corridors made a purple tubelight near the double doors flicker every time the mechanical hum suddenly speeded or slowed, and where the hanks of cable looping under the studded ceiling plates were nobbed along their length with glimmering transparent lumps called "ice"—which had something to do with water, though he didn't know what.

Once he was told to make a special trip at four-thirty in the morning out to the relay station to pick up some readings, only the man who told him was new and pointed in the wrong direction. He knew it wasn't right, but he thought that's where they wanted him to go anyway. So he walked for six hours while the sky went from starless black to cloudy red in flaming streaks above the sand, brightening to orange and becoming hotter.

And hotter.

And hotter . . .

They found him, sitting, his feet moving a little, one, then the other, as if still trying to walk, his eyelids swollen closed, his lips dusted gray, cracked here and there, the blood in the cracks dried to black, and the black dusted gray again, his huge hand over the embossed lizard, protecting it from the sun.

They had come after the bag, of course. It had a signal-locator built in that let them find it anywhere, and it might have had some things in it they needed. No one had known for sure what it contained when they'd discovered it was gone that morning.

They took him back too.

He lay on an old piece of canvas in the sunscreened rear of the transport with a wet rag in his mouth. One or the other of them took it out every few minutes and re-wet it so that he could suck it.

No one ever asked him why he'd gone the wrong way—though he could have told them. After that they just said he was very stupid.

Even for a rat.

One night during his third year there, three of the porters sleeping on the sand beside him began to shiver, vomit, and make strangling noises. After four hours, while he lay awake watching, first two, a few minutes apart, then half an hour later the third, died.

The next morning the woman first in charge of the station beat him with a steel pipe:

"You *brain*less, mor*on*ic, *worth*less . . . ! *Why* didn't you come *in* and *wake* somebody *up*! You idi*otic*—!"

The man second in charge pulled her away by her loose, sleeveless shirt. "Come on, now! Cut it out!" (Whatever had been done to him six years ago, though it had stopped any necessity to respond to pain with expressions either of fear or defiance, did not make pain hurt any the less.) "They only do what you tell them. Nobody's ever told this one anything about q-plague."

"Then what does he think the rest of us are all up here *studying* it for! . . . I know: he *doesn't* think!" Before her, plastic careened and swerved and rattled. "But seventy-six SI-units apiece those three cost me! And they actually had some skills." (By now he knew he'd only cost twenty-eight.) "Why couldn't *he* have gotten infected! He's been here longer than the rest. You'd think—" Then, not thinking, she struck him again, on the knee, so that he finally fell to the mottled thermoplast flooring, one hand over his bleeding ear, the other feeling around his agonized patella.

"Come *on*, now! Just leave him a—"

"What I want to know is how the virus got out into the rat cage anyway. I mean nobody was supposed to—" Then she turned, flung the pipe away—it rolled to clank the baseboard—and stalked off. The man second in charge put him back to work an hour later, where he heard three of the other men talking outside behind the station:

"Did you see the way she went after that damned rat? I mean I was just up the hallway when she lit into him, man!" (Rat was what you called someone who'd been to the Institute: man was what you called someone who hadn't.) "With a steel pipe! I thought she was gonna kill him!"

"It's working for a woman, man. That's all. I just never was that comfortable working for a damned bitch." (Bitch, on that world, was what men called women they were extremely fond of or extremely displeased with when the woman was not there.) "It just isn't right."

"Well, you know the boss. She's been under a lot of pressure, right through here. And I've worked for worse."

"I know, I know. Still, it gets me, to see her go after somebody—even a rat—that way." Shaking their heads, they went on talking.

Their lozenges tinkled.

He took down the work gloves from the rack of gloves along the hangar door's back and pulled them on. One fraying pressure bandage deviled the bottom of his vision along his right cheek. The other was bound just a little too tight on his left leg. He rolled orange-rimmed drum after orange-rimmed drum to stand beside the lift rail of the thirty-meter sled.

". . . as soon as a bitch gets any power, man. And with a damned rat . . ."

He walked back for another drum and did not think: They talk of me as though I were invisible. But as he tipped the container to its rim, he saw the woman (besides the woman who was first in charge, she was one of two others—excluding rats—on the station staff) who directed the loading. She stood about two meters from the men, a hank of strings hanging from her fist. Threaded on each were the dozens of tiny cubes about which were glyphed the loading, packing, and shipping orders for the station. She had turned her wire mask around on her head so that the intricate plastic shapes, translucent and opaque, hung by her ears.

Her naked eyes were green.

In the lined flesh about them (she was not a young woman, but she must have been handsome once, for she was not above five feet tall), he read an expression he recognized as one that had, from time to time, before all this, fixed his own face. (Since the vestibule console had been dropping its oversized message-cubes into his hands every morning, hieroglyph on one side, a simple picture explaining it on another, and on still others the totally mysterious alphabetics, he had been learning—for they had *not* changed who he was, and he had *said* he could learn things—to read.) He could not have spoken what was written in her face now.

"Hey, man," someone called to her from the corner of the sled, "you better check out your stacking schedule . . ."

What he did think was: a damned bitch . . . a damned rat. . . . He watched her watch him. Slowly she reached up. Strings swung, cubes *clisked,* plastic clattered as she twisted her mask to place. She breathed out, making no sound and taking a long time doing it. Then, wrapping the hanks of string efficiently around her forearm, she turned to go after three other rats struggling with a distillation unit just inside the hangar door.

He began to roll his drum.

In his sixth year there, an important personage came to inspect the station. He noticed, and did not think about, the titters and whispers passed on station rampways and at turns in the halls. ("I don't care *how* tall they look! You better stop talking like that, or somebody just might start wondering about *you* . . . !") The day before, the woman first in charge had suddenly resigned, and he had heard men talking in the corridors, behind purples and

greens and blacks and yellows: "She told him she was
going back south and commit herself to the rat-makers! I
mean, can you imagine someone who's reached *her* position doing *that* to themselves? She's got to be crazy, man.
I always told you she was crazy—although you have to
respect the bitch." And the other woman had left the
station a long time ago anyway.

That night, he turned over on the ground, waking, to
see the station's back door open on a silhouette in yellow
light. (Inside the station the halls were always illuminated
with yellow tubelights during the hot polar winter.) A
body-sheath of gold—possibly a silver that just looked gold
in that mustard glow—a tall cylindrical mask, black and set
with dozens of reception and projection lenses, black boots
with decameter-thick soles . . .

He did not know, nor did he wonder, which lenses
worked.

"Well . . ." The short laugh was mechanically distorted. "I just thought I would come out and see for
myself."

Around him on the ground lay an oval of blue, which
came from one of the lenses. At one edge was the foot of
the rat sleeping to his left; on his other side was the blued
elbow of the rat to his right.

"I always check with the Institute before I embark on
one of these expeditions to the outer reaches. Shutting
down a station like this, this far away from civilization, is
never pleasant. Still, you'd be surprised what you can find
in the rat cage if you look. For example, the Institute told
me before I came that you—yes, you—and I share complementary predilections that might have resulted in an
hour or so of pleasure for us both." The mechanical laugh
again. "I'm afraid, however, I hadn't counted on—" The
glow around him changed to red; nothing else happened—
"your looking quite like that. Your face . . . ! Well, I shall
simply retire to my rooms. And perhaps cut my stay here
short by a day or two. Sorry to have disturbed you. Go
back to sleep." The figure in the high-soled boots retreated, tottering, behind the door and closed it.

He lay on his back, curious at the warmth flickering
low in his belly, in his thighs, a flickering which, as he
recognized in it an almost forgotten arousal, ceased.

He slept. And woke with a gentle shaking of his

shoulder. He blinked in the orange dawn-light. A thick
sole rocked him back and forth. Above, the speaker-distorted
voice said: "All right, up you go. Time to get up." The
masked figure moved on to kick another rat awake, but
gently—which was not the way they kicked him awake
other mornings. "All right. Everybody up. Well, rats,
what do you think of the new job you're going to, hey?"
The figure stopped to brush sand off the shoulder of one
woman porter.

"Think . . . ?"

The figure laughed. "You *can* think, you know—though
they don't encourage it in places like this." In the tight,
metallic suit the man moved among shambling rats. The
cylindrical mask revolved. Lenses retracted; lenses appeared. Then the figure paused. "Didn't they tell you
yesterday that all of you had been sold?"

One rat said, "No. They didn't tell us."

The cylindrical mask revolved again. "I hate it when
they treat rats that way. It isn't necessary. They could
have told you. I hate it." A light behind one lens changed
from deep red to green, but under the streaked sky it
wasn't that noticeable. "Well you *have* been sold, the lot
of you. Most of you are going north again."

It was another underground station with sandstone
walls up to the wire mesh below the ceiling. The masked
figure was with them.

He stared at the lensed headmask, unblinking—not
feeling any of last night's lust but remembering it, wondering if it would come again. The creature behind the
lenses didn't seem to notice at all—until the car roared up.

"Okay, inside you go. Inside!" and the little hand
reached way up to give him a friendly push on the shoulder. "Sorry, rat. . . ." Then the door of the transport shut
behind him and he was in the dark with the others. (There
should have been some lights. But they probably weren't
working.) He nearly fell when the car moved.

Many hours later, they shot from darkness into pale,
blinding blue. With his eyes squinched against the glare,
forcing them open, closing them, then forcing them open
again, he realized that the curved roof and the upper half
of the walls as well as large parts of the floor were
transparent.

Between the rings that, every few seconds, flashed

back around the hurtling car, he saw cloud and, way below, rock. Here and there, something flickered as though the stones were afire. Hundreds of meters or hundreds of kilometers ahead a mountain wall drew closer, darkening.

Red and brown rocks towered about.

Moments before the car smashed into the stone-face, he saw the hole with still another ring around it.

Another rat in the car mumbled: "Another world . . ."

They plunged into it: darkness.

He'd known his world contained cities and sand. But the canyon, with its rocks and rampant clouds, made him, though he could not have said how, change his vision of what a world was.

After the ride there was another station, another shower. The man who ushered the hundreds of rats who'd been collected here into the hangar, under water nozzles along the ceilings and walls, stopped him long enough to say, "Jeeze! *You* look like you ain't been washed since you *got* to the Institute!" (The rat cage in back of the polar station, though it had been disinfected and deodorized once a month, had not had any water for washing rats.) After the shower they were issued more clothes. (The ones he'd been given back at the Institute had, down at the polar station, come apart, bit by bit, first at the places they'd been too tight, then all over, now a sleeve falling off, now a pants leg torn away; for the last year he and the other porters had done their work naked.) He was fed from another trough.

Under girders and wires and behind round windows that distorted things at their edges, he'd worked for three weeks at the industrial yard before he associated the frequently repeated name *Muct* with the unknown hieroglyph above the doors and on the first cubes of all instruction strings and stenciled in yellow on the brown and green enameled machines. There were seven engines from which he had to clean the soot and soiled lubricant that blackened his hands and stiffened his clothes. Unlike the polar station, here he was fed twice a day, washed every three days, and his work togs changed biweekly. Around him, thousands of rats serviced the great city full of machines, called Muct.

The man in charge, of him and some thirty-two others, told him many things, now about one engine, now

about another, told him the things softly, simply, clearly—
told him to remember them; and what he was told to do,
he did. In six months, he had learned how to drive two of
the machines and how to repair four others so well that
frequently he did not see the man who was in charge for
three and four days at a time.

Sometimes the man came in to where he was working, with another man who himself was being trained to be
a rat trainer: "Now who says they can't learn? Look at this
one here, for instance. You just got to know how to teach
'em, is all. They learn better than an ordinary man. I
mean, you tell them to do something, they do it. And they
remember it—*if* you tell 'em to remember. You just got to
know what to tell. I always say to you new guys, you tell a
rat to take a shit, you gotta remember to tell 'er to pull her
pants down first and then pull 'em up afterwards. Or you
gonna have a rat with shitty pants." (Most of the rats back
at the polar station and most of the rats at Muct were
women.) "But some guys don't have the patience. You
gotta be patient with a rat. Man, I can get these damned
rats to do anything a damned man can do. I can even get
them to do things you wouldn't think a damned bitch
could do. Once I taught a rat to cook food for me, just as
good as a man."

"Oh, I know women who can cook!"

"Well, yeah. But those were exceptions," the trainer
said. "And I mean, a damned rat . . . ?"

"What else did you teach her?" The interlocutor's
lozenges tinkled.

The man in charge, who didn't wear a mask (like a rat
himself), just grinned as they went out.

Sometimes between work shifts the man would sneak
several rats into his own quarters and tell them to do odd
things. Several times other trainers came and kidded him
about it or, occasionally, yelled at him about it. Sometimes
he kidded or yelled back. But he didn't stop. "I mean," he
said, "they all do it too. Even some of the bitches. It ain't
nothing. It goes along with keeping you rats in line. I
mean, what's a damned rat for, anyway? I ain't never
heard one of you complain about it—hey, rat?" And *he*
wasn't one of the rats the man took off with him, anyway.

He had a sleeping pad again. During those hours of
the afternoon or night when his shift was not working, he

sat on a long bench, watching a high screen, on which were projected stories about men and women who wore the dangling masks. Somewhere before the end of each story one man or another would rip a woman's mask off and the woman would turn her face away and cry. If the wrong man did it, the right man would kill him—or sometimes kill the woman.

A month after he got there, they fixed the sound on the projector; after that the stories made more sense.

He worked and watched stories for three years; then one morning the man in charge came to kick him awake.

He pushed himself up to his elbow.

"They sold you!" The man kicked him again, about as hard as he'd ever *been* kicked, so that he fell back down and had to push up again. "How you like that! They sold you out from under me! I've really *worked* on you, too, you mindless rat! You don't treat a damned man like that. You don't treat a rat like that, either!"

He thought the man was going to kick him again. But he didn't.

"They said they needed some rats with some kind of experience down in the south. You didn't *have* no damned experience when you came here. You didn't know a thing. Now you got some you can use to do something useful, and they're gonna take you off, who knows where, and use you for who knows what! It ain't fair, not after all the words I shoved into your dirty ears! It ain't fair!"

The man went away. But that evening, after work, he came back. "Come with me, now."

So he got up off his pad and went.

The man's quarters were not large. The other male rat and the five females they had picked up on the way almost filled the cluttered cubicle.

"Okay, okay, get your clothes off. Get 'em off, now." The man was tall (almost as tall as he was), and he put an arm around his shoulder. "This is going to be a going-away party for our friend here. He's been sold south, you see. He's going away tomorrow—and it's a damned shame, too. It ain't fair. So come on! Get your clothes off, now. Put 'em over there. There're some masks. Put 'em on—no, on your *head*, shit-for-brains! Come on, you been here before. You remember now, for next time. Put on the masks; then you can feel like real people for a while." He scratched his ear. "I don't think it does a damned rat no harm to feel like a real bitch—excuse me—" (to a rat who'd dropped her splotched tunic to adjust a wire head-frame from which more than half the plastic pieces were missing) "—or a man. Myself, I think it makes 'em work better. And it don't hurt 'em much, don't care what they say. . . ."

That night he was told to do some odd things. ("I want you to do just like you'd 'a' done at this kind of party before you come to the Institute. Exactly like it, you understand? You can use that one, or that one, or that. Only not her—she's my favorite, right through here, you see? Unless of course she's got something you really like a lot.") The man in charge never did put on a mask himself. For much of the evening he made love to one of the masked women while the other masked male struck him on the shoulders and buttocks with a piece of frayed copper wire and called him "a tiny rat" and other things.

There *wasn't* much he'd have done at this kind of party except sit, watch, and bite at his cuticles and nails. (As a boy he'd been to a couple like it.) So that's what he did. After half an hour, the man in charge, who had spatters of blood all over his shoulder blades by now, looked up and noticed. "Okay, then," he said. "I want you to play with yourself until you come. You too—" which was to a female rat.

So he did.

It felt astonishing and surprising and pleasant—the most powerful thing that had happened to him since the moment he'd said, "Yes," at Radical Anxiety Termination. When the man in charge sent him outside to go back to his sleeping pad, the female rat had not finished.

The next day some women in plain beige face-covers got him and took him to another station where he was put on another car. Days later he got out at a station with sandstone walls, wire mesh on the ceiling.

Among the men who came to pick up the six rats who'd been delivered, he recognized one: and after a few minutes, while he was checking them for hernias and bad teeth, the man recognized him. "Hey, this one was here six years ago!" he said to his companion. "A real idiot! *He* couldn't do nothing right! I think they sent us the wrong rat! The order was for rats with some experience of what

we were doing up here. But I didn't mean just any rat
who'd *been* here before and couldn't *do* anything!"

"What're you gonna do? Send him back?"

"Naw. We can use him for porter work. That's what
they used him for before."

He worked at the polar station, which had been re-
opened, doing pretty much what he'd done—carrying the
bag back and forth to the data station—for seven years
more. Lots of things were different, at least at first. There
was another man in charge. Though he didn't know exactly
what, the station was now studying something other than
q-plague. Now there were several large, spidery instruments that sat out in the sand with great arms yearning
toward the orange sky. And the wall behind the rat cage
had been painted blue.

For a while the rats at the station were given clean
clothes each month or so. But they missed the laundry
more and more frequently. One morning, when their clothes
hadn't been changed for three months, a man came out to
the cage. "Okay, come on. Take 'em off. We're going to go
back to the old way. Naked's better than walking around
in that stuff." Feeding went back to once a day after that,
too.

Coming back across the sand, by the power pylons, he saw
the green transport sled and walked by its high, sand-
scarred flanks into the station vestibule to lift up the
lizard-embossed flap of his canvas bag and empty the
elliptical spools of data tape into the receiving slot. About
an hour later, someone called him and three female rats
into the office of the man in charge.

Years ago, it seemed, he'd been in the room to take
out tubs of old message strings and bits of discarded packing foam. Today the walls were blue, like the back wall of
the rat cage.

A very tall woman sat on a cushion on the black tiled
floor, one sandaled foot on the desk's lowest shelf. Her
heel had overturned a stack of multicolored cubes. Some
had fallen to the ground.

"You know that what you're asking is illegal."

The woman made a barking sound, becoming a laugh
that would have set her lozenges shaking—only for some
reason she'd taken off her mask and tossed it on the tile so

that the colored bits lay in a tangle. "You think a bitch like
me doesn't know that? Do you think a bitch like me would
come in here and ask what I'm asking of you if this station
were three thousand kilometers closer to the population
belt?" She pulled her foot off the shelf. It dropped to the
black, along with three bright cubes. She smiled, as if she
knew that behind his plastic bits the man currently in
charge smiled back. "What kind of bitch do you think I
am?"

"I think—" The man coughed. "Well, really, I don't
know why I'm doing this. It's irregular—"

"I only said you should bring them in and let me look
them over." She drew her heel back to the cushion and
put her arms across her knees.

"And I have." The man coughed again. "I have. There
they are . . . but I don't know why I'm doing it. It's
irregular, and it's illegal, and—"

"I'll tell you why you're doing it." The smile softened
on her dark face. "The economy in over a third of the
equatorial geosectors is failing. Neither the political swing
towards the extreme Yellow, the insurgent Crazy-Grays,
nor the Free-Informationist backlash is going to mean a
return to the soft-money economy that will benefit any of
the polar projects, north or south. I took a look at the
shape your rat cage was in before I came inside. Hot stars
and cold magma! You men haven't been properly staffed in
three years, and getting rid of another mouth to feed—
even a rat's—is going to be more help than hindrance. You
know it. I know it. And that's why you'll do it—"

He didn't know why she paused, but he expected her
to pick up her discarded mask and put it back on now:
that's what the women on the projection screen at Muct
had always done after they paused meaningfully. But that
had been years ago, somewhere else in the world.

This woman still smiled, face still bare.

The masked man behind the desk took a silent breath.
White hair moved on his chest under his shirt's soiled net.
"You're quite a woman."

"I'm quite a bitch." She threw back her head, and her
hair, which was dark and wiry, did not swing. "That's how
you'll say it when I'm gone. Say it to me that way now."

Behind the swinging fragments, the man coughed
again. "Well. I guess you are." He rose, stepping from

behind the desk. "A bitch. At any rate. These are the ones
I can let you choose from."

She turned on the cushion, rising to her knees. She
had an expression of great concentration now, an expression the women in the projected stories never wore. After
seconds she stood. "I told you I was interested in males."
She touched her chin with her fingertips, moving them a
little as if scratching some half-felt itch. She was a good
head-and-a-half taller than the man in charge.

"Well, we have more females here." The man
shrugged. "These are the ones we can spare."

"Mmmm," she said, as though she knew that already.
Then she said: "Which more or less limits me to this one.
Tell me—" She turned to face him— "are you ready to
come away with me to strange climes and stranger lands
and be my slave forever, to obey my every command, to
fulfill any and every whim and caprice I should articulate,
no matter how debased or lascivious?"

He did not know what "articulate" or "lascivious" or
some of the other words meant. "Yeah . . . ?"

The man in charge coughed once more.

The woman chuckled over her shoulder. "That was
mostly for your benefit. He isn't exactly what I pictured, I
admit." She turned back, reached forward, touched his
naked cheek, grimacing as if she questioned some terribly
important point to which he was oblivious. "But you'll do.
You'll have to, won't you? It's cut into your brain now,
that you'll do . . . do what I say." Her hand fell from his
face, a finger brushing his collar bone in the fall. "How
much do you want for him?" She turned to the man in
charge and, stepping over fallen cubes in her scuffed sandals, took out a coil of silver string from her leggings
pocket and began to unroll it, silent lips counting the
evenly spaced black beads along it to which cubes could
be clipped.

The man mentioned a price so far above twenty-
eight-SI units, he simply decided that they weren't discussing him after all.

The woman kept wrapping silver around her fist, kept
counting. Finally she popped the credit cord, rolled it
from her palm with her thumb, and put the SI payment on
the desk. "You know you're overcharging me by even

more than some black market slaver might in some mildewed equatorial bazaar." She still smiled.

"You know," the man said, "the only reason I'm doing this at all is because—"

"—is because you think you can get away with it." She put the remaining credit roll back in her pocket and bent to pick up her mask with a swipe of her arm. "That's why I'm doing it too." Lozenges clicked and tinkled on tangled wire. "Would you like me to take him out the back? We'll attract less notice that way."

"Yes," the man in charge said. Then he said, "Just a moment." He reached behind the desk, opened a lower file, and pulled out one of the yellow canvas bags with the embossed lizard. "He can put his things in this." He handed it across the desk.

"Thanks." She took it and slipped the strap over her arm. "This way?"

"Yes," the man repeated. He came around to the front of the desk to pick up the cubes she'd knocked from the desk shelf. He knelt. "The back way. Yes, that would be best."

In the narrow hall with the badly tacked up roof repairs shredding above them, she asked: "Do you *have* any things to take with you?"

"No. . . ."

She looked down at the canvas bag hanging at her hip and shook her head. "The condition your cage is in—" She gave a bitter grin— "I'm not surprised." She put one hand on his peeling shoulder as they walked out the three-layered hangings at the hall's end that kept in the cool air.

Over hot sand the sky was a hotter orange.

She walked with him through the heat.

Sand streaked between the evenly spaced bolt heads; the transport's green metal wall dropped its shadow over them. She opened the door in the side. "Get in." She followed him up and closed the port.

Tossing the canvas bag into the clutter behind them, she slid under the padded restraining bar and into the seat. She reached forward to rub at a smudge on the transparent sandshield with three fingertips pressed together. "Sit down."

As he sat beside her, she asked, "Did you know you

have to sit down, in these things here, before I start driving?"

"Yeah."

She sucked her teeth in mock disbelief, pulled some lever sharply down, kicked at some pedal under the instrument board. A motor began to rev, then, at another pedal, to rumble. "Have you any idea why I bought you from the station, there?" She heaved the steering bar around. Outside, the world turned slowly, then began to move back. The transport shook across the sand in a direction he'd never walked before.

"No." The seat shook against his back and buttocks.

"Oh. Well, you will." She turned in her plush seat to face him. "I think the first thing is to get you washed down. I read that if I got one of you from any but the big industrial complexes up at the equator, that would probably be the first thing I'd have to contend with." She frowned. "Tell me, do you know how to use a sonic cleaning plate? That's what I've got in the back."

"No."

Outside the plastic windows long dunes shifted. Her look grew puzzled then, oddly, nervous. She gave a little laugh. "You don't?" The self-assurance from back in the station office had fallen away somewhere, as if in their short walk across the sand, pieces of it had shed onto the desert. "Well, do you at least know how to use a damned squat-john? All I need is to have you pissing and shitting all over this hulk like it was your putrid rat cage—" Suddenly, with the thrust rod in both hands, she leaned forward, her face between her arms, and began to shake. She took great breaths, and he did not know if she were crying or laughing. "What do I think I'm . . . by the hot stars overhead, by the congealed magma, oh jeeze . . . ! What do I think I'm—it's crazy, I . . . I can't, I—" Possibly steered by its automatic mechanism, possibly not, the transport moved on.

"Yeah."

She looked up. There were tears on her face, and great confusion under them.

So he told her again: "Yeah."

The grimace again. "Yeah, what?"

"Yeah, I can use the john."

She held the rod, looked at him, and finally took a long breath.

"But they didn't have one at the station. For rats. So they told us to use the cage. Then we slept in it—"

"Jeeze . . . !" she repeated. "All right, when you have to," she said, with another breath, "please do. Use it, I mean. The john in back, there. I . . . I know I've got to tell you everything. And tell you very clearly. For heaven's sake, I've got a whole carton in the rear compartment full of instructions on how to handle rats—and I've been afraid to read more than a cube or two of any of them for fear I'll come across some incontrovertible fact that'll tell me this whole thing just *isn't* going to work! And then—" She looked away, glanced back, looked away again— "I've got this machine that's supposed to make all those instructions unnecessary anyway, or close to it, and—" She took another breath— "and I'm terrified!" She blinked at him, dark eyes near the surface of a dark face, while he tried to remember which emotion terror was. "I mean, if you could only. . . . I mean, could you— If you might just put your arm around me, hold me—firmly, and perhaps even love me just a—love? Oh, what am I *talking* about! If you just wouldn't *hate* me—"

She stopped, amidst her uninteresting (to him) confusion: because he'd moved over on the bench, put his arm around her, and held her, firmly.

"Shit. . . ." she whispered. After a few moments she asked: "You don't hate me for making you do . . . this?"

"No."

Outside the windows, near dunes moved quickly before distant ones. On the instrument board, red and yellow needles quivered on blue and black dials.

She put her head against his shoulder, took another long breath, then raised her head again. "Then I guess anything's possible in this man's universe, right?"

He didn't answer because, again, he didn't know. But she didn't hit him or yell at him as had often happened back at the station and sometimes even at Muct when people got upset around him.

What she said finally was: "Well, I guess there's nothing to do but get on with it." Apparently that meant, for the next five hours, driving over the beveled sands. Ten minutes into them, she said, gently: "Take your arm away now and sit back where you were, please." So he did.

An hour after that she said:

"You know, even with two families in Kingston and three very fine jobs that took me back and forth over almost half this world, from Ferawan to Gilster—do you know, I was miserable? Miserable! I thought about suicide. I thought about becoming a rat myself. I went to the Institute once, sat there for a whole day, watching one pathetic creature after another push in through that black leather curtain and not come out. I must have put my own number back and taken a new one from the end of the list over a dozen times, before it hit me: I don't have to *become* a rat to solve my problem. I could *get* a rat. For myself. I mean, that would have to be better. For me, for what I wanted. So you see . . ." and was quiet, then, for more than an hour.

Then she said: "Look at the way the light glitters on the grains caught at the edge of the sandshield." She nodded at a corner of the window. "And there, at the horizon, sometimes you get that same, vaguely prismatic effect, a kind of colored glitter in the basic tan—like you do when the grains are up close. That's because human beings are the basic height we are—if we were less than one meter tall or more than three meters tall, it wouldn't happen—and because this world is the diameter it is, so that the horizon is the distance away it is from people who happen to be about as tall as we are, and because the average sand crystal here is as big as it is and because the atmosphere filters out the particular frequencies it does. One of the two great poets who came in the second colonial ship to this world noted the phenomenon, worked out its parameters on an early computer, and said, in a beautiful poem, that this effect would define the lives of humans here as long as we stayed. I suppose he didn't realize how fast there would be sandless cities all around the equator. You know, I learned the poem by heart when I was ten, but I never saw the actual thing itself until three months ago, when I took this transport and struck off from the population belt here toward the south pole. And now, though I remember the poem and the story about it, I can't remember either the poet's name or the poem's title. Do you know—? But no, you wouldn't know things like that. Not on this world. Still, it's a beautiful thing to watch and realize that someone else, two hundred fifty years ago, watched it too; and thought it was beautiful."

And hours later she said:

"This is crazy. This is more than crazy. It's stupid! If they catch us, I don't want to think about what'll happen. What I want, you're just not supposed to have, here. I never thought of our world, with its endless deserts and orange sky and multilayered equatorial cities and great canyons and underground waterways, as coy. But it is! It makes slaves, then says that individuals can't own them, only institutions—because somehow institutions make slavery more humane! Well, I *want* a slave, my own slave, to do exactly what I want, the way I want it done, without question or complaint—a slave to do what *I* want to make *me* happy. The Yellows are going to win this coming election. I know it—everyone knows it! Well, *we're* heading for Gray territory. We'll hole up there for two weeks. After the election, during the resultant confusion in the Gray sectors, records will vanish, order will disappear, and who knows what moments of freedom might occur in the chaos or for how long they'll hold stable. Happiness! Yours?" She grinned at him. "Mine? No, not yours I guess. But if I could, I'd *make* you free—before I made you serve me! I really would. Only I can't. So the only thing left is for you to make me free." She snorted. "Or happy. Is it the same thing? *Is* happiness slavery? That's what they tell you at the Institute, isn't it? Slavery is happiness. Accepting slavery, becoming a rat, is happiness. Well, I don't believe it! I don't believe it at all! And even though you're a slave, I hope you learn that! Learn that from me. I swear, if I thought I could teach you that, I'd turn you loose this instant and be on my way. There *are* some things more important—than I am, to me. Nobody else believes me when I say it. But it's true. Do *you* believe me—? No, don't answer. I don't want you to say anything now."

Later she said:

"I have this machine—have you ever heard of GI? General Information? Tell me: have you?"

"No."

"Well, I'm not surprised. It doesn't really exist on this world. It does up on others, though. They've even got it on our larger moon. But they've legislated against it here, planetside. Oh, there're other worlds where it's common. Can you imagine? Living on a world where, if you want to know something—anything, anything at all!—all you have to do is *think* about it, and the answer pops into your head? That's supposed to be how it works. Even our Free-Informationists are scared to go that far. They think we'd slide over into Cultural Fugue in a minute! Well, we just might anyway, the way this world rolls. But you see, I have something that does almost the same thing. It's even more illegal than stealing you—they'll call it theft, you know, if we're ever found out. I had to come near killing three times to get it. And worlds with as many ways of killing the mind as this one has don't take kindly to killing the body. Anyway, around the population belt there're lots of computer-generated data broadcasts all over the place. Some of the sorting and decoding is a little difficult, but with some of the standard encyclopedic programs and . . . it's for you, you see? Do you understand why?"

"No."

"Well, I suppose I don't, either, really. But some people think that the only thing you lose at the RAT Institute is information—not just facts and figures, but information on how to process the information you have, how to deal with the new information that comes in. And if you can replace or supplement . . ."

She stopped again.

She looked at him a while.

Then, without talking, she drove some more, like someone who'd been telling a very complicated story about themselves only to find, in the middle, they did not believe it either.

Hours later, she said:

"When I was a kid, my family co-op broke up, and I got shipped off to a platechtonics study group in the north—because none of the adults really wanted to take all those seven- and eight-year-olds with them. I've read that *most* worlds where humans live today are basically deserts, of one sort or another, like ours. Wet worlds are rare, and us human beings are supposed to have come from a world that was largely water. That's why—at least I used to think so when I was nine—it seemed the most colossal waste to live in the middle of a huge industrial tinkertoy where every day I offered my minuscule help to the basic project which was pumping millions and millions of gallons down into the fault lines in order to hydraulically relieve the pressures that built up and caused those catastrophic monthly earthquakes the northern mountains were so famous for back in the days of the first colonists. I mean, though we'd just about stopped the earthquakes, nobody *lived* there. Anyway, at night I used to ride out on a sand-scooter from the compound into the desert—a very different kind of desert from here, with purplish rocks all over it, and little scratches on them that for a while made the geologists believe there might have been life on this world before we humans got here. In the north, sometimes you get breaks in the second-layer cloud level; and when it happens at night, you can look up and actually see stars—other suns, where you know, with some of them, other worlds are circling, where other humans, and maybe even aliens, are living in entirely different ways, in entirely different cultures. I would park my scooter in the dark, climb up in the headlight glare onto some slanted rock, lie down on my back, and gaze at a star. Even with the platechtonics station relieving the pressure by pumping all that water, you still got little rumbles and quivers every few hours or so. Sometimes, I'd feel one underneath me while I lay there in the night, and I would think: suppose the platechtonics station just broke down, and there was a pressure buildup along some major fault line, and suddenly we had one of those giant earthquakes we used to scare each other with, telling stories about when I was a child at the equator—an incredible earthquake, where the whole skin of the northern desert was cracked up and hurled into the sky, and me, lying on my rock, I'd be hurled up with it. And suppose I was thrown so hard I went up into the night, all the way to one of those stars, one of those other, better, different worlds. . . . At nine, I thought they all must be better than this one. I really used to want it to happen, in some kind of vague and awful way. And I also used to wonder, lying there, searching for holes in the nighttime clouds, if there was anything that I, nine years old and alone in all that desert, could think or do that, without an earthquake, would actually *reach* one of those other worlds and change it, affect it in some way so that everyone on it would look up and realize that a world away something as important as a

great poem had been written or a new technological
infrasystem had been solved . . . poems and infrasystems,
that's what we studied at the platechtonics station when
we weren't pumping water. At nine, I didn't even know
that more than half the people in the population belt of
this world probably didn't know what a poem or an
infrasystem was! Today, I wonder what all that childish
night yearning did for me. Gave me grandiose ambitions, I
guess." She laughed. "Only not so grandiose anymore. I
don't want to make another world sit up and take notice—or
even this one. I just want a little pleasure and satisfaction
in my own . . . world? Should that be the word for it? I
don't think so. Maybe if I hadn't wanted so much as a
child, I wouldn't have wanted . . . well, you. Today. This
way."

He didn't know what a poem or an infrasystem was
either, but for some reason the memory of the canyon,
with its rocks and clouds he'd once shot through, returned. He tried to put both words with the memory, as
he had once tried to speak properly the signs, *Radical
Anxiety Termination*.

She frowned—possibly because his lips were moving,
in much the way that, years before, his feet had gone on
shifting in the sand after he could no longer walk.

She pulled the braking lever. Through the sandshield,
brown and red evening reached in to color dials and
switches.

The transport stopped shaking.

The desert stopped moving.

"Well," she said for more than the fifth time, "let's
get on with it."

Sliding from under the restraining bar, she pushed
some small bubble-switch with a foreknuckle.

Behind them, six metal bars fell into the floor, and
the bottom of the left wall swung out an inch. Pneumatic
arms on the ceiling flexed, and the wall swung up to make
an awning over the sand.

Heat slathered in over the top of his foot, flopped
against his shin, slid in between his fingers spread on his
knee. Then, under the awning's shadow, sand divided as
though a blade, parallel to the floor, had sliced it, as some

force shield went into operation. The regulator thrummed; cool returned.

"Come on," she said.

He turned in the chair, not knowing where she wanted him to go.

The wall-become-roof shaded a flat of sand scarred on three sides by the shield's bottom.

She walked to the cabin's cluttered rear, tugged aside one carton, pushed another with her sandal toe, stooped over a third, and pulled out a circular plate with worn straps on one side. Slipping her fingers through, she stood and walked back to the middle of the studded floor as, plugged to some many-jawed connector on the plate's rim, the pink cable dragged from the carton, flopping coil on coil. "Well, let's get—"

She paused. Then, with a frown more to herself than to him, she said:

". . . I mean, get up from your seat and go stand out on the sand there."

He did. It was a jump. The sand inside the shield markings was cool.

She came to the floor's edge, and stepped down the half meter, awkwardly, one knee stretching her frayed pants there, her other foot making a wide print, sliding where it landed.

She walked towards him, fingering the plate.

A coil flopped over the floor's edge to mark the sand.

"This may tickle." She did something with two fingers at her wrist; the plate hummed.

He watched her pass it over his shoulder. It more than tickled. It burned—for a moment, then reduced to a faint vibration in the skin.

On his shoulder where she'd brushed was a streak of gray-brown powder, which she beat away with her free hand, revealing clean, red-brown skin and its feathering of hair. "My lord! You *are* filthy!" She moved the plate down over his arm, around it, beneath it, brushing the powdered dirt and skin away. "That's amazing. I honestly hadn't realized you were that color." Her skin was brown with little red at all.

She rubbed the joint between his upper and lower arm, now on the blackened elbow, now on the crook where veins wriggled across the high-standing ligament, banded with paler creases—till, with the third pass, it was all one color.

She rubbed his hand, the back, the palm. It made the sides of his fingers itch. Once she turned the plate on its strap to the back of her own hand and took his two great ones in hers, stepping away.

One arm glowed clean in evening light. His other was the fouled grime-gray that, since his return to the station, he'd never thought of as other than part of him.

"Rats aren't supposed to forget stuff they knew before they went to the Institute. Do you mean to tell me you've *never* used one of these before?"

"I didn't . . ." he began, unsure if the question was about meaning, telling, or use.

" 'Let's get on with it . . .' Your father never called you in from some social therapy group like that? Where I grew up, that always meant to a kid it was time to come in and get clean—with one of these."

"No." He frowned at her, realizing she wanted something more. "Didn't have no father." But he wasn't sure if that would do.

She dropped his hands, stepped up again, reversed the plate again and moved it over his cheeks, his hair, his forehead. With a quick turn she troweled its edge along the crease beside his left nostril, beside the right, now up behind his right ear, behind the left, across his eyebrows— "Close your eyes." (He already had.) —brushing off the slough every two or three passes. "Pay attention to what I'm doing. Because I'm going to want you to do the same thing to me, later. Having someone give you a clean-up like you were a little kid is the most sensuous thing in the world, I think." She passed the plate on to his chest, down his stomach, along his hard, dry flank. "Does it feel good?"

"Yeah."

She gave him a grin and a small push on one shoulder. He sagged backwards a little and came forward again. So she said: "I meant, turn again."

He started turning.

"Eh . . . stop. With your back to me. No, like that—"

The tickling dropped down one shoulder, began again along the valley of his spine, then repeated down the other. It moved about one hip, circled on one buttock.

And stopped. "Wait a minute." She stepped past him.

He watched her put the plate down on the transport floor and climb back in. Again she squatted in the shadowed clutter. When she stood, stepping back to the edge, she held a . . . black, ragged glove? "We might as well try this, too." She jumped to the sand with the awkwardness often shown by the very tall. "Hold out your hand. No, the clean one."

His knuckles were large as sun-wrinkled fruit, his wide nails still as gnawed as in childhood.

Both forefingers in the wrist opening, she slipped the glove over his hand—not really ragged. It had been slit in a dozen or more places, the bands held here and there by lengths of metal fixed inside. He felt them slip over his fingers' broad crowns, his knuckles, under his palm's callus.

Elastic bits stretched.

His hand distended the bands as far as they would go, so that what had been a glove was now a web of black ribbons across the rayed ligaments that ran from wrist to knuckles or over the veins that raddled across them.

"Let me turn it on now—" which apparently meant snapping the metal clasps together at his wrist:

What happened next was fast and complex, but he followed its parts as though he were being patiently taught and rehearsed and taught and rehearsed again in their workings by the most skilled Muct instructor.

A pedal voice— ". . . stupid, stupid, stupid . . ." —that had begun sometime in unremembered childhood whenever he'd been asked questions he couldn't answer, that had continued whenever he'd been asked questions he'd had to answer "no," and that had finally come whenever he'd been asked any questions at all or even had to ask them, suddenly became audible. A tiny voice, still it had insisted as relentlessly (and as unobtrusively) as his own heartbeat, at least since the man in a circular desk had told him to say, "Yes."

But the reason he heard it at all, now, was because another voice, which felt and sounded and settled in his mind as if it were his own (but *had* to have come from somewhere else), suddenly took that small voice up and declared: ". . . stupid," on the beat, and then went on, off the beat and overwhelming it: "stupidity: a process, not a state. A human being takes in far more information than he or she can put out. 'Stupidity' is a process or strategy

by which a human, in response to social denigration of the
information she or he puts out, commits him- or herself to
taking in no more information than she or he *can* put out.
(Not to be confused with ignorance, or lack of data.) Since
such a situation is impossible to achieve because of the
nature of mind/perception itself in its relation to the functioning body, a continuing downward spiral of functionality
and/or informative dissemination results," and he understood why! "The process, however, can be reversed," the
voice continued, "at any time. . . ."

The plate circled his other buttock. He felt her slide
the edge between them. She paused a moment and said,
"Jeeze . . . ! I never . . . well, I guess they just didn't
think about toilet cloths for you guys out in the cage!" But
what he was much more aware of was that they stood in
some tiny, shielded space of coolness on a scorching desert, over which, if you went long enough in one direction,
you'd encounter a magnificent canyon, while if you went
in another, you'd find a huge city with filthy alleys and
deep underground passages and the RAT Institute in it,
while a journey in still another would take you back to the
polar station; and that there were tunnel tracks between
them—he knew all this because someone he didn't remember had once mentioned in his presence that his
world was round; and knew also that he could go to any of
them, because he knew how to drive this particular transport: its controls were identical to one of the ones whose
workings he'd been patiently and repeatedly taught, along
with its care and maintenance, by the man in charge back
at the Muct.

Another voice, begun even further back in childhood,
had, in the interstices of ". . . stupid . . . stupid . . ."
been muttering, "I know . . . I know . . ." And though the
man at the Muct had reinforced this second voice by
telling him, "You know this, now. Remember, you know
this," he had never really heard it before. But it too
became audible because the strange voice that sounded so
much like his own took it up: ". . . I know, knowledge:
another process, finally no different, in its overall form,
from the one called stupidity. Information is not taken into
the human organism so much as it is created from the
strong association of external and internal perceptions.
These associations are called knowledge, insight, belief,

understanding, belligerence, pig-headedness, stupidity.
(Only social use determines which associations are knowledge and which are not.) Only their relation to a larger,
ill-understood social order decides which categories others
or yourself will assign them to. . . ." And he understood
that too! Like a genius, he thought; and amidst this new,
responsive excitement, the disgusted comment of someone to whose care he'd been briefly entrusted when he
was ten came back: *Well, he's sure no genius!* "Genius,"
the new voice took it up, "is something else again . . ."

She said: "I guess it doesn't make too much difference, does it?"

Her cleansing strokes against his thigh, his shin, were
firmer.

"No . . . yeah . . . I don't know . . ." He looked
down at her bushy hair, on which was a powdering of his
scurf. "I don't know how to say."

Frowning, she sat back and looked up.

"Not 'no.' " He said: "I . . . know. . . ." It took an
astonishing effort to put words to that internal voice while
the other drummed (". . . stupid . . . stupid . . ."), meaningless now, yet no less insistent for its meaninglessness—an
effort that made the back of his neck, his inner arms, and
the rear of his knees moisten, not with the sweat of physical strain, but rather the sweat of fear—though fear, along
with pain, was something he hadn't been afraid of since
the Institute . . . no, he did not know how long ago now.
Nor did he know how he might create that information
from what, as yet, he had in mind. "I know," he said, out
of momentum, "but I can't say." Though that was a response to something his mind had abandoned . . . long
ago, it seemed.

Long ago.

She sat back on one knee, with her powdered hair,
looking at him with a series of slightly changing frowns,
some of which called up expressions he'd seen on other
faces from so long ago there was no way to remember what
those frowns meant nor what their order might signify,
though their opaque suggestion without resolution seemed
marvelous and baffling.

"Do you *feel* any . . . different?" she asked.

"I don't know how to say," which sounded hugely and
hopelessly inadequate (". . . stupid . . . stupid . . .") so

that he turned to some ancient feeling in him called rage
that welled through his body but, because of what they
had done to him, connected with nothing, breaking instead like a water jet in some city fountain, reaching its
height to fall in white foam, flashing drops, gray spray, and
falling, falling . . .

Rage, which he could name now, had been erupting
at least as long as the voices' drumming.

"Ah . . ." which was more guttural than the syllabic
with which it was written—the words moving through his
mind were *all* attached to a bevy of written signs! "Radical
. . . Anxiety . . ." he whispered, and took a breath; "Termination . . ." pronouncing the three words clearly, seeing
the three supernumerary hieroglyphics that supplemented
the syllabics and alphabetics which, till now, had merely
been marks on cubes that danced on the fountain's ever-
shattering tip.

She blinked. "You mean that it really . . . ? Well, I
guess the transition must be kind of . . . difficult!"

He watched her decide she could not comprehend
what he was going through. Those were the words that her
frowns, finally, had led him to. She went back to cleaning
his thighs, his genitals, his shin, his ankle.

"Transition," he repeated. "What is . . . ?"

Stupid, stupid, *stupid,* it roared, because he was asking a question. Not to know, to have to ask, was stupid,
stupid, even while the new voice explained, yet again,
that that was knowledge. But—and this came with words
too—whatever the glove had done had not changed who
he was any more than the invisible gamma lasers had
changed him years back; and for nearly fifteen years now
he had been a man who was not afraid of the most astonishing and monumental inner occurrences including his
incomprehensible stalling in the great desert of no occurrence at all. He asked, "What . . . is transition?"

"Change," she answered thoughtfully (though the glove
had already told him), running the plate's edge under the
inside of his foot's ball, then the outside, then beneath his
toes. "It means change. The change you must be going
through is probably quite hard. I think your feet are
beautiful." She brushed them off. "I've never been much
of a foot fetishist, but I've known a few who were. Here,
give me the other one."

He did; and gave her also, "I have to use the words I already have, to speak." He gave it because he heard silences around him in a new way now, as though voices moved and pulsed in them that wanted words. To listen to those voices and speak them was easier than remaining silent before the older, ritual drummings. "The new ones, like 'transition,' take time to . . ."

She blinked, surprised. ". . . settle?" she offered back. "Settle in place?" She stood.

Settle wasn't a word he'd used often and not for many years. ". . . to settle," he said. "In place."

"I think I . . ." she smiled—"understand." Taking up his other arm, she passed the plate down it, and down again, now over, now under, brushing away powder, now brushing her own hair.

Powder lay in a ring on the sand about them.

"What is it," she asked, "that you want to say?"

". . . didn't have a father," he repeated, because something brought back the words he'd said before—the momentum that had impelled speech since his arrival at the Institute, if not before.

⎰I know.
⎱Don't want to know.

The doubled voice made a stutter in his mind, in the middle of which, between *know* and *want to know,* desire for knowledge bloomed and fountained and obliterated rage, to which, at the instant each question posed its interrogative tingle, the glove responded with a million tastes that, on no diet at all, he'd never known existed; he shook his head to get away from their overwhelming bitternesses and sournesses and saltinesses and sweetnesses and burnings.

She dropped his other hand, clean as the one in the glove now. "What is it?"

"I think," he said, "in this world it is very important not to have a father if you want . . . to know anything."

She gave him her most confused grimace. Then laughter broke through it (while his own mind began to catalogue reason after reason why his statement had been preposterous, meaningless, inaccurate, interesting, suggestive, insightful, right, wrong . . .); she said, "I think that's very wise. Only I haven't the faintest idea how that could have come into your head. I mean now, here. Nobody mentioned fathers to you. What are you talking about?" But she was pleased. "Here," she said. "Please . . ." slipping the plate off her hand. "Please, I want you to clean me now." She looked back and forth between his hands. "I guess you put it on the . . . Well, no. You decide."

He took the plate and slipped it over his bare hand, recognizing and wondering at the approval that wrote itself from bottom to top of her face. (Moments later he realized her approval was because she most likely thought the gross currents in the plate might have interfered with the workings of the glove had he put it on the other hand; she had taken his choice as sign of the glove's success.) He felt a small surge of pleasure at her response, even as the glove informed him by a series of angular pronouncements and diagrams, slapped blindly across his mind, that she was wrong: the glove contained enough stabilizing circuits and bracing units so that it would not have been bothered by the plate's impedance at all. The pleasure was as unconnected as the still towering rage—yet he enjoyed it even if enjoyment meant as little as the rage did.

He reached for her shoulder with the humming plate, brushed her shoulder with his other hand—but nothing much to brush, which made her laugh. Anyway, she'd brushed every two or three passes.

"You do that very well." She closed her eyes. "Almost as well as I do. And that's nice."

". . . good," he said. In her smile and closed eyes there had been a request (rather than a question) he could not read; and for years he had been someone who'd feared questions and answered requests.

"You're *not* the same rat I brought from the polar station!" Suddenly she opened her eyes with a kind of delight. "You know that, don't you?"

"I'm the same," he said, and was confused because that wasn't what she wanted, but what she wanted was not what he knew. He ran the plate's edge beneath her left breast, then her right: she took a surprisingly large breath and closed her eyes again.

The strap was very tight around his hand.

The upper part bare and the bottom part in pants and sandals, her body was oddly interesting. There was a small scratch on her ribs, and he realized he was unused to seeing scars on women's bodies. Certainly in the rat cage and in the city he'd seen injured women—but the women in the projected shows at the Muct were never scarred, so that the . . . stereoptical view (and *that* was suddenly a concept he understood well enough to make a metaphor out of it—and metaphor was another concept, a stereoptical concept . . .), which that gave him, blended to blur the real through the idealizations/flaws inherent in any representation.

All sensations, as well as the faintest memories associated with them, were given a word and three written versions of it, in syllabics, alphabetics, and ideographs, each of which dragged behind it connections, associations, resonances. . . . He'd known about the ideograms and the alphabet; but he'd never known his written language included syllabics before.

The new condition was not so much an alternate voice loud enough to drown the voices of childhood as it was a web, a text weaving endlessly about him, erupting into and falling from consciousness, prompting memory and obliterating it, that was simply more *interesting* than the drumming voice asserting or denying ignorance or knowledge.

She said, "Remember, you're cleaning a truly extraordinary bitch. I want you to do exactly what you'd do if a beautiful . . . female asked you to clean her—before you went to the Institute, I mean. Wait a minute—" She reached down and unsnapped her pants, letting the flaps fall open, pushing them down her hips a little. "And you can pretend I'm wearing my face," which was what, in that language, the wire masks were sometimes called: though he'd never known that before. (But the glove now told him.) "Myself, I can't stand the things. So I don't usually wear—"

The feeling was in his body; and perhaps he moved his body, in the course of moving the plate over her shoulder, to locate the feeling more clearly; discomfort was the word that joined it, followed by a correction: sexual discomfort.

"Yeah," he said, knowing as he said it that it would also not be what she wanted. So he changed it to, "Yes," a form of the word he hadn't used since that day at the Institute.

She frowned at him. (She too must have thought it odd.) "Don't tell me you got to the Institute before anybody ever got to *you* . . . ?" She touched his face. "The scars there, from the epithelial herpes—you must have had it rather badly. Frankly, though, you see so much of it these days, once the actual sores are healed, like yours, I find the pits and texture rather attractive." She paused again, dropped her hand. "How old *were* you when you went to the Institute? I know they don't take you under fifteen. . . ."

"Nineteen." He lifted her arm as she had lifted his, to clean beneath.

"Just how many sexual encounters did you *have* before you went to the Institute?" She still frowned.

The rush of accurate memories, enhanced by verbal tags, produced a strain he hadn't known since becoming a rat. "Fifty. . . ." The strain made him speak slowly, while the figure was corrected within the muscle of his tongue: "A hundred fifty . . ." which was obliterated by more fragment memories, averages, extrapolations, approximations. "Maybe two hundred fifty. Maybe more."

"Well!" She laughed. "You certainly outdo me! I doubt I'm *that* much younger than you, and I think of myself as quite a sophisticated woman—with a mere twenty-seven men behind me. I don't have to worry about *your* knowing what to do with a bitch!" But the frown battled through. "How many sexual encounters have you had *since* you went to the Institute?"

"One . . ." he said after a different rush of words, of concepts, memories of the little man in the tall mask, the tall man at the Muct, of approximations no less complicated than the others for all the difference. "Two, maybe. You're—maybe—the third."

"Oh. Well, like I said, I want you to do whatever you would have done in any of those situations." She closed her eyes. "You can do what you want. Anything. Anything at all. How does that sound to you? No, don't answer."

He lifted her other arm, trying to understand, in the play of signs, memories, and facts that stuttered about the glove, what answer she might want. The silence that for years had hung about words uttered in his presence filled with ordered comprehension. Yet there was another silence, a cube bare of all inscription, outside the answer she'd made clear she did not need or want, that as clearly was wanted, was needed. Many people purchase slaves for sexual reasons, the man at the Institute had said. Recalling it now, however, was his new knowledge's result, not its cause.

"Do what you want," she repeated. "You'd better do it, too." She closed her eyes again. "Because, afterwards, I intend to do *just* what I want with you." She opened them, frowned.

He said: "I'm not . . ." The word rocking his tongue in his jaw's cradle was one he'd heard before but, like so many, had never tried to say. ". . . Not het—heterosexual." As though the glove responded to his difficulty, a host of colloquial synonyms flicked up from his hand to beat about his head. "A front-face . . ." He said that one, while the list continued: *a quick-in-and-out,* which was a term he'd actually used before he'd come to the Institute, but was not one he would ever have thought of using *to* one of them, even a bitch. So instead he said one further down the list: ". . . not a stiff-stuffer—"

"Yes?" she said, blinking. "Oh, shit . . . !" She took the smallest step backward, small enough so that the glove said it was the swaying of a larger than usual breath coupled with the slightest movement of one heel, but— because he had not changed—he chose to read it as a stepping back. "Wouldn't you know! *My* luck. . . . No, you don't have to say any more!" Then she stepped six inches over sand toward him.

He swayed, moved his heel. But did not step back.

"Look," she said. "Whatever you are, you still *know* what a dog would do!" And "dog" was a term he'd occasionally heard that some women used about men when the men were not there; but of course no women had ever used it to him. "You can do it . . . ? Sure you can! Go on. . . ." Here, she grabbed her breasts and pressed them upwards, which he found both confusing and distracting— though moments later he remembered one of the projected stories at the Muct where a very bad woman had made something close to the same gesture.

The glove had nothing to say.

So he did what she asked.

Surprisingly, it wasn't hard, as long as he stayed relaxed; and staying relaxed in the face of most things had been assured him at the Institute years ago. To do it, he just had to think about the same kinds of things—indulge the same fantasizings, the glove offered him as paraphrase—he would have with a man her height. Still, his erection was something of a surprise to him. Moments before he came, she suddenly pushed him off, rolled him over on the edge of the transport flooring (that's where they were lying), and demanded he be still—though he wasn't moving—while she unplugged the plate and hit him on the back with the end of the wire. What she wanted to do, it seemed to him, was not much different from what the man at the Muct had wanted done to him. Still, he did not find it pleasant. And it distracted him from all sexual thoughts, so that for a while he tried to stop thinking altogether.

With the glove, though, that was impossible.

She lay against him after a while, holding him tightly, which was uncomfortable because of the edge of the transport's floor under his hip. When she got up, she was breathing hard. "You can get up too."

So he did and turned to her. Some of his blood from the little nicks had smeared over her breasts and down her side. She moved about uneasily, teeth now and again clenched. "No . . ." she said several times. "No, that wasn't quite. . . ," And once, suddenly staring at him: "More than two *hundred* . . . ? I've only had a chance to do *this* maybe three times in my *life!*" She took a breath. "So you can't blame me if I don't get it right the first time, huh?" After that she climbed back into the transport. He stood looking out through the force field at the sand, smeared over in long streaks now, messy with sunset, till she called him inside and put down the wall.

He sat beside her, watching the instruments' glow, green on her neck, under her chin, on the roofs of her eyesockets. Outside cloudy night rushed them, split by headlights, to slap to at the side windows.

He thought: She's tired.

He said: "I'll drive for you."

She glanced at him. "You know how to drive this?"

"Yeah."

"Is that the glove?" She touched an auxiliary current knob as if to adjust it, but didn't. "You're not supposed to have any skills at all, they said at the station. Those were the only rats they'd sell."

Through wired velvet, dry flesh between, with wide fingertips he felt his knuckles. "I can drive this kind," he said. "I learned before . . . before I came back." Then he said: "They didn't know, though. They never checked . . . my records."

"Part of the Free-Informationists' platform in the upcoming election is: 'To be a slave *is* to be used inefficiently.'" She grunted. "Inefficiency. That's what *they* think is wrong with slavery." She pushed some pedal; some gear below engaged. "I wish they were more of a threat. But they haven't got a chance. I mean . . ." She paused, long enough for him to decide she'd stopped talking. Then she said: "I mean even me. I didn't want you here to drive. I don't need you for porter work. And if you hadn't put on the glove, you probably never would have said that much about yourself and I'd never have thought of using you as a driver. I want you for one illegal, very selfish—and, now that I know the kind of pervert you happen to be, very inefficient, I suppose—reason. . . ." In the dark, she laughed. Green shook on the underside of a breast, a nipple, her collarbone, chin, lower lip, septum. She was like a city, entered at night, created of small green lights—which was a memory from age fourteen, when he'd been running away from some place or other again, a memory that had remained as the canyon he'd shot through had remained, but which he hadn't been relaxed enough at the time to understand because the man driving (as she drove now) had been *so* much shorter than he was.

When he was fourteen.

She said, shocking him because now he had some comprehension of shock's sexual nature: "I wish you were about two and a half heads shorter. They say all bitches ever think about is sex, you know . . . ? 'Think about; and never do.' Which is what everyone else says. Well, there *is* one other thing I want you for—" The bits of light on her changed position hugely as she yawned. "One other thing," she repeated, "before I let you drive for me. Maybe this is just as inefficient. But since that damned

glove works, I might as well." She made a gesture with
her chin over her shoulder. "Back there I've got a carton
of catalog cubes from the Inter-Sector Broadcast Library."
She lay two fingers on his gloved hand. "Thanks to that,
you're tuned into the compressed textual band. Do you
know what that means?"

"No."

She snorted. "What are the four largest geosectors on
this world?"

"Abned, Rhyon, Cogonak." He paused to question
why she wanted to know. "And Emenog . . . ?"

She answered: "That's the sort of question any bright
twelve-year-old in this world—with the right education—
could answer. Though he probably wouldn't have given
them in ascending order of size, the way you did, but in
the order they were established—"

"But you asked which were the biggest—"

"Which are the four smallest?"

"Mesetin, Hebel-E, Tinert, and—"

"—and Eudo is *the* smallest," she said, while he said:
"—Eudo."

She said: "*Every*body knows Eudo's the smallest, of
course—don't ask me why, it's just one of those facts—but
I don't think anybody but a professional geographer could
tell you the other three. You see, in terms of data at hand,
right now you're on a par with the Skahadi Library itself—"
which, when her tongue lifted for the initial sibilant, he
had never heard of before but which, by the time it fell
from the final vowel, he knew had been founded in '12 in
Lower Cogonak, back when it had still been officially a
part of Abned, before the Severance Decision of '80—which
was when the Yellows had won their first major electoral
victory. "You're in touch," she explained, "at this point,
with a good deal more information than I am. I certainly
couldn't have told you the *four* smallest. Anyway, I figured we'd put all that to some use. Like I said, the
carton's filled with catalog cubes—about five hundred of
them. They're not there at random: they're all texts I've
wanted to read but never got around to. There're more
than a few in it I've discussed in great detail with various
people, just as though I *had* read them. There're a whole
lot that I've read the first chapters of and have meant to
read the rest for years. And there're lots I read when I was

much too young and have been intending to reread. Oh yes, and there're about ten or fifteen I've read and reread a lot and just like a lot. Anyway. The instructions on the box your glove came in say that I—ordinary mortal that I am—can only absorb texts from the broadcast band at about one every ten minutes. But, as you may have figured out by now, I'm a lazy bitch. It says that if you've been through Radical Anxiety Termination, you can absorb them about one every point-thirty-two seconds; that's without turning your mind into wet sand. You see, what I want to do is *talk* to somebody who's read everything I should have read. I want to control such a man, make him lie down in the sand and lick my toes." She grinned in the dark. "The glove will give you the texts verbatim. On hot, hazy nights, I'll let you recite choice passages to me so that I can pick and choose. I can always get them myself with the glove later. But I think this way is more useful, more interesting." She pushed another pedal. "Don't you?"

"Yeah."

"Go in the back," she said, "and read a few dozen books. Then come up here, and we'll discuss literature while I decide where to drive us tonight." She pushed a switch on the dashboard. A pale ceiling plate behind them put hands of light on her shoulders.

"I . . . I don't read too good."

She smiled. "Yes, you do. Now." In the dim cabin her lips were still underlit. "Besides, all you have to do is read the titles. The library broadcast takes care of imprinting the text on your mind. In half a second. Go on."

He moved from beneath the bar and stood, slowly. The transport's shaking was mostly in his knees. Turning, he walked to the back.

The carton was obviously the open octagonal one, stuck about with packing tape. Upside down against it, flap open onto the floor, the lizard-embossed bag leaned where she'd tossed it. He squatted, knees winging either side. With his gloved hand, he held the box's ragged rim. With his naked one, he pushed down among the dice and pulled one loose. The cubes were not smaller than most people's fingertips; but they were smaller than his. He turned the smoky die between his great crowns with their bitten nails and read: *The Nu-7 Poems*—the collected poems and poetic fragments that a mail-routing engineer, Vro

Merivon, had stored over many years in the unused Nu-7 memory bin of her communications department computer, perhaps seventy years ago now. Their wit, their bright images of wind, cloud-forms, and various structural materials for highways, all used as metaphors for certain highly abstract mental processes, he learned about from the introduction. But the more than seven hundred poems themselves, ranging from a few lines to many, many pages, well . . . somehow, he realized as the cube fell back into his hard, dry palm, he had, suddenly, *read* them . . . !

Understood them?

Perhaps some phrases here, some few lines there. But he had read *every* word of the carefully chronologized and annotated (by Merivon's nephew) text!

He blinked.

The cube fell from his horny palm back into the carton. He stuck his hand down inside to retrieve it, to find out what it was, indeed, he *had* read. The cube he pulled out now announced on its black faces in white hieroglyphs: *The Mantichorio*, the epic narrative whose origin had been a subject of scholarly debate since the first incomplete copy had been discovered by the second wave of colonists in an abandoned outpost on the site of modern-day Kingston-prime, left by some of the first colonial wave sixty years before (again, the thirty-thousand word introduction): Were its great battles between the winged monsters and the children, its radioactive treasures in the sunken, red-walled caves through which rushed foaming black rivers, a fantasy of this world or a more realistic narrative surreptitiously brought here from some other? The 207 Cantos of the poem itself? (Cantos 199, 201, and half of 202 had been irretrievably lost in the early At-Man Devastations; Cantos 71, 72, and 73 only existed in the prose summaries that had survived the Censorship Acts of '87.) What he knew, however, was that, out of the 137,000 lines of alternating heptameters and hexameters that were now an immediate part of his memory, the Nu-7 poet had consciously (or unconsciously) rewritten more than a dozen phrases from it into her own poems.

He scrabbled for another cube, hoping he'd find the first one but pulled out instead *The Sharakik Years*, a compilation of letters, documents, and diaries of people around the outlaw Ky Sharakik, who had roamed and

robbed the disputed territories between the Forb Geosector
and Hykor Canyon—from its description, it must have
been the chasm he'd once shot through! The 260,000
words of biographical commentary that Redyh Snurb-Nollins,
who'd compiled and edited the three volumes, had inter-
spersed among the documents, told a jaw-dropping tale of
the exploits of the five-foot, white-haired, seventeen-year-
old Sharakik, who'd amassed her gang of seven- and eight-
foot criminals from the rejected dregs of several cloning
projects that had been instituted in the early days by the
Yellows as part of a later abandoned population push.
Sharakik herself, illiterate, probably psychotic (though in
the last months she had sent more than three dozen extraordinarily eloquent letters to the Ferawan Senate, which
she had dictated to the second-rate poet Seb-Voy, who
had recently joined the gang and who, numerous commentators still felt, was the actual author of at least some
of them), had finally been captured, had been tortured,
had been ultimately killed at age twenty by the Yellows'
"Gray Group"—though for years afterwards a myth had
persisted that she'd been torn apart by her own rebellious
gang before they scattered among the new cities, a myth
that had only been exploded by the researches of Sargu-4,
Redyh Snurb-Nollins' immediate predecessor.

When he plunged his hand in again, he was looking
equally for the first-rate Vro Merivon as for the second-
rate Seb-Voy, but came up with *The Lyrikz* of Megel
B'ber, which baffled him, because they were brief, beautiful, elegant, and more or less comprehensible, with few
words or references he did not understand—because the
last three tomes he'd managed to absorb (which were also
the first three things he'd ever read which were not delivery instructions) had, among their thousands of sentences,
managed to use most of the same words and grammatical
constructions. He still found himself catching his breath:
the scant sixty pages of the ninety-seven-year-old B'ber's
Lyrikz, in that tense and quiet voicing that seemingly
made any object named shimmer so in his mind, were the
most beautiful things he'd *ever* read! And he had read so
much . . . ! Another cube: he read through the classic
stories of Relkor, with their astute observations of tech-
nocratic life in the Jamhed Complex and their underlying
note of surreal horror. Another: he read the Metropolitan

Edition of the novels of Sni Artif—*Wind* ('15), *Road* ('17), *To the Black River* ('20; in Chapter VII of which he learned in the conversation of the tall girls and short boys who defied their teachers to indulge in long, drugged conversations behind the plastic sand-carts in the evening, that, though many people talked about it, unlike him, almost no one ever actually read the *whole* of *The Mantichorio*), *Sand* ('22), *Air* ('22), and *Time* ('24). Sni Artif, he learned in the afterword to the first novel (the fact then repeated in the introductions to each of the following volumes), had eventually committed suicide by burying himself in the dunes of the Nyrthside Range, before what turned out to be a futile and easily repelled attack of the Meyth in '28. And the next cube was, oddly enough, Kysu Jerzikiz's *The Sands*, a famous memoir written at about the same time as Artif's *Sand*, but on the other side of the world, about the exploration of the intra-geosectral divides, during which some of the most famous technological infrasystems had been discovered, some of which, the afterword explained, had been recently disrupted because of later human development as the equatorial population belt had begun to close on itself. He read the seven-volume psychoanalytic biography of Hardine, the legal philosopher whose work had been so influential in the organization of the Vresht Federation, which, only thirty years ago, had included twelve geosectors. Toward the beginning of volume three (*Years of Noon: '92–'01*) he learned the full story of the deep friendship between Hardine and Vro Merivon; it had been Hardine who had, after Merivon's death in '95, rescued the poems from Nu-7 and overseen their first publication. He read Okk's incendiary odes of jealousy and ennui, *Hermione at Buthrot,* apparently written offworld, which had supplied as many allusions for B'ber as *The Mantichorio* had for Merivon. He read the complete extant work of the twenty-two-year-old prodigy Steble, her five multicharacter dialogues, the handful of papers on algebraic agrammaticalities, the surviving fragment of her journal for the '88–'89 concert season, and the final impassioned letters, sent from her deathbed in the disease-infested Jabahia Prison complex, to her old teacher, Seb-Voy—the same Seb-Voy who, ten years later, would go off to fight alongside Sharakik between Farb and the Hykor. He read Gorebar's thirteen dazzling *Sketches*—and read, in the introduction to that volume for perhaps the fifth time now (somehow it had come up in the introductions to a number of other books as well), about the nine other volumes of verse Gorebar had published, all of which were completely pedestrian and without writerly value—which only made him plunge his hand down among the cubes again, in hope of finding one of those nine so that he might read them for himself.

And came up instead with Byrne's *Marking/Making*, her three-quarter-of-a-million-word experimental novel, a cascade of names, numbers, isolate phrases, and single hieroglyphs that created a kind of hypnotic, sensual experience in itself, unrelated to anything he had read before, but which, as much as any other affect now inscribed behind the bone of his forehead, had been clearly produced *by* the reading. Blinking, he placed that cube carefully back in the carton and picked up . . . Wevin's classical cycle of twenty-six novels, written over half that number of years, until her death by fire in the printing plant where she molded cold type: *Scenes on the Capitals*. The opening three books, the introduction informed him, had been widely popular since their initial publication, though the middle cycle of seven were as unread as any great works from *The Mantichorio* to *Marking/Making*. But one after another the tales inscribed themselves across his mind's eyes, ears, hands, volume on volume. In six of them, he was surprised to find, the tragic hero or heroine ended by going to the Radical Anxiety Termination Institute; and the narrative of the third from last turned on the abduction of a young man who was illegally made a rat and then rescued by some well-meaning social workers three years later. He read Demazy's series of tender and distanced novellas and a collection of the first three powerful novels by Horeb, who he knew now from some other introduction was a pseudonym for Saya Artif (a second cousin of Sni, though they had never met), a younger disciple of Byrne's. Indeed, he found himself recognizing, in her stripped-down sentences with their sudden grammatical lurches (was this an analog of what Steble had meant by agrammaticality . . . ?), the same sentence forms that had run through *Marking/Making*. There, of course, almost wholly a-referential, in Horeb they were used to describe, with glimmering exactitude, dawn forays out from the early spaceports across the equatorial dunes, or evening fires below the awnings of the dark transport machines parked about the newly sunk foundations of the Selm Chain of urban complexes. (For almost three decades in the previous century, the introduction commented, Horeb could arguably have been ranked as the most popular writer in this world.) While he put that cube down to pick up another, he wondered if the similarity marked the success or the failure of Byrne's experiment. . . .

He had just finished a six-volume set, *Classics of World Philosophy* (selections from the major works of Tondi, Fordiku, as well as the complete proceedings of the Vedrik School, Seminars and Publications for the years '82–'89), when she said: "I know you *can* do it at that speed now—" (He looked up because she had touched his shoulder—) "but I want you to stay sane so that you can appreciate some of the things *I* want to do later." Her fingers moved against his neck. "Stand up, now. Come. Come with me." He stood—the pains in his knees that came with squatting over the last years still surprised him.

Had it been days he'd squatted? Or hours?

In the dim light she looked at him with a kind of bland approval. Suddenly her face twisted. Her full lips puckered. "Phttt!" Saliva struck his cheek, the corner of his lip. At the same time she grasped his shoulders, thrust him out so that the back of his heel hit the carton. He heard cubes fall over cubes. Then she pulled him against her. "Yes . . ." she whispered. "Yes, the look on his face—your shock, your shame, your humiliation, your revulsion, your astonishment . . . I don't know. It does something to me. Breaks my heart, I suppose."

He'd felt no shock, no revulsion, only the mildest of sympathetic pains above his buttocks at the sudden standing, the slightest surprise at her action, the faintest curiosity at her motivation. Over her shoulder, he reached up to wipe his jaw with the hard heel of his hand—

"Come." She released him, stepping back. "No, *don't* wipe it off. Let it dry there. Come, come with me now." Holding his wrist, she led him back toward the instruments. "Tell me, what have you been reading at so diligently for the past three minutes?"

"I . . . ?" Perhaps, unlike the Institute's gamma lasers, the glove *did* change who you were. He certainly did not feel like the same person he'd been . . . *three* minutes ago? Years and monsters and ages and cultures and kilometers and feelings ago? "I read *Sand* and *The Sands* and *Lyrikz* . . ." and when he'd recited a dozen more titles, she stopped him with a laugh. Sitting in the driver's seat, she lay both hands on the thrust rod. She must have stopped the transport while he'd been crouched at the carton.

Outside, on low, headlights lay dim orange over sand and pebbles.

"What a strange view of world culture you must have!" She leaned forward and shook her head. "When I was packing those, I called myself taking all the important, profound, and indispensable titles I could—nearly filled the box. But one of the more eccentric librarians at the internment compound I'd gotten permission to rifle had put up a whole shelf full of cubes of women writers or texts about women. She was convinced nobody could be truly educated unless they'd read them—though nobody I ever met had, except her, maybe. Anyway." She pressed another pedal again. Outside, headlights brightened. "I decided I might as well take those too, as a lark, and loaded the box up with cubes from her special shelf. I'm afraid they were the top three inches in the carton. From the titles, it sounds to me like that's what you got stuck in!"

"But . . ." he began.

She pushed the thrust bar. The transport lurched on into desert night.

"But Horeb—Saya Artif—" he said, "was the most famous writer . . . in the world." He added: "For almost thirty years," and felt odd making a contestatory statement about his *world*; till now it had never occurred to him he'd had one.

"She may well have been," the woman said. "But that thirty years was many years ago. You can be sure: most people today haven't even heard of her—which I suppose was my eccentric librarian friend's point in putting that shelf together in the first place. You say you can drive this. I want you—" She leaned forward and punched a lot of buttons below the e-output meter— "to get me to these coordinates." She frowned. "Can you?"

He leaned forward to look at the numbers that had

appeared on the locale screen. "No. . . ." The coordinates were six-figured ones, and the only system he was used to from the Muct was the two-figured one for finding your way around within a city. But, certainly, it must work more or less the same way as the two-figure system. "Yeah." Coordinates were coordinates. He could figure them out. "I can."

"Good." She slipped from her seat. "Then I'm going to sleep, in the back."

He slid over onto the driver's plush cushion and, with gloved and naked hand, took the bar.

He drove for an hour or more and did not look back because, finally, he had not changed very *much* from who he had been before. Then—once—he did, because he was curious about where she was sleeping, and curiosity was, in itself, a curious emotion and, now, nowhere near as frightening as it had once been.

She'd pulled out a piece of canvas and lay on it, on the plastic flooring, snoring, one canvas corner pulled over her shoulder: a bed, he thought, harder than sand.

The town was one of those old-fashioned attempts at ecological self-sufficiency in a world with no ecology to begin with. The description was not his, but had been written by an off-world woman a hundred years ago to describe her entrance at dawn into a town more than four thousand kilometers east. Recalling it, however, made him want to look out the transport window more clearly. (It also made him want to return to the carton.) This town was five observation towers—and places where, no doubt, a sixth and seventh, now fallen or pulled down, had stood—with forests of gray-green elephant lichen between.

Dawn streaked green and blue behind them under a dark red sky, still awaiting day's orange. On the locale-screen, the first four mobile coordinates had closed with the stasile ones she'd punched out last night. They rolled in on a worn road walled with wire mesh to hold the lichens' wrinkled hides back from the shoulder. He watched the delta discrepancy in the last two figures decrease.

Above, on high trestles, great translucent plates would cast down their blue or red or green light onto the rippling vegetation later in the day. He had seen them as a child in the great city parks in which, from time to time, he'd slept. It was only a little surprising to look at them now and know, for the first time (because Seb-Voy had once explained their workings to Sharakik), what they were for—though now the light slipped under them, rather than fell through, to put copper trim on the raddled edges of the barky growths.

Delta dropped from twelve to eleven, which meant their destination should be visible in another minute.

Through the side window they passed a yard stacked with wrecked transports like the one he drove. Out the window across, he glimpsed an acre-wide silt-vat, through which crusted mixers spattered back and forth in the organic slush. He rolled over a stretch of road gouged about with kids' graffiti, as were many roads in the southeastern geosectors. He had seen such things before—old transport yards, roadway graffiti—in the much larger cities in which he'd grown up; but now, because the Nu-7 poet had written a poem comparing the passion of young love to a blind child's exploring such a junked transport lot, and because the villain of *Sand* had drowned the enraged clone-dogs in such a silt-vat, and because Fordiku, on a dawn not so different from this, when hiking out of Kingston, had stopped to talk to an adolescent girl busy cutting graffiti in the road just like the ones which, moments ago, had made the transport treads go thump, and from the encounter had begun to construct her time-and-text theory that had dominated—well, not all of world philosophy, but at least one narrow, academic strand of it for nearly a century, he saw them not as so flat and so unknown you could not even call them puzzling, but rather as historical and curious, specific and resonant.

The delta dropped from two to one and began to roll down through point nine, point eight, point seven. . . .

The plaza entrance he pulled through was littered with desert slough, even this far in. Acrylic greens and yellows chipped or lapped loose from peeling advertisement statues. The transport halted on asphalt covered with large red circles, indicating parking. (At Muct, it had been small white ones, but that was in another geosector, in another part of . . . his world.) He sat a long time, looking out the scarred sandshield.

A bank of mobile lichen furled and unfurled slowly

below the chin of a woman's giant head, cast from some sort of flesh-toned ceramic. Panels of colored metal hung before her. Now and then one, turning on its cable, revealed a smile's corner, a great nostril's curve, an eye's iris.

A tall old man stood in a doorway whose metal hinges, even from here, looked loose. His naked chest was snarled with white hair. His brown head, within a circle of white, was bald. Over the next ten minutes he picked and prodded and pulled at the wires that, twisted together, made up his belt buckle, till his pants fell to his ankles. He stepped from them, looked till he found the green rag he must have hung on the door handle minutes before, and, trying to tie it across his face, stumbled unsteadily across the yard, to disappear among the signs.

Minutes later, two astonishingly short men, in thick-soled wedgies, hurried across the yard, plucking at their masks' clips behind their heads, one laughing as his came away, the other bumping one shoulder into some stay-wire supporting an old sign for soft drinks.

The sign swayed.

He watched the yard a long time, before he heard her turn over behind him, dragging canvas.

He did not look.

Canvas fell on plastic.

She grunted.

Then her hand fell on his shoulder. "We're here," she said, recovering from a yawn as, now, he glanced up. "So. You actually got us here. That wasn't too hard."

Outside, two very short women with elaborate head-masks ran into the enclosure, giggling and poking at one another, turned, and ran out.

Crossing the yard, one either side, a very tall man and a very short man, both with naked faces, glanced one at the other as the other glanced away, the both of them elaborately feigning not to see each other.

They walked perfectly in step.

Holding his shoulder, she frowned: "What is this place?"

He said a slang word that, before he'd come to the Institute, had been a frequent part of his vocabulary, though he had not used it since.

"Oh," she said, while he reflected that in the whole of

his reading, only the Nu-7 poet had used the word, and that only once, comically and obliquely. "You mean," she said, "here, we've driven over three thousand kilometers in a night to some little belt-border town, to wind up in a . . ." (She, he noticed, mispronounced it.) "I guess you about-faces are all over the place. Well, it makes sense. We're fugitives, and when I bought my fugitive coordinate pattern, I guess I should have figured the people who did the kind of traveling we were going to do would use this kind of place as a stop-point." She gave a kind of laughing snort. "I'm going to punish you for this."

He was curious why, but did not look at her curiously.

"I mean," she offered in nervous explanation, "here I am, indulging all my kinks—and I intend to keep right on. You might as well indulge yours." Then she *humphed*; or coughed. "Three thousand kilometers in toward the population belt . . . all you expect to do is just brush civilization's rim. And here I am, stuck with a microphile in the middle of an erodrome—" *Microphile* and *erodrome* were technical words whose meanings seemed not so much concerned with their referent as with the gesture of her using them as compensation for the slang term with which, he realized, she was far more uncomfortable than he— "just as if we were in central Kingston. Get on out," she said, and reached over his shoulder to press a button.

He couldn't remember, he thought with some distress, if that were the switch that released the transport's side or not.

Catches on the single door fell away; the door swung out.

He stood up, looking at her.

She said: "Go on. Get out there and indulge your foul and unspeakable desires." She gave him a quick smile. "When you get back, I'll indulge mine."

He smiled, knowing he wouldn't have a day before. But that was because, in his reading, he'd found the word "indulged" nearly a dozen times, and recognizing it felt . . . well, good.

He walked toward the entrance.

"Really *do* it," she called after him. Humor and nervousness tripped over each other to get control of her voice. "*Do* it, because the punishment will be exquisite!"

Without using his hands, he shouldered out the door as if it were some institutional hanging.

The morning was warm and dry. He stepped down on the powdery ground, scattered with gravel, plastic bits, and the tiny black grommets whose source or use, for all his reading, he did not know any more than he had before the Institute had shipped him from the city years ago.

He walked across the clearing, pausing to look back, but the sun, still low, put a red glare over the darkened glass so that he could not tell if she watched him or not.

He went first to the doorway the old man had stood in—and was surprised because it was locked.

He dropped his hand from the circular entrance plate and looked down at the man's discarded pants. One brown leg dangled across the entrance sill. He turned and walked back.

The archway stood behind two statues—a new one, a great sphere in luminous blue, whose hieroglyphs advertised some drug he had never heard of, and an old one behind it, a peeling red and orange bucket that told of a distant water-station.

The arched darkness glimmered along its edges with some sort of weak-energy heat shield.

He stepped through, onto downward stairs. Somewhere in the wide, dim corridor water dripped. Shafts of light fell through the high hall's cool dusty air.

Near the step's bottom, a very short man, wearing . . . well, it was *like* a wire headmask, only there were not dozens but, seemingly, hundreds of colored pieces. Some of the wires curved as far down as his ankles. Naked beneath it, the man danced slowly, alone.

Which was when he remembered it was after sunup in some tiny town at the very rim of the population belt. Few men were likely to be out at this hour. He might as well turn around and go back to the transport.

He didn't.

And the men who were out, well. . . .

Over the next three hours, moving around through the dark rooms, he had sex seven times, twice with unexpected satisfaction, and four times after that with an indifferent adequacy that slipped him into adolescent memories undisturbed for years. The last time was with a man taller than himself—a partner he'd never have considered when he'd been a child. But the encounter proved to have a gentleness and satisfaction that drew his second orgasm of the morning up from behind his knees to rage like a large lake filling below his belly, while his shoulders shook, till, unmarked time later, with words whirling and falling in his head, the wonder, pulsing and pulsing from spine to genitals, settled slowly into the wordless memory of wonder.

"You look like you haven't done that for a long time." The man rubbed his shoulder and held his face close.

He said: "Not for a . . . a couple of hours," and patted the high shoulder back, clumsily, with his glove.

The little man, who'd stood near watching, lifted his immense contraption of swaying wires back onto his head and again began to dance.

So he left.

He came out behind the water-station sign, stopped to take a deep breath, and started across the grommeted dust.

The single door to the transport stood wide, the diagonal rod at the corner in place to hold it open, which was not (he tried to reason why) the way he'd have expected her to leave it. But he was still not really used to reason. Hers or anyone else's.

He stopped, moving his hand to the side of his face, to scratch some itch there, which became a conscious curiosity at how best he might move the dark cloth first from the tip of one finger and then another to bite on the nails there. Still wondering, he stepped inside.

The cabin was empty.

What he did next had the same insistence with which, for years, without thought, he had raised one finger and another, thumb and little, to pick and chip with his big teeth at crown and cuticle, or, indeed the insistence with which, for three hours, he'd stalked from encounter to encounter while all thought had been toward leaving in a minute, in three, in no more than five.

He went to the octagonal carton, squatted, plunged in his hand, pulled out a cube, and read *Seven Comic Dialogues* by Cher Ag, most of whose humor escaped him, but which, especially in the fourth and seventh, managed to pass through some jarring and bizarre social configurations that caught up all his thinking; and tossed that back and pulled out the long-story *Mutations*, which, the afterword explained to his surprise, had been written in collaboration by two women, one of whom had been a rat. And put that back, pulled out the next, and to his greater surprise reread *The Mantichorio*, marveling both at how much he remembered and how much seemed wondrously new, as familiar characters, who, in his mind's eye, looked entirely different from memory, engaged familiar battles and said familiar lines, their motivations and arguments so changed— so much more, indeed, like his own might have been, now, here. Still, it was amazing how the black ripples under the children's long oars on the underground waterways were lit, this reading, by torchlight of such a different gold.

Then he read an anthology of poems by women connected with the *Tarcarto Publications*, and for the first time found himself responding to individual lyrics as good or bad, instead of simply comprehensible or confusing.

Minutes, seconds, ages later . . . ?

He was in the midst of a huge, desertlike novel, subtly contoured with the palest shifts in tone, as satisfying as a walk on warm sand at night—partially because it dealt with the Tarcarto itself. Its secondary heroine was one of the more eccentric poets whose work, so recently, he'd read. Then, through the half-consciousness in which his perceptions of the transport cabin around him hung, he heard a footstep; several footsteps; then: "Yeah, that's him. Get him."

The leisurely narrative resolved with its closing meditation on the dawntime of a young world—

Someone grabbed him by the shoulder and spun him back.

He lost balance, went down on one knee. His other struck the carton, which overturned, spilling cubes. The cube in his hand fell among the scatter. His buttock hit the plastic flooring and his gloved hand skidded behind him.

He looked up at baggy beige suits and at official beige masks.

One of them said: "And get that thing off his hand, will you?"

That's when he saw the canvas bag with the lizard on its flap hanging over the small one's shoulder. His first thought was: How odd to find such a carrier this many kilometers across the sand from the polar station. Then he realized there was no bag lying beside the carton. The two thoughts interlocked to become recognition of how they'd come looking for it.

The first man in beige, who had bent down while he was thinking all this, jerked his forearm up, hooked a forefinger under the wrist of the glove, and yanked: cloth and small metal links tore—

And his world and all thought about it tore from his great hand.

Qualitatively, the feeling was somewhat like being in the midst of an involuted argument with a particularly complex point to make, only to open your mouth and forget what you were about to say. Quantitatively, it was so much more intense than simple forgetting that anyone who'd undergone the experience would probably question the qualitative as a metaphor to convey the quantity of that shattering erasure. For what had been stripped, wrenched, excised from him at that tug was all in him that could have understood the very description of it. Left was only a tingling that worked through every cell of him, more completely than her plate (whose name he could not remember) when she'd cleaned him.

Breath came out, slowly and continuously, as though hands, huger than his, had taken him up and wrung him. For moments air caught in his vocal cords. For moments it slipped through them, unvoiced. Sometimes it stuttered between the two: " . . . gggggkkkkkgghh . . . aggggghhh . . . k-k-k-kggggg. . . . "

"There," the man said. He looked at the black rag with the bits of metal in it, turned his fingers down through the ribbons, and jerked his elbows apart.

More ribbons and wires ripped.

One asked: "Where do they get these things anyway?"

The short one with the bag said: "I wonder what she did to him." From the voice, it was probably a woman.

The tall one said: "You'll never know. I mean, a damned bitch. That's what gets me. With a man, it doesn't seem so weird. But I can't stand it when a damned bitch does something like that with a damned—"

"Hey, watch your language, man!" the one holdi̵ the ripped glove said. "You don't have to talk that w̵ front of the kid."

"Oh, yeah, man," the other one said; and to the young woman, "I'm sorry, man."

"That's all right, man," she said. "I just wish I knew what she did to him." She reached down, got a hand under his arm, and tugged. "Come on, Rat. Time to get up."

He slipped, so that one knee went down to the floor on a cube's corner. Pain shot from knee to thigh, as the woman said:

"Oh, jeeze, look at those cuts on his back, will you? Maybe it's just as well we *don't* know. . . ."

Leg throbbing, he stood.

The tall one said: "Can't we find anything to put over his face?"

The one with the ruined glove said: "You don't need to do that. He's just a rat."

"I know," the other said. "But a guy with a face like that—those scars on it. I got some of them myself. It ain't right."

"The cuts. On his back," the woman said. "Do you think she beat him . . . ?"

"With perverts like that," the one with the glove said, "they'll do *any*thing. You just be happy it's against the law to ask."

"A damned bitch—"

"Come *on* now, I said! Watch it."

"Oh, yeah. I'm sorry."

"It's all right," the woman said.

"Can't we get something to put over his face—?"

"Let's just get going."

They led him outside, into the rubble-strewn yard. Now the square was almost filled with people in beige, some standing, some strolling in pairs. They led him ("No, *this* way, you stupid rat!") to the entrance and out among the lush, gray vegetation, where a smaller transport waited.

In the back, through the grilled window, he saw her. The woman's arms were strapped to her sides. There was a large bruise down her cheek. Blood had run from her hair.

A rag had been tied decently, if haphazardly, across her face; but there were no eyeholes.

"Come on. Get in."

"Shall I strap him up?"

"Naw. He won't do anything."

They put him in the front seat, then slid in beside him. One began to maneuver the controls.

One said: "Hey, that thing you took off him? Does that really make you know more stuff?"

"Naw. It just makes you *think* you do. It can make you real sick, too—you see the way he was when I took it off him, moanin' like that?"

"I didn't hear him moaning," one said. "What do you mean?"

One said: "Can't we get *something* to put over his . . . face?"

"They told me back at headquarters," the one who still held the ragged glove said. "If it was a normal man or woman, you couldn't just take it off him like that. It would probably kill him. Something in the head. That's how bad it is for you. But with a damned rat, it don't do that much."

"I don't know," the other said. "I'm not from around here, like you guys. I just can't stand it." He'd found a piece of blue, oily cloth under the transport's seat. "Let me get this on him, huh?"

After that, he couldn't see where he was going at all.

"You understand, a woman like that could've been dangerous," the man in charge said with a harshness that had grown each time he'd told the story of the way he'd tricked her into taking the carrier bag with its signal generator—three times now.

He picked up bits of foam, torn paper, crumpled lengths of red packing tape, handfuls of orange sand, discarded cubes, blue shreds fallen from the peeling walls and ceiling, putting them all in the triangular carton, while they went on talking and he paid almost as little attention to them as they did to him.

"Still, I couldn't just let her take him off like that without doing *some*thing."

"You had to do something," one man said.

"He's been back three days, huh?" said another. "I wonder what she did to him? Well, I guess we'll never know. That one's too dumb to tell us, even if asking *was* legal."

". . . dangerous," the man in charge repeated. "You never know in a case like that."

"Well, she must have done something," a newer man said. He had taken his mask off of his clean, young cheeks. "It's like he's just not the same rat anymore."

"What do you mean he's not the same rat?" another asked. "He looks the same to me, man."

"I worked with this one before she stole him, and I've been working with him since we got him back." The new man (six months) was short, brown, and smoothfaced as some bitch, and oversaw the worst jobs at the station—always going around without his face like a damned rat himself. "He's doing all *sorts* of dumb things."

"If it's the rat I think it is," another said, "he ain't never *been* too smart, you know? You mean this one here, now—"

"I don't mean dumb-stupid," the unmasked man said. (Many of the other men didn't like him.) "I mean dumb crazy."

"Like what?" the man in charge said.

"Well, you know where they have the work equipment all racked up along the inside of hangar doors—they got the work gloves sitting up on a rack of pegs so you can just take 'em down when you need them? Anyway, I was reading over my packing orders while about six rats were unloading supply drums. But I had to go get a replacement string from the vestibule console because the computer had messed up the printing on one. I guess they must have finished up the first tier of loading. When I got back, he had them rats all standing together in the hangar doorway; and he'd put one work glove on each one of them, on himself too. Just one, you see? And they were staring across the sand like they were waiting for something to come over the horizon."

"Man, I think you better put your mask back on." One man laughed. "You been getting too much sun."

"No, I mean it. You should've seen 'em. And he was right there, at the head of them, in his one glove, with this funny expression on his face; if he was a man and not a rat, you would have thought he was going to cry—"

"I've worked places where they don't let the rats run around with their faces all naked like that. Why don't we—"

"How'd you know he was the one who did it?"

"I asked. A rat don't lie, man—least if he understands the question."

"Look, I been here a lot of years, now—and when I got here, I used to do the same job you're doing. Back when we were studying q-plague. First of all, I *never* seen a rat, dumb or smart, pay attention to no other rat, much less give 'em a . . . work glove! Second, *that* rat—and I worked with him back before the station got closed down and opened up again—that rat is the *last* one who'd do something like that."

"Like I say, man, it's as if he wasn't the same. When he got taken off, something happened. He come back different. I don't mean he's turned into an ordinary man or anything. But I mean it, he's different. If you used to work with him, you could see it too, I bet."

"Aw, come on. . . ."

But he was finished cleaning now and dragged the three-quarters full carton behind him out into the station's low-ceilinged hall.

Over the next few months, he did a number of things equally stupid. One afternoon the rat-keeper went to kick up a shift from the cage and found him missing—he was already at his station, working. Once, instead of getting his carrying orders from the console, he pressed some other buttons and got some other random cubes and was found standing before the station computer, turning them over in his great, fouled hands, with a puzzled look on his long, pitted face.

The other things he did, however, were all just as harmless; and as they occurred less and less frequently, they elicited less and less comment.

Things happened at the station.

During the election the station's men cast their votes through the station computer; but he never learned who won, Yellows or Grays. Shortly the station changed over its function once more; new equipment was shipped in and set up. New staff came; some old staff left; they got two new rats. For a time the cage feedings were dropped to once every two days. And the new man, who was

actually pretty bright, was promoted to second-in-charge
and wore his mask more.

But these things did not noticeably affect the rat.

For the next seven years he worked at the station,
doing much the same as he had always done.

One evening during a dark, red sunset, one of the
women at the station (there were three on the staff now)
told him to take the lift down to the sub-basement refrig-
erated storage crypt and bring up one of the new machines, a model 184. He didn't know what model 184 was
used for, but it had a lot of mechanical claws dangling from
it, and many little lights flashing about it. It weighed some
twenty-six kilos, but though you had to carry it up steps
and over the ice-clotted thresholds, it would follow you
along any smooth surface if you threw the toggle under the
red flange circling it.

Behind him 184's treads had just gone thump again
on another doorsill.

As he turned to free it, there was a huge roar. The
striplights along the ceiling went out. Suddenly he was
thrown to the chill, steel-mesh flooring, scraping elbow
and hip.

Metal grated on rock above him.

The temperature rose twenty degrees in ten seconds.
In the dark something fell over on him, pinning one leg,
something bigger and heavier than 184. And in a conflagration that lasted some seventeen hours, all life on the
surface of his world—a world whose name in all his forty-
one years he'd had less than a dozen opportunities to
speak, a world he'd known only from the most impoverished perspective, a world whose coordinates in the Web's
encyclopedia of habitable worlds he had never even heard—
was destroyed.

MONOLOGUES

Visible and Invisible Persons Distributed in Space

ONE

From Nepiy to Free-Kantor

The first I heard of Rat Korga or the world Rhyonon?
(Look. Listen.) Large and blue, a woman who tended to
come apart into jellylike pieces only to flow together about
the translator pole, my current employer₁ said: "Thank
you. Thank you, Industrial Diplomat Marq Dyeth, thank
you for delivering these heteromer sheathing samples."
Heteromers are very big, very broad, very flat, and in
places very active molecules; but it had taken me the first
three days of the journey with all my delivery ship's GI
resources hard by to get even that far; they're also very
difficult to put together from just a recipe, unless you
actually have some of them against which to check off the
million-odd atoms that comprise them. "Thank you for
delivering them to this beleaguered geosector of this wide
world, this world of Nepiy." She went from pale sky to
indigo.

    Within many-layered transparent gold gloves and some-
thing filmy that seemed like a parody of the alien bubbling
about the pole, the other woman (this one human) stood
off beneath the dripping roof-stones and looked on with
intense approval.

    My employer₁ said: "May I ask, ask you a favor?"

    "Well, I—"

    "Please, Marq Dyeth. Please. Your shuttle flight does

not leave for some time yet, not for a while. I want to explain, explain something to you; then I want you to explain something to me—"

"Well. . . ." Feeling uncomfortable, I smiled my most diplomatic smile, fairly sure what was coming. "You must understand that an industrial diplomat often finds herself—"

"I want to show you this, this most recent atrocity in this atrocious fugue." (I was right.) "Because you're not from around here, not from our world, not from our geosector, I merely thought you might take a certain understanding, a certain knowledge, certain information away with you . . . ?"

The assumption is that because you're not "from around here" on such a cosmic scale, you couldn't possibly know what "here" is like. Always true; but it means that after a while an ID has seen more of this sort of thing than anyone could care to.

"My friend will take you in the skimkar." She indicated the other (human) woman. "He's a careful driver and can answer any questions you might want to put." The "he" made me flex an imaginary lip bone—which, a human myself, I do not have. But I've known lots who did.

"Very well." I nodded, wondering what a nod meant on this world, at this spot on it.

The human stepped forward, and we started through damp veils, streaked pink and blotched brown, along the entrance, while my employer$_1$ came apart and collected herself behind us.

As we came out under the loud, dark sky, she said: "He's quite something, isn't he?" (The second "he" made that imaginary lipbone of mine unflex.) "If you knew even a tenth of the work he's been putting into our emergency situation here, you'd be awed. We've had to go to the stars when we can't even get help from geosectors five or five-hundred kilometers away!"

"Oh, in just the day I've been here, I've been able to get a rough idea." I think she looked questioningly at me on the word "day," but I'm not sure. "Yes," I said, "she's quite a woman. And you've got quite a situation to deal with here, all of you."

The dark sky crackled with red lightning, and a moment later thunder, which had punctuated my stay almost every twenty minutes, trundled across the low, ragged peaks. "Is it always like this?" I asked, loudly.

Trailing gauzes around her, she glanced at me, her face glimmering as through washes of (human) blood. "Oh, we have whole fifty-and sixty-hour periods when the lightning is blue."

"I mean over all of Nepiy."

"Oh, no," she answered. "You only get lightning here in the western equatorial band. A thousand kilometers toward the poles in either direction, and you don't get any lightning at all. Just black."

We climbed into the kar.

Strung into the pilot's net, the woman pressed and pulled and pushed.

The kar broke through the power shield into the hot, dark, ululating silt.

"Do you have anything like this at home?" Now she wore lots of layers of lensing plastic over her face.

"No," I said, thinking of our southern hotwind season, which comes close. "Not really."

"There—" she said suddenly, pointing through the grillwork over the window plate. "Can you see it—?"

I couldn't, which is pretty usual in such situations.

"Over there . . . ?"

After a few minutes I thought I could. Which is also usual. General Information got me through, though: apparently those dark, fuzzy slashes were where kilometer after kilometer was acrawl with a rugged, rotting vine that decayed into polluting vapor, whipping about the strong wind in yellow blades—like my home world's -wrs gone wild. The vines had been intended as high-yield bean bushes that would bear seven distinct types of bean, each with a distinct and different flavor. But as the genetic designs had been shipped from world to world, star to star, somewhere along the way a few triplets had fallen into the DNA specifications that, in conjunction with a high-sodium environment, upped the possibility of viable mutation: and this particular bit of Nepiy desert had been all salt marsh sometime before its very superficial planoforming. The triplets hadn't been detected, or rather hadn't been recognized for what they were. At about the fifth generation, the bushes had suddenly metamorphosed into this lethal and virulent sport.

"Within thirty kilometers there are three urban complexes that are on the border of starvation, with a com-
bined population of twelve million women—of both races,"
my driver said glumly.

"I see." Outside the window, the fields were dark and
dim. "Still, I find it a little hard to understand how three
whole cities are dependent on a single product, to the
point that its failure threatens them with starvation . . . ?"

She glanced at me through many lenses. "It's more
complicated than that, of course. But you have to leave in
a . . . day. Do you have time to hear the last fifty years'
history of this geosector, or the last eighty years' history of
the Quintian Geosector Grouping, of which our sector,
here, is the smallest, or of the two hundred twelve years'
history of Nepiy's whole colonization . . . ?"

"Given the time we have, I probably wouldn't be able
to follow it." History is one area that General Info is
notoriously poor in imparting, I reflected, while I made a
mental request from GI for any special usage information
about the word "day" in this particular area of Nepiy.
"And I wouldn't be likely to remember it for very long
once I left."

"Then you'd better just accept the simplified version.
The beans don't grow; the cities starve."

Day, GI informed me, while still part of most equatorial Nepiyans' vocabulary, has become largely a literary
word, due to the overlying cloud layer, and is seldom used
in ordinary conversation. [Cf. *The Silent Polar Fields*,
whose famous opening line, "Alone here, she turns under
day . . ." is frequently quoted over almost the entire world.]
The more usual reference to time units is in periods of
hours, their number usually divisible by ten, with twenty,
thirty, and sixty the most frequently mentioned. . . . There
was a little mental *bleep*, which meant that the last GI
program I'd summoned up hadn't been completed yet.

I acknowledged mentally, and learned that the original genetic designs for the bean bushes had been prepared
on the north of a world called Velm—which happens to be
my home, though I come from the southern reaches and
have spent almost no time in the north. Diplomatically
enough, I suppose, I didn't say anything.

My driver looked uncomfortable, but, knowing its
codes, its historical complexities, she could see more on

her world than I could. "I heard there was some similar problem about three thousand kilometers to the north, with the genetic designs for some mineral pulverizing viruses that didn't work. I wonder if they're connected—although those designs were put together right here on Nepiy."

"It's possible," I said. "They could both be similar manifestations of a worldwide informational warp. Though it would take a lot of work to find out—and the fact is, it's not likely. But I'll make a note to report it to the Web, and they'll at least have it on file. If they don't already."

"A few days ago my friend was up on the moon where he heard a perfectly horrible story about—" My driver stopped, as though it really *were* too horrible to go on with. She grunted. "By Okk, what a world this is. . . ."

We looked out the glass at our little patch of what, GI informed me, was a good hundred eighty thousand square kilometers of this one; and I smiled to hear that most familiar exclamation in this most alien environment.

The skimkar skimmed.

The clouds hovered.

(Listen. Look . . .)

2.

"If you're hungry," my employer$_1$ said, "I'd be highly complimented if you'd eat some of me. Indeed, if there's any of you you can spare: body hair, nail parings, excrement, dried skin . . . ? Really, our two chemistries are very similar, notoriously complementary. One speculates that it's the basis for the stable peace that endures between our races throughout the lowlands of this world."

I'd accepted such an offer when I'd first come; I would accept it again before I left—as GI prompted. But now I was told to ignore it as a phatic exchange that required no more than a nod to avoid offense. (Oh.) I nodded.

And after a moment of blue self-collection, she went on. "What I would now appreciate, what you could really do for me, what I so deeply desire—" Blue bubbles broke in my employer$_1$ around the vibrating translator pole— "is for you to explain this spreading horror, this war with no sides, this disastrous ruination of the quality of life that brings pain and desperation to all women—"

"—the fugue," the human who'd driven me said. "That's what he wants to know about." Gathering up her veils in her gilded gloves, she reached up to rub her upper lip with gold fingertips. "We all want to know."

"I can tell you this." I took a breath. "Though it may seem to have aspects of Cultural Fugue to you, it's not the big C."

They both waited, breathing, bubbling.

"You have a catastrophe here, a real, desperate, and life-destroying catastrophe. But it's not Cultural Fugue. If it's fugue at all, it's fugue with a very small f." I wondered what the translator pole did with that one since this was a world where—as GI had reminded me already on several occasions—writing was only a tertiary method of text production.

"How do you know?" my employer₁ asked. "Can you tell, just from the feel of the sky above you, from the lowest frequencies in the thunders' rumble?"

"I can tell because the Web's report on Information Deployment for your world is open to me through GI: there's not one sign, but at least a hundred seventy-five, that would be visible if you were moving anywhere near a CF condition."

"The violence, the death, the anguish on our world, not only here, but many, many other places, have been immense," my employer₁ said.

I said: "I know. And I don't blame you for asking. But you should know this, too: in the many, many worlds I've visited in my capacity as an Industrial Diplomat, where there was some problem that stretched from horizon to horizon, if you talk to anyone in the middle of it, among the first things they'll want to know is if their world has gone into Cultural Fugue." I smiled. "It's little consolation, I know. But horizon to horizon—which is hard to remember when you're standing on the surface—is still a very small part of a world. A whole world, that's a big place. For a *world* to go into Cultural Fugue—for the socioeconomic pressures to reach a point of technological recomplication and perturbation where the population completely destroys all life across the planetary surface—takes a *lot* of catastrophe. There are more than six thousand worlds in the Federation of Habitable Worlds. And Cultural Fugue is *very* rare."

"Forty-nine times in the last two hundred eighty years," the human said.

"And our years are a bit longer than Old Earth Standard," said the alien. "I was up on our moon only days ago," she went on, "when I heard that a world perhaps a third of the way around the galactic rim was just destroyed. There were hardly any survivors."

(Look. Listen. Did you catch it? I didn't. The reason, I suppose, is simply that I'd have thought someone in my profession₁ would have known about that already had it really happened. But there, on alien Nepiy, I'm afraid I read it as something between a glitch in the translation and mere myth or misinformation to be expected in the general anxiety among women under such pressure.)

"Were they with the Family or the Sygn?" I asked; and I'm afraid I smiled when I asked. "Or were they just unaligned in the Web?"

"They didn't say," said the alien.

"They didn't say," said the human.

Which only confirmed my suspicion. And I thought, as I had so often on my own world: when women of different species say the same things, you are most aware of their distinctions.

An hour later I was on my shuttle flight towards Free-Kantor, listening to the thrum of ion pulsers beyond green plastic walls.

3.

Free-Kantor? In terms of light years, it's not so far from my home. But that doesn't make it notable, now.

"Free-Kantor is a world in itself," I've heard spiders say.

But it's not a world.

At all.

One of thirty information nodes built as free data-transfer points about the more heavily inhabited parts of the galaxy, Free-Kantor began as three ice-and-iron asteroids herded together and locked in place by force fields (so quaintly called), webbed between with numerous tubes, girders, and strutwork scaffolds. One is some nineteen kilometers in diameter, another twenty-six, and the third nine.

They circle a star with no planets to speak of, and though I've been through it a dozen times, I've never managed to find out its sun's name.

Coming into them on an ion shuttle, watching from the simulated view windows, I've often thought of a cluster of dyll nuts with their pitted hulls and feathery sheathing, hanging in the dark, sun-reddened on one side and webbed with sharp shadows, among which, now and again, some polished plate, catching the proper angle, flares with starlight.

We hung about in an invisible cloud of ships for almost four hours, waiting for a landing slot. When Kantor was built three hundred years ago, there were not yet a thousand inhabited worlds. One suspects that an odd and old argument had . . . well, not raged here so much as it had been mumbled and muttered over most of that time: freighter ships were just not Kantor's first priority, so that if dispatch were needed, they could go someplace else. . . .

We waited.

There *are* other free transfer points of course, but none of them were really any more efficient; so if I was going to wait, I might as well wait here. Myself, I've always suspected it was part of the general Web strategy to discourage interworld travel.

We landed.

Three hours later, I was sitting on a bit of frozen foam under a transparent blister, shadowed with girder work, half the night blocked out by a mini-world hanging a few kilometers above me, pricked out with lights and blacknesses, waiting for connecting passage with my home world (which ship GI said was going to be nearly twenty hours late), my thoughts not so much ahead on home as behind on Nepiy.

I had been on Nepiy only a fraction more than a day . . . that is, a thirty-hour period. Chances were I would never visit it again—as I would never revisit more than a fifth the worlds my job$_1$ took me to. A geosector of Nepiy had been ravaged by its complex misfortune (that I only knew about in a simplified version): I couldn't have charged them full direct-line energy costs and full information-

exchange rates, which was why I was returning home via
Free-Kantor now; there are more expensive ways to travel
from sun to sun, world to world, and an ID usually takes
them. But after all, I'm a woman.

The romance of a free-data node and, I suppose, the
reason why I finally consented to come this way, had to do
with what *was* Kantor's first priority: information.

GI on Kantor dwarfs any on any given world. To walk
in the weak gravity by the great aluminum and ceramic
banks in hot and cold storage is to walk past macro-
encyclopedias—encyclopedias of encyclopedias! I recall my
first time through, when I stood on a plane of scarlet glass
under an array of floating light tubes and thought out:
"What is the exact human population of the universe?"
and was informed, for answer: "In a universe of c. six
thousand two hundred inhabited worlds with human populations over two hundred and under five billion, 'population' itself becomes a fuzzy-edged concept. Over any
moment there is a birth/death pulse of almost a billion.
Those worlds on which humans have the legal status of the
native population and little distinction is made among all
these women present statistical problems from several points
of view. Thus 'exactness' below five billion is not to be
forthcoming. Here are some informative programs you
may pursue that will allow you to ask your question in
more meaningful terms. . . ."

Does Free-Kantor or, indeed, any free-data transfer
point contain all the information in the human universe?
Far from it. On such a scale, data-quantity itself is even
more fuzzy-edged than population. But in the way that an
urban complex soon becomes a kind of intensified sampling of the products and produce of the geosector around
it, so a free-data transfer point becomes a kind of partial
city against the night, an image of a city without a city's
substance, gaining what solidity it possesses from endlessly cross-filed data webs.

On my hard foam, still puzzling over Nepiy, I'd thought
to question a bit of curiosity that had tickled me since I'd
left it—what, *there*, did that unseemly "he" signify?

On any world which took Arachnia with it from the
Web for its basic tongue, language often changed and
changed quickly under the pressures of a new environment. It was easy to see how, with foreign global condi-

tions, the term might enlarge or shift its semantic category to include, say, certain postures of respect, certain social hierarchies, or even personal affection.

I put in my mental GI request for Nepiy language patterns, Arachnia, linguistic shift: What's the special meaning of "he" among the women of that part of that world?

Surprisingly, I got the hiss of mental white noise that means—as a compensatory message confirmed seconds later—all information channels are currently in use and/or overloaded. Please, stand by.

Well, it's happened before. But the brainy hum that makes it too hard to think too much about anything went on, and on . . . and on!

With that roar in your head, you lose concentration. I could have disconnected, of course, but that requires a complex set of access codes, one of which I wasn't sure of anyway—you'd usually get it from GI. But I kept thinking it was going to end in another minute.

That was the state in which, quarter of an hour later, I wandered around the black and silver partition into the sloping hall with its arched roof. Lit by small orange lights down near the floor, walls and clear roof converged in the black toward a worldlet a few kilometers off.

Wandering over the dark rug, I realized where I was when I saw the women standing a few meters down from me in the dark. Perhaps it was because part of my mind was obliterated by the overload; perhaps it was simple curiosity:

I wandered on.

Both human, both female, shoulder to shoulder and with bright squares of red glass taped to their foreheads, two women strolled up to me. "I think that's him . . ." one announced.

"Perhaps for you," said her friend. "For me, while she's quite a pleasant looking male . . ."

"I'm complimented." I smiled. I nodded. "But while I'm indeed male, this woman is going to refuse your proposition!"

"Me? Propositioning *you*?" said the first. She laughed again, a little sadly I thought, shrugged, and turned to leave.

"Tell me," I asked the other, "who is that over there?"

Faint light pulsed around an immensely fat woman in

a black jumpsuit, sitting by one of the belts that lowered little trays of warm, boring food-curds down from the darkness into the fluted plastic flange on the carpet.

"Ah, a sad story," the remaining woman said, "and I don't want to tell it. Why don't you go over and ask? I'm sure she'll give you *some* information."

So I did. (Was it the hum in my head that made me act so strangely . . . ?) She turned up a huge face, large pores about her nose and above thin oily eyebrows.

"What are you doing?"

"Eating myself to death on uncooked food," she whispered. In her hand, with its depressed knuckles and upper finger joints twice as thick as the next ones down, she held a paring knife, with which she seemed to conduct unheard musicians.

"Oh . . . ?"

"It will take several years. I'm in charge of the whole station, you see. Its administration, that is. I stay in the pits between the worldlets. Never go down, in any of three possible directions. This is where I $work_2$."

"And the overload . . . ?" I asked.

The face was too thick to register with any precision the expression bone and muscle within pulled and pushed it towards. But I think she was surprised. "Overload—? What, another?"

"Yes," I admitted, and wondered if my $employer_1$ back on Nepiy had been as odd a woman of her species as this woman was of mine. "It's going on right now." I rubbed the back of my head, as if to remove the hum.

Perhaps she guessed what I was thinking. "At home, this behavior that you no doubt find so strange would be most ordinary—even unto my protesting its ordinariness." She speared something off a rising tray and nibbled at it. "I'm very competent at both job_1 and job_2. It's just $homework_3$ that defeats me."

"You're not connected to GI?" I asked.

"Oh, good-night, no!" She nibbled from the knife. "No one is who actually *works* here."

"Let *me* have him." Two hands closed on my arms from behind, warm and callused. I looked at them. Large, engagingly grubby, they belonged to a smiling male, with yellow hair that lazed over forehead and ears. "There's been one overload condition or another, four, five hours a

day now for months. Come away to my little world to see
if we can find an hour or so of pleasure for us both . . . ?"

And I thought: he's not so bad.

"Take her! Take her!" said the obese administrator.
"Let me get back to my debauchery."

I took his hand. "Hello. My name is Marq Dyeth."

"I'm Seven. Forty-six of us were cloned during a
population drive on my home world: A to Z, AA to MM,
and One to Eighteen. Would you believe, not one of us
works at home any more? I'm an electrical mechanic. So
were most of my sisters. . . ." Talkative, friendly, he took
me along the dark corridor, where I glanced about at
various sights within and without the transparent covering;
marvels of architecture hung like some intensely alien
statuary along one of my own world's runs.

Gravity shifted.

Instead of bounding lightly uphill, we were leaning
back against the faintest slope down (artificially maintained),
till he led me off into some hangar's gigantic workroom,
hung with odd-looking torches and grapples. The smell
was interesting, but sex—as it so often turns out with such
folks from newly and intensively populated worlds, was a
hopelessly complex affair involving so much equipment
that by the time he was a-crackle with sparks from the
low-amperage high-voltage electrodes that he had me play
across his handsome, lithe body in its various manacles
and restraints, I was more working off the overload than
against it.

All I can say is that, like some diplomat himself, he
was as obliging to me as I was to him, with only one or two
quizzical and good-natured inquiries, while I managed to
drink his semen and induced his rectum to drink, as it
were, mine—he held me with hard arms and legs and
said: "Oh. . . ." And, minutes later, "You're a very interesting woman."

"So are you," I said, though it was more camaraderie
than critical judgment.

"Have you ever thought how vulnerable we are here?"
she (as I could only bring myself to call her now) asked,
coiling up wires and pushing machines about the parti-
tioned flooring. "This isn't a world, you know—though we
all try to pretend it is. But it could go up like that—" She
touched an electrode to some metal plate, so that it sparked

and snapped— "and we'd all be gone, except the dozen or so of us who could get to the nearest ship." She pulled a strap of her coveralls over one hard and dirty shoulder. "Ten thousand people gone, like that—with only a few hundred getting out."

"Yes." I raised an eyebrow. (Do you see, with the frequency of such speculations why I discounted those of my employer₁ on that other—what was its name? Yes, Nepiy—world?) "I suppose."

"And yet—" She stood— "we never do. It's probably because here we have no Family, no Sygn."

"You know—" I smiled, recalling how worried the women of Nepiy and fifty other worlds had been— "for Cultural Fugue to take place, you have to have a culture . . ."

"True," she offered.

"I bet you grew up right in the middle of the Family."

"And your world was a Sygn world, wasn't it?"

"True," I returned. "At least my part of it." While both of us wondered how we knew, she went with me to another well-lighted corridor in the rhisome of corridors that webbed Kantor's three little worlds. "Odd," I said as we walked, "but just a while ago, someone mentioned a whole world to me that recently got destroyed. Just a few women survived."

(You've been looking. You've been listening. No, I knew neither Korga's name nor his world's, yet I *had* heard of them, and had already passed the information on.)

"Mmmm," said my tall mechanic, as if she'd been given something fine to eat. "Was it a Family world, or with the Sygn?"

"They didn't say," I said.

We turned another corner.

So she said: "This will take you back where you want to go." Then, with the goodwill and self-confidence only people who know for sure they are largely liked by lots of women can show, she said: "A whole world . . . !" Then she made a funny little hand motion (which, I suspect, would have meant the same as if I'd shaken my head) and turned away.

Broad, breezy, full of detours, underpasses, and overhangs, the hallways I walked back down to ground level through were an allegory of the informative complexities that Free-Kantor both was and was made for.

And the overload hum was *still* going on!

That I've *never* known to happen. Information overload in a major GI sorting system is something that's supposed to stop after a second or two, maybe ten at the very most, certainly no more than ten minutes. This jam finally concluded with a sudden burst that brought me up short over the large red and blue plastic panels of the water fountain where I'd just bent to drink, with the declaration:

In Arachnia as it is spoken on Nepiy, "she" is the pronoun for all sentient individuals of whatever species who have achieved the legal status of "woman." The ancient, dimorphic form "he," once used exclusively for the genderal indication of males (cf. the archaic term *man*, pl. *men*), for more than a hundred-twenty years now, has been reserved for the general sexual object of "she," during the period of excitation, regardless of the gender of the woman speaking or the gender of the woman referred to.

Which is to say, on Nepiy "he" meant exactly what it did on my own home world or, indeed, here, at Kantor, far off it.

But somehow during the overload, the question had become misfiled or misplaced in my own mind, so that for a moment I felt as if I were being given the answer to a perfectly irrelevant query instead of what, an hour before, I'd asked.

The disorientation, even more than an hour of oppressive hum from the overload, completely struck me away from the feeling that, I realized as it ceased, was probably the reason why I'd come to Free-Kantor in the first place, braving all her inconveniences: here I was in the center of the night—which now, while the water bobbled slowly over the huge, plastic sheets, changed to the conviction that, lost in darkness eternal, I was (at least for the moment) nowhere at all!

TWO

The Flower and the Web

One of my earliest memories—

But I must interrupt to ask: does the above disorientation and estrangement return me to this early moment in the mode of terrified retreat, or do I come to it through a broad and relaxed sense of disinterested aesthetic contrast? Both terror and aesthetics no doubt fuel memory to spear night and time to that morning thirty (standard) years before, but in what form, combination, interplay? Perhaps the answer is in the account itself. Or is it likely that women are just more complex than can be made out by starlight alone?

—the memory: crawling the soft nursery loam between the furry bodies of my schoolmates, some of whom were beginning to get dark scales on their backs; being licked a lot and occasionally licking (though it struck me even then as silly), I wondered at all those tongues that spoke so much better than mine but said such silly things: "The sunlight falling, oh, my goodness! You're not {a shell, oh {"A house?
{never! You're not my goodness either. Ha! Ha! . . . That's
{   called
{Never will you taste like a shell or good either!"
laughter, and this is sun, and this is sand. . . ." (How many dozen evelm playwrights have used the speech of

the nursery to lend poetry, poignance, and whimsy to politics and passion?) Crawl a little. Sniff a claw (or a hand); sit back and laugh. Listen. Look. Crawl. For all our world, I suppose we looked—as real adults of both species are always pointing out—like innumerable miniatures rehearsing the movements that will go into future homework3 along the corridors of some shadowed run, trough to trough, statue to statue. Finally I got to an area where a naked (like me) human (like me) male (like me) was kneeling in the dirt. Through the leaves above the nursery's plastic roof, Iiriani light dappled the unfamiliar figures. Differences between us? Well, the child was two years or so older than I, and at that age such seems an eternity of wisdom and power. The hair was yellow and smooth. (Mine: rough and nappy, the color of wet sand.) The face was round, with bright brown eyes not deep at all in the friendly face. (Mine: the lightest tan, they peer from non-epicanthic caves.) As I watched, he—and I can say that honestly now—dug up handful after handful of dirt. I remember thinking how pale and strong his hands were. Perhaps six? Maybe seven? Myself, I couldn't have been more than five.

The child was an appalling nail-biter, which is a habit humans can have and evelmi, as far as my experience of their claws goes, cannot. The dirt had darkened his knuckles and put a black line about the wrecks of those nails, harried back from the grubby crowns toward cuticles that had thickened in defense against even more gnawing. He looked up and smiled.

I smiled back and watched, fascinated, while he patted and pawed the hulk of some marvelous sand castle to shape. At that age, I did not know that at one time perhaps a fifth of the human race had such pale skins and such colored and textured hair—and were called Caucasian, nor that over the six thousand worlds today well over half have such marvelous eyes as his, once called Mongolian. The other children, some human, some evelm, whispered and gamboled around us. . . .

Sometimes I think I watched him only a moment; sometimes I think I stared at him an age.

Then: a black claw descended, like the huge limb of some mechanized sculpture falling into activity.

The youngster looked up to grin at some hovering parent (like mine): rough and grainy where they emerged from the bark-black hide, becoming metal smooth as they curved to needle tips, iron-colored talons spoke only to me of distance but not of specific origin.

The child reached up.

Claw and hand grappled—

I couldn't have watched that juncture more than a moment. Even then I knew the tussle of a parent picking up a child to go off somewhere into the city—home, for me.

But for him? Really, then, I knew little of the two kinds of flesh joined there, or of the disparate organic body chemistries that, some places on my world, sunder the species and at others are the parameters about which everything that is human and everything that is evelm are in play.

They were gone.

I was left, amidst the other children, furred or fleshed, fingered or clawed, to tell myself endless stories over the next years as to why, for a few hours, that child had been there. The most obvious answer? He and a parent had been passing through Morgre and the child had simply been left off at the nursery to play a while. But not a year standard has gone by when, in some lone moment, I haven't enhanced on some recomplication of a human child's and a black-scaled beast's adventuring together across my world, during which, momentarily, I glimpsed an instant of it: their joined hands within a strange nursery under leaf-shadowed light.

2.

A grandmother of mine was an Industrial Diplomat. So was one of my mothers. But though two of my female siblings share the vocation, I am the only male of my ripple to take on Industrial Diplomacy as my primary profession—a profession$_1$ I sometimes slip into thinking of as the Dyeths' traditional calling now for three of our seven waves. And suddenly this memory—recent, adult, insistent, yet trivial:

Walking across the green terraces, home from some job$_1$ or other, both eager to see them and uneasy over the prospect of all that food and fellow feeling, as the oestern

court's black and silver wall rose on its humming treads to
reveal some visiting aunt, who turned ponderously behind
the Dyethshome ampitheater's ornate railing, a long fork
waving from one midclaw, to call first with one tongue,
then with another: "But of course!" going from vibrant
basso to treble: "I know you! You're one of my marvelous
little human relatives! Now you're . . . ?" and couldn't
remember my name to save herself.

But with this interruption, among all possible stream-
ing memories, I find myself turning to another, again,
earlier.

The true possibility of my becoming an Industrial
Diplomat (Marq Dyeth, auntie! Marq Dyeth!) no doubt
goes back at least to the year I spent offworld with my
grandmother Genya. Well under one percent of the population of any world will ever set foot on any other. Vaurine
tours satisfy the wanderlust of the rest. Still, *we* could; and
she thought it was a Good Thing. So we went a star away
and I waited on the wet moon, called Senthy, of a gas
giant that, itself, had no name but only a number, while
Genya snarled and unsnarled herself from the Web, and I
mooned about the rust-blotched plates of the administra-
tive hangars' tall doors outside the new space port, mum-
bling over lessons fed directly into my mind by a voice
with a strange accent and prompted by visual aids—the
image of some locally engineered amphibious kangaroo
stopping you on the crumbly black path—whose colors
always seemed too intense for the green clouded horizon
against which they were projected.

A year later we were back on Velm, in the Fayne-
Vyalou, at Morgre, Genya happy to be home and angry at
the Web policies that had made the return so precipitate;
and I settled into a more usual routine—usual for someone
like me in a situation like mine on my particular world. In
my particular place on it. Only now I'd had a year to see
how unusual, in universal terms, my usual could be. Certainly such knowledge ripened me for the memory I wish
to recount:

Twelve years old, then, and studying with the tracers,
I find this persists as strongly as the memory from the
nursery. An apprentice, I was assigned to accompany some
older cadets down into one of Morgre's lower interlevels. I
remember cables moving above us. I remember echoing

breaths and wide wings. I remember mica glimmering in the rock walls under the burning purple of the shoulder lamps.

A manufacturing union had used the upper shelves of this space for storing several tons of corrosive muck that should have been carried out to the desert months before. Turned out to be more corrosive than they'd thought. Next thing, the report arrived that it had dripped, dripped, dripped, trickled, then poured down through the eaten-away container bottoms and shelving onto some V-lifts, ratchet diggers, and transport sleds stored below. Most of them had been ruined, and tracers$_1$, roused from their sleep before dawn, had come in, tasted, tested, and foamed the place with blacklime to neutralize the corrosion. Now our group of tracers$_2$, cadets (and one apprentice: me), were coming to dig out what had to be dug and send what had been tagged, with little green plastic disks, swinging off on the salvage lines thrumming in the dark. Two males, both of us human, were among the winged females and neuters that day. I guess people notice such things, but where do you learn it's not necessary to comment on them?

Not, apparently, where the other human male was from. This one? About twenty-five—possibly thirty. It was certainly old enough to me, and the behavior was that which I would later come to associate with many humans from my world's north. A tracer$_1$, this male had taken a temporary job$_2$ here while traveling in the south. Oh, there was much of making it clear that our friend's sexual tastes were for the greater winged neuters, with much bantering apology to the smaller, gorgeously winged females, allowing how, on the part of our world *she* came from (Katour?), interracial heterosexuality was, indeed, the most prevalent perversion; but *she* was different and liked them big . . . at the same time, demonstrating much parental affection for me, as a young human: hugs, jokes, her rough black gloves with their simulated steel claws on my shoulder a lot. (She'd had scales set permanently into the flesh of her muscular back, which, as I had never seen that before, I found it both intriguing and mildly repulsive.) Boisterous, bumptious, and—to perhaps a third of the women there—charming in one way or another. Still, as far as anything I might have considered true intercourse there was nothing for me.

In purple glimmer, we found the mucky mess.

"Here, yes. You, little one," the woman in charge said with one tongue: and with two others:

{"You hold this, Dyeth."
{"I mean hold the light here."

So I did, leaning against some unsteady slab of peeling plastic, while the rest slopped forward among sticky industrial units. The foreign male pulled off her gloves, which chittered up to her belt on little chains wound into spring pulleys there—

Then somebody knocked against something; something started to topple.

"Catch it! . . . Hey, watch—! . . . What the—! . . . Hold it! Hold—" from a good many more tongues than cadets.

My beam was focused on tight, and it swung up to catch claw after claw reaching to hold back something large, metallic, and filthy. Among the claws, slipping and pushing, a pair of human hands grasped the riveted edge. Big, soiled fingers: another nail biter, he—wouldn't you know? I thought it just like that, the shift in pronoun coming just that simply, with a warmth and pleasure flowering in the danger that had already begun to resolve:

"Yeah, steady! steady! . . . We got it. . . . No, just a—There, there, now! . . . There it is!" in multiple, languid bassos, with the occasional human pitch cutting through.

Among the evelmi claws that moved about his (yes, that's what I thought), over his, or that, now reaching for another grip, his moved over, one claw had three of its talons smashed from some former accident, so that they were just splintered bits of horn sticking from the black hide. It kind of made me wince, and I wondered which of the women *that* claw belonged to.

As they settled back upright whatever it was that had almost fallen, I twisted the light beam into a wider circle, so that it expanded to include the dark-scaled heads, the rearing arms, the wings, the midlegs supporting the metal further down its runny side. And suddenly I stopped— thinking? Breathing? *Some*thing unquestioned and headlong within me had come up short:

The human hands were *not* the foreign male's—who was standing, I saw now, a little ways away, head shaking, neck rubbing, the gloves back on, as if replaced to fend the anxiety of nearly being crushed.

A muscular, human female, whom I'd hardly noticed among the several in the group, let her big hand slip from the dirty metal plate, to laugh with relief among the rest. And the claw with the broken talons belonged to a wingless male, who backed away on hind legs now, turning a bony head and tasting the air with this tongue and that, the three sections of her black-scaled chest heaving, the front four legs peddling the darkness among the gesticulations of the other tracer$_2$ cadets. . . .

The foreign male stood, grinning, dirty. . . .

In a kind of shock, I waited with them while they dug out machines and muck, while they pulled weighing scales up. I helped position refuse crates on them till I was told I was too young to do that and had better just watch. And come on, Dyeth, hold that light up now. Later, I went to the run I'd frequented since I'd been back home, because it welcomed both youngsters and oldsters, and stalked those dim halls the whole evening with a desperation I've heard adults say is common among the excitable youth, though I've never felt it to the same extent before or since. I searched up and down its mile and a half for hours, and only stopped when I found what I assumed, from their dirt and daykits, to be some returned dragon hunters who'd come here and had, drugged on what I didn't know, fallen asleep in an alcove. The human male in the party, who I rolled over on his back, was stocky (like me), bearded and hairy (like I would someday be), and not much taller than I was, with thick hands still stained with the sands from outside the city. When I finished with him, only half-responsive in his interrupted sleep, he folded those hands around my chest; and I slept against the stranger for an hour, while claws padded about us, a tongue now tasting my foot, my ear, my hands, or his; and all that watched us were the statues' faces, some with eyes, some without.

When I got home I did something I've done only perhaps six times in my life: I cut my nails, usually a normal length, usually clean (like now), as short as I could, till the nubs hurt, some of them even bleeding a little, and squatted on the green flags to rub them painfully in the dirt beside the pool in the front yard before our yard—till my mother, Max, came out to ask what in the world I was doing.

All I could do was say that, honestly, I didn't know.

I wanted to tell you just of those two images, you see: the hands—human and evelm—I saw in the nursery and the hands—evelm and human—that I saw struggling together in the interlevel in my beam. The curve those fingers made, those talons formed, were parentheses marking out something I've always felt totally within me, solid as home itself. Yet what is between them works to disrupt that totality, both *from* home itself and from worlds beyond it. The same goes for what is outside them. Why, for instance, are they split by the memory of that aunt (if she *was* an aunt) who could not remember my name? Perhaps because, with the Family trying to establish the dream of a classic past as pictured on a world that may never even have existed in order to achieve cultural stability, and with the Sygn committed to the living interaction and difference between each woman and each world from which the right stability and play may flower, in a universe where both information and misinformation are constantly suspect, reviewed and drifting as they must be (constantly) by and between the two, a moment when either information or misinformation turns out to be harmless must bloom, when surrounded by the workings of desire and terror, into the offered sign of all about it, making and marking all about it innocent by contamination.

3.

Which brings me to the second time I heard of Rhyonon or Rat Korga.

Jump weeks, worlds, stars away from them all—my home, Free-Kantor, that plain of rotting vines.

The new job$_1$ was herding machines up and out of the frozen ammonia sludge of southern Ydris across one thousand seven hundred light years to the butane winds roaring about the canyons of northern Krush. What kind of machines? The large mechanical sort, with moving parts and switches you couldn't just talk into opening or closing.

In my tiny cell of the tremendous stellar freighter, I suddenly began to receive those distressing messages that basically suggest that the job_1 is being woven through by all sorts of restraining strands from the Web. Finally, there on some station hovering among Krush's six moons above that deep green disk (a coppery sand, not vegetation), much to the blustering frustration of my new $employer_1$ somewhere down on that heavy world below, the whole thing was called off.

Spiders purred: "When you began, the Sygn was up and the Family down in that geosector of Krush. But since then, it's reversed. And I'm afraid the conflict has necessitated terminating your project. . . ." So, despite all my descriptions and redescriptions, the hulking, clanking, greasy cargo was shunted off toward Krush's hot little sun into which it would never actually fall because it would have already vanished, blown away as so much scalding mist.

Then the so friendly invitation from a high-ranking Black Widow that you cannot afford to refuse if you want to stay in my $profession_1$: "By Okk, I think you should come to a little conference the Web's holding out about seven light years in toward the center! We can bring you up to date on what's operable and what isn't in this particular cluster." It's good business since they have to pay the kill-fee on the job. "It changes so rapidly in this situation. . . ."

The "situation," of course, *is* the conflict between the Family and the Sygn: in their differing methods of preventing Cultural Fugue—largely on worlds (as more than one commentator has noted) where it wasn't very likely to happen anyway. Still, as the interstellar agency in charge of the general flow of information about the universe in many places, the Web is near to being torn apart by the fracas. The first ripple of Dyeths sat just on the edge of that fracas, watching, yes, but (according to one version) completely above such adolescent hugger-mugger, or (according to another, that you have to go rather far afield of any Dyeth to hear) green with envy that we were not in the center of those romantic schemes. After all, my seven-times great-grandmother Gylda Dyeth worked for the Family potentate, pontiff, and poet, Vondramach Okk, doing for her, I like to think, much of what I do now for $employers_1$ all over the habitable worlds. Common sense, however, tells me it must have been a much darker enterprise she was involved in. Vondramach herself, with her own dark beginnings and darker demise, was at one point sole ruler of seventeen worlds—*four* of which destroyed themselves in Cultural Fugue (and that's a lot!), while the Sygn, in those pre-Web days, was the most famous institution in the worlds. That's *real* wealth; that's *real* fame—of a sort that simply can't exist today. The Web won't let them, thank all the star-flung night!

At any rate, you go off those seven light years to some glass and plastic L-5 station, some baroquely subterranean conference center (from inside you might confuse either one with the corridors of Kantor; and you don't see much outside these days) and attend seminars and discussion groups and rapid briefing sessions in everything from local ecologics to interworld legalistics, all spiced with endlessly varied teaching aids and opinion-nudgers. You absorb and file away and forget vast amounts of data about what information is, in certain situations, as well as what information is or is not acceptable in this or that part of this or that world.

It was at one of these that I struck up my acquaintance with Clym. I question now if it *was* desire that first made me notice . . . him, the bald little gorilla with the tattoos. Perhaps, despite those leafy emblems above his collar and below his cuffs, it was just easier, in an alien field, to want someone with ankles and cheekbones so much like my own.

When I first noticed him, he was deep in conversation with a very tall woman whose epicanthic folds flattened a brown, round face. She had a broad nose and an awkward, animated air. They sat together in one of the apricot lounges, gossiping softly, leaning together, smiling a lot, his short muscular body all in black, she, towering and shirtless, wearing a skullcap tight enough to suggest that underneath she had as little hair as he did. The only phrase I actually caught from her was: ". . . by my roots on Eurd, Skychi Clym!" which suggested that she'd spent time around the Family. Well, I thought, if *I* had, I wouldn't advertise it at an official Web function.

Then, only hours later, she passed me in the hall. Her green metallic pants were probably meant to suggest she was with a world-based advisory group connected

with, but not of, the Web—which also seemed incongru-
ous: on a chain around her neck, hanging on the bony
place between her breasts, she wore a cyhnk. (This one
was a two-centimeter gold bar with a tangle of gold wires
at one end, on each wire's tip a ruby.) Well, she *could* be
a member of the Sygn. It all seemed ludicrously contradic-
tory. More, it seemed rather naive, if not impolitic, to
flaunt emblems of either—not to mention both—mutually
antagonistic faction on what should have been neutral
territory controlled by an adversary (the Web) of both.

But I was talking of Clym. More out of boredom than
real lust (for his hands were just like mine), I finally
announced: "Yes, I believe I would like to make love with
you." (He had the learning booth just behind mine, and
we were always bumping into each other—literally—when
we reported for briefing sessions.) Mine the usual trepida-
tion about approaching sexually someone from, probably,
a highly different culture. Clym refused, politely enough,
I suppose. But he also became far more friendly over the
next few days. It was he, finally, who suggested we take a
shuttle off somewhere else—anywhere else—during the
next break. "Why don't we go hit rock?" was his quaint
suggestion.

4.

The landscape we ended up in was all red sand and brown
stone. Minuscule atmosphere was kept over us by obviously artificial means: an indigo glow ribboned the horizon. A sun was about to rise—or perhaps had just set. We
must have been on some large moon, or small world,
awaiting planoforming; but I honestly don't remember
which. "I do believe," Clym sighed, heaving back his
shoulders in their tight black covering, "that we're actually
out of Web security. Isn't it nice to know nothing you say
here will be used against you?"

"That's assuming both of *us* can be trusted." But I
smiled when I said it.

Clym glanced at me with very blue eyes—a flower
tattooed on his cheek pictured some exotic bloom in different greens, with red and yellow highlights. The faint per-
fume about him, he'd already told me, was the crenna

blossom's scent, implanted in his sweat glands at the same time the image had been inked under his skin. "I know you're an ID—so you probably have your problems with our data-spinning hosts too. I doubt you'll be offering them more information than they ask for."

I've said the Web discourages interstellar travel; it also frowns on excess interstellar imports, which means such importers' minions, Industrial Diplomats, are considered a necessary evil; and there are days (if a job_1 is stymied the way my last one was) when I think of the Web in much the same terms. But probably for that reason I hadn't mentioned my $profession_1$ at the conference so far. "And what do you do_1?" was all I could come back with, while I wondered in which folders and fiches he had gone prying to find out.

"I'm a free-agented $professional_1$," Clym said with a businesslike smile. Sporting spikey leaves, the stem of the crenna went under his jaw, down his neck, and disappeared beneath the black collar. "What the good women of this universe would call a psychotic killer."

"How fascinating." Well, he was not the first I'd met; and I assume that while I'm in the $profession_1$ I am, he won't be the last. I wondered if his friend knew. "When's the last time you killed somebody?"

"Really want to know?" Clym scratched his ear with thick fingers. In orange, black, and gold, a multifanged beast's head ornamented the ham of his thumb. The creature's neck wrapped his wrist to disappear under his cuff. "You remember, during the morning session, when I slipped out of my booth for a few minutes, presumably to go to the john . . . ?"

I nodded "yes" with no memory of it at all.

Clym nodded back with deep and knowing seriousness.

"Oh . . . !" When caught in the pleats, snags, and politics texturing the surface of a world, the Family/Sygn feud can get intense. I've said my seven-times great-grandmother possibly shared my $profession_1$. In soberer moments I assume what she did for Okk was closer to Clym's calling. "At least you folks only do in one or so people at a time." Part of a diplomat's job, even an industrial one, is to be able to say something nice about everybody. "Not so long ago—oh, very far from here—someone was telling me about a whole world they thought had just gotten done in. Of course, being in my profession₁, I didn't really believe—"

"You mean Rhyonon." Gold nap hazed Clym's roundish skull. His hand went up to scratch it. "In the Tyonomega system. The seventh world out. Rhyonon."

"Was that its name?" A moment of Nepiy's loud desolation was superimposed over the quiet waste before me, bright as some GI prompt, while the possibility of belief organized itself uncomfortably. "The women who mentioned it to me didn't say. They were too concerned about the possibilities of Cultural Fugue on their own world. I wonder if this Rhyonon had gone with the Family or the Sygn?"

Clym looked at me strangely. "Then you *don't* know anything about it . . . ?"

"No. I don't, really." I'm sure I looked pretty strangely back.

"A world is a big place," Clym said, sounding like a GI prompt himself. "I was on my way to do a little job there, right when Rhyonon bought it. For the next month of my life it was all I heard about, talked about, or thought about. It's a little odd, not a month after that, to meet someone who doesn't even know for sure if it happened."

"You mean it *did* happen. . . ." I got chills, while on Clym's blondly hairy foot, a mechanical beetle with copper pincers crawled amidst tattooed green and yellow crenna roothairs, to disappear under his pants cuff. "You were there? When was it? What happened?"

"What can I tell you about Rhyonon?" Clym shrugged; and I thought, as I always do when someone begins that way about a world: What can you say that's not contradicted or obliterated by any given continental plate, geosector, county, horizon-to-horizon bit of beauty, monotony, or horror? "It was a sandy world—" (Like most—) "with a double-rotation axis, giving it an irregular day/season alteration—" (Rare; but after six months the inhabitants don't even notice—) "as well as a hot, fairly consistent temperature over the whole of it. A few canyon systems gouged about in it. Most of the population was concentrated at the equator. Lots of geological activity in the north—mainly earthquakes—that were kept down by a number of strategically placed hydraulic stations. Nothing but sand in the south. Two moons, too small to see from the surface. And a dust layer, rather than a cloud system, that reddened the day and blotted the stars at night over most of it. No indigenous life, though in the north there were the usual signs that possibly there'd once been biogenic activity. But nothing so conclusive as a fossil. There were the usual genetically tailored, imported lichens—mostly grown in the cities. And the deserts were rife with the usual atmosphere-generating bacteria that had been brought in to keep the sulphur and ammonia down and the oxygen up. A conservative, moderately populated world, it wasn't on any important data lanes. It didn't have much to offer in the line of information *for* anyone else, and it responded by claiming not to want to know anything *about* anyone else. They wouldn't even allow a GI system on surface; only a paltry one they let the Web establish on the larger moon—"

"I'm just curious," I said. "Had they aligned themselves with Family or Sygn?" I guess one just likes to know these things.

"They were still in Interplay." (That's the official name, in case you're wondering, for the state in which a world is making up its mind.) "When the first troubles were beginning to get out of hand, some conservative political party, called the Crazy Grays, which had just won a landslide election, had summoned in the Family, and immediately a radical group known as the Free-Informationists began to explore the possibilities of the Sygn. That's why I'd been asked to come there, actually—"

"You mean they'd been alerted to possible Cultural Fugue condition, they'd called in both Family and Sygn; and they *still* did themselves in?"

"I can only tell you what I saw." ·

"Tell me what you saw," I said, wondering where exactly one stands to see a world destroyed.

"You understand, I never set foot on the place. If I had, I probably wouldn't be here. Everything I've told you up till now is just from my GI prep on my way there." Clym took a breath. "I was coming in on a slow shuttle, looking like your usual flowered business woman, aiming to land on a moon. We were in the viewing lounge, when a very large, very black woman stood up and pointed through the bubble dome: at the planet, with its tan tea-cozy of dry mists—only there were burns, glowing red, patchy, slowly pulsing, glimmering all across it. You could actually *see* them moving over the planetary surface! We all kept trying to translate that motion across the visible disk into a wall of heat rushing across deserts and canyons at hundreds of kilometers a second. And didn't have much success. Then, of course, there was a swarm on General Info. Which, as you might imagine, was in chaos by now, since, as I said, it was based on a moon. At last one of the ship's captains was finally able to get through. She read out the GI report as it came over: About twelve minutes before, in the neighborhood of the equatorial complex of Gilster, a sudden flower of flame had bloomed to some three hundred kilometers in diameter. Within minutes, fireballs were springing up all around the equatorial band, with incendiary sheets rushing north and south, burning the surface dust itself."

"Fireballs? It wasn't something as primitive as atomics—?"

"Ah, but you're not letting me tell you the most interesting factor."

I frowned.

"The Xlv . . ."

My frown deepened. "What do you mean?"

"Ever heard of them?" Clym smiled over a leaf.

I suppose some movement in my cheek or knees or shoulders, or perhaps the breath—"The Xlv . . . ?"—I breathed through that vowel-less clutch of fricatives let him know I had. "That's the other race besides humans who've developed interstellar travel."

Clym nodded. "A fleet of Xlv ships had been circling the equatorial belt of Rhyonon at perhaps a hundred fifty kilometers altitude. As soon as the conflagration started, they rose to three times that height and continued their circle. The fleet, apparently, consisted of three hundred sixty—"

When Clym was silent for seconds, I asked: "Three hundred sixty what?"

"That was when General Info cut off. So we don't know—one assumes it was three-hundred-sixty-odd of their mysterious, alien ships." (The Xlv are truly alien. In this epoch of brilliant translation devices that have broken through to hundreds of species on dozens of worlds, *no* one has managed to establish any firm communication

with the Xlv.) "Though it may have been three hundred
sixty million. But for the next seventeen hours, General
Info was open for no questions beyond elementary multiplication tables and what is the time at fifteen degrees
longitude on Hephaestus VII—while Rhyonon burned itself out above us."

"Presumably they were still giving out basic naviga-
tional data?"

"Presumably. Though, from then on in, the trip to
that moon was so bumpy I wouldn't be surprised if the
captain was navigating us in by hand."

"Were the Xlv responsible? I mean, Cultural Fugue
is one thing. But for another species from another world to
destroy—?"

Clym's shrug—and perhaps his expression—halted me.
"A day later, I was holed up on a very hysterical moonside,
with a very strange planet lighting up our sky—which is to
say, it looked pretty normal again. Everybody who had
been heading for her, of course, was held up in a kind of
limbo-style detainment. Everyone had the same question
you did. But when GI came back on, however long it was
later, any request for information about the big round
world up there—who named it, when it was settled, what
its population was—or the Xlv, got you nothing but an 'All
information pertinent to your query is undergoing extensive revision.'"

"What do *you* think must have—?"

"In the Tyon-omega system, where Rhyonon was the
one habitable planet among twelve ammonia-covered, super-
large, super-hot, high-gee gas giants, all information as far
as I know is still under 'revision.' And if you were to
request any information, anyplace else in the known galaxy, about Rhyonon, you will get a really astonishing run-
around of cross-references that, as you go pinning them
down, will finally result in your question being declared
nonsense."

"You're telling me all references to an entire *world*
have been removed from all the General Information systems on six-thousand-plus others?"

"I can't believe all six-thousand-plus *have* General
Info. But on the twelve I've visited since Rhyonon that
do—which are pretty widely flung worlds at that—it seems
to be the case."

"Amazing," I said. "I'd be curious to see how they've set up the run-around circuit. I've seen some that were really quite clever." They're frowned on by the Web but sometimes are necessary with information the kind of commodity it's become. "I think when we get back to the conference center, I'll just casually put in a request for data about—"

"Don't." Clym gave me one of those strangely inappropriate grins that are the hallmark of his profession₁. "I've been called in now more than once this month to dispense a couple of folk who, among other things, did. When you do, anywhere in the known galaxy, your security status automatically changes in your Web-dossier to one that, even if it doesn't get you killed, will probably make your professional₁ life difficult, to say the least."

I frowned. "Clym, are you telling me something I don't really want to know?"

Clym shrugged. "You brought it up."

During the silence I wasn't saying anything in, Clym squinted off into the indigo, took a few steps forward, shaded his eyes, and turned his head left and right, for all the world like some dragon hunter out of my childhood on Velm (radar bow on shoulder, scanning the dawn for the flights of the more beautiful beasts). He was probably checking out some satellite schedule. I watched him with nostalgia and distrust. Since I couldn't say, *But why are you telling me all this?* I asked instead: "What about the survivors, Clym?"

His head swiveled back to lock my gaze with sapphire eyes.

"Clym, a world *is* a big place." (Agents are carefully programmed psychotics—hyper-rational on all macrobehavior, but, when push comes to shove, crazier than any number of coots.) "I mean, *some*where across Rhyonon's entire surface some shuttle boat must have just been taking off with half a dozen passengers for a moon; someone must have been at the bottom of a mine shaft and sealed in, only to be clawed out by a Web rescue team in low-heat suits; someone must have been hauled up from the bottom of an ocean in a research bathosphere that happened to have its own air supply . . . ?"

"Rhyonon had three extensive artificially maintained underground river networks—comparable to seas. Their coverings were blown away and their contents were boiled off in the conflagration; their basins are now craters of fused and bubbled slag . . . as is about thirty percent of the planetary surface."

I lowered an eyebrow. "I thought you said General Info was dead on the subject . . . ?"

"We are both—" Clym gave a little snort that sounded like my favorite younger sister's nervous laugh, which still gets on my nerves— "in professions$_1$ where information leaks. The survivors . . . Why don't *you* tell *me* about a survivor?"

"Well . . ." I frowned, wondering what exactly he meant. "Like we said, worlds are big. You say moderately populated. But I have no idea what Rhyonon's population was. A third of a billion, if it was an average industrial world around for more than eight or nine generations. A few hundred million, if it was still being explored. If it was just an experimental station, it could just be a few thousands—"

"It wasn't an experimental station."

"All right," I said. "Your average survivor on your average world: she'd be about forty or forty-five years old, your normal fifth generation—" I stopped. "No. . . ." (Clym's eyes were bright, sharp.) "I have this sudden picture, this image: she'd be the lowest of the low, the person most people would think the least likely to survive such a catastrophe, perhaps some kind of mentally retarded idiot, who only came through because of some fluke that happened to . . ." Then I laughed—it may just have been embarrassment under Clym's bright, narrowing gaze—because I realized another image was fighting my imagination. "Another possibility: she's a great sage, a genius, a hermit, a woman who's fled the coils and toils of her society, living alone in some burning valley, or on top of some freezing mountain—at any rate somewhere as far away from the population centers as possible, busily devoting herself to the acquisition of spiritual knowledge, who, long ago, because she saw through the sham of her society's pretensions, sequestered herself. And now, all at once, flames on all sides, above her, below her, around her; and somehow, miraculously, she remains untouched. . . ." I faltered, feeling the frown at work through my features.

Clym said: "None of us knows anything about the survivor."

"*The* . . . ?" I said. "There's *only* one?" (Look. Listen. . . .)

"If there's one or a hundred, we don't know anything about her—or them. And yet, notice how we go on talking as if there were, as if there had to be."

"But to imagine the population of a *world* completely de—"

"Exciting, isn't it?" Clym's hand suddenly came forward to touch my neck. His voice dropped. "Within seventy-two hours, my friend, if we still know each other, I am going to take you by force, chain you in a special chamber I have already equipped for the purpose, and do some very painful things to your body that will possibly—the chances are four out of five—result in your death, and certainly in your permanent disfigurement, mental and physical." (We live in a medically sophisticated age. You have to work very hard to permanently disfigure any body.) "I've done some checking on you and found that you are a strange human being—at least to me: your sexual predilections run toward only one gender, and only of a few species. You make distinctions between pain and pleasure that are baffling to me yet highly interesting to contemplate violating. You've informed me of the nature of your desire for me. It is only fair, I feel, to inform you of the nature of mine toward you. You are, of course, free to absent yourself from my company. But if you do not, what I speak of *will* happen . . . though another woman, male or female, or any of several species of plants will replace you if you decide to leave. These are distinctions you make in your desire and pursuit of the whole that I, fortunately, am not encumbered with. Do you understand?"

"Just tell me," I said, my throat dry, suddenly and uncomfortably so, "is this part of your job₁ or just your way of being friendly?"

"Though my sexuality is not part of my psychosis, they have been integrated carefully by some very clever people." She moved one and another finger (and from then on, "she" was the only way I could think of her) against my carotid. "As of now, the distinction between work and pleasure is one I do not make."

"Oh," I said.

5.

We got back to the conference with no further breach of
politesse, at least as far as I could tell. I asked for an
immediate transfer to another section of the seminar, meeting some sixty million kilometers away. Minutes later in
my room, my callbox beeped approval.

As I was hurrying down the hall to catch my shuttle
boat, a tall figure, suited from feet to face in scarlet, ran
up to me. "Skri Marq . . . ?" She made a few wriggling
motions and scarlet fell away from her black cap, her
silver-shot eyes (contact lenses? corneal tattoos?), her neck,
her shoulders. Scarlet peeled from breasts, arms, sides,
and belly, to float out about her waist like a bloody crenna.
"Skri Marq, have you seen Skina Clym?" I didn't recognize the particular honorifics. Worlds that have them,
have them by the dozens. But whenever you come to an
official Web function, there's usually a note somewhere
among the cards, tapes, and fiche-crystals they present
you with as you arrive asking you, please, while in Web
territory, not to employ them at all. "I really must find
Skon Clym. She's such a fascinating woman. I *am* totally
fascinated by her, you know. I only hope she is as fascinated with me." She dropped her head fondly—and a bit
quizzically—to the side.

As red petals began to close about her, I suddenly
touched her arm. "I'm sure you will. But you *must* ask her
to be *very* clear about her intentions toward you. Remember that. It's very important."

"Oh, Skyla Marq!" (Apparently my status had changed;
perhaps after one has answered a question . . . ?) "Do you
think . . . *he* really might . . . that someone like Skoi
Clym might even . . . !" And the star-flung night alone
(and maybe a population of sixty or seventy million) knows
what a *Skoi* might be. "This whole experience here, in the
Web, has been so thrilling, so expansive, so growth-
provoking!" An open smile hung beneath her filigreed eyes
widened above. "And, by ancient Eurd, to think that someone like Skyotchet Clym might even be interested in . . ."
Red sealed in it and her cyhnk.

"No one likes advice. Still, remember mine. Please."

I suppose I had been overcome with an image of the naive worldling, lost among such intrigues as bloom and blossom in the Web. Clearly she'd been displaying every emblem she could think of to impress the spiders at their spinning, while understanding none of those emblems' import. "Take care of yourself now. Take very serious care. But now you must excuse me." Then I went sixty million kilometers away.

And wished it were sixty million light years and in another sun system.

The weeks passed. The seminar ended. Then light years, finally, obliterated mere interplanetary distance.

What can I say?

Things like that happen in my profession$_1$. I don't mean worlds getting destroyed. I mean encounters with the odd creations of our epoch, like Clym. I know about security reclassifications. If I couldn't check out General Info about Rhyonon, then there was nothing to do but put it out of my mind—sort of.

THREE

Visitors on Velm

Which is what—sort of—I did.

Until I got home.

Home?

It's the place you can never visit for the first time, because by the time it's become "home," you've already been there. You can only return. (You never go home, only go home again.) *My* home?

Star-system: Iiriani/Iiriani-prime. (Yes, a double.)

World: Velm. (No, we never have two solar blobs high in the sky. Iiriani is our sun, and sometimes Iiriani-prime is a blazing star that blues a few degrees of the night or, during some of our days, puts a nova-point in the greenish blue. Iiriani has two more worlds beside Velm, a large one and a small one, neither good for much. Iiriani-prime has a single ball of iron and ice swinging around it called Micha, into whose interior have been sunk a few research stations. And Velm's got two small moons . . . like Rhyonon.)

Geosector: M-81. (What else? Well, we call it the Fayne-Vyalou, locally, after the two large plains, one raised, one not, which makes up most of it. It lies surrounded by Velm's southeastern mountains and mineral oil swamps.)

Urban complex: Morgre. (The seven levels of the city—four of them underground—are sunk between a hot

-wr and a valley in the Myaluth Range. The upper levels, irregularly spaced at different heights, with their great pylons supporting one atop the other atop the other, are recreation areas, spacious parks. . . .)

Morgre?

Let me tell you about Morgre.

2.

Among urban complexes it's the third largest in our geosector, which, in world terms, makes it an astonishingly unflamboyant place. If you come expecting one of the great cities of the north—Melchazidor, Ahrun, Katour (with its Grand Triple Run), Eblevelma, or even more southernly Farkit or Hanra'a'sh—you'll be disappointed.

I don't know where the basic design for our world's urban complexes came from. Still, the notion was that, given a certain amount of successful planoforming, the complexes themselves should be ecologically more or less self-contained, which means they could be sunk just about anywhere—and, over most of our world, they are.

But Morgre's site was chosen with some care.

Where the red rock drape-forms of the Myaluth Range end, a ribbon of hot-swamp—the Hyte-wr—winds out onto the pitted Vyalou Plain. Dozens of species of indigenous gnats, gold, black, and red, swarm above the Hyte's brackish sludge. During the day the blue erupting fumes are visible for kilometers.

Years before Morgre proper was sunk, several furniture and tool-making collectives organized themselves along the Hyte-wr's oestern bank, then called Morgre. (Oh, yes: for reasons no doubt lost in colonial archives, our world has five points on its compass: north, east, south, oest, and west—instead of four or six like most others.) The industrial collectives used the swamp's natural heat to run their machines, while the tolgoth trees (closer to a kind of cactus) foresting the Hyte-wr's north shore provided their almost unworkably hard pith for lumber. Processed by an ore-smelting co-op ten kilometers up the narrow Myaluth Pass, sponge-copper and heavier metals were worked into blades, wires, switches, and chips. Chained to their slippads with the old-fashioned, black, flat-sided links, the

orange ingots had been hauled in along a monoline running part of the three hundred kilometers in from Helk'um
Port, where the space shuttles still come in on the lavid
plains that hold the circular ridges of ancient craters,
eroded away over most of the rest of the world.

The old monoline's pentalons have been down for fifty
years, but their star-form supports are still clamped, in
clusters of five, to the pebble-pocked rocksheets. As children, we used to scooter out over the sarb-grass and
silvagorse mortaring the porous stones that footed the
Myaluths and, wandering among them, guess at what those
meter-wide claws grasping the ground could possibly have
been, while the black and green coaches of the present
monoline whistled above us on humming cables down into
the city.

The nematode farm on the southern edge of present
Morgre claims an unbroken line in their service cooperative going back well before the sinking of Morgre itself. Its
founding year is proclaimed in silver letters over its gates:
2521 Web Standard. Silver is common on Velm—about as
common as calcium was supposed to be (according to
Family historians) on Earth. For years, 2521 was the most
repeatedly mentioned date in Morgre's local facribbons,
which, after the six o'clock, two o'clock, and ten o'clock
shift-breaks, twisted and blew along the edge of the ground-
level alleys where the workers$_2$ discarded them—wafting
toward the gulping grills of the quietly bellowing cleaners,
for all the world like the blue smokes curling over the
Hyte.

When I was ten (proportionately more stocky, substantially less hairy), I joined a chemistry study-group in
which two of my older groupies worked on the wormfarm
with their parents. Soon, half the kids in the group had
trial jobs$_2$ there. For me, it was sorting spawn samples into
glass vials on a dusty plank table, while the shadow of the
window pole, from Velm's larger moon, swung across the
floor to give way to the dawning light of, first, our larger,
then our minuscule, sun. I thought then that the huge
cooling pits outside, the racks of ten- and fifteen-meter
strainers casting checkered shadows over the broken fields,
and especially the dirt clotting the underground support
beams holding up the roofs of the kilometers on kilometers
of catacombs where most of the adults worked, must all go

back to the founding. Everything, including you, stays so dirty on a nematode farm—which, to a kid like me from Dyethshome, was half the fun. Later, as a teenager, I saw some pictures of the original farm co-op, c. 2,521: a bunch of grinning, grimy women, some human, some evelm, in odd-looking work outfits (bare chests; oddly paneled skirts), toiling on land a fiftieth the size it is now, using hand-strainers and pick-axes on a bit of yield-soil the size of the skene in the Dyethshome amphitheater.

Such violence to the known turns home into history.

What actually brought Morgre here, however, was the Retreat of the Arvin. I've never thought of my world as one where the Family had real influence, yet I know (human) Family adherents from the north first came to the sparsely populated south and built their retreat on the site where a few local evelmi vaguely thought an ancient temple may once have stood. (Which is the Family in a dyllhull for you.) Its glacine cases housed the gold inch, the silver meter, the platinum centimeter bars, the vibrating quartz crystals measuring out nanoseconds and Standard Years, the plastic molecular models of human DNA, all lovingly imported (supposedly) from world to world, their origin supposed to be the original Old Eyrth. Completing a swing that had already finished in the north and that had no doubt driven those settlers here, the religious revolution which made the Sygn the official dogma of this world arrived in the south; but it was carried out in our area fairly peacefully, well before anyone thought to construct a city. A bunch of locals—some concerned evelmi, some enlightened humans—came round, so goes the tale, and said with lots of tongues at once: "Get this tasteless garbage *out* of here!" and unlike some places throughout the six thousand worlds I could name, there were no staunch objections. (The riots in the polar caves of Minjin-IX; the burnings, the mass slayings among the floating labyrinths on the magma fields of Nok Hardrada . . .) Of course the Sygn wanted to find the name of the deity or dedicatee of the "temple" on the original site: Arvin is Velm's smaller moon, which by night looks no larger than Iiriani-prime by day. And Arvin was the best they could come up with, since concepts like "temple," "deities," "ancient," "dedicatees," and even "name" just didn't fit into the local evelmi culture at the time the way humans might have expected. What replaced the imported holy objects in the newly-renamed-with-its-more-or-less-old-name "Retreat of the Arvin" was, among other things, the earliest vaurine library in the area—where, two hundred fifty years later, I went to see the old projections of the wormfarm, actually. Indeed, some of the original measurement standards—in their original cases, say the little cards under them—were eventually returned to the museum. Since the Sygn is concerned with preserving the local history of local spaces, the Family occupation of the retreat was now part of that history.

So there you are.

Indeed, I only learned the dogma actually practiced there was part of the Sygn after I'd spent that year offworld with my Grandmother Genya on Senthy. (The long, thin parks with their sudden curves at the end, where the pockmarked fisherwomen, waiting for work, walked up and down, up and down, under the high transparent roofs stained a perpetual brown by Senthy's rusty rains.) There I'd seen rituals, cyhnks, and services so vastly different from the ones here at home as to be unrecognizable: then the return, to discover that the Sygn itself—which is only a name, pronounced a thousand different ways, spelled differently in a hundred different languages—was all it was: but one of the Sygn's most widely spread tenets (and, like everything else in the Sygn dogma, it, too, no matter how wide, does not obtain everywhere) is that history is what is outside, in both time and space, the current moment of home. And without history, there is no home. A second tenet that usually (though, like all else, not always) goes along with the first: when you go to a new world, all you can take of your home is its history. And if you are a woman, your choice is to take it knowingly and be its (and your new home's) silent friend, or to take it unknowingly and be its (and your new home's) loud slave.

And "slave" is one of those words in Arachnia that, amidst a flurry of sexual suggestions, strongly connotes the least pleasant aspects of "master."

But even compared to other spots on Velm, our Sygn retreat here at Morgre was quite modest. Our local Arvin produced no famous mystics, no writers of profound tracts, no multivoiced orators, or even thirty-tongued preachers—and few brooding sermons. But it served as a cultural and social center for the Morgre area when there was nothing here, beside the Hyte-wr, but a loose association of labor communes and cooperatives, nestled at the foot of the Myaluths. Still, many of the primitive statues in the Arvin's meditation gardens, rich with wood (pith, really), metal, and local gemstones decorating the basic plastine forms, made up in invention and passion what they lacked in sophistication: the itinerant evelm (and sometimes human) artists, who traveled from retreat to retreat in those days, leaving a sculpture here or a net-tapestry there as offering for their fare and lodging, had a sense—the best of them—of what would widen a local's eyes. When the retreat was moved three hundred meters south to make way for the sinking of Morgre proper, only two of the meditation gardens were reconstructed on the new site. (The statuary from the other three is now at Dyethshome.) In my own too infrequent visits to the Arvin, where it currently stands, its pale blue walls set with carved portrait faces, licked over with reddish schist-moss, gazing out onto Morgre's South Plaza Market, I doubt I've ever seen more than six people at a time using either one of the remaining gardens for actual inward-communion. But tradition has it that, in the early days, area meetings were held there in which four or five hundred workers$_2$ would come to vote and discuss local and geosector policy and offer replacement ones. Presumably hundreds among them stayed to meditate—though where hundreds might lie down to pray, even in five gardens, always puzzled me, since I could visualize no more than twenty people at a time using the ones they still had.

The seven levels of Morgre were sunk into the scrumbly stones of the Vyalou in 2,588 Web Standard. Its northern edge just touches the three artificial spurs that had been dug off the Hyte. The Myaluths to the west offer substantial protection from the hotwinds that tear over most of three months through the otherwise balmy climate in this geosector, bringing scalding grit and the stench of acetone all during the season of the pearlbats.

Hotwinds make the above-ground parks and recreational levels of a number of the larger urban complexes further oest and north pretty much a joke. Five hundred kilometers away in Farkit they put out warning signs half an hour before a blow is expected—and *every*one goes underground. Here in Morgre, because of the Myaluths, with goggles and a good sandsuit, humans for an hour and evelmi for three can actually walk around in one, though it's not fun.

And in the same year as the sinking of Morgre, on what is occasionally called Dyeth's Rise, by Whitefalls— one of the three waterfalls the Sygn was able to coax from the underground water springs about here, whose streams join in Morgre's Central Park, to flow away and finally mingle with the hot oils of the Hyte—at the end of the path of polychrome clays, flanked with topaz cactus, Mother Dyeth, who had just resumed a job$_1$ as a foreman at one of the furniture communes and had taken a job$_2$ as a spiritual advisor at the Arvin, instructed the great offworld ships and cross-country transports that sidled up beside the already bustling cranes and diggers and crawlers and loaders furiously laying in the underground levels of Morgre complex (and the ships and transports all bore the insignia of Vondramach Okk) to erect the astonishing gift she had been presented with, a gift so large its implication may never really have penetrated to the folk with whom she had worked in this area five years before.

But that's to get away from Morgre proper and turn to the castle going up—and down—by the waterfall to the east. And though that castle, Dyethshome, is my home, that's not yet my plan.

3.

Just off Fayne-run, centered in Morgre's fourth layer down, Dylleaf Crescent has got to be the dingiest street in the city. Up between slanted black columns, high ceilings had once displayed elegant frescoes. But during a long forgotten industrial overflow, a union lower down had requisitioned the roof for storage space, bolting up their ribbed and rickety gondolas. Eventually some of them had been removed. Some had simply been emptied, but still hung there. A lot of the frescoes had come down with them, so that blotches of dirty yellow plaster now patched what was left of the gray, green, and gold.

The street cleaners must have been on the blink again, because facribbons had been trampled into mulch and kicked against the stone walls, too wet and wadded for the air currents to lift and carry toward the waiting grills. (Sometime soon, tracers$_2$ would arrive with their wide blades to scrape them away. . . .) I ducked through a stone gate a head too low for me.

And I'm not tall.

But the gate had been put up generations ago when it was just assumed no human would ever live here—though once, on a labor$_2$ sabbatical, I'd had my living room only meters away.

In the dusty floor, six limen plates made a hexagon. Overhead, four of the six viewing lights worked, thrusting misty pillars down from the darkness.

I stepped onto one. "Santine," I called, "are you at home?" (At home my own viewing light wasn't working so I couldn't see who was at my plate.) "Santine?"

"Oh, just a second, will you. There . . ." and I felt the sensation that is something like rising but more like falling, in a column of light. . . .

"So." Santine reared up on her hind fours and dropped her black, scaly head to the side. "You're back from gallivanting about the stars and have decided to pay a world-bound friend a visit."

"Actually, I've been back for three days. But my job$_2$ caught me up immediately out at the home and I've just only been able to try any new tastes since this afternoon."

"Well, come in. Come in, and I'll find us something interesting to suck on."

I stepped off the plate onto the gray and blue clays that stretched off to the hedges of silvagorse and on for desolate kilometers toward the middling cliffs. At the horizon was Morgre, in which I had been only seconds before. The city lay, like a toy of girders and plates, dark and miniature in the west. The sky to its left was still copper.

Under indigo air, pole lights stood at half-illumination about the semi-tiers of stone into which Santine's room was hewn. Out of season, five or six pearlbats flicked at the tallest. Outside on Dylleaf there'd been the warm bellow of the street cleaners; here there was natural breeze.

"Sit. Sit." With bluish claws she plumped a pile of cushions covered by an antique web-work tapestry she'd brought with her from Hysy'oppi in the north, years before I was born. "All safe for you. Sit."

I went over and dropped on the soft seat, while she went to rummage in the white cabinets that stood about the room. "So, you folk out in the prestigious rim of the city have decided to pay a visit to the center. Ah, riches! Ah, poverty!"

"Oh, come now," I said. "Someone of your profession₁ has been many times richer than I five times over." Santine was a tracer₁, and the exchange was one of the rituals that had grown up here in the south to integrate the human concern for wealth with a culture that had no concept for uneven-distribution-of-exchange-power (so that it took its neuroses out in much more interesting—to humans—ways). "I've been meaning to pay you a visit ever since I got back. And now I have!"

Santine found one stone on one shelf, licked it, then found another—tried that one. "How're the rest of the worlds in the universe rolling along?"

"Oh, well enough, I suppose—though a month or so back I was on a world called Nepiy . . ." But Nepiy took me to another world that no longer existed and that I didn't want to talk about. "Well, *they* had their problems! But then, why talk about unpleasantnesses here. Popping around the universe the way I do, the only thing that still surprises me is that there're so many humans in it."

"Billions," Santine said, picking up a third stone. "Over how many worlds? Thousands of worlds, you told me once."

I leaned my elbows back on the cushions. "The truth is, Santine, I don't have any *real* concept of how a billion differs from a million. Or a thousand. At least in real terms. No human does."

"I've heard—" Santine turned, on her hind legs now, flavor stones on all four foreclaws— "that, other than by abstraction, none of you can really count above three."

"I don't know about that," I said. "But just for an example, I've walked into the Dyethshome amphitheater when it was three-quarters full and then again when it was four-fifths full and had no immediate sense of the difference." The amphitheater at Dyethshome has ninety-nine tiers of seats rising about the central skene. I looked about the eleven tiers of stone that rose around Santine's room, on the bottom of which I was sitting now. "Crowds . . .

large numbers . . ." I shrugged. "They're mostly things
one finds today doing metaphorical work in bad poems."

"I suppose it's because I'm one of those," she said
with one tongue; and with another, "women that humans
fascinate, in all the ambiguity the phrase allows in our
language(s)—" She added the plural with still another
tongue evelmi usually only used for tasting, then picked
up the sentence with still another (whose relation to the
first I could no longer figure I'd blinked)— "and it still,
after all the intercourse between our cultural discourses,
does," and, with another tongue, "doesn't it," and concluded with the traditional tongue for endings: "Yes?"
Then she laughed. "As a foreigner to this city, I know
there is a grammatical mistake in there somewhere. Here,
my young friend: taste." With the deep, disturbing rumble that was evelm laughter, she came to me.

I kneeled up to lick first one stone (peppery, with an
aftertaste of mint), and another (the cool inertness of most
rocks), and another (the ashy saltiness not of sodium chlo-
ride but of some potassium substitute). Santine gave me
the fourth to hold and taste at my leisure, and I leaned
back on the cushions, much more relaxed now that I had
experienced some kind of familiar greeting. "Santine, you
know what I heard not so long ago? In the play of the
universal machinery, another whole world has met its
destruction." So much for what one doesn't want to talk
about. "A whole human population—" somehow I just
assumed it was an all-human population—"was annihilated."

"Yes, you humans do that to your worlds from time to
time, don't you?" Santine mused. "Were there any survivors?" She moved off again to her shelves.

"There had to be some," I said. "One. Or a hundred.
Or a thousand." I adjusted myself on the cushion. "Isn't
that an awful thing to have to think about while you're . . .
gallivanting about the stars, as you put it?"

"It's not a terribly pleasant thing to think about while
you're bound to the surface of a single planet," she said.
"Sometimes you do it to other people's worlds too."

"Mmm . . ."

"How happy I am that the processes of thought are so
different between my race and yours. We love you."

"We love you, too," I acknowledged. Another ritual—
indeed, I'd never questioned what it meant. But it always

made me feel good. "How long has it been since I've seen you now?"

"Not long. To me. Years. Standard." Santine, instead of sitting, was pawing about in another set of shelves. "And not many of those. And in that time, I have been looking over the book you lent me."

I frowned. "Book . . . ?"

"I suppose I shall some day become accustomed to," she declared with one tongue; and with another, "the religions of you humans: they fascinate me. Only," and a third took up, as she turned from the shelf with a familiar object in her midclaws, "the book you lent me has little to do with religion. It seems, from all I can find out either from it or from General Info, to deal exclusively with art and life. Which, as I first said to you when you were a two-year-old, doing knee paintings on rough fabrics about your mothers' claws: I do not understand your race's concept of art. Nor am I that secure about my own race's notions on that intriguing topic."

"Vondramach Okk," I said, because I recognized the leather, glass, and aluminum volume in Santine's claws. "I remember loaning it to you. You said you were interested in Vondramach's religious thought; so I lent you her poems. I just suspected you might find something in them to illuminate her theological notions. I've always felt the poems provided an interesting commentary on her religious period."

"Nothing." Santine clicked her bluish claws on the bluer clay. Where she came from, that was an ironic sign for negation, though evelmi in the very far north make the same gesture for intense agreement—while those who grow up near Morgre don't make it at all. "They suggest a virulent critique of everything religious, yes."

I laughed. "Well," I said, "for humans, the declaration 'God is dead' is just as religious a comment as 'I believe in God'; and the infant, innocent of all theology, seems as holy as the studied saint. Do we humans have a broader notion of religiosity than you?"

"Merely less refined." Santine arched her upper gum ridge, which was a smile. "Vondramach intrigues me because she had tasted the bitterest sins. Such flavors authorize the highest, the deepest, the widest religious feelings that pull us away from all social centers. But these poems,

as you call them, are things made with the taloned claw
rather than the perceiving tongue."

"I think," and laughed while I both thought and said
it and so probably distorted both processes, "that because
you evelmi have more tongues than fingers—or taloned
claws—you will never understand us humans, really."

"And that is why you humans kill us in the north,"
Santine declared. "Ah, yours is a political statement if I
ever heard one. Well, your Vondramach was a mistress of
politics as well as art and religion, yes? But in those two
fields, she leaves me far behind."

I didn't say (indeed, I probably didn't think): That's
why we're killing you in the north. Rather I found myself
simply uncomfortable with this, from one of my oldest
friends. I was about to question this discomfort as diplomatically as I could when Santine lunged forward.

"Here is your book."

I pushed myself up on one elbow, took it, and reached
for the chain hanging from my waist. "Thank you." There
was a ring on one side of the volume, which I snapped to
the ornate clip at the chain's end—

—and thought of a row of small yellow lights in the
distance.

"Oh," Santine said; she had obviously thought the
same thing. "I think you have a photocall."

"Excuse me," I said. I stood up from the cushions and
looked about for a stone wall. Near the wall, connections
are always better. I walked toward the mound of schist
beside the lowest tier of seats, and thought through my
reception code:

"Oh, Marq!" My mother, V'vish, clasped her foreclaws and declared with two tongues at once:

{"Where have you been, Marq?"
{"Where are you, dear! Please,
the Thants are here and we don't want to insult them!"

I took a deep breath. "Is it formal?"

"Oh, no. Just come home, please. We don't ask much
of you, but we love you." And with another tongue: "And
we'd love for Santine to come, if she would."

"I'll ask her," I said—then tried to change my voice a
little, which is a habit we single-tongued humans here get
into in childhood, but which, except when talking to my

parents, I've mercifully (almost) broken. "And I'm on my way."

I turned from the wall as V'vish vanished.

"They want you, don't they," Santine said. "Do they want me too?"

"They do. Will you come? It's an informal party for some offworld friends. The Thants . . . ? But I know you've met them."

"If it's an informal affair, I'll be along in an informal amount of time. Tell your parents, won't you, to expect me?"

"Yes. Of course."

"Good." And with her broad, beautiful wings unfurled and boisterously beating, she shooed me toward the entrance plate. "Get on with you then," she cried; and with other tongues: "Get out . . . ! Get out . . . !" and with still another: "You'll see me later in the evening. I look forward to seeing you at your home!"

"Yes, Santine," I said, as the night breeze and the air from her contracting wings, in the midst of the rising fall, joined the roar of dark Dylleaf's cleaning winds.

4.

Up a level, across the park, down one run and along the roller way—which once had seats but now only has the worn pentagonal spots where the cleats had been removed.

Thoughts while rolling through my hometown:

On Morgre's lowest level there are, today, twelve- and twenty-rack vegetable farms, with huge metaquartz light-conduits leading down from the overground parks. There are distilleries for the liquor we make in a number of Velm's southeast geosectors from the wild sarb-grasses. There are swimming pools, design mills, a dozen fine cheese houses, which still make their various wheels and stars of green-, yellow- and orange-rinded cheese from the fine nematode milk the out-city farm produces. There are ceramic works and aquaria, and what has slowly gained a reputation as the finest manufactory of personal electronic musical instruments in the hemisphere. (The biannual music festival held at Morgre, in which composers come from all over our world to have their works performed, was one

of the joys of my adolescence.) On ground level and the
first sub-ground level, three quarters of the population
still lives. Wide alleys twist between and up and down the
roller-ramps and stairs about them. Those who live above
ground mostly have skylights in at least one of their living
rooms. (Those below, I've always noticed, have so much
more varied holoramas outside their window-walls or in
their surround rooms.) Rolling walks take people beneath
the girders supporting the parks above, past the various
outlets of the various service unions. Broadlifts are always
going up and down, their rails sliding closed, and the
young and old women of both races are always disappear-
ing up into, or appearing down from, the upper, vine-
hung parks.

It's more or less inevitable: those who work$_2$ in the
out-city communes and co-ops ringing an urban complex
always feel themselves slightly superior to those who work$_2$
within the complex itself, especially when the out-city
co-ops are so old and well established as the furniture
factory, Dyethshome, or the Farm. . . . Yet there are so
many advantages to life within the city—more parks, more
runs, more pools, more dancing areas, more, and more
varied kinds of, sex, greater varieties of social and cultural
stimulation, more adventure, and more play—that the
twin pulls, of prestige in one direction and excitement in
the other, keep the general population moving both ways.
In an efficient bureaucratic anarchy—our most common
form of government on Velm—there are very few jobs$_2$
that one keeps for more than five years. (Your job$_1$ is
another story.) And since your job$_2$ is pretty much the one
that determines where you live, a good third of the population is constantly moving out to live in the outskirting
co-ops when the outer-city jobs$_2$ open up; or, by the same
cycle, are moving in to sample center-city life. And it
tends to be a different third all the time. Still, I was no
more than thirteen and a year back from Senthy when I
first realized that somehow those in my home, Dyethshome,
were exempt from this cyclic flow—though I'm sure the
council-board who, seven generations before, had author-
ized Mother Dyeth to accept the gift that Vondramach had
offered her, saw it as nothing more than a large out-city
commune, even if the idea of a commune that was nothing
but a work of art struck them as unusual—and might even

have aroused downright hostile suspicions in that board's ancestors on their other worlds.

Myself, though I've lived in Morgre and other urban complexes on Velm (and off) many times, indeed loved life in the inner city with the passion of a youngster loosed from the toils of tertiary homework$_3$, I was always on a labor$_2$-sabbatical when I lived inside, never on a job$_2$. My friends there tended to be others with as much free time as I, though they might have been in all or any other jobs$_2$, inner or outer, only weeks before. All *my* jobs$_2$ have ended up in the out-city communes, where frankly I feel more at home when I'm working at anything other than my profession$_1$: diplomacy.

I'm not the only Dyeth to whom this applies.

Because of this, from time to time, close friends—like Santine—have remarked I have a different manner about me, something other than just my being human. They more or less find it amusing. When I was younger, I would look within myself when women said this, to seek out the pains of being different and to wonder how I'd been wounded by my isolation in the outer-circle's older labor co-ops. Yet off-world folk like the Thants take the same manner—which for us Dyeths marks a hurt, a failure, a deprivation—and read it rather as a mark of privilege. Which in turn makes us find them somewhat amusing.

Among its three free-standing, two-hundred-meter multichrome walls, their transparent panes gone dazzling at Iirianiset, on the eastern rim of Morgre just beyond the blue tiles of Water Alley, by Whitefalls, rise the courts of Dyethshome.

5.

I rushed up the steps across green flags, wondering where the Thants had been on their way to that had allowed them to stop off at southern Velm for a visit. You understand their world is very different from ours. (Their sun system: Quorja. Their moonless world, sixth out: Zetzor. Their city, called 17, is blasted among myriads into the rock wall of a three-kilometer-deep canyon that worms and branches and doubles back and rebranches for several thousand k's about Zetzor's permanently dark north pole.

Yes, Quorja is about sixty-eight thousand light-years around
the galactic rim from Iiriani.) I've said that interstellar
travel is expensive? To promote cultural interchange, some
of Zetzor's larger geosectors finance one of their reproductive communes to unlimited fare for travel anywhere about
the galaxy. (Myself, and every other ID, has to get a job$_1$
where fare expenses are taken up by the employer$_1$ requesting the import.) Once, I made the mistake of asking
Thadeus Thant how she and her spouses and her offspring
had been chosen for such an honor. Somewhere behind
careening metal, she laughed. "Well, considering that we're
chosen from the population of an entire world, you can be
sure the selection isn't *entirely* fair. . . ." I raised an eyebrow and (diplomatically?) changed the subject. At some
point in their random travels they'd met my mother Egri
(also an ID) just before she retired about ten years ago.
Striking up a friendship, they've been dropping in to see
us once or twice a year standard ever since. A visit from
the Thants at Dyethshome—Death's Home is how it's still
pronounced, though vowels have shifted and, in the last
hundred years or so, space and punctuation have fallen
out—is ebullient good will, lavish and humorous gifts (that
the Thants buy or have made, by the bye, *after* they get
here. The importation of offworld gifts? Even their lavish
geosector government can't afford to go that far.) It's
Thantish awkwardness, if not downright insincerity, growing from their reception and friendship with a stream so
old and august, at least the way it tastes to their tongues,
as Dyeth.

"That—" Alsrod Thant put her small brown hands behind
her, gazing up at the crystal column— "is your grandmother, your seven-times great-grandmother, the source
of your stream, Gylda Dyeth?"

I chuckled. "It's what they used to call a simulated
synapse casting. All the soft lights and multicolored flashes
inside *supposedly* reproduce her personality, in crystalline
form."

The glimmering pillar rose from its ornate metal pedestal to soar beside the wall decorations next to the blades
of the door, till it disappeared into the equally ornate
capital, one with the court's roof, where silver tracery

pictured what one evelm artist had thought she'd seen in
our stars.

"Shall I tell you the story connected with it?"

Alsrod's hands came before her to clasp in mimed
ecstasy beneath her brown chin.

I put my hand on her shoulder. "Mother Dyeth lived
well into the fourth generation of her children. The casting
was taken right at the old lady's demise. A decent length
of time after her bodily passing, when it was turned on, so
we've all been told, the capital speaker up there announced:
'Now, I'm a mechanical reproduction. Not the real thing at
all. I know it. You know it. You were fools to get this thing
made in the first place. Frankly, I'd turn it off if I were
you and let me *stay* dead,' which was so uncannily like
Mother Dyeth in life, everyone was quite astounded at the
synapse caster's skill."

"Did they obey?"

I nodded. "I don't think there's anyone among us who
knows *how* to turn it on today—though when I was a
child, sometimes we would stand around, my sisters and I,
and all try to put our arms around it, not quite able to
touch."

"Telling me this," Alsrod said with, suddenly, a very
pleased look, "you're just doing your job_2, aren't you?"

"Yes." I smiled, a bit puzzled. "I am. That's by and
large what I mostly $work_2$ at."

"Does that mean that you don't really *want* to tell me
such things?"

"Ah," I said, "but I like my $work_2$ as well as my
$work_1$. And I like my $work_1$ a lot." Then added, because
this seemed the moment to do so: "Perhaps we should go
back to the others . . . ?" I turned with her to walk toward
where her sisters waited on one of the stone benches,
while talk trickled about in the hall behind them, between
my parents and theirs. Alsrod Thant, the youngest Thant,
fourteen standard years now, bony, brown, and delicate
eared, her head shaved—really a rather genial child—and
this was her first trip to another world with her parents.
(She'd assured me with studied modesty that she'd been to
moons before . . . no, not Zetzor's. Zetzor doesn't have
any.) Though she knew us and we knew her from numerous vaurine projections, still it was the first time we'd met
her in vivo. I'd found her charming. For all the circles in

dull aluminum that hung around her neck and waist and shoulders and calves, I couldn't help thinking of her as a younger me.

I sat.

Alsrod sat—between her older sisters, Fibermich and Nea. My sisters Alyxander and Black Lars came up at that moment to sit by me. A little ways off, George Thant scowled, arms folded over her big metallic chest, like some colossus from an artistic tradition I wasn't quite familiar with.

Across the room I thought I heard Thadeus declaim: "A world, you see, called Nepiy . . ." and my attention turned.

But Fibermich brought it back with a continuation of some conversation which we'd apparently joined. "Let me tell you." Her brown hand hovered and quivered, like an object intended for steady focus, but which, because it held too much energy to remain static, kept blurring into a faster time frame. "We were on Bragenvold, in some northern geosector. Incidentally, they really don't *think* in geosectors on Bragenvold because the political alliances are between interconnected and interwoven nets of city-states: the Blue Net, the Red Net, the Green Net, the Orange Net. Well, there we were in the capital burg of the Green Net, kilometers underground, and with the capitals of the Red, White, and Tyrian Nets less than a day's work away with a jackhammer on three different sides of us. (Oh, they *are* labor-intensive in those underground caves. And the people in hand-arm intensive societies look so different from those in leg-foot intensive cultures—don't you find?) As we rowed down the city's central canal, there was a circular facade, carved into the rockface itself, oh, maybe seventy-five meters high. Painted above the narrow doorslits, in the local color-code syllabary: *Do not profane your origins on Eld Eyrth.*"

Fibermich and her seated sisters rocked in unison, laughing their different laughs at their different pitches in their different rhythms.

"And once," declared Nea, recovering, "we were on a world called Kra, where, in a particularly depopulated area, they had just put a legal limit on how much material an architectural structure could employ—" She looked about us at the sprawling levels of our ball court where so seldom, these days, anyone danced. Her hands, sheathed in foil and joined in her lap, tried to tug from their nest in her thighs. As she spoke, she leaned to the left (tug), to the right (tug, tug, tug . . .): they did not come loose, though I felt that the rooves themselves might peel from the sky if she overcame her own gravity. "There in the desert—" (tug, tug—) "we saw the rim of an overgrown crater, where we'd heard the Family'd been established. Sure enough, the flame-speakers around it were blaring, both in the High Musical code as well as the Low (ironically pitched two octaves above the High one): *Lest I forget thee, Oh Urth!*"

They laughed; they rocked.

"And on a moon, once—" I suppose Alsrod had some previous knowledge of the conversational path pursued by her sisters; but frequently with the Thants, if not all folk in stressful situations, I get the impression they never say anything new. "Once—" Alsrod's hands were clasped on her knees. She swayed forward on the bench like a figure of struts and ropes, invisible thermofoils yanking at her shoulders as some undetectable hotwind whipped them back and forth, pulling her about as they whirled and snapped, collecting their energetic bounty and directing her intense movements below. "Once, on a moon, I passed a tiny office in a narrow corridor, through the transparent wall of which I could see it was all staffed by the local aliens—"

Fibermich, Nea, and George all turned to her reprovingly.

"May the ant and the worm take dinner in my vitals, I speak the truth," Alsrod protested. But one hand came loose from her knee and raised before her face as if to protect herself.

"Go on," my sister Lars said, perhaps as a representative of our own local aliens, and arched her lip bone.

But I don't think Alsrod saw it through her spread fingers. Her eyes were closed. "—staffed by local aliens," she repeated in a voice respectfully devoid of emotion. "And on the wall, written clearly in incised letters—" Here her hand returned to her knee which had jackknifed up to catch her boot-heel on the bench's inlaid edge— "*Fail not the eternal presence of Eurd.*" Her eyes were still not open.

They laughed.

We smiled—which we assumed they would take as a comparable gesture . . . if they asked GI about such things. They frequently did.

"On Zetzor itself, in the south, there used to be a whole museum complex. Took up half the city of Q. Had folks handing out little cards on the cross-corners of cities all over our world, from 17 to 70; from A to R. Visit their paltry showing, and it stated in woman-high letters sunk into the piazza before the main rotunda: *Forget not your debts and beginnings on Earth*—and they meant, you know, the famous Earth, the sixth world so named after Old Earth itself!" (I'd never heard of a particularly famous Earth, sixth named; but I didn't interrupt gleaming George, who'd stepped up to join the conversation.) "We had the complex shut down. That is, Eulalia did. Thant Eulalia—" and without unfolding her arms, she nodded in the direction of the jeweled extravaganza, her mother, across the room by the sculpted half-walls, surrounded by our (and her) other parents. "That's what *we* think of the Family on Zetzor. And their countless corrupt slogans."

The three seated howled wildly, swaying with the precision of three broad leaves of sarb-grass in a single breeze. A scowling brass giant, George watched attentively over their performance.

"Now, of course, you can't set this against the problems of Nepiy . . ." I heard again from Thadeus. Indeed, hearing the name before, I'd assumed it was just a trick of the ear. Even now it occurred to me that, with six thousand worlds to choose from, it was more likely that they were discussing some planet with a similar name than that they were discussing the actual world I'd so recently visited.

The evening drifted by.

I drifted by people; people drifted by me.

Then Santine made her entrance, on a rag-rope platform that creaked, in ancient gilt fringe, down from the informal stars. She stuck out one of her tongues to receive me, and I thought she said, in one of her voices that I happened not to recognize: "Do you really enjoy these affairs?"

I grinned, and was about to say—but it was not Santine aping a human voice. It was Alsrod Thant, in her aluminum circles, who had just stepped up beside me.

I said (because frequently the truth provides the most diplomatic answer): "I don't believe I've ever attended one since I was your age where I didn't feel, beforehand, an oppressive dread at the isolation that can reign in a large enough group of even the most intimate friends, much less an admixture of intimates, acquaintances, and strangers. Still, so much of my social education has been effected in such gatherings, so many true friendships have had their beginnings in meetings much like yours and mine, that I feel these affairs must not only be endured, but negotiated with a certain energy, if not commitment." I dropped my head a little to the side and gave her a grin. "They can be fun."

Alsrod just looked at me.

Below her shaved scalp and high forehead, brown eyes blinked. The pupils were large enough to suggest either drugs or the slightest genetic divergence in human evolution. Suddenly she raised her hand, palm facing me. Before her face, brown fingers spread: "Oh! The force of a criticism whose reasons I can no longer spelunk throws me into the neotenous posture of the tadpole, the caterpillar, the newt!"

I had never heard of any of these beasts, and neotenous I knew from nothing. I opened my eyes rather wide, but I guess I was still smiling.

Alsrod dropped her hand and grinned back. "There." Suddenly she pointed to my thigh. "What's that hanging by your leg?"

"This?" I ran my hand down the chain from my belt.

Three tongues out and one of them, I knew, tasting the taints and feints that humans could communicate through body odor alone if our olfactory systems had not fallen by the evolutionary wayside, Santine regarded us with the steadfast attention it had taken me years to learn did not (when *she* did it) mean offense, and to which Alsrod seemed all but oblivious in a way that made me wonder about her. But she was from another world. . . .

"This—" I turned the leather binding over to the ground-glass screen; on the back was a set of finger-tab switches, set within gemmed circles— "is what they used to call a book." It was a beautifully worked object, well read (the leather around the controls was worn smooth), and no bigger than my palm. "My friend Santine here just returned it to me, earlier this afternoon."

Santine nodded, licked, and watched.

Alsrod blinked at me some more, considering, I suppose, whether to go into another song, another dance. Finally, she said: "I know it's a book. We have a whole library full at home. What's it a book *about*? Unless—" Her large eyes lowered— "I have broached yet one more of the infinitude of topics my ignorance of your laws, land, and life would bar to any polite transgressions from a poor—"

"Oh, now," I told her. "Of course it's all right to ask!" A library of books on Zetzor? This one was an odd offworld object that had somehow gotten into a basement at Dyethshome. I'd found it as a child just back from my first year offworld at Senthy. As far as I knew, it was the only book, at least of this particular technotype, on my world. "It's a volume of Vondramach Okk. The poems, not the religious tracts. Apparently she used to joke that since nobody ever took the poetry of political rulers seriously, it didn't matter what language she wrote it in. So she used her own made-up one. This book contains all her privately published volumes of verse, a selection of her letters, her complete private journals, about six contrasting critical studies, and an official biography—as well as a lot of allied papers and documents that don't get too political."

Alsrod stepped around me to see; I touched a playback button. The screen became pink haze, above which formed the most frequently reproduced holo of Okk: sixty-seven standard years old, tall, black-skinned, and gawky, she wore a maroon cape, blown back from a naked shoulder. Her breasts, emptied with age, hung against her ribs. Belt aslant sharp hips, she stood, in dark pants and darker boots, on a lime-pocked ledge, gazing pensively (and poetically) down on some absent landscape, one hand on her waist, one lost in the red folds of her cape, jaw, ear, one shoulder, and belt buckle roughed by a sun thrice the size of Quorja or Iiriani.

"From what I've studied of *your* local culture, however, in preparation for my coming—" One hand holding her opposite elbow, Alsrod gazed at the twenty-five centimeter figure glowing above the book plate— "I would have thought that was a piece of theater, or perhaps a sculpture—if you hadn't told me, that is, it *was* a book."

That made me laugh. I hefted the object in my hand: the image above it stayed steadier than its projector lying in my palm. "I can see that. It does have a stage, I suppose. And half the statuary you see about today is some kind of image projection. But this is just one of the book's illustrations. Besides, it's not a technofact of our world—at least it's not common to this area of it."

"And I never knew Okk wrote," Alsrod added. "I mean poems. What an interesting-looking woman. And you must think so too." She blinked rapidly at me.

I nodded. "Most of the holograms we have of her come from the years she was in exile on Pretania. Like this. Once before, one story has it, she actually ordered all visual reproductions—of anything—destroyed over a whole world. There were too many of her, and she didn't like the slant of her nose or something. Or maybe she just felt she'd become too recognizable. Another ruler would have dealt with the situation by having her own features altered— and she did that too, from time to time. But on Pretania, when it seemed, at least for a while, her political career was over, apparently she stopped caring who took pictures— and wrote her baker's dozen greatest poems."

It's easy to read, in that image, the aging poet pondering the coming stanza of one of her brooding, crepuscular cynghanedds. The biography, however, tells us that the fifteen planets she had finally annexed three years before had, through the successful revolt of the Regunyi, just dropped to twelve. She was much more likely contemplating the coming battle of Granger-9 where, in a six-month interstellar encounter, the Pretania exile would end and she would sweep into her grip five new worlds (one of which would destroy itself in CF within the year). I wondered what Alsrod saw in it.

"Was she a major or minor writer?"

I smiled. "Personally, among poets, she's my favorite. There're a good number of study-groups devoted to her work, here and on many other worlds. But there are many thousands of poets neither of us will ever hear of with greater followings among people who, themselves, have never heard of her. In her youth, actually, she was quite stout. Only in her last decades, on Abnerangc, Pretania, and Tartouhm, did she develop that gaunt and austere appearance most of us associate with her today."

"She was an impressive-looking woman," Santine said appreciatively, as I've heard her say a dozen times in as many years.

"I've studied many major—and minor—poets on *my* world," Alsrod announced; she inclined her head to add: "What poems did she write?"

With my middle finger I pressed another switch on the book back, already set at one of her most accessible lyrics—the third from that sumptuous second volume, *Lyroks.* Runes formed above the screen; Vondramach faded. "One of the things that makes her particularly interesting is that the language she invented—actually she made it up when she was a girl on that large macro-life station where she spent a good part of her invalid childhood—employed both a phonetic and an ideographic writing system as well as a whole series of shiftrunes—"

"Shiftrunes?"

"Letters that are pronounced one way on their first occurrence in a text, another on their second, another on their third, and so on in a fixed sequence. It gives the poet an interesting technique to exploit: she can have pairs of words that alliterate visually but not phonetically as well as pairs that alliterate phonetically but not visually. And she can play the two off against each other. At any rate, most of Okk's really interesting work is written in this language: the two epic-length pieces, the *Onerokritika* and the *Energumenika*, as well as the series of lyrics and love poems, *Hermione at Buthrot.* And of course both the early and late satires. If you like, I'll give you the access code and you can take half a minute, learn the language from GI, then take a look at some of the poems in the original—"

"I'm afraid that my impetuous youngest sister—" Nea Thant stepped up behind Alsrod. She placed her metal-covered hands not on Alsrod's shoulders but centimeters above them— "as this is her first trip to your world, has not been rendered compatible with your local General Information service—"

"I was going to get it done last week," Alsrod said, "but I guess that was when Mickey and me were off on that—" Then, assailed by astonishment, her hands raised to, but did not touch, her face. She rocked her head from side to side, intoning, while aluminum jangled: "Oh, repentance! Oh, regret! Oh, retribution for the way of life a youth indulges among rocks and ice and icemoss!"

"Really," I said, "it's probably just as well. I mean, here at a party more than likely isn't the place you'd want to go off in the corner to sit for half an hour with a—"

"But you are the host!" declared Alsrod. Her arms jangled to her sides. "I want to submerge myself in your world, your life! Your interests for the duration of my stay are mine! Your theater, your sculpture! *Please* tell me about your grandmother, Gylda Dyeth!" With Nea behind her projecting her fixed smile above her head, Alsrod's intensity fairly glittered. "I mean, she was a great friend of Vondramach's wasn't she? Vondramach was the one who gave her all this—" she swept her hands about, indicating all around—"Dyethshome?"

Beyond us, the column glimmered.

"Yes." I smiled again, because some of what had been mysterious had become clear for me—we'd been through this in one way or another with every Thant as we'd met them, though it still surprised me, I suppose. "I'll tell you, if you'd like."

"Oh, please, yes. It's your work$_2$ anyway. You said you liked your work$_2$."

"I do." The Thants have always been excited by the connection between Vondramach and Dyeth, the older just as much as the younger. Yet it still shocks me when that excitement erupts so blatantly. "What would you like to know?"

"How they met? What did they do? How did they part? And then you must tell me about the stream which runs from them to you!"

I laughed, thinking how much I enjoyed the story, yet how much it always seemed that any time it's told to the Thants, the tale was doomed to misunderstanding. Yet enjoyment won out. "All right. My seven-times great-grandmother, Gylda Dyeth, came to Velm when she was nineteen standard years old on a colony ship of eight thousand from a world called Klaven that I have never seen, but that a goodly number of the inhabitants at the time thought was on the verge of Cultural Fugue."

"But it wasn't," said Alsrod, who no doubt had al-

ready received one version or another of the tale from her
siblings and parents, if not from her home world's GI.

"True. Eventually Klaven managed to get itself together again—but not before a number of its inhabitants
had also managed to get themselves a new home, Gylda
among them. She'd probably been some kind of free-
agented professional₁ before she came here, though we
don't have much information about that period of her life.
On Velm, she lived a while in the north, didn't like it,
moved to the south, and did. At one point, however, she
was up on our smaller moon, Arvin—"

"Ah," Alsrod sighed, "moons—yes, wonderful, tiny,
attenuated moons, where night and gravity are stretched
nearly to the breaking."

It had so much the sound of a quote from some poet
I'd ought to have read, I didn't even bother to ask GI to
identify the allusion.

"Moons," Alsrod repeated. "We don't have any moons
around Zetzor. It's a great sadness to me."

"Well, we have two," I said. "Moons are smaller than
worlds. People stay closer together on moons. Vondramach
Okk and her entourage were en route from one star to
another, when she stopped at Arwin's relay station. In
spite of her security, she and Gylda met. The middle-aged
tyrant was much impressed with the young woman colo-
nist and hired her right there. Gylda worked for Vondramach
over the next half-dozen years, traveling with her and
without her about the galaxy, with a freedom that, from all
reports, was rather like yours with your government's gift
of unlimited space-fare. At the end of her services—"

"—Vondramach gave her Dyethshome!" Alsrod supplied, looking about the high-ceilinged court. "As a reward
for her faithfulness!"

"I've always suspected it was a bit more complicated
than that." I looked about my home. "Vondramach was
one of the great proponents of the Family. Gylda was an
adherent of the Sygn—as was most of Velm at the time. It
probably wouldn't have made that much difference to
them, as both of them were personally very tolerant, but
one of Gylda's major reasons for retiring was that she
wanted to raise children for a while. Sometime before she
left Klaven, she'd suffered several massive radiation con-
tacts. She had so many smashed and shattered chromo-

somes only a complex enzyme therapy kept her from blooming into rampant malignancies three or four times a week. She'd been sterilized when very young—probably under unpleasant conditions. Because of that old radiation bout, she couldn't be cloned. But Gylda had a kind of single-mindedness—not unlike Vondramach's, I flatter myself in thinking. She had all of Dyethshome to let kids run around in; and believe me, that's some running. When she came back to Morgre and moved in here, she adopted two human females, Lane and Neza, and a human male, Vrach, from the north of our world. They'd been orphaned in the early conflicts between the native evelm and human colonists. She brought them up, here at Dyethshome, while she collected the art works and cultural artifacts that gave this place its purpose in the culture of Morgre. Over the next fifteen years, Gylda and her three children survived all seven visits Vondramach paid her—I mention it because not everyone did. When Vondramach came to visit, she brought not only her entourage but her whole lifestyle, which included assassination attempts, strategic murders, political intrigues and factional hugger-mugger of precisely the sort Gylda had left her services to get away from. On Vondramach's sixth visit the killing of Secretary Argenia occurred right there in Dyethshome's north court at a formal supper party of a hundred guests. Today we hardly ever use it—I'm sure the custom goes back to the Argenia assassination. Visiting students are the only ones who ever go in there now. There was never any doubt in Gylda's mind that Vondramach herself was responsible for the murder. On her seventh visit, Gylda suggested that Vondramach not come back. This time there was quite an argument. But the tyrant refrained from bombing Dyethshome, blowing up Morgre, and blighting the land for a hundred kilometers in all directions—all things she was quite capable of doing when she got riled. But she never returned. Five years later she was overthrown. Three years after that, she was dead. And Gylda went on with her life here. The only one of Gylda's children interested in raising more children was the male, Vrach. Vrach Dyeth and her lover, another human male, Orgik Korm, took over Dyethshome. They had two male children cloned from the germ-plasm of a friend of theirs on store in a local plasm-bank, a former lover of both of them, who had been killed some years before in a local mountain slide up in the Myaluths. These clone-twins, Cyar and Hashe, began the third wave of Dyeths to live here at Dyethshome. Vrach and Orgik later adopted a human female also from the north, named Jekk, which completed that wave's ripple. There's some unpleasantness connected with Hashe, the details of which I don't really know. She went off and did something nobody approved of, but what it was I'm not sure. Jekk and Cyar decided, when they were in their late fifties, they wanted to carry on with Dyeths for another ripple. Both of them had jobs₁ as evelmian ethnologists. They worked with an ethnological commune that was then helping the native evelmi who were fleeing from the north— human/evelm relations have always been strained up there. Dyethshome was given over to their ethnological commune, so that the place became a laboratory as well as a museum in those years, and all the humans and evelmi who worked here became the next ripple of Dyeth parents: Gubba, Rhis, and Wee are some of the names of those adults. And their children—all adopted and all native evelmi, included Kee'fa, Jatch'jat, another Vrach, Large Maxa, Ari, and Liji. . . . Gylda lived a dozen years into this fourth nonhuman ripple of the Dyeth stream. She was very pleased about it, too. People often wonder why evelm/human relations have been so much better in the south. Myself, I think it's because both populations are smaller here—and we always have the north's appalling example to instruct us. Ari was the first of that ripple to decide on more children, and she brought in as a child one of my own grandmothers, Genya, who, as an adult, joined with Large Maxa from the generation before, who's also parenting for this generation as well—but you know, evelmi mature more slowly than humans and live longer. So actually numbering ripples beyond this point gets confusing. The point is, however, there are no direct egg-and-sperm relations between any ripple of parents and any ripple of children at Dyethshome—nor have there ever been, since Gylda began the stream, seven ripples ago."

"But when there are so many paths and parameters," Alsrod declared, or rather, as I recognized a few words into it, quoted, "along which and around which women— young, old, human, evelm, male, female, and neuter—can develop both community and communion to be passed on to others, why should you restrict yourselves to direct egg-and-sperm relations? That's wonderful!"

"Well," I said. "It may not be all that wonderful, but it's the way our particular nurture stream worked out. More than half the streams here in Morgre have used direct genetic reproduction in some form or another at least once a ripple, since their founding. Perhaps in Gylda's time there was active resentment against it as a method. It smacked too much of Family Life, which had already proved disastrous in the north. But there isn't today. Egg-and-sperm relations between stream ripples? Myself, I like to think of it as a method we just haven't gotten around to yet."

"And now you must tell her why you call it a stream—instead of a family with a small 'f'," Fibermich said, stepping up beside her sister, with great approval beaming in her face.

"Well, I—"

Fibermich immediately darted away again.

"Oh, please," said Alsrod, while I looked after her. "I *want* you to say it!"

I laughed again. "If you're really interested. But I know you know it already. All right. Velm is a very dry world. Water is rare here. The propagation of nurture has always been highly respected among the evelm. But none of their local languages ever developed a general term for reproductive lines. 'Stream' was the term they used for their educational paths, their universities, which extend all over the planet. When the human and evelm cultures melded, here in the south, the appropriation of the educational sign to the nurturing situation was one result."

"And *now*," declared Nea, peering at me over her young sister's shoulder, "you must tell her the conceptual ways in which a stream differs from a family."

"Perhaps we should leave that till . . ." Even someone who likes to talk as much as I do and works$_2$ at it eventually feels a sense of occasional strain when running on too much. "I mean, I'm *sure* Alsrod already knows it, so that—"

"But I must hear it in your own voice," Alsrod exclaimed. "It's what I have come light years for!"

"All right," I said once more. "But there're so many ways that a stream differs from a family, I don't know where to start. The father-mother-son that makes up the basic family unit, at least as *the* Family has described it for centuries now, represents a power structure, a structure of strong powers, mediating powers, and subordinate powers, as well as paths for power developments and power restrictions. It's also a conceptual structure as well, a model through which to see many different situations. The Family has always been quite loose in applying that system to any given group of humans or nonhumans, breeding or just living together, so that you can have lots of fathers, lots of mothers, lots of sons; and any woman of any age or any gender can always fill any of the roles; I'm sure the right Family analyst could reinterpret our nurture stream or your reproductive commune as a classical 'family' without an eyeblink, just by assigning one or more parts to one or more women. But if we agreed to the model, no doubt we'd begin to stabilize the power structure it controls. But there're other power structures that can apply to nurturing groups. For instance, in the Family structure, the parents are seen to contain and enclose the children, to protect them from society. In the stream structure, the children are the connection between the parents and the society. To become a parent is to immediately have your child change your relation to society. Suddenly you have to deal with nurseries, nutrition co-ops, study-groups—a whole raft of social institutions. Because most children don't generate from within streams, the stream structure conceives of all children as gifts from society, as gifts to society. In the stream structure—"

"Now translate!" Alsrod suddenly cried.

"Excuse me?"

"I know that Dyethshome used to be the scene of marvelous theatrical productions for all of Morgre—all of M-81. And I have come here to see one—metaphorically speaking, of course. And you are so generously providing it! No, I have not read Okk's verse, but I've studied the works of one of your greatest playwrights and musicians, Jae'l Bazerat, whose finest productions were performed here in the amphitheater at Dyethshome. She wrote of the streams that ran across the deserts and swamps of your world—the universities—both before and after humans left their pawprints here."

"That's true," I said. "Among academic playwrights she's considered—"

"Yet Vondramach is *your* poet, Marq Dyeth!" Alsrod beamed once more, as though some extremely important point had been made. "Now translate for me." She pointed to the book I still held but which, in the course of my disquisition, I'd forgotten. "You mean this . . . poem?" The runes of the long-dead tyrant, whose childhood friends had called her Dramach and whose adult intimates had addressed her as Vondra (a word which, in her own language, meant "the taloned claw"), hung in the air above the stage my hand made. I wondered whether Alsrod's abrupt change of subject was an expression of boredom, a social custom, a logic alien to me, or simply personal avidity. "Well . . . this one is from her series of participatory poems. She added to the sequence all her life. Its title translates 'The Strange' . . . or maybe better, 'The Awkward.' But the word can also mean 'The Exotic,' or simply 'Another Person'—or also, 'Another System.'" (Somewhere in her journals, Okk writes: *Poetry is what is avoided as it is surrounded by translation*. In her own language, however, it only takes three words, all beginning with the same sound, 'ch.') "Anyway, she provides one half-line and a single letter that you have to work into a word in your own version of a second half-line. . . ." But how could anyone who didn't know Vondramach Okk's private tongue appreciate the participatory works? Beneath the book I fingered the random selector: runes flickered till I released the touch-tab. "Now this one . . . yes, happens to be another of my favorites. The title means 'The President,' or maybe 'The Ruler,' though it *doesn't* come from a word root meaning either measuring, straightening, or presiding. The particular root word—which she also invented—means 'stroking softly' or, in some cases, 'mangling.'"

"Is it autobiographical?" Alsrod asked.

I was surprised. "Many commentators have taken it to be—though she wrote a much earlier draft of it when she was still a child at the hospital station at Jryla. But really, Alsrod, perhaps the next time you come you'll be wired for local GI compatibility and we can . . ."

Nea still stood with her hands poised above her sister's shoulders. I saw Fibermich off and joking uproariously with a bunch of parents, for all the world as though she were barring them from our conversation. Then I turned and saw what, in the corner of my eye, had given that impression: her metallic figure chased at forearms, temples, and calves with high veins, George Thant stood up on the bench by the spillway, arms folded, legs apart, staring over the milling heads between at Nea, Santine, Alsrod, and me. George frowned intently. At any intergeosector party people always do strange things and other people try to remain oblivious. At a party for folk of different worlds, both the strangeness and the obliviousness can reach surreal proportions. People milled about George's knees, occasionally tossed a quip up at her, occasionally didn't, and drifted on.

"*I* would like to be a ruler, a president, or a mangler!" Alsrod announced beneath her sister's smile.

"And I would like to be a poet." I laughed. "But I'm too far along in my life to start another profession$_1$; and fortunately there are laws and institutions today to prevent rulers from becoming manglers, at least on Vondramach's scale."

"Weren't there laws and institutions two hundred years ago?" Alsrod asked.

Santine chimed in with one of her tongues in one of her more cajoling voices: "When one actually starts the historical research, it sometimes seems as though there weren't. Now I have never been to another world, except once in a vaurine tour. Most likely, I'll never go in vivo. Would you tell me: how do *you* find the flavor of the experience hangs in your mouth, my young wanderer?"

"Well, with all this talk of poetry, it's a shame to bring up a cliché, but a vaurine tour *is* more educational— and fun. And I suppose . . ." (While Alsrod searched for the proper metaphor, I beamed all astral thanks to my old labor$_2$-mate for letting me out of the frying pan.) "Well, a vaurine tour simply serves up richer, better prepared, and more carefully orchestrated flavors than live chance possibly could. . . ."

Without looking, I fingered another button on the book's bottom to turn it off, and let the chain slide down through my fingers.

Alsrod stepped out from under the foil epaulets Nea's hands had become, to continue her conversation with

Santine. (The book bumped against my calf.) Nea still stood, still smiled, and still kept up her hands, as though preserving a cave into which her sister might retreat should she accidentally and irreparably disgrace herself.

An image: Fibermich and George, now that Alsrod had turned from me, coming together to join Nea in a toe-to-toe line for a precise and ordered bow. (Behind Nea I could see a stone cyhnk that had been brought here from the Arvin to decorate the room how many decades ago now: Nea's arms, in their fixed position, looked like two more of the religious symbol's branches transferred from the living trunk.) But before I could find out if my vision was simply fantasy or social prediction, laughter exploded across the room.

Thadeus Thant came toward us, followed by my sisters Bucephalus and Tinjo and my other sister, white-skinned and livid-eyed Maxa. A swarm of three-centimeter metallic disks careened in a suspensor field maybe a decimeter away from Thadeus's body. Blue, gold, copper, silver, and black metal whizzed about; turned on low, the privacy cloud was a convocation of comets. Between, now and again, you could see within, up here an aged eyelid, down there a parchment kneecap, higher a collapsed pectoral with its folded dug. "What are you youngsters plotting over here? How are you planning to do in your parents this time?"

We all laughed now.

"We're plotting to steal time itself from you," declared Fibermich. "We're going to spike it to the floor as it slips by. And just as you come over to see why it's so still, we'll pull it out from under you—"

"—and send you spinning off around the galaxy's edge," my sister Alyxander took it up, "on your grandest adventure yet, Thad!"

"We're planning to pluck all the best stars out of the sky and stuff them in our pockets," I said, "so that when we meet you once again and thrust our hands deep inside to hide our embarrassment, our fingertips will smart on them, as if they were desert grains, caught down in the seams, and we'll smile at you on your way to a glory that, for all our stellar thefts, we shall never be able to duplicate."

"Respect!" Thadeus said loudly, in that great, brassy voice—though the corporeal Thadeus always seemed so little inside the colorful cloud. "Yes, that's respect!" I believe this eldest of the three Thant mothers was honestly happy young Dyeths had taken time to learn at least some of the rituals from the polar geosector on a far, far world. "Now why don't you—" Thadeus waved an arm toward us seated children, though I only glimpsed a wrinkled elbow, a vein curving a wrist. Bright metal swooped and careened— "*you* show the kind of respect these youngsters do," and comets flew on across the pulsing colors on the pastel floor to join more of our parents.

All of us looked at each other; and all of us smiled; because I really think we all—Thant children and Dyeth children—in one way or another loved the old creature whom, because of the privacy disks always in flight about her, we saw so little of.

As such encounters do, this one dissolved our conversational group, and the fragments moved to reconstellate. I heard Santine say, as she moved off with Thad: "But you were talking about Nepiy? Young Marq mentioned it to me not so long ago. . . ." Curiosity would have moved me off after them.

But there was a motion by my eyes—then shadow. I stopped, surprised.

Alsrod had stuck her hand before my face and shook it. I blinked—but it was just a way of getting my attention. "That," she said, dropping her hand once she was sure she'd got it, "is a cyhnk, isn't it?" She nodded toward the carved stone medusoid, which, moments ago, her sister had stood before. "What does it mean? I mean this particular one?"

"Now you know a cyhnk is the sign of the Sygn," said Fibermich, stepping up to rejoin us in her lace of small chains, clearly deprecating her younger sister's disingenuousness: but she flashed a huge and toothy smile in case I didn't know she was part of it.

"The Sygn is the veritable and virtual enemy of the Family on all, or almost all, worlds among the six thousand," concluded Nea, strolling up on the other side. As she moved in her armor of foil, studs, and leathers, a sly look suffused her dark, full mouth, to let us know she knew we knew she knew.

"No, I mean," Alsrod insisted, "this cyhnk here. I know they all mean something different."

"It's an old piece," I explained, "dating from about two and half centuries ago. It comes from a local monastery, the Arvin, at the south of Morgre." I glanced over at the statue. On its black display pedestal it was grotesquely handsome: a four-foot stone trunk that branched into seven writhing arms, each ending in a gross red gem. "At the Arvin, they used to teach that the cyhnk symbolized the difference between its own, unified trunk and its many-branching head, a sign of the difference between the one and the many. Myself, I was always quite sure it was a stylized presentation of one of the tolgoth cactuses growing on the other side of the Hyte: but even our local retreat stressed that the image didn't come from our world or any world near it—though that was rather hard to believe with a forest of the things only a kilometer and a half away . . . at least that's what it seemed like when I was eight or nine or ten."

"When did you learn," Alsrod asked, "that the meaning of the cyhnk was not the same everywhere in the universe?"

"Only about ten years ago, actually," I told her. "On a world whose name I don't recall, I came across an older Sygn retreat. Right behind them some looming temporary factory had just gone up that for twenty months would be hot-stamping out large, ceramic, ugly things so that the murals I had come to see in my free three hours before my ship took off—they dated from the time the building had been an exploratory outpost five centuries before—were gummed over with black, protective elastic to absorb the shock and keep them from cracking. Anyway, once I doffed my airmask inside the irregular and blobbed transparent walls, distorting the starscape and rockscape outside, somehow a priestess got to explaining that the shape of the cyhnk I was familiar with back here on Velm was only one of many a cyhnk could have. On some worlds, apparently, it's a trunk with just two branches, both quite straight. On others—the one I was on for instance—it had five branches, each of which was a regular helix. And on some—though I forget the significance of the number—it is simply a cluster of a hundred and eleven twisting spokes; then, on others, it's only a single bar with a jewel at each end; and on still others, it's a jeweled sphere—while on still others, it's a plain one. These wise women in their deep robes and

the grilled mouth-speakers they wore to disguise the indi-
viduality of their voices told me that on many worlds the
cyhnk signifies, as it does on Velm, a difference between
one part of itself and another. But on other worlds—for
instance, theirs—it signified the difference between one
cyhnk and another, the difference between the myriad
kinds of cyhnks that exist on myriad worlds, the difference
between the myriad dogmas, each one different for each
different part of each different world, that make up the
institution so frequently known as the Sygn."

They all laughed again, this time, oddly, all on one
pitch. One after another and each at a different speed,
they began to rock, at first Fibermich, at last even George—
who had come up to join us somewhere in the midst of my
recitation. And though I now requested explanation from
the sociological GI program I always keep on tap with
visitors from different cultures (as they no doubt keep one
on me), I could not learn the significance of that alien
motion.

From the metal cloud that was Thadeus, once more
her brassy voice boomed: "Respect for the old and appreciation of the new, that's what the name of Thant is all
about! And that's what I found on Nepiy, too—that's what
made it such a wonderful world! Oh, if you'd ever been
there, you'd remember Nepiy: chalk-white deserts under
an onyx black sky, stretching to the horizon in all directions, with orderly crevices dug into them, where women
live in harmony and goodwill in the dwellings cut into the
stone—oh, no! Not like the zigzag canyons of Zetzor, but
rational, orderly, precise. The gestures of civil intercourse
there have a clarity and lucidity to enchant whoever ap-
preciates the fine heights that human civilization can reach.
A fine world, a wonderful world—I had a wonderful time
there! Someday you must visit it. Oh, yes! You must!"
Thadeus laughed again, hugely and generously, while
Eulalia, through the array of my own parents and siblings,
trailing her clouds of metals, gems, and lights, moved
around and around her co-spouse, miming gestures that,
in our own world's theatrical tradition, at any rate, indicated here obeisance, now mockery, there despair; or joy.
And I could not help thinking that, although Thadeus and
I may have been on the same planet, because, no doubt,

we had been on it months and geosectors apart, we had
really been to different worlds.

The evening drifted on.

When, for the tenth time, my eyes had gone ceiling-
wards—not to examine constellations but to imagine the
real stars far above their argent representations—I finally
decided I'd had it.

Standing by a decorative wall of falling water from the
spillway upstairs, I waited out the end of a story from (of
course) Clearwater Thant, and (it was a rather good one),
laughing, excused myself. Dark hands came up, but not to
halt me so much as to push me on my way. And Clearwater's own light laughter followed me as I threaded from
the thrumming falls. But I'd taken as much as I could of
strangely behaved, too easily impressed, boisterous, familiar friends.

I went to my room.

6.

Way down and away from anywhere else, it had once
belonged to a Dyeth mother, Ari, two ripples before. I'd
been ten and had just returned from that first extended
visit offworld to the giant moon, Senthy: Egri had taken
me there to stay with my grandmother Genya for nearly a
standard year, and my memory still swarmed with images
of those tall women, their fur parkas drawn tightly around
their pitted faces as they poled their boats in toward the
high steel docks. Into those reveries, made suddenly exotic by a simple trip of twenty-six light-years home, my
mother Maxa inserted the hard fact: I was of an age to
choose up a local habitation and a name. The last was easy.
With a bunch of my parents, I went down to the record
union in Morgre's lowest level, the knots in the polished
pith walls recalling faces on another world, and registered
the "Marq" which people had been calling me all my life.
The habitation, however, took some trips over and around
the area to search out a proper spot—I wanted something
rural, with natural rock, water, and all the technological
comforts a rather spoiled twelve-year-old could imagine.
My temp-parent, Kelso, was with us; and after several
hundred k's cruising about, she suddenly declared: "Look.

I know what Marq wants! Do you remember Ari's old place? Whatever happened to . . ." Back home, there was the scrabble through the closet full of discarded domestic cassettes. . . .

Today, honestly, I don't know if I love the location more or the fact that it's been a living room for Dyeths as long as it has:

Twenty-foot fire cactuses rose behind the ornate rail at the polished planks' oest end. (Shells and rocks, rocks and shells.) Overhead, a few night clouds pulled away from the brilliant oversized star that is our larger moon. The rocks beyond the rail were tufted with giltgorse. An orange carpet on the dark wood gave under my bare feet as I walked from the fading entrance column. Beyond the platform, through the tolgoth growth, the stream plashed. How many times a week do I open the railing gate, take some text-crystal from the fiche-board standing below my bed (six carved legs, with strange ball-claws for feet, rumpled sleeping mat over it), along with a portable reader (what we have instead of clumsy, beautiful books), to go and sit, to sit and dream, my back against some velvet-barked elephant lichen, to dream and read, with warm water washing my ankles?

Between the hills that gentled the horizons to the north, the crazy jewelry of Morgre-complex's upper park levels—my night light all through those strange years when childhood gives way to the beginning of adulthood—glittered like a little cyhnk; I was as far away from the city now as Santine's room, but in another direction.

In the platform's center stood a round desk—old, locally crafted, a horror to look at, but ridiculously efficient. Its reddish top was cluttered with gaming pieces, editing blocks, lengths of tape, and the reassembled skeleton of a small creature resembling a desert skate but indigenous to one or the other of Velm's polar wastes. Suspended above it all glowed a globe that, besides serving as a lamp, was also the central star in a double-sunned orrery—no, not Iiriani/Iiriani-prime—of ten planets (thirty moons among them, one of which was, yes, giant and nostalgic Senthy, circling its huge, useless world, NRJ-6B), all rotating and revolving on their hugely slant and varied orbitals.

On the desk, the comscreen was still up out of its slot,

a pile of dice in front of it; a piece of string on which I'd
been practicing whed-knots (an art performed by a small
northern tribe of Velm natives with their hind feet; and I
was improving) lay across it. Scattered before it were some
text crystals from my seven-times-great grandmother's un-
readable memoirs which, that morning, I'd once again
taken from the Old Library.

As I approached the desk, the bench rolled out from
under it; the bench-back swung up and took the proper
curve and angle. On the comscreen, which for some reason hadn't turned off when I'd left, the pale colors of the
ball court still pulsed: within the pentagonal frame, among
the laughter, I watched Thadeus Thant (voice like a cracked
claxon, a gentle, jovial, jealous creature, who, now at age
eighty, has learned to turn jealousy into ambition), Clearwater Thant (the quietest, smallest, and blackest of the
Thants—the most prolific, in years the oldest, but looks
not a day over fifty, my favorite, and by me the one with
the dryest sense of humor) and imperious Eulalia Thant
(an impressive redhead surrounded by more jewelry than
I think all of us Dyeths owned, kilos of it floating out on
suspensors that kept it turning slowly about her, as she
turned about her children, her spouses, a woman with an
insight into human motivations both cultivated and uncanny), and Fibermich, Nea, George, Alsrod . . . all bobbing about among human and inhuman Dyeths and friends
of Dyeth.

I sat.

I watched.

I pondered the performance below long enough to
sense what an odd feeling familiarity is, consisting as much
of the dark things that attract as it does of the bright ones
that repel. Was it simply all that warmth and those good
wishes? Sitting there, I felt it swinging at my side, and ran
my hand down the chain to retrieve it: the pink light still
glowed above the leather bound screen. Runes swarmed
as I lifted it, giant gnats swinging about it as the book
swung. (But I *thought* I'd turned it off . . .) Apparently in
my haste I'd just flipped the random selector to still another poem. It had been on all this time.

On my cluttered desk top I set the book that could
have been stage or sculptor's pedestal. Above it hung dark
runes that could have been a statue or a performance.

Between them I watched the comscreen, bright with the party.

Before I tell you which poem was on, I want to tell you something that the title (in lower case runes at the very bottom) brought immediately to my mind. An evelm philosopher once wrote: "Almost all human attempts to deal with the concept of death fall into two categories. The first can be described by the injunction: 'Live life moment by moment as intensely as possible, even to the moment of one's dying.' The second can be expressed by the exhortation: 'Concentrate only on what is truly eternal—time, space, or whatever hypermedium they are inscribed in— and ignore all the illusory trivialities presented by the accident of the senses, unto birth and death itself.' For women who adhere to either position," this wise creature noted, "the other is considered the pit of error, the road to injustice, and the locus of sin." At this point, I must explain that by "human attempts to deal with the concept of death," the evelm philosopher in question meant only those humans who happened to have lived in this world, Velm, up in the beleaguered north or here in the calmer south, for the last three hundred and eighty years. This philosopher was no doubt unconcerned with that greater death, Cultural Fugue, and if someone ever told her that the first attitude more or less categorizes the Sygn and that the second is indicative of Family, I suspect that this venerable sage would have returned a look to remind any human that the evelmi are, indeed, alien. (Of course: the perfect translation for the title of Vondramach Okk's early participatory poem, even though the connotations differ: "The Alien." Why hadn't I been able to think of it with Alsrod?) The title of the poem I *had* accidentally opened to translated clearly and simply: "Stranger."

I didn't read it.

Fingering my scrotum, I felt my penis move on the back of my hand, till some unspecified desire began to weight and lift my genitals with blood. I waited for that desire to fix on some current masturbatory image. When it didn't, I briefly thought I might leave my room, my home, and seek one of the city's runs. But apparently whatever I was feeling could not express itself through public copulation any more than through private satisfaction. Desire died. What replaced it was a GI access code.

Had I really been thinking about it during the intervening time? I turned off the book and pushed it aside. I'd carried Clym's warning about with me, anent security reclassifications contingent on inquiries after Rhyonon. But there was another operative in the tale that could be inquired after.

Why did I think about it now?

Perhaps it was simply because I was feeling I shouldn't be feeling so at home?

I thought: *Non-human life forms,* and my mind filled with another lengthy access code of numbers and colors. I read them over to myself. They cleared away, and I thought—

7.

—Xlv.

From the bottom of some distant GI storage bank— rank upon rank of the tiniest, brightest metalloids submerged in some super-chilled, coal-black, linearly conductive syrup—the information welled into my mind like memory: Among the many forms of life discovered in human world-hopping, a surprising number of them clearly intelligent, many of them culturally advanced, and even a handful with extraordinarily ingenious methods for getting between the planets and moons of their own sun systems, the Xlv are the single species besides humans who have an efficient means of interstellar travel. For many years their starships were mistaken for natural objects: massive, black, irregular as meteoric rubble, here and there a huge multi-faceted crystal face glittering—through which nothing is visible.

Inhabitants of at least two hundred gas giants throughout the galaxy, the Xlv still cannot be designated a race with whom we have "established communications." Our ignorance of them is oppressive. Do they have [a] language[s]? Can the term intelligence be applied to them? Do they know of our existence? There is still a raging debate on whether they construct their ships as humans do, or whether they secrete them in some way similar to the way certain insects secrete the waxy material for their nests. . . .

As I reviewed their tripartite plasmoid biology, learned of their odd colonies that may or may not be floating well down in the atmosphere of gaseous planets almost large enough to ignite into small stars, reviewed the rare space encounters between human and Xlv—so baffling as to leave moot in almost every case whether an encounter had or had not occurred—I recalled Okk's absent half-lines in *The Alien/The Awkward/The Exotic*.

For most women, the Xlv are a complete question mark, nor are we even sure which direction that question mark faces. (They are a shiftrune whose sound sequence remains unuttered.) When our instruments detect Xlv on one world, how are we to know their social or political relations to the Xlv on another (Do they have societies? Cultures? Politics?); not to mention the relation of Xlv on one ship to the Xlv on another. (In the conflict between Sygn and Family, if one does something appalling to a neutral party—as has more than once been the case—the other certainly doesn't want to take the blame.) What kind[s] of government[s] do they have? Which kinds get along? Which kinds are constantly falling into tension situations? Is interstellar travel for them analogous to the human discovery of the potter's wheel, paternity, the solar system, or the semiconductor?

Among six-thousand-two-hundred-plus worlds and thousands of billions of humans and aliens, there are probably hundreds of thousands, even millions, at any moment, exploring aspects of the Xlv, scattered across any hundred or five hundred worlds. That is still a microscopic percentage of humanity as a whole.

If only because there is so much to know in our human universe, the working assumption you can go on is: You may assume, about absolutely any fact (how many transuranic elements are there? why does cold water remove human blood stains faster than hot?) that nine hundred and ninety-nine people out of a thousand do *not* know it—which goes for the working assumption too. And the Xlv, who, after all, *are* alien, touch an even more microscopic percentage of human lives than most things. Thus: "There is an alien life form that travels between stars" is simply another little-known fact—because in our human universe, of necessity, *all* facts are as little known as the works of great poets.

The green light bar before the comscreen on my desk was blinking under the tape rumple and through the dice. Some sister or parent or cousin was calling to find out where I'd gotten off to, jovially to demand I return to the ball court and watch the presentation of some elaborate gift, hear the recitation of some florid toast. Beyond the rail, fire cactus tittered. The warm breeze tickled my neck. Among cold stars a single light moved in a trajectory between moons—a satellite catching and throwing back a fragment of my world's communicative complexities.

What would the Xlv mean to the Thants of Zetzor, the Dyeths of Velm, to the women, human or other, of (approx.) six thousand two hundred worlds?

What about the fact: There is an alien lifeform that may have destroyed someone's world . . . ?

What did that mean to the Xlv?

The call bar blinked green again. I started to press it, but for a moment I looked over the railing about the patch of mine that filled my after-dark horizons; and felt strange—estranged, really, as though considering the demise of one world made me a stranger to this most familiar spot on my own.

Might the ravines and marshes, the urban complexes and universities and hive-caves of Velm, I wondered, flare suddenly and broil away before a world-wide fire wall . . . ?

With that smile we prepare so easily for friends, for stream, for anyone we love (and which always feels so odd in the ligaments of the human face; though the evelmi among the Dyeths say they do not know this feeling), I pressed the answer plate. "Hey, Clearwater . . ." I said to the familiar face forming. "Look, would you tell V'vish and Shoshona I'll be back up in a while? Don't worry, I haven't finked out on you yet."

At the same time the column of light that was the entrance to my room came on in the platform corner. I glanced at it as George Thant materialized, with that artificially metallized skin, looking very like a polished bronze statue, every one of her movements suggesting pyrite heated to that near-white temperature where the form begins to crumple like hot wax; and Zetzor is so cold.

She was laughing and rocking. But since she was outside (more properly, inside) the door (more properly, the column) and my viewing light had, finally, been fixed,

I could see her; but she couldn't see me. On the comscreen
Clearwater was saying: ". . . and come downstairs, Marq,
before George gets there and makes a nuisance of herself."

George is probably the strongest person I've known
from any world, physically speaking, who does not use
artificial muscular additors. "Marq! Hey, Marq!" She was
flexing her brazen hands as though one or the other of
them might be clutching a rock, a neck, an ice shard.
"Come on and join the party. We want to see you!"

"All *right*, George," I said. "I'll be down in a few
minutes!"

"Look, only one of your beautiful sisters is still around.
Egri is doing her lizard routine. *You're* supposed to be the
guy who knows how to make strangers here feel at home.
Come on down and be hospitable!"

"George," I said, this time loud enough for her to
hear, "you would be at home in the pit of a volcano or on
top of a glacier"—both of which are structures common on
Zetzor and unknown on Velm. "Look, hang on to your left
tit and I'll be up when I damned well feel like it, you
metallurgist's reject!" It fascinates me what makes some
people comfortable.

George roared with laughter and turned in the column unsteadily, like someone a great deal drunker than I
suspect she was.

"Now stop cluttering my doorsill, gnat-brain, and leave
me alone!" And we do have gnats here. And I don't like
them. There's an energy about the Thants, every one of
them, that fascinates us Dyeths—almost every one of us.
We regard it, watch it, discuss it endlessly. I wonder if it's
analogous to their fascination before our age and tradition.
George is also the least sexually exciting human I can
think of, which has always struck me as odd since strength
and size are usually positive factors in my erotic schema.
But in her great body, they just sat together wrong. I
suspect the Thants surround for me all that is, or could
possibly be, alien. ("The alien is always constructed of the
familiar," is as good a translation as any of "The Alien"'s
opening half-line, though it lacks all music.) And I know
that's because any request for a false parity, where Dyeths
might play a congruent part in the Thants' schema, is
simply not to be met with. Still, the fascination—much
more than the simple desire to *use*—exists on both sides;

probably exists less on their side than on ours, which is
the wonder.

"Yes, Clearwater. I won't let George bother me. I
hear you. Thanks for the warning. Thanks a lot . . ." as the
entrance column went dark in the corner around retreat-
ing bronze. On the comscreen Clearwater's black face
melted, glittering, like all night.

FOUR

Rescue on Rhyonon

Cut through the galaxy's glitter; slice away all night. What thoughts did I dole out to that world (out of the six thousand, which, according to a rumor that had crept worlds and worlds away, corroborated only by a certain certified psychotic, may have been) destroyed by Xlv?

Certainly I thought about it.

Yet after a week, after a handful of weeks, now at home, now away, somehow the rational part of my mind had accorded it much the weight one gives to the most insubstantial notion.

I was finishing up a fairly simple job$_1$—though today, none are easy. The folk artists in the temperate wastes of Yinysh—a world whose polar caps are sheeted with black ice—make vast mosaics out of tiny laterally sensitive tiles: changes in light cause them to change not their own color, but to transmit a color change to the tile beside them: by fine maneuverings, this can be worked into a mosaic whose picture moves and changes with the changing sun. Four thousand seven hundred light-years along the rim, an architect in the equatorial stone fields of Batria—a thin-aired planet where atmosphere is released from volcanic fissures in the north and shipped in orange plastic tanks to the planetary midlands—heard of them. As she was also a religious leader for three geosectors, nothing would do but to import the actual tiles to decorate her new pantheon's sunrise-facing facade. The expense was undertaken in the name of interworld relations. I was hired for expenses (huge) and a modest fee (modest) to shepherd those cartons of glittering hexagons across five thousand light-years of dark. We had paused on some vasty station orbiting one of Batria's Lagrange points. I was off ship in a library cubicle looking up information that I thought might come in handy for a job₁ that I saw a good chance of picking up once I got down to Batria (What's *my* whimsical historical document turns out to be *your* immoral, tasteless, obscene . . . Anyway, there's one reason they need industrial diplomats), when my call number slid up the green tube running past my cubicle, stopped at eye level, and bonged.

I swung the reader away from my nose and turned. The call, when I thought through my reception code (visualize yellow fading slowly to green, while hearing the first three digits of my home-mail routing number recited in my sister Alyxander's voice, followed by the sudden stench of burnt plastic) ran round the tube in imperative pink: Report instanter to the Web Official at Level Two (that's quarter gravity), coordinates 12-17.

Curious as to what could possibly be questioned this time about my cargo, I hauled myself out of the cubicle and kicked off through the enamel and silver hall (the library was in the free fall level), from time to time giving myself another pull on the wall railing.

Accelerate in freefall, and you always have the vaguest feeling you're rising straight up; decelerate, and you have the equally vague feeling you're falling straight down.

I fell (straight down) at a lift cable, grabbed it, and lifted (straight up and at right angles to my former down) through the side wall. Moments later, I stepped off with the blobby feeling one gets in quarter-normal, and strode unsteadily forward, taking giant steps, over the yellow pebbled flooring and under blue hanging gewgaws, with large-leafed plants waving either side.

12-17 was a forest of reflecting panels. I stepped among them, worked my way around layer after layer; the floor itself became flats of glass over lower flats of mirror. My own reflection reduplicated away from me in myriad directions, heads all turning as I turned, feet all stepping as I stepped. And suddenly I was surrounded by, and confronted with, and interwoven among a woman who looked up at me from her desk and said:

"Marq Dyeth." She smiled with the face of a friendly mule. "I haven't seen you for years."

"Japril!" The new blue, green, and red rays around the sunburst on her shoulder told me she'd moved up some in the Web's hierarchy since we'd last chatted together behind the protective plastic shields on the flame beaches of Shahng-al-Voyard. "Honestly," I said, "you are not whom I expected to see here."

"I'm not here, actually." She turned in her seat, pushed the desk, which drifted aside on silent rails, and crossed her silver leggings.

2.

I sat on the floppy purple thing inflating blobbily behind me. "Just how far away are you?" It firmed beneath me.

"More than nine thousand light-years." She toyed with something that was gold and thin, black nobs on both ends. (Pencil? Microphone? Letter opener?)

"That's a rather costly hyperwave projection just to say hello."

"We have forty minutes' conference time, Marq. A few seconds out for nostalgia won't hurt—though I doubt if it will help either. We'll let it go at that."

I had some good memories of Japril: her insight, her ambition. I also had reason to wonder if some of her memories of me were not so pleasant. "I'd thought you'd be somebody calling to chide me about my current cargo. But this has got to be about some past crime of mine, if not some crime to come." Spiders all think industrial diplomacy is a crime; they may be right.

Japril went from smile to grin with those big teeth of hers. "Actually, it's neither." Her fingers came together on the golden bar. (Calculator? Energy knife? Water purifier?) "Relax. What do you know of Rhyonon?"

A memory of Clym; and a chill. "Only that no one is supposed to know *that* much about it." Funny thing about that chill. It didn't subside. There's something permanently scary about an entire world's death, even in rumor.

"What do you know about the rescue operations? The

few thousands we got out, say, or the few colony ships the
Web managed to load up in hours and evacuate during the
course of the disaster? The survivors we managed to pry
out of the peripheral ruins and smoking wreckage once the
major conflagration was over?"

The Web *is* information; it's silly to lie to a spider,
especially one with that many rays rainbowing her sunburst. "Nothing."

"I know," she said. "There weren't any. At least of
those."

See what I mean.

"You want to know where I am." Japril's fingers moved
absently on the stick. (Sound recorder? Cosmetics case?
Musical instrument?) Possibly having something to do with
it, possibly not, mirrors blanked out among us; reflections
vanished. Behind Japril a wide, indistinct window looked
out on a brown landscape, boxed and blotted with architectural oddities, some angular, some freeform, many connected by arching tunnels. The sky was salted with stars.
"I'm at a rescue station on the sixth moon of Chyvon, in
the Tyon-omega system; Chyvon's a gas giant one out from
Rhyonon. Within an hour of the catastrophe, a rescue
station was set up on Rhyonon's nearest moon and an
overflow station here."

"Then some *did* get out . . . ?" hearing, as I said it,
how ridiculous it sounded. With two years' planning, you
can lift a few thousand women from one world and relo-
cate them on another. How many can you evacuate within
minutes?

"The station on Rhyonon's moon was closed down to a
skeleton staff within a hundred hours after the catastrophe."

"I would have thought that the majority of the
refugees—" I felt strange calling the survivors of an entire
world refugees— "would have been brought to the nearer
station."

"The reason we maintain the skeleton staff on Rhyonon's
moon is at least to suggest—to those who're suggestible—
the possibility of a small refugee population there."

"But there isn't one . . . ?"

"As far as illusions go, it's pretty paltry. Believe me, I
wasn't in favor of it when it was decided on."

"Japril," I said. "Are there any survivors at all?"

She took a long time to say: "Yes."

"And they're not on Rhyonon's moon, but rather on that moon of . . . Chyvon, with you?"

She took an even longer time to nod—throwing me to all those far-flung cultures where a nod does not necessarily signal affirmation. But they were not Japril's.

Nonchalantly as I could manage, I asked: "How many?"

One reason Japril became friends with me in the first place is because of her uncanny ability to see through my diplomatic masks. "Why don't I tell you, instead, your relation to this survivor, Marq?"

"You mean this woman is a factor in my life of an order other than rumor?"

"It's a notable relation. And don't discount rumor. It's the real order of business this evening." (Where I was, I was thinking of it as afternoon. But no matter.) "I've noted that relation—"

"And the Web wants to exploit it. Which is why you've called on me to talk about it—across nine thousand light-years." One reason I became friends with Japril is because of how quickly her ambitious and devious plans open all their exfoliations to my view. "There *is* a survivor, isn't there? At least one." Really, I was thinking of Clym far more than the various suggestions Japril had all but thrown in front of me.

"We've had Rat Korga here at the station for . . ." There was relief in her voice as she said the name to me for the first time; and I got a sense that this was something she had not talked about with many people; and that to talk about it with someone outside a very limited circle was something she had wanted to do for: "—well, for a while now."

3.

"Let me tell you about Rhyonon, Marq. Sit back and I'll catalogue the horrors. I've done it in enough reports that I can recite it in my sleep. The flame shell," Japril said, "where it roared across Rhyonon's surface, was over fifty thousand feet high—which effectively did in any passing air travel. Most of the actual holocaust was confined to the equatorial areas. So was ninety percent of Rhyonon's population. The resultant gaseous toxins alone, not to mention

the incredible heatstorms that went raging out north and
south, pretty well did in the parts of the world that were
not directly burned. Winds over the whole planet rose to
nearly six hundred kilometers an hour. In ten hours, the
major flaming areas had more or less burned themselves
out, with twelve percent of the planetary surface fused and
the atmosphere radically deoxygenated. How's the reception over there where you are, Marq? I just got a flicker.
No, don't say anything. Just let me go on. In seventeen
hours, there was an average drop in temperature recorded
over the general surface down to a hundred degrees celsius, or even below that, here and there; and the average
was falling. Because we have to mark it somewhere, this is
now considered the official termination of the catastrophe,
though there were still seas of hundred-fifty-degree muck
bubbling around, on places that had never seen temperatures above twenty-five degrees celsius before. Choosing
the real moment of termination over something the size of
a planet is rather like deciding where the edge of an
atomic mushroom cloud is with a ten centimeter rule. But
less than twenty hours after the disaster's commencement
we were actually flying through that planetary murk. Marta
was glum; and Ynn was putting out the forced cheerfulness
that only makes the glum get angry. I called myself keeping my mind on the controls; and never have bothered to
ask what I looked like to the others in the rescue boat. It
only took us half an hour's flying over thousands on thousands of square kilometers of lava fields, in the midst of
which had once been some of Rhyonon's major civilized
cities of millions, to realize it was a pretty useless search.
And how many hours was it after that, our scouting ships
veered north and south toward the poles? How many
scouting ships were there? And why was ours, among the
hundreds called down to quarter and requarter the assigned areas, the one to make the strike? Suddenly our
radar, peeking through the blackened air, came back with
the ruin of a building. You have to understand that in
places where a day ago there had been urban complexes as
big as Vongle or Rimena—" Japril and I had met in Vongle
afloat on Pattuck's southeastern seas— "there were only
puddles of boiling mud. Large puddles, too. The deserts
in the south had just been scorched—which is to say, that
for a few hours a wind somewhat above the temperature of

boiling water had raged at several hundred k's an hour over them, which was enough to do in any but the staunchest surface structures and pretty well all animal life; not to mention plants.

"And there was . . . a ruin!

"We sat our three-girl boat down beside it. The air was unbreathable—we had to go clomping out through the portal tube in heavy heat suits, because the temperature even here was still in the neighborhood of sixty degrees. Walking across the sand toward the broken walls, Ynn's boot toe struck a pile of rubble falling away from something which, as we gathered around it and kicked away more dust, was clearly some desiccated transport machine.

"Within the roofless walls themselves, there was sand almost a foot deep over what turned out to be thermoplastic floorplates. There was also almost a complete lack of information about what function the station had served or who its inhabitants had been.

"Only one of us—Ynn—had bothered to learn any of the local Rhyonon languages in the minutes before we'd taken off. You and I, Marq, would have probably considered Rhyonon a fairly primitive place. They didn't have a General Info system, for what seemed to be essentially religious reasons. They'd even been trying to legislate against the one the Web had set up on their nearer moon and not succeeding. On one of the few strings of cubes lying around that hadn't melted beyond decipherment, on which they did their hieroglyphic insect-scratchings, Ynn found mention of a hermetically self-sealing underground refrigerator and storage crypt. Should we investigate? (Since the air was too thick to see through, inside what remained of the building, we watched each other in stereo schemata formed of little colored squares, reduced from infrared reflections, on stereo face plates inside our masks.) Why not? Back outside, where everything was scrimmed with dirty gold, and the stereo plates could be raised for simple glass—as long as you weren't trying to make out details on anything more than a meter away—we hauled out the excavators. The blades dropped, began to churn sand. And that's when Marta, inside the ship for something, called out that the biodetectors, which till now we'd all but forgotten, were blipping and pinging like mad.

"Something was down there—and alive!

"Marta's first guess was that it was some kind of plankton farm below—perhaps the bacterial decay that had gotten started on the remains of some par-boiled algae. But the fine-tuning on the detectors told us the major form was almost certainly animal, not vegetable. Mice? was Ynn's suggestion—they've gone with humanity everywhere else. Fleas? Some local paramecia who'd managed to escape frying? We tunneled and delved, furious as banshees, at the same time refusing to believe what the detector—with each ton of sand and slag the excavator's blade heaved up over the crater's rim—was insisting. You have no idea what it's like to come upon something the size of a world where less than a day ago there were a quarter of a billion people, only to discover that now everything even resembling a molecule of ATP has been reduced to salts, gas, and water. Marta was putting up heat screens and clean-air traps as fast as Ynn could push away the rubble with the excavator. Using relay lines to the lunar GI system—the local signal jammers had been knocked out by the catastrophe—we'd all managed to become experts in any number of fancy rescue and medical techniques over the previous three hours. I was darting in and out of our ship, looking over the edge of the pit— swirling with smoke—then running inside again to see it on the screen in infrared, which cut out all the haze and where you had the advantage of being able to vary the focal length. 'We're through!' Ynn called over the earphones; and Marta brought in her last bubble-dome, digging various polyisoprene walls well down in the sizzling sand. (I was out again.) Through plastic panes I saw sand fall inward.

"What came out into the bubble was immediately analyzed and the bubble itself was flooded with a gas mixture five degrees cooler and ten percent richer in oxygen—we figured no matter what was in there in the line of animal life, that would have to be an improvement. Then we were scrambling down ourselves and through the floppy plastic envelopes, with all sorts of suspensor stretchers, medical kits, flares, and stun-guns bobbling along behind us. In our great mittens, we climbed down through the welter of twisted pipes and cracked masonry, shooting cool air around us with super-handy-dandy portable air conditioners. It was over forty degrees in there when we

went in. We sent out beams of white, blue, and green
light among the collapsed lattices of crumpled supports
and broken pipes. It had been seven minutes since we got
the first life-reading—but we'd all been working with ×5
time-dilation drugs, which had made it seem to us just
over a leisurely half-hour. Yellow, orange, and red beams
converged. In the resultant glow, we saw, not moving,
under a scatter of rubble, a leg.

"Ynn set loose a handful of diagnostic bugs that attacked our find like killer bees. But even as we were
closing in, it was pretty clear that something fairly awful
had happened.

"I started to say something was pinning the leg down—

"But, frankly, there wasn't much leg left. Twenty
seconds later (divided by five) the bugs reported, on the
little screens flickering on the left sides of our vision
plates: our survivor was also blind.

"Other reports were coming back now from the host
of analyzers flitting and humming around the crypt, taking
their readings and making their correlations: some time in
the first few minutes of the catastrophe, one of ten giant
refrigeration coils had ruptured and for seconds the space
had been flooded with fluorine, before the gas had been
removed, a minute later, by the sluggish purifiers, their
efficiency hugely reduced by the high heat. Fortunately,
for most of that minute, the survivor had not been
breathing—otherwise the trauma to the mucous membranes of the respiratory system alone would have been
fatal. That minute, by the bye, was to give us a lot of
trouble over the next few days.

"But we got our survivor bubbled, sedated, aerated,
and suspensored. In the midst of sealing up the plastic
shield over the stretcher, there was some ghastly, basso
grunt that threatened to topple towers and shatter ear-
drums—a human groan, but to us, thanks to the drugs,
five octaves lower than uttered.

"Then we were pushing the stretcher along and up
and between broken ledges. Outside the shield, flying
dust had already peppered the transparent plastic with
enough grit to blacken whatever we had been able to see
before in the gray and mustard mists. And time-compres-
sants were winding us down from the dilation drugs. (More
than ten minutes is bad for your heart—and terrible for

your kidneys.) In the sealed stretcher tube, the fellow was already being ministered to by threads of light that had pretty well woven around what was left of that right leg, growing a new one for him from the remains of the old. We got the stretcher out of the envelope flap, floated it across the sands (I swear the dunes had been blown into entirely different shapes in the minute we'd been down) and through our ship lock. Bubbles coursed the pale gold liquid that filled the container, carrying newly cloned cells to the proper locations and flushing away the damages. The survivor . . ."

"Japril," I said, after moments when she had remained silent, "I've heard that term before. Now you've said it, I have to say: I can't believe that over the surface of an entire world, any catastrophe short of the whole planet's physically blowing up could manage to do in *every* member of the population with only *one* exception—"

"The survivor was, by now, being monitored and observed by twelve hundred other rescue workers still searching and quartering Rhyonon's steaming, storm-scoured surface, looking for others with one added grain of hope lent by our success." (Yes, I was thinking: You could bring in twelve hundred workers to look for survivors in *one* undersea magma-mine disaster. A world . . . ?) "Our ship lurched up, and we rose above that noxious desert, bearing what we would soon learn was a hugely ruined creature, healing now in our biotic tubs."

"And you brought her here," I said. "Which is to say—there, where you are. But why are you—"

Japril's foreknuckles came together on the gold bar. (A work of art? A medical device? A child's toy?) "We're talking of *this* survivor—the survivor that concerns you."

FIVE

Rescue Continued

"Japril," I said. "I don't know why I keep asking. But I suppose it's because the implied answer just always seems wrong. Tell me—or tell me why the Web doesn't want me to know: exactly *how* many survivors were there from Rhyonon?"

"Marq," she said, "you should know if anyone does: it's your question that's impossible. Three thousand volunteers in a colonial ship bound for the Mie-t&t VII colony had left Rhyonon's surface six hours before the holocaust commenced. All of them are alive today; and none of them knows what's happened to her former home. Were they survivors? There are thousands upon thousands more, born on Rhyonon over the last hundred years, who now live on a moon or a world or an O'n-colony circling some moon or world, having left a day or a year or a decade ago. Are they survivors? Or the how-many from other worlds, other moons, within hours or minutes or days of visiting or returning to Rhyonon, whose flights were then canceled— not to mention the seven hundred and fifty-eight incoming offworld flights that we were able to deflect, within minutes of the disaster's commencement, to moons or other planets. Were they survivors?"

"What about the five, or fifty, or five hundred you couldn't?"

Japril got that angry look I've always liked her for. "I could give you two answers. First, it's not my department. Second, there were two-hundred-seven of those. In seventeen cases, the Web was actually able to effect some midair transfers of passengers and crews that, if there's going to be any excitement about the Rhyonon rescue operations, ought to be at the center of it."

"All right, Japril," I said. "I hear what you're saying. With a population as large as a world can have and a disaster of Cultural Fugue proportions, 'survival' becomes a kind of fuzzy phenomenon; it's not the hard-edged fact of local fires, floods, and hurricanes. Go on and tell me about my relations to—" I laughed. "You know, I'd started to say 'my' survivor."

"Our survivor," Japril said ruefully, "presented a host of medical problems, once we lifted that bruised and ruptured half-corpse off the steaming silt and sand and slag that was, now, much too much of Rhyonon.

"When we got a full diagnosis of the blindness, we thought we had hit the major medical hurdle." (Something General Info has returned to us: one or two people can see a whole project through from start to finish, even if various stages in it demand three or four or fifty fields of extensive specialized knowledge. That the Web is the most constant utilizer of the newest facets of GI should be no surprise. They invented it.) "The whole front orbital surface, of both whites and corneas, was corroded—thanks to that fluorine. And inside, the retinas had been perforated in half a hundred places and the humors generally congealed as solid as boiled albumin—which can be dealt with. But the interior eyeball lining had become granulated and would clearly become a suppurating hive of problems in no time, even if all the works were restored. You *can't* deal with that. Which meant the eyes themselves had to be replaced. Ynn suggested a Rhyonon-manufactured optical prosthesis might be best. There were actually some around, since we were only a moon away. Marta hit up GI for some quick courses in optical surgery and wired them in. . . . Under dim light, Marq, the new eyes look like black-backed globes of clear glass. In ordinary light, they are your usual, faintly veined white with irises of a green substantially more vivid than the true irises originally were. In bright light they turn a disquieting silver. You know—"

Japril frowned— "there's an odd thing about the sociology of prosthetic devices. When a culture first develops the technology to counterfeit a human function, the counterfeit is usually awkward and jarring. But when the culture reaches a technological stage beyond that, the prostheses are made to look as much like the original organ as possible. Now when a stage beyond *that* is reached, suddenly the prostheses are consciously constructed to call attention to themselves in aesthetically interesting ways. In fact, limited technological stages can be meaningfully described as exhibiting just such variations as I've—"

"Japril," I said, "you are telling me, in your own inimitable way, Rhyonon's culture had reached a level two stages beyond that needed to create a functional optical prosthesis. But *we* only have a limited amount of conference time. You haven't told me—"

"We set the survivor's waking for an hour after our own next day. Rest is still the best cure for that kind of bodily trauma: new leg, new eyes. We came into the rotunda of the rescue station here, wondering if the pale blue walls and the wall window, beyond which sprawled only lunar schist and craters, were really conducive to the best revival. Had we done certain neurological tests? Certainly. Had we done others? Well, now . . . we'd done enough to determine that we had no major deficiencies to deal with. There were signs of the most minor prenatal brain damage that may have been due to potassium starvation in the bearing parent. But neural paths had been established by normal growth to compensate. We had neither a genius nor an idiot on our hands. That we knew. How did we go about telling someone in the huge range we humans have generally set out for ourselves as normal that their world is . . . gone?

"A hundred lights, each a different color, died in the froth of glycerine that washed about that human-shaped bath. Tubes drained off the puce and fuchsia biles that, in a sort of antidigestive process, had, by their chemical actions, healed; had, by their tidal actions, exercised. Molecular gradients were read across sheets of tissue; neural charges were positioned down to the synapse and detonated.

"The right arm twitched.

"For a moment the left hand's knuckles were four

bubbly islands in the trough's syrup. A knee flexed from thick liquid.

"Then, dripping, the survivor sat.

"You understand, Marq, I had never seen such a waking, but GI had given me the recalls to call on of seventeen experts who'd each watched this process many times—watched the coughing, the shaking head, the neural twitches as the nerves came on again, the unsteady motor orientation of an old nervous system taking over a radically reprocessed body, the ten-to-twenty minutes' limping to accommodate the inevitable discrepancies in neural firing times of the nerves in the new leg, the two-to-five hours of increased blinking to acclimate to the just-connected optic nerve.

"The survivor sat, to the waist, in foam.

"The survivor coughed.

"The survivor raised both hands and, with two thick and awkward forefingers, rubbed away the juices from each lid in a single downward motion. The tub began to tip, and Ynn automatically stepped forward to give a hand, that, clearly, as our healed creature stepped forward among the railings and handholds now, was not needed.

"There was no stagger at all.

"The eyes—bright green under our lights—were wide. With all that lubricating syrup, physiologically there is no *need* to blink for a full three minutes. Still almost any human waking from such a bathing blinks. A lot.

"The survivor didn't; but rather looked about. Marta made a gesture with her hand beside her face that showed she was empathizing with the queasiness we knew was being felt but, did not show. With a supporting ring in each large hand—so very tall—the survivor stood, for all the world (the world . . . ? which world?) like someone waiting. No questions, no curious glances, no self-orienting looks; naked thighs streamed, and the drain gurgled behind wide heels.

"I said softly to Ynn: 'Perhaps that brain damage . . . ?'

"Ynn said sharply: 'Who are you? Tell us your name. We want to help you,' in the most common of Rhyonon's six languages. We knew that twenty-four percent of Rhyonon's population was—or had been—bilingual, with the most common language either the first or second tongue of that quarter.

"The survivor was looking somewhere between Marta and me . . . not with any particular intensity. Still, because that face so clearly wasn't paying attention to what Ynn was saying, it made me want to look over my shoulder to see what those eyes were seeing, even though I knew it was only blue plastifoam.

"Ynn said: 'Who are you? Tell us your name. We want to help you,' in the second most common of Rhyonon's six languages.

"The survivor said: 'Korga the Porter . . . Rat. . . .'

"The last was a term I didn't know, though by now I'd been programmed with four advanced courses in Rhyonon linguistic patterns—enough to locate that accent as a pidgin version of the speech associated with the urban equatorial slums. Though just *which* slum, I couldn't tell.

"The survivor still didn't look at us.

"There was something about . . . the height, the roughness of the body, the stubble darkening the male jaw, the unexpectedly steady gaze of those eyes we had just given—"

"For a moment, Japril—" I laughed— "I thought you were going to tell me my relation to this character was that I happened to be her perfect look-alike, or perhaps among six thousand worlds' population, we happen to have turned out genotypal twins. And male, you say. I'd just assumed—"

"Rough, black hair," Japril went on, "sun-darkened skin . . . from what we know of Rhyonon's demographics and colonizations records, chances are almost thirty percent of the ancestry was white. The face, Marq, was uneven and pitted—"

"Sounds like the scars of a very rare disease called acne," I volunteered. "When I was ten, I encountered a population where it was rife. On that moon, in fact, both the males and the females considered it a mark of great distinction—" which was not quite accurate. "I've always agreed."

Japril's smile said more things than I could read in it. "There was something about that face—though I only thought about how to express it later. Consider a mask of terra cotta. Now take a jeweler's hammer, strike it from behind, then, before the first cracks appear on the surface, catch a picture from the front. There was that about the face, Marq. The survivor stepped forward, now, unsteadily. The disorientation we expected from fear, from displacement, from remembered terror at whatever had happened a world, two eyes, and a leg ago was just not there. Those eyes now looked at Ynn, at Marta, at me.

"Over seven feet tall: two heads taller than me and almost as tall as Ynn; and the distinctions among those long, long muscles were different from the ones a woman's take on in a gymnasium program to bring out the body's lines.

"I've seen worlds where women's physical labor was a prime commodity. The physicality was much more like that than such a—"

"And I've seen women from labor-intensive geosectors on low technology, or unevenly dispersed technology, worlds, Japril. You make this survivor very vivid to me."

"Do I? To me, it all was a bit horrifying. There was a solidness, a dullness, an unresponsiveness that lay out on the ceramic flesh, still glazed with our oils, like an underfinish keeping the surface glaze from exploding. Though I knew I was watching a human, I kept trying to decide what genus, what species—"

"Japril," I said, laughing, "I know some Sygn priests who'd call you a blasphemer."

"When a world is destroyed—a whole world, Marq— there are so *many* fuzzy-edged phenomena that to speak of the event at all is to broach blasphemy. I watched, Marq. And what I sensed, Marta saw. She said something to Ynn, who glanced at me, then looked back. What can be talked of clearly, General Info can teach you in under three-tenths of a second." (That's the time for neural firing throughout a cubic-third-of-a-centimeter of brain material, case you're interested—the amount of time required to memorize with GI, say, the *Oneirokritika* by heart.) "The rest one must mumble about, either loudly or quietly as is one's temperament. Marta began to make quiet mumbles— as do most spiders from any of ten worlds I can mention in her home Web-sector—punctuated with the likes of '. . . severe disorientation . . . sociopathology . . . no clearly damaged . . .' while Ynn said in her high, sharp voice:

" 'Well, of course, Japril, after all the trauma suffered, there have to be, almost predictably, some unpredictable results. We found that slight brain damage, supposedly compensated for. But that isn't normal neural material for a normal neural reaction to waking with no

world on a strange moon. Our charge's world has been
destroyed. None of us knows that world by anything but
report. The truth is, in subjective terms, we *don't* know
how strange this place is. We may be dealing with neurological or psychological upset, any combination of the two,
and at any level of resolution.'

"And Marta shook her head, whispering: '. . . remap-
ping of neuronal deployment . . .'

"After several hand signals, indicating hope and despair in her own religion, Ynn depressed a small pedal:

". . . and the survivor's eyes closed.

"The knees bent.

"The metal floor tipped back to topple the figure into
the tub, while the drains reversed to become gargling
tributaries. As the body bobbed about, we went through a
dozen access catalogues, had a dozen GI programs erased
from our minds, and took on some thirty more between
us. And we remapped the survivor."

2.

"For the next three days we remapped.

"We viewed through diverse screens and measured
with sundry meters each neuronal center and margin,
plumbed and monitored and analyzed the chemical context in which each synapse drowned; our computers recorded the ionic dance along a billion nerve sheaths. Our
simulators produced conglomerate vector templates in four
dimensions and thirteen colors at half-a-dozen different
depths of focus.

"But it was only what GI so quaintly calls a 'footnote'
to an auxiliary program Marta had added almost as an
afterthought that finally guided us to the answer: 'Something very odd has been done, Japril—probably done a
long time ago, too. What's more, if it *is* the synapse-
jamming the footnote says it is, on most worlds it's illegal!'
We gazed, regazed, reprobed, and reread among the synaptic net-patterns' possibilities of meaning. (They unpack,
like any text, not always with what has been packed into
them.) Then we turned to the Web's Basic Galactic Information map of data-deployment to see if we could locate

the proper data-node that would explain the particular biotechnic operation all our researches seemed to indicate.

"The particular method for taking the living brain and doing the kind of synapse-jamming that had apparently been done—perhaps some twenty standard years ago—to Korga the Porter, Rat, was first invented on a world in the seventy-eighth cluster some four centuries ago, and then again, in the forty-third and forty-eighth clusters simultaneously and independently (as far as we can tell) about two hundred and eighty years back—just prior to the time of Vondramach Okk, as a matter of fact."

"Should I say something?"

"It's relevant," said Japril. "You'll see why in a moment. The information had spread slowly from its first source, hindered by law and the civil outrage that can accompany any human discovery women find destructive; it had spread quickly from the latter two sources, camouflaged by a far more liberal attitude toward research when not simply hidden in the information glut that has been the hallmark of more recent times—the glut that is the reason, purpose, and responsibility of the Web. The three data-flows converged on the worlds of the fortieth sector some fifty years ago.

"Such data convergences on the worlds of a single star system from so many directions frequently make an information-stable node that is very hard to control. If the information is highly destructive, frequently when the Web thinks it is under control, it simply pops up under another name in the same place—or right next door. The particular synapse-jamming procedure that we had on our hands in Korga, once we recognized it and traced its diachronic trajectory through the fortieth cluster's general épistèmé, had proved particularly tenacious. And because Rhyonon was a world out of the main data channels that are central to the Web, not much energy had been expended on it. The synapse-jamming technique first surfaced on a moon of Rhyonon's cousin world, Jesper, here in the Tyonomega system, as a medical method for dealing with certain social intractables. It was squelched by the Web as inhumane and was finally superseded, on that moon, by a program of drug therapy that was easier, cheaper, more efficient for its purposes, and—for that particular moon—ecologically sounder.

"It reemerged on Rhyonon itself as a rite in a political movement that had begun gaining wide adherence several hundred years ago. Then there was a political shift—from Yellow to Gray, which may or may not have had something to do with the early conflicts between the Sygn and the Family—and immediately it resurfaced as part of the practice of an extremely violent art form: for some twenty-five years during Rhyonon's second century many of the artists in various geosectors of Rhyonon's southern hemisphere, when the emotional stringencies of their craft became too great, would voluntarily subject themselves to this form of mental suicide—during which time the practice gained great social prestige.

"The Web launches, as you probably know, a very different kind of campaign against an aesthetic institution from the sort it launches against a medical one—some say the former is no campaign at all. We try to contour an alternative aesthetic stream away from conceptualization and toward representation. Periods of high-resolution representative art, in whatever field, seem to be local phenomena on any world at all. They never last. But the swing, when we tried it on Rhyonon, was enough, according to our records, to make us think we'd won.

"Again, you must remember that Rhyonon was, as are most of the worlds in the fortieth sector, a terribly unimportant world in the Web's scheme of things. It was uncommitted in a conflict that had already taken over nine percent of the six thousand two hundred worlds. It had no General Info system, and its approach to offworld information in general was unsympathetic to say the least.

"The synapse-jamming technique came back once more, this time as a gesture of public philanthropy. The destitute of Rhyonon's most impoverished social classes, about thirty standard years back, had apparently been allowed—by inter-geosector law—government-subsidized access to this most sophisticated technique of 'Radical Anxiety Termination,' as the Institute administering it was known."

I nodded. "If museums are open to the public, then we must make available as well all the strategies the artist uses to contour the particular problems of her life. I've encountered the syndrome before."

"It's not a privileged one," Japril said, which I just assumed was her spidery way of telling me that, in her presumably multilensed eye, some industrial diplomat's odd datum was not privileged either. "So now we had a good statistical context within which to read the signs we had been presented with. Given what we now knew of Rhyonon, her language deployment, and Korga's accent, we had established a good statistical probability that our survivor, though found at the pole, was from the sociopathic dregs of one of Rhyonon's equatorial slums. At some time in the past Korga had apparently been offered, by a benevolent society, a chance at what had been up till recently, on his world, the *ave atque vale* of artists and priests: the chance to have the paths in the brain through which worry forces us to grow closed over forever and detours about those troublesome crossroads left permanently open."

I raised my chin, which is a sign to continue in the language spoken in the west of Japril's home world (I wondered if she remembered telling me) and, in many languages of many others, communicates negation and/or doubt.

She said: "The rest of the statistical range—much smaller—includes the possibilities of artist, religious thinker, philosopher, or even an industrial entrepreneur who, after having amassed a fortune but never having bothered to correct her accent (such corrections were apparently done in urban equatorial Rhyonon), suddenly opted for the Termination treatment."

I frowned. "Radical Anxiety Termination . . . Does that have anything to do with his name, Rat . . . ? An acronym of some sort?"

"'The Universe is overdetermined,'" Japril quoted. "About seventy-five years ago on Rhyonon, an ideographic writing system was instituted worldwide, in an attempt to clear up the confusion of some five alphabetic systems and syllabaries that had come with the various colonial groups. Since then, all official business had been conducted in ideographics. But such slang and many old terms are best explained by one of the older scripts. The second most common language of Rhyonon as well as its seventy-five-years-now discarded alphabet are closely related to the interlingua you grew up with—though I doubt whether Rat Korga would understand the explanation."

"I'm not truly sure I do either. Go on, Japril."

"When doctors think they've eradicated a disease, they stop looking for it. So if the disease itself suddenly shows up again, they may not even recognize it; they may even mistake it for an entirely new one. We were lucky to have diagnosed the synapse-jamming for what it was as quickly as we did—since on Rhyonon it was not even considered pathological. But the location of the proper antidote, in such cases, can be even more difficult than diagnosis."

"Why *does* the Web consider the situation pathological, Japril?"

"You must remember—" Japril was smiling again— "Rhyonon had no General Information system. It's precisely those 'anxiety' channels which Radical Anxiety Termination blocks that GI uses both to process into the brain the supportive contextual information in the preconscious that allows you to make a conscious call for anything more complex than names, dates, verbatim texts, and multiplication tables; and it also uses them to erase an information program in such a way that you can still remember the parts of it you've actually used consciously."

"What you're saying is that Rat Korga can never get all those little neurological transmitters wired into the crevices of the top five vertebrae that will hook into whatever local GI system happens to be around." I frowned. "Coming from a completely destroyed culture into something as complex as the Web, not to mention other worlds, and without the help of GI—that could be hard."

"Even harder when you consider that Korga began with what you and I would call a hopelessly impoverished information battery. The thing anyone dealing with Rat Korga must remember—and 'Rat' you understand is . . . *was* a kind of title, and, on Rat's own world, a pejorative title at that—is that this woman was a hugely informatively deprived individual from a generally informatively deprived world. That much was clear however we mapped the synaptic deployment. As Korga bobbed quietly in healthful juices and restorative fluids, we came to watch at, and lean against, and look through, with our palms up beside our cheeks, the slanted viewing windows—their lower sashes sloughed with froth and squamous scum.

"We had discovered the problem in three days—No,

just let me go on. I don't even want to tell you how long it took to discover the answer."

I dared: "What was it?"

"Ynn found it—and by an accident that, as I remember now, seems no more probable than the one by which we discovered Korga himself. You and Ynn share an enthusiasm, Marq."

"We do?"

"I mean the period some two-hundred-odd standard years ago at the height of the Family's power and the reign of Vondramach Okk over the seventeen worlds."

"I wouldn't exactly call it enthusiasm," I said. "There are some traditions among the Dyeths, yes, about the time when all that was going on. And I like her poems. But for me personally, the period's hardly something I could even call an interest," which is not quite accurate either. There *is* Dyethshome.

"Well," Japril said, "back when you and I were more friendly than of late, you mentioned it to me enough times so that when Ynn came up with this I thought of you."

"What exactly was it?"

"For Ynn, this period is an enthusiasm, a passion, an obsession—as, indeed, is everything connected with the life of Vondramach. Relaxing one evening in her living room, it occurred to her to run an exhaustive GI crosscheck between all the information currently at hand on Rat and all the documentation on her personal hobby, Vondramach. All she was looking for, she told us later, was metaphorical similarities that might provide an amusing hour's musings. She sat down on her hammock, thought over the access numbers, replayed the code, lay back, and let GI do its work. Then—there it was in her mind: the access numbers to a loosely documented historical program on Okk's youth that she had never run into before. Even for an expert, of course, there'd be thousands of those—"

"Japril," I said, "I've spent all my life on worlds with extensive GI systems."

She suddenly shook her head. "Really—you must forgive me. I'm beginning to wonder if I haven't been closeted with Korga just a little too long. One gets into the habit with Rat of explaining everything. Anyway, there it was, beeping like mad and demanding a referential check.

Later Ynn said she had been familiar with a number of loosely documented accounts of Vondramach's youth referring to the early experiments with mind-distorting and dilating drugs, neural-tampering machines, and medical-based consciousness-bending techniques. What she hadn't known was that before the age of twenty-three Okk had indulged in enough such to kill permanently anyone with less access to such an extreme restorative medical technology as Vondramach had available. Through self-mutilation and other fun things she'd had to replace most of her vascular, muscular, and skeletal systems, as well as a good deal of neural matter, several times over. And when the synapse-jamming techniques we're talking about, spreading from the seventy-eighth sector, first reached Vondramach's attention, she was fascinated by its possibilities. Even then—especially back then—it was billed as a permanent change. But things like that didn't bother her. One morning she went in and had her brain jammed. Predictably, after a few days, she decided she didn't like it. And there were already other things she wanted to inflict on herself. But the jamming takes place within synapses set fairly deep in the brain, kept open or closed by setting up a small, naturally self-reinforcing feedback loop that is at once extremely delicate and extremely tenacious. It can be started by the merest brush of a finely modulated gamma-ray laser over the proper chemical gradient in the myelin sheathing of the nerves adjacent to one of the cerebral pelvises. The only way to stop it, however, is to surgically excise the neural material, or to short it out totally—the side effects of which are not only unpleasant but frequently fatal. And the most disconcerting of the side effects is that the whole pattern, if it is erased in one part of the brain, tends to be remembered by the rest and—assuming you survive excision or shortout—usually reestablishes itself somewhere else almost immediately."

"It's one of *those* . . . ?"

Japril nodded. "You don't know *that* much about neural cartography, Marq." She smiled. "And you know that the one thing *we* know is just how much you know about practically anything. Anyway, Vondramach Okk, unlike Korga, who only had what Marta, Ynn, and I could ferret out of GI to help, was directly in touch, even by then, with the complete medical resources of eight high-technology worlds—five of which, even at that point in her career, she officially owned. That technology had already generated the beginnings of what was to become GI's direct neural access system. Vondramach gave an order: 'Fix this mess, and fast . . . !' or an order that boiled down to the same thing. It was the kind she had given many times before. According to this particular loosely documented report, she got what she wanted.

"We've borrowed it."

"What did it turn out to be, Japril?"

SIX

Rescue Concluded

"Finding it began with a reference number to a sealed storage chamber in the uninventoried sections of wing seven of the Okk Museum on Tartouhm." (I once spent a week in a vaurine projection of *one* of the Okk Museum's twenty-nine wings—the one where they put the Louvre, the Palazzo Vecchio, and the Vatican Library collections that Vondramach had exported, building at a time, to the wing's lower rotunda, from the ruins of Old Eyrth during the first days of the Seventh K'Tong. [And where they'd come from before that is anyone's guess.] A momentary memory of those six hours a day touring, absorbing the most minor fragments of the age my great-grands used to gossip about.) "We opened it up," Japril said, "and looked inside."

I raised an eyebrow. "Physically?"

"We sent a message to open it, had the contents described minutely; and the description and vaurines sent back. You know Vondramach Okk: when she ordered something done, she didn't just have it done once. When she needed a prosthesis—and throughout her life, what with assassination attempts, not to mention some of her own more bizarre pastimes, she went through quite a number— she usually had between fifty and a few hundred made up, each slightly different, from among which she took her pick." (We've mentioned several times how big a world is? Now imagine owning some.) "What was inside that neglected vault? A set of ornate finger rings, several hundred of them, ranging from a dozen that were small enough to fit a three-year-old child to another dozen big as bracelets for that same child."

"What did *they* turn out to be?"

Japril's left hand danced on what might have been a piece of jewelry, the key to—or the catalogue of—her personal wardrobe, or the next month's orders for her and the spiders in her nest. "They were hard-circuitry replacements, of an astonishingly sophisticated kind given the year they were constructed, to counterfeit the usual operations of the jammed neurons. They feed the results directly back into the nervous system, but with large informative nets added in. The rings get their 'information' into the brain by using the sheathing impedance of the whole neural web as its general neural receptor."

"Could you use them on Rat?"

"We wondered about that a lot. Unlike our Korga, Vondramach Okk was not, for all her failings, an informatively deprived sociopath. If anything, she was a hopelessly privileged psychopath—and by almost any account a genius. The two shared few or no deep free-afferent synaptic configurations. The rings, however, were not constructed with the individualized synapse tailoring we use today to hook the neural receivers and transmitters into children to connect them with GI, or to allow them to use mentally activatable equipment. Instead, they bombard the more complex neural webs with blanket information matrices at every free entrance point."

"Was the technology available to recreate them for you?"

"Once we figured out what they were—with the help of the little booklet stashed down in the case—we had a set of them from among those that were the proper size shipped out."

"*The* rings Vondramach wore?"

"That Vondramach wore some of, some of the time, from among some of those that would fit her. Whether she wore them permanently, or whether some more refined neurological compensation was eventually developed for her is just one of those things about her that isn't documented."

"I gather there were times she could get passionate about privacy. Every once in a while, so the Dyeth tradition has it, she'd destroy quite at random great portions of the records that accumulated about her—"

"—and still managed, at least for most of her adult life, to be the most documented human being in the universe." Suddenly Japril laughed again. "But the thing you can be sure of in this day and age is that no one is the 'most' of anything; just the 'most' you happen to know about. Marq, we had the rings imported—"

"This survivor, Korga, is *very* important to the Web. . . . Who was the ID on the import job, by the bye?"

"No one you're related to, or who would be likely to let you pump them about the matter."

"Perish the thought!"

Japril let several odd and unsettling expressions flow along her long, handsome face. "We've already talked of the 'fuzziness' about the concept of a world-survivor. But there is a simple second-rate truth that you've probably suspected, if not known, all along." She settled on one with the corners of her mouth way down. "Whether the phenomenon is fuzzy or not, a growing number of people, despite all the Web has tried to do to prevent it, consider Rat Korga the single survivor of a totally depopulated world."

"Backtrack a little, Japril." I admit it. Vondramach *had* pricked my curiosity. "What sorts of information were *in* those rings?"

"Very basic stuff." The corners of Japril's mouth went back up. "Remarkably close to a first-order GI series, actually: mathematical tables, general vocabulary accretion lattices, metonymic multipliers, some spatial and temporal prompters, temporary term retainers, and mnemonic nudges—the sort of aids that would make anyone seem brighter, without necessarily influencing their basic opinions about anything."

" 'Nothing to influence opinion,' " I quoted an early critic of the GI system, " 'and everything to alter belief.' Were there any data reverse-retrieval systems?"

"Quite a lot." (Those are the subconscious systems by

which you decide whether other people possess a context for understanding what you want to say or not, and, if not, for adding appropriate contextual material to your own communication. Another name for it is—you guessed it— diplomacy.) "Data reverse-retrieval seems to have been one of Vondramach's prime concerns, if one can go by the rings' contained programs."

"I'm not really surprised. So . . . these are the things that are erased from the normal brain by the synapse-jamming process?"

An even stranger expression took over Japril's face. "These are among the things thought to be able to compensate for *some* of the jamming effects—back in Vondramach's era." The gold bar, with its two black knobs, suddenly went into a side pocket of Japril's vest. I actually felt a regretful hitch that now I'd probably never find out what it was. "When we were checking out accounts of the synapse-jamming in the first place, we found that a number of people had advanced the theory that the jamming produced, by artificial means, the neurological state achieved naturally by certain saints, mystics, and holy women. Presumably, they would go through alternate intellectual and spiritual disciplines to get there that would perhaps produce slightly different results—at any rate, the saintly bit was the part, of course, that interested Vondramach."

"Thanks to her Family connections, I know there were people who considered her a religious leader. But I don't think anyone would call Vondramach a saint," I said, "even for three days—or however long she was jammed. After you got the rings, what happened when you revived Korga again?"

"We emptied our survivor out of the slopping coffin. . . ." The frown on Japril's face was suddenly readable distress. "Korga stood among the supports, not holding any of them, green eyes wide. Marta walked up, took the wet wrist, and slipped one, another, and then another of the rings on one and another great finger." Japril joined her empty hands—which was what she used to do frequently when someone from the north of my world would simply sigh. "They fit.

"It was only a blink. Marta started at it; and the head turned a fraction to see her."

"Ynn stood among the support loops, holding Korga's

fingers, still wet with our juices, bound now with metal,
like something alive. . . . I described those great, rough
hands, later, at least five times as '*like* something alive'
before Marta said to me: 'But Japril, Korga's hands *are*,'
and I had to paw over my memories of the waking to find
what made me react as though they were not.

" 'Who are you?' Ynn asked.

"The lips met, parted, halted.

" 'Rat . . . Korga,' Ynn said with an inflection that
questioned as much as it stated.

" 'Rat Korga . . .' The repetition, in the deeper, balder,
flatter voice, somehow reversed the weights of stated and
questioning emphases within the single name.

" 'What are you feeling, Rat Korga?' Marta asked
from where she stood by aluminum and plastic struts.

"Korga turned his head to look about our strange
machines (Why were most of them enameled green or
yellow?), at our walls (Who decided they should be blue?),
out our windows (What was the *use* of windows in such a
moonscape?). Where those alien eyes that we had loaned
now looked, we interrogated everything. The eyes turned
to Marta's, to Ynn's, to mine. 'I feel . . . more fear than
I've felt for . . . many years. What do you want? Why
have you brought me here?' Korga was a terribly strong
male; and the hours of our ministrations had no doubt left
her body stronger. But both our native logic and borrowed
expertise said that strength should have been awkward in
its newness. Korga seemed so easy with that awkwardness.

"Korga looked at me; and, while I tried to untangle
the survivor's unspoken questions from mine, Ynn, on the
stand, said suddenly:

" 'Your world, Rat. It's gone.'

"Korga looked down where Ynn pressed those big
fingers, heavy with new knowledge.

"Ynn stepped back, her own hands wet with what had
healed.

" 'What . . . world . . .' Korga asked in a voice whose
hoarse accents already spoke to us of old wounds in that
throat we hadn't even noticed. 'My . . . world . . .'

"And suddenly, looking at Rat—tall, naked save a
handful of rings—we felt cluttered with our own accoutre-
ments: silver suits, bright insignias, recorders, calculators,
reading machines hanging at belts and wrists.

" 'Your relatives. They're all dead.'

"Rat said, still looking down: 'I never had any relatives.'

" 'Your friends. They're dead too. All of them.'

"Rat made the diagonal movement of the head up, that we had learned, in Rhyonon's second most common language, indicated negation. 'I don't have any friends.'

"I said: The people you worked with, the place . . . it's gone, Rat Korga. Everything you've ever known . . . your work, all the things you didn't know that made what you did know what it was. Your world, it's gone.'

"That big-boned, red-brown face watched me with a concern lacking all suspicion, with a vulnerability lacking all hostility. Their absences made me realize how used I was to ignoring them in the looks of others.

" 'My world . . .' Rat repeated. 'My work wasn't much. All that's gone? Is that all?' Once more Rat looked around the room, at a machine, at a window, at one of us, at a floorlight. 'Now I am not as frightened as I was.' The various observation lights, set around the floor, threw up amber illumination to underhook a knee, to catch in the foreskin's wrinkled cuff, to shadow the curve of a vein along the scrotum and snarl in the hair above and around the genitals, to burnish the flesh below the naval's cave and light that cave's roof, to underlight a nipple and the roofs of smaller pits and dermal irregularities about the jaw, to illuminate beneath the brows. I watched and wondered where the hormonal tides and impedance gradients and saline shifts that constitute fear inscribed themselves on that lank body.

"As Korga watched us, ringed and unringed hands came together. Once, Marq, on a frozen outpost where spines of black rock were strung with vines of a substance we were not sure was really alive or simply crystalline, a small, white, furry, and many-legged creature—definitely alive and insistently friendly—became my companion. She was silent, curious, and affectionate. And I was alone. One day I found her pulling herself between the rocks—she had fallen. One of her legs had broken. I picked her up in my thin gloves and carried her back to the compound, under the grainy sky. I called up three different GI programs on her alien anatomy, ethology, and convalescent patterns, which only confirmed what I knew and put off my doing it another minute. I took out a plasti-splint from the medicabinet, bent it to shape, peeled it apart, grasped my little friend under one arm, and pulled straight her injured limb while ignoring the others' flailing. I secured the two pieces of the splint on either side of her limb. As the splint grew back around it to form a plastic sleeve-cast, I set her down on the floor and picked up a tranquilizer bulb that, admittedly, I should have administered before I put on the splint. When I turned back to my friend, I was in time to see that she had secured all her working limbs behind the splint's collar. With one gesture, she slid the splint off her broken leg—and that gesture, I realized, was the signature neither of trust nor distrust, but rather of a completely alternate code for what was mete and un-mete: the splint, which she neither knew, understood, nor even questioned, was simply . . . un-mete.

"And Rat Korga, in a gesture that brought back to me the grained sky, the chill rocks, and the ribbed and slanted compound walls on a world I hadn't thought about for fourteen standard years, with bunched fingers, slid a ring off one finger.

"The face changed.

"The heavy features' disruption brought home my inability to read the expressions on either side of their quiet violence. But because I was human and Rat was human, I assumed the former had been some complacency while the latter some distress.

" ' . . . all the things I didn't know that made what I did know what it was,' Korga repeated. 'When you said that to me before, I understood it. Now . . . I can remember the words, but not their meaning.'

"Rat looked at the removed ring.

"I think that particular thin bronze circle bore around its inner face the bifurcation circuitry that allowed the stabilization of terms amidst reflexive descriptions.

"Rat looked at us.

" 'You have taken away my world . . .' On the great hand were still several more rings that controlled complex hierarchies of metaphorical organization. 'You have taken away . . .' Then, in a gesture all of us later agreed communicated urgency, but within which we could find the tell-tale radicals neither of speed nor intensity by which urgency usually signals itself—his movement was slow, deliberate, and *still* urgent—Rat pushed the ring back on. 'What have

you given me?' Korga asked. 'What have you taken away?'
Looking around the room, Rat took three steps among the
support loops, now resting her bare hand on one, with a
touch that told how superfluous that support was. (Ynn
turned, watching.) 'This . . . this is not my world. On
what . . . world are we?'

" 'It's not a world at all,' Marta said. 'It's a moon. Of
Chyvon.' Then she frowned, because that pitted face remained unchanged. 'Chyvon's a world about sixty million
kilometers from yours, that also circles Tyon-omega.'

" 'To be sure,' I said, 'what we call Tyon-omega, Rat
calls simply the "sun." And "moon"? Let's just say we're
someplace very far away, Rat.'

"Korga looked at that hand, at the metal bands and
their settings, raised those fingers—and began to bite at a
nail. While Korga chipped and bit and red stones and
green stones between the still-wet knuckles glittered to
the chipping, those eyes watched us. Biting, Rat spoke—
and must have heard that the speech was unintelligible
with the gnawing; so stopped biting and spoke again: 'I
had a world. But it is as true to say I never had a world.
You have given me . . .' He paused to gnaw again while
agate or garnet obscured a word: '. . . possibility of a
world. What world will you give me?' The fingers, bent
above opals, went back to the teeth—big, straight, more
ivory than white. Still biting, still chipping, now at the
thumb, now at the little finger, Rat came to the ramp at
the stage's edge and started down, leaving dark footprints
that dried in seconds on the spongy floor. Was that slow
gait menacing? Did we read menace into it? Korga
wandered—and in that room, less than five by five meters,
that gait, broad-hipped and great-shouldered, as upward
lights swung round the drying body, was, itself, to me
what wandering was.

"Ynn turned, watching.

"Marta turned, looking for buttons and pedals that,
she must suddenly have realized, Rat was now too far from
the emptied tanks for her to use; she turned back. And
watched.

"Did Rat read her intent?

"The hand dropped. 'What world will I have? You
know: Whatever you have given me, it does not correct
the radical . . .' Rat paused, tongue struggling with the

syllables, missing as many as it caught: ' . . . radical anxiety termination. It only compensates. This is not like before, on the desert. So you see, now you *must* give me a world. Or I may take ten, thirty, or a hundred. And then what would you do with me?' Rat raised the bare hand now, to gnaw again. Knuckles turning, veined ligaments taking shadow and losing it, Rat watched us above shifting joints, stopped beside another floorlight. The ringed hand, fallen to the thigh now, was so still one bloody facet flung its flare up to my eye, unmoving, for five, six, seven breaths.

"I moved—and blood slid to green to white to orange.

"Now that their charge had been gone from them for more than a minute, the tubs and shields and meters behind him on the stage, which had washed and watched Korga, began to autodegrade into their liquid states, flowing along the guiding troughs into the waiting flanges of their red and black hexagonal canisters. And Korga was walking again, toward the high archway to another room with the teaching games, and program-courses, and visualization screens, and educative therapy pads, and mobile environmental simulation units which we'd hoped would teach some comfortable movement among the cultural patterns of any number of worlds Rat had never known.

"Ynn stepped down nervously from the stage. Observation lights withdrew into the floor. Illumination cords, looping about the ceiling, began to adjust color and brightness.

" 'Now what could Rat mean, "give me a world"?' Marta asked, from where she leaned against the freeform aluminum decorations set out from the wall.

" 'Look,' I said, 'Rat's only had these language skills for—' I glanced at the colored time scale pulsing along the stage's edge—'about three minutes now. Don't expect any real accuracy for another three weeks.'

"But we had all seen the glittering stones from among those which, once, had weighted a tyrant's hand.

"Ynn came down the ramp from the arch; I fell in; Marta followed.

"Hearing our bootheels click the plastiplex, Rat dropped hand from mouth, glanced back at us. (Rat's own bare feet were silent.) 'What world will you give me?' then turned back to squat, examining an inset floorheater beneath its plastic grill.

"We spent the next days, Marq, trying to find one in which Rat could, with help, fit—one that could fit Rat. We decided, Marq . . . finally, on yours."

"*My* world?" I asked. "Dyethshome? Morgre?" I tried to corner the careening astonishment and it was always just beyond me. "I mean, the Fayne-Vyalou? All the other three hundred geosectors on Velm?"

"And in exchange, we've decided to give you Rat's."

"Rhyonon? Japril," I said, and what I felt was the sudden pervasive yet almost unrealizable anger you'd better be in touch with if you don't want to ruin three out of four diplomatic missions$_1$, "what do you . . . what do you *think* you mean by—?"

"You've been an ID over a dozen years, Marq. Perhaps half that time you've spent on Velm. But the other half you've spent on any number of dozens of other worlds. So your 'world' is a bit more complicated than Dyethshome. Or even Velm."

"But you said—"

"And as far as giving you Rhyonon—well, yes, there is a charred and smoking planet whirling about Tyon-omega in an orbit that was Rhyonon's. Perhaps in a decade or three, when some of the acids have sifted out of that cayenne sky, when some meteorological stability has reasserted itself, the Web may actually reexamine it, give it a new name, and consider—very carefully—another bout of planoforming, another influx of colonists. But as far as Rhyonon is concerned—the *world* of Rhyonon, the complex of information that was that world: well, as you have already heard, Rhyonon no longer exists." Japril stood up, stepped from her chair, and turned away from me. She joined her hands behind her back. "I said I was going to tell you about your relation to our survivor." She spoke to the window.

"That *is* what you said."

"The relation's very simple." (Listening to someone speaking towards someplace you're both facing has always been hard for me. But people have stranger customs than that with which to decorate what they consider important statements.) "Besides being the single survivor of Rhyonon,

Korga happens to be your perfect erotic object—out to about seven decimal places."

2.

"What—?"

While I frowned, behind her back Japril moved the fingers of one hand into a little bud of four with the thumb about an inch away—a sign, I suddenly remembered, on her world for something highly amusing. "More to the point," she went on, voice perfectly deadpan, "out to about nine decimal places, you happen to be Rat's." Hadn't she once told me folks on her world frequently make that sign of amusement without even being conscious of it? Oh, a diplomat's life is not an easy one.

As Japril turned back, I thought: What a strange thing to hear on an afternoon's library research session ten thousand light years away from anywhere—maybe seven hundred thousand k's if you happen to think Batria is someplace; and I'm sure the odd three-quarters of a billion do. "How do you *know* what . . . ?" but stopped at the memory: dozens of times in an ID's life fairly complete synaptic maps are made of the brain; and such things as Japril spoke of can as easily be read from my maps as from Korga's—though admittedly mostly no one cares to. While I sat there, I actually recalled Japril, once when I'd told her I found males who bit their nails sexually exciting, asking me just what my ideal sexual type was. Go look it up in your files, I had said most curtly.

She had.

"It occurs to me, Japril," I said, wondering why, on top of that anger, I felt so strangely disoriented, "that in one version or another, I've been hearing references to this Rat Korga over half a galaxy now. Sex is no longer the mystified subject it once was. What you are saying, in a word, is: Rat and myself are sexually attracted to males. Also: Rat and myself both fulfill a number of tricks and turns of physical build, bodily carriage, and behavioral deployment that would make making love with each other not only fun but . . . well, rewarding. Now that's part of the simple truth—"

"The truth is not simple. I am saying a great deal more. And you know it."

"Still—" I put up a hand, which in this gestural language means "halt," in that one "full speed ahead," and, in still another, "I have to go to the bathroom." "You brought up the idea: as flattering as the concept is, with the universe as large as it is, I can't believe I'm in a unique position."

"The most precursory run through the Web's most accessible files of women directly or indirectly connected with us—"

"The ones you happen to have the dope on."

"—show that there are some nine hundred eighty-two billion persons who fulfill the erotic preferences of Korga out beyond three decimals."

"Let's see. That's short, stocky, hairy, blond, kinky-headed, and male—if we're to judge by me."

"I said we go to a number of decimal places. You're still talking in gross description parameters. Now there are about seventeen billions, in those same files, who would find Korga sexually satisfying to three or more decimal places—before you ask, let me tell you: that represents a very small proportion of those whom we've actually *got* on record. And, if we ran the same cross-check on the average woman, or male—you, for example—we would usually expect to come up with about two hundred billion takers delighted to get her."

"And only seventeen billion for Korga? That's not your ordinary eroto-star, then. Well, I've never seen one I'd cross the street for—when I'm somewhere where there are streets."

"So your synaptic mappings suggest."

"You understand, Japril, I spent some of my younger days on some very strange—"

"Spare me. We all did, I suppose. Like you said, your reality isn't privileged either."

"What I want to know about, Japril, is the overlap."

"Between the persons Korga's attracted to and the persons attracted to Korga?"

"Just in your most accessible files. You said 'perfect' and talked decimals."

She regarded me a moment, and I could read nothing in her face. "About twelve million."

"Well . . . I *said* I wasn't unique. Tell me, have you informed *all* twelve million of us on the list that Prince Charming has just been rescued from a blasted world and that—dare anyone do the wake-up routine with a kiss, the chances Korga will melt with reciprocal passion have been computed out to here?"

"The metaphor suggests a cultural reference I may have missed. Nevertheless, there were only two names out of the twelve million that I was acquainted with personally."

"What would we do without quick GI surveys," I said, not asked.

"I'd never actually met the other person—only heard the name. There certainly seemed no reason *not* to keep this in the family." (Yes, I listened awfully hard; but that "family" definitely had a lower case "f.")

Then and there, you know, I got scared. It was a salty fear that brined the saliva at the back of my tongue. And below that, the disorientation. And below that, still, the anger. . . .

I took three deep breaths and asked: "Does Rat Korga know as much about me as I know about—" Well, I didn't see any reason not to— "him?"

Japril nodded, which means "yes" in one gestural language, "no" in another. She said: "Yes, he does," and I wondered whether the nod was confirmation or ironic comment.

Can I think of ten questions I *should* have asked? One: *Why* does the Web want me to know all this? Two: *How* am I supposed to . . . Oh, you fill them in. The one I came up with was:

"Who is this other guy?"

". . . can't remember," Japril said; or ". . . off on some expedition to another galaxy . . . won't be back this lifetime," or something else maybe, but anyway to that effect.

I guess that's friendship.

"All right . . ." Still the anger, still the fear; and the absence between them which must be where desire lies. "You've told me that this Rat Korga actually exists; and you say you've told Korga I . . . exist? What . . . happens now?"

"Oh, you'll walk down a street, on a chance that you'll

meet; and you'll meet . . . though, after all this set-up, you'll know it won't be all *that* much by chance."

"The rhyme suggests a cultural allusion that I'm not fami—"

"What's important—to you, to Rat, and to the Web—is that you *will* meet. And I think we've almost reached the end of our conference time." Japril sat down again in her bobbing chair. "You now have the information we find necessary for you at this time. Would you like a recording of this interview to go over at your leisure?"

"Oh, thanks. No. . . ." Full vaurine recordings are expensive. Besides, the particular Yinysh folks with whom I'd been working recently are one of those cultures where everybody is always offering you everything just to be polite. And to be polite back you'd *better* refuse—or end up garrotted. "Really, no. It's not necessary."

Japril smiled. "As you like."

And I began rueful years of regretting my idiocy. (Spiders, and especially Japril, offer very few things just out of politeness; and as an ID, I am well schooled in what these are likely to be: friendship frequently, sex infrequently, and hyperwave vaurine recordings, broadcast across light-years at tremendous expense, never.) What came to me then was something both daring and obvious—obvious because, after all, the business of spiders is to know what is known. But when I said it, I was more aware of the daring: "Japril, what about Cultural Fugue—or *was* it the Xlv?"

She regarded me with one of her more mysterious expressions. (Were I someone from her world, would that long face with its broad mouth and small eyes be totally clear to me?) "Some time ago, you were informed that any GI inquiries after Rhyonon could lead to serious reappraisals of your security status. Well, for now, just consider that extended to cover the Xlv as well, at least as far as you're concerned."

"Oh," I said. *Have* I said? One thing I hate is anyone telling me what I can or cannot know. "It's like that?"

"In your case. For now. From now on." Her hand moved toward her pocket—for a moment I thought to pull out and wave her magic wand. But before she completed the gesture, she began to fade. I stood up with my most diplomatic smile—to find myself in a rectilinear garden of me's—up, down, left, right, and diagonal. (It's even more unsettling in weak gravity than it is in full.) I wandered along with, and through, and among a thousand ambling selves, till at last I was walking on yellow pebbles.

3.

What do you do with information like that: Somewhere in the known universe is the survivor of a world, possibly destroyed by inscrutable aliens—whom you've been given specific orders not to scrute—the information itself blotted out of the Web, yet still trickling along from world to world, star to star. Oh, yes: the two of you just happen to be made for each other. And he wears the rings of Vondramach Tyrannus.

If you're as busy a person as an ID invariably is— well, you don't dwell on it. For very long.

Nonstop, I dwelt perhaps six hours.

During the next seventy-two, in which I got my tiles to Batria and my new job$_1$ wrapped neatly up, my thoughts returned to it, oh, perhaps a hundred, maybe a thousand times. Dwelling? Well, don't we all live with some such idea anyway: Somewhere in the known universe is the perfect woman for me?

Maybe now I tried to visualize him—for that's what he was, now—a little harder than one usually does. You can come up with *near* perfect that way.

But perfect?

At thirty-six years standard you know it can't be done.

Which I guess is what desire is all about.

SEVEN

Home and a Stranger

I was back on Velm.

Library sojourn and Japril's message had, like all things, tumbled weeks and light-years into the past.

My world?

I had seen the friends I had wanted to see—Menek, Santine, F'namara. I had been at Dyethshome long enough to reach that state with parents and siblings where, if one is a traveler by nature, one withdraws a little in as friendly a way as possible, thinking on far pleasures while indulging near comforts.

I'd taken a surface trip to a place, among Velm's western geosectors: Beresh—I'd only heard it existed weeks before. (Worlds *are* big places.) I had gone to it, had looked at it, had loved it—had wrestled with its strange slang, its austere foods, its complex social rhythms. Velm's world government is bureaucratic anarchy. That's the plurality governing structure among the six thousand—the thirty percent of them that have world governments. Syndicated communism comes next; then benevolent feudalism—which any communist who's spent time in one will tell us is never all that benevolent; then oligarchic collectivism; then industrial fascism; and by now, we are well over halfway through the seventy percent that *don't* have world governments . . . just remember there's no majority.

Bureaucratic anarchy means a socialist world government in which small sections are always reverting to some form of feudal capitalism for anywhere from a week to two years standard—the longest we'll allow it to last. Though I'd been hearing of these enclaves all my life, Beresh was the first on Velm I'd visited: verticals of blazing blue chalk, bright portable living-rooms lying all over, some clustered together into small court groups of five to fifteen, others stacked maybe two hundred high, next to ersatz elevator towers, from any one of which at any moment a woman or a child might emerge to engage me—lurking about in my tourist reds—in bargaining for some part of my travel credit, for which they would perform in return bizarre and fascinating services.

Then the trip home: fourteen hours by ten-propeller flying platform; another six by monorail.

Home.

And we remember what a complicated . . .

2.

I checked to see if my baggage was properly tagged with the little green disks that would conduct it through the interlevels and on, then loped off the rickety old rollerwalk, crossed the broken blue bricks of Water-Alley, and sauntered between the heavy columns flanking the entrance to the local outlet of the Butcher's Union. Inside, high on the shelves, behind copper webbing, racks of cloned flesh thrust pink and red through the hooking rings. Longpig over there, shortpig—our term for the native flesh—in front of me and on the far wall, a host of more exotic insect, lizard, and worm meats. Prime cultures, says Si'id, who supervises$_1$ the kids working$_2$ this shop as well as the next outlet down; she'd go on for hours about the various pedigrees and provenances if you let her.

I never go into a butcher outlet anywhere on Velm, or anywhere else for that matter, no matter the geosector, without recalling the first time, during my fifth trip offworld, that I was dining with my employer$_1$ and her spouses for my third job$_1$. (The feathers on *every*thing; the very unsubtle music.) I was charmed when they served the meal on narrow plates, about three inches wide, curved around in a circle. You worked your way along from portion to portion—cunning I thought—eating with your fingers; though getting the tastes and smells so confused with one another would never go at home. There was the meat; and I began to tell them about the butcher outlets on Velm, and just what the cloned longpig I'd been raised on was, realizing as I spoke they were a little shocked. I picked up my own bit of roast, bit down—something hard was in it. . . .

Then I realized: Bone!

This meat had once been walking around with a skeleton inside. Although I didn't, many times when I've told the story, I've *said* I left the table.

Inside, the stained-glass skylight lay reds and greens over the chipped stone flooring. Three other women waited with their director disks ready in claw (or hand), while the little human redhead who'd been working$_2$ here as an apprentice for a standard year now, swung and slashed with her broad bright knife; and the two other apprentices behind the glass wall were preparing outgoing orders: one kid, another human, with long tanned arms, the other, evelm, with gold claws on tufted greenscaled ones, tossed the packages into a clinking chain net that carried them out through the sphincter flange.

Minutes later, I'd sent a kilo and a half of flesh, tagged with a green disk, on ahead of me. (Shoshana had said: "Marq, if you're going to come home unexpectedly, *couldn't* you at least see about your own food?" So I was going to see about several of the folks' today.) I was out the door again, through the gate, and onto the roller walkway—clink, clank, clunk, halt, bounce, go again. Blue noon-sky between the platforms of the two above-ground park-levels, like the scraps of dark blue cloth we cut up as kids to make patchwork maps of imaginary counties, clear and smokeless.

Then overhead platforms pulled away.

From the rollerwalk rail I watched pale cactuses drifting on my right, and the high boulders nearer and nearing on my left; we came around the cliff edge, to see the falls broiling on the rocks, and there beside it, its three free-standing multichrome walls rising two hundred meters each behind it, the black and silver pile: Dyethshome.

3.

I stepped off onto yellow sand, walked through a break in the lurid growth, and turned onto the variegated clay. Stone steps led up to the terrace flags—the same green stone fronting most of the older manufacturing communes all around the city. Three of my siblings were playing in the pool by the rocks that turn white down near the water. Spray splattered the olive flags. Tinjo flopped Bucephalus, splosh! Bucephalus wagged her scaled tail, sheeting out meters of droplets. Small Maxa jumped up and down at the pool edge, afroth to her chest.

Tinjo saw me—or Bucephalus smelled me; Tinjo squealed and the same moment Bucephalus was out of the pool and up by the carved railing on all sixes, shaking her scaly head—Large Max swears Bu is the finest looking of all this generation's children, human or evelm. Bu lolloped across the stones, the wet tufts on her legs dripping about her claws, the scales on her back a glister of purples and browns. She leaped against me, bronze claws hooked over my shoulders (yes, the gold-clawed apprentice in the butcher shop hails from a different continent than Bu), small tongues playing over my mouth. I opened wide, so she could be sure to taste me properly. Her eyelids signaled madly the sign we had both agreed on, when we were fifteen years younger—me sixteen and just emerging from human adolescence, she fifteen and just emerging from evelm infanthood—would be my name to her: *Marq Dyeth*, I read. *Marq Dyeth, Marq Dyeth* (I blinked back *Bucephalus Dyeth* for all I was worth), while with her nether tongue, the one below the three she was tasting inside my mouth with, she was saying in that slow-motion basso: "Marq, you're back! Where have you been? What did you see? Tell us how many stars you've swallowed since I last saw you? How many worlds have you chewed up and spit out—" which started me laughing, since I'd only been gone for three days two thousand kilometers to the oest-east. I almost bit my (and her) tongue.

Then Tinjo, all of ten years old, was shoving Bu aside and, holding my shoulders, jumped naked and wet against me. And, of course, nothing would do her but to lick my face too. "All right, Tinjo," I said. "From you it's just sloppy."

"Well, I got your meat," she said. "*And* took your bags inside." Where she had them on her, I don't know, since she was stark naked; but she held up her wet hand, in which were my green identidisks that had dragged my parcels home.

"You're a love." I licked her wet hair. But she must have thought something was very funny. She began to laugh, and her face was burned darker than dragon's urine by our white sun, all around her black eyes and watered lashes.

I pocketed my disks.

Then Small Maxa, who is an albino and will not tan—they had to do something to her skin to keep her from burning and insert darkening lenses behind her livid irises—stepped up in front of me. I bent down, and very seriously she mimed licking my face.

Something is wrong with her.

She hates to be touched. But at twelve, she wants to do what everybody else does. "Hello, Marq." She grinned hugely, creasing her white face like an old human's. "I've been building a toy mine that I want you to come see; I love you." Then she held out her hand to me and I held out mine—about an inch away from hers. We made motions of shaking. Some of us think she might be crazy in some serious way. But we respect it.

And Tinjo and Bucephalus were tearing off after each other around the terrace again, now down the steps, now into the water, now up the rocks.

"I'll come and see your mine after I've gone to my room a while. And do you want to see some vaurine recordings of where *I've* been?"

"I love you. Yes, Marq." She dropped her eyes; her hands made small ivory fists at her hips—which I always thought meant she wanted to hold you but didn't dare because the contact would be too unpleasant.

"I'll see you in a while." I put my hand about an inch from her cheek and mimed petting. Still grinning, she blinked, saying nothing by it, save some obscure physiological comment on our dark blue sky, our wide white sun.

I turned away and walked through immense silver petals, blooming around me in the black wall, turning red.

Inside, the crystal pillar by the door disappeared top and bottom into black pedestal and capital.

Large Maxa (my mother the biogeneticist[1], evelm) sat on her perch, where she usually does these days, blinking about the hall with quiet, gilded eyes, her gorgeous wings folded about herself, their polychrome membranes rustling in the draught from the high grate to the south court. Egri (my mother the industrial diplomat[1], retired, human) squatted beside Max, forearms about her knees, her toenails slightly yellow, her biceps sinewy, her long hair—slightly yellow—thinning over her freckled scalp. A childhood memory of the two of them, engaged in endless discussions in three languages about the complexities of the world and interworld information field, its signifying ramifications, its semiotic specifications. Now they just sit together, keeping each other company, looking up at the balcony platforms across the hall, down through the transparent stretches of flooring at the ball courts below, out at the rest of us.

Lurking there in the entrance hall—which is the way evelmi from Maxa's part of the world sit around in their own home caves—they've always struck me as probably a little daunting to most visitors.

But they like it.

"Marq?" Shoshana (my mother the architectural consultant[1], human) came up from the spiral stair through the star pattern in silver set in the maroon clay. It represents an astronomical cluster, called *Mu*-3, visible in the skies from Velm's northern hemisphere but not, unfortunately, from Morgre. "Glad you're back." Shoshana has hair like a salted helmet. "Lights were blinking on the console downstairs. Two students just arrived in the south wing." Shoshana's knuckles are silver berries, ripe and wrinkling in her sixty-eighth year; her hand, over the black globe that was both newel-nob and clock, half obscured the time. In the dark glass the time in Morgre, the Zevia-n-complex a third of the way west round Velm, and Katour, one of the three largest complexes in our world, way off in the north, glimmered in—respectively—brazen, emerald, and carbon light.

"They're two hours early," I said. "I called myself rushing to get back here so I'd have some time to myself." Regularly, groups of students come to study at Dyethshome, for which, over the last three generations, we have provided the south court. Orienting them is—yes—my job$_2$ while I'm here. "I suppose I have to get to it, then."

"I know you want to go to your room and rest, Marq," Large Maxa rumbled, showing a splinter of her wings' scarlet lining. When I was five and six, she would reward our good behavior by unfurling them over us while we hissed our delight. "You see to them, make them comfortable."

"Sure, Maxa."

Egri blinked, sighed, and really looked more like an evelm than Maxa—which Egri claims is what fifty-four years as an ID$_1$ will do to you.

"I'll get them set up, Shoshana. Then, after I've taken a break, I'll go back in when the others get here." Have you noticed? Whenever you come home, your folks always find *some*thing for you to do within the first three minutes.

I trotted over the reliefs at the foot of the ramp circling above the spillway. We only flood it for parties. The carvings along the spill bottom, done by and of the native evelmi—well before any evelmi married into the Dyeths, or even before there were many evelmi in M-81; only dragons—have always been my favorite. Large Maxa, Kal'k, Sel'v, and N'yn, my evelm parents, were always a bit condescending toward the human kids' delight in them. For one thing, as far as carvings go, they don't taste like anything. And N'yn and Sel'v once took all of us, when I was thirteen, on a trip to the R'Rtour-wr, way up north, to see the cliff carvings there, where evelmi live in a squalor and violence which, though I'd heard about it, along with the horrifying tales of human exploitation, I had never seen before. Licking those slime-covered stones to taste the cinnamon and sandalwood—neither human scent really covers the evelmi palate—beneath that dribbling mucus . . . !

As I reached the ramp's crest, I peeled away my tourist reds and got most of them on the suspensor hooks at the first toss. They pulleyed off to be cleaned and folded away. Catwalks circled off toward the balconies.

The ramp ended in a flowering of mirrors.

I walked into them.

4.

Mirrors swung back and up and out and down; I stepped
under the irregular stone arch, traced with emerald guano.
(I've mentioned the pearlbats . . . ?) High Iiriani behind
one of the towering multichromes flung parti-colored dap-
plings down through the transparencies and over the amphitheater's tiered stones. Low Iiriani-prime was a diamond
at the edge of one of the others—did it lend enough light
to pale those hues? I could hear the falls, but all I could
see from here were a few fountains, the thin jets deflected
by suspended vanes.

I walked down the cracked steps, squinting up among
the theater seats' ninety rows.

Each month's student load is about twenty-five. It can
be as low as twelve; it can be as high as thirty. They come
to study the art (endless), the architecture (exemplary),
the history (frequently embarrassing), or the technology
(extensive) of Dyethshome—sometimes some combination
or interface. They usually arrive in the late afternoon on
the north monoline spur, which takes longer but doesn't
go through Morgre proper; lets them off within sight of
the rear grounds—except during hotwind season, when
we have someone meet them at the central station and
take them here by an underground route. When I come in
to meet them, they're inevitably scattered up around the
top ten tiers. I call them down, and after an hour's orientation, during which I tell them about where they'll stay in
the six stories of galleries, tunnels, halls, corridors, ramps,
lifts, and lounges below the amphitheater, comprising the
subterranean part of the south court, discuss study aids,
research guides, and various ways to get into town, tell
them where they can cook, eat, wash, and shit, describe
the more and less interesting runs for sex through Morgre,
note the public parks offering the most joyous and the
most somber dancing, the pools around which the conversation is the most and the least subtle, we're usually all on
a first-name basis and fairly happy.

At the foot of the stairs I stepped over the grate;
below it water glimmered. Barefoot and naked, I wandered onto the middle of the skene.

Despite Shoshana's lights, the amphitheater was empty.

Trying to make sure I hadn't overlooked someone sitting or standing in the very top row, I walked to a side aisle, stepped on the bottom stair, and ran the service number through my mind three times—before I realized I had it wrong.

I corrected it—and the right side of the steps, on which I was standing, began to escalate me up.

I looked about the falling rows, left and right.

Still no one. Passing tier forty-four, I glanced over at the entrance corridor. The light above it was out, which meant no one was still down inside. The globes along its ceiling, as well as the blue lights at both ends, turn on when you enter and off when you leave. I looked back down over the seats, over the rounded roofs of the oest court, across the upper parks of Morgre, to the pitted crust of the Vyalou. Here and there, purple patches wound through the orange east from the fuming Hyte. (Amphitheater: half-theater. The other half should always be kilometers of calm sublimity.) When I reached the seventieth or so tier, I stepped off and started walking behind the backs of the seats. At the next aisle, I didn't bother to start the escalator. I just walked down. I was thinking of calling out, was not sure what to call, and found myself amused at my own hesitancy.

In the center of the twenty-first row is the polarized chamber—built with the amphitheater for those people who wanted to see the performance or the landscape but who did not want to be seen seeing. Invisible from the outside, it appears only as the smallest gap between the row's two center seats, perhaps an inch wider than the space between the others. It deflects light and sound around it, so that two people can sit in those two "center" chairs and hold a whispered conversation with each other and never realize that they are some twelve feet apart. The only thing that doesn't work is leaning to touch your friend's hand. Our great joke as children was to have our friends count the seats in that row: though they seem to correspond seat for seat with the row behind and the row before, the count always comes out to ten short, which, after you've counted the three tiers five or six times to check, tends to unnerve both evelmi and humans. Students who come here have frequently done their GI homework pretty thoroughly and know of nooks and crannies in this place even I've forgotten.

Just to check, I walked over to the place where I could see nothing but seats and stepped inside.

She stood up from one of the high-backed chairs. "Marq Dyeth . . . ?"

He remained cross-legged on the cushioned bench, watching me. And did not blink.

"Nea . . . ?" I said. "Nea Thant! What in the worlds brings you here?"

Through ornate ceiling panes, Iirianilight, twice colored, caught in the crevice between white gem and silver setting above his thumb's deeply ridged knuckle. He breathed; and the glare detonated at my right eye's inner corner. I swayed back a little. Perhaps my eyes narrowed. But I didn't blink.

"Hello, Marq!" Nea held out a hand, gloved in red foil. (I took it.) "This month I'm one of your students. I wanted to get here early, though. I needed a chance to say hello, to talk—"

Beneath the line of a roof tessellation's shadow, lopsided like a mask, his eyes were black holes out of whose eerie absences he looked at me from under rumpled brows. For all Japril's explanations, I could only think: But why here . . . ?

"Marq Dyeth, I had to come!" Nea said, with the growling intensity you should reserve for statements made just before committing murder, but which the Thants use to underline a tenth the things they say. "I had to talk to somebody . . . somebody who would understand. I flew here. I flew across sixteen thousand light-years, alone and terrified, to tell you. It's about—" and somewhere on the other side of dazzlement I heard her voice lose all voicing, her breathing go all breathy— "about our reproductive commune, Marq. That's why I came. There's a small, unimportant world, Marq, that no one's ever heard of, called Nepiy. Oh, if you know its name at all it's because Thadeus mentioned it last time we were here—at your lovely party. But it's a world with many problems among its impoverished lowlands."

He put one great bare foot down on the stone flooring. He leaned forward to put his elbows on the frayed knees of his canvas pants: unhemmed at waist and cuff, belted with some ornamental chain, they and his rings were all he wore. The big hands, one naked, one weighted

with metal and stone, hung between his knees from heavy
wrists.

"There's been talk, in many of Nepiy's geosectors, of
the possibility of Cultural Fugue," Nea went on. "Just
recently fifty-two of its hundred-seventy-nine geosectors
voted to call in the Family to reconstruct some of its social
functions in a less volatile form. Of course there's some
opposition from some of the lower lowland areas more
oriented toward the Sygn. But the Family has approached
Thadeus and our reproductive commune to serve as a
Focus Family—for all of Nepiy!" She caught her breath.

He breathed.

"You mean they want you to become Focus Family
for an entire world? For Nepiy?" I tried to remember
what I could of that strange form of rule by celebrity, by
media, by notoriety. "Does Thadeus want to move from
one world to another? Do you all want to be bothered with
all that publicity and attention?" I remembered to breathe.

Again.

"Thadeus thinks it would be exciting. Eulalia wants to
do whatever Thad wants. And Clearwater doesn't care,
which amounts to the same thing. Thadeus says it's our
duty; she says it would be exciting. She says when a whole
world calls to you in need, you must put aside personal
considerations and rise to the occasion. We would be
virtually the most important . . ." she paused . . . "important family on the entire world. Its rulers, for all practical
purposes. In the early days of Dyethshome, among your
interstellar visitors there were several visits by Focus Units
from various worlds. In the time of Vondramach. So I've
come here to study them—and yes, I *know* the study is all
pretense. I just want to talk to someone who knows something about interworld relations."

And I thought: How could his fingers, even that big,
hold so many rings? Three iron ones; four bigger ones of
bronze; some were narrow and copper; three, of pale gold,
on different fingers, were set with shards of different jades,
two, on the same, of bright aluminum, with both agates
and opals; the platinum one on his thumb was cast in a
shape very like one of our local dragon's heads, big as a
dyll nut and gnawing a mistrock as big.

"Zetzor is a very different world from Velm, Marq.
And Nepiy is different from them both. But one thing that

Zetzor and Velm share—at least your part of it and my part of it—is that they both function under the Sygn. We have never been seriously religious any more than you have. But to be asked suddenly to adopt a religion that, in a sense, we've never really known; to be asked, suddenly, to abandon one world for another, to leave our home—" A nervous motion took her a step to the side—in front of him. And I think I actually saw her for the first time, while he became only a brown canvas knee, creased and with a worn spot, the brown curve of a shoulder, reddened further from the ceiling panes, visible at her side, all equally and confusingly astonishing. She looked down at the loose flags, pushed at one with her baggy boot's soft leather. "I love the Thants, Marq. And I'm terrified for us. I'm terrified that Thadeus will get her way. And I'm just as terrified that she won't."

"Nea . . . ?" I said, and did not take a great step either to the left or to the right. "Look, maybe we should go inside and talk to Egri about this." I think there was a slight ringing in my ears. Low in my abdomen it was as if a bubble had suddenly blown up to push all my organs around into uncomfortable positions. I mean, what do you do when you first see your perfect erotic object and have been assured, by unimpeachable sources, that the perfection is mutual? (The one thing I can vouch for; I never had the slightest question *who* he was.) "Come on, Nea," I said. "Let's get out of here!"

With neither nod nor smile, and my ears and knees heating with diplomatic embarrassment, I fled the chamber.

Nea came after me. (Did she look back at her companion and excuse herself? I didn't hear. I didn't see.) She caught up to me when we were halfway down to the skene. (And from the invisible chamber, he watched me with his invisible eyes.) As we stepped out onto the amphitheater stage, me naked and her in leather and foil, I think I was about to turn around and rush back, when Nea said, in a funny kind of voice: "What a *strange* one, Marq . . . ! I could tell you felt it too!"

"Nea," I asked, and felt like a fool for it, for somehow with all I knew, I didn't know at all: "Who *is* . . . ?" I began but was afraid to place before her the pronoun that would place me with . . . him.

"She *is* rather odd," Nea said, confirming what, I was unsure. "She's just another one of your students—at least

I assume so. We got to talking on the monoline down. In the whole trip, I didn't manage to get her name. But I gather she's from *very* far away." Then, as we stepped across the grill and started up the cracked steps, she gave a great sigh, and I could almost hear her thoughts travel thousands of light-years off. We reached the top of the stair, beneath hanging green. Mirrored blades swung in and out at us.

5.

And missed.

"Max! Shoshana!" I called from the ramphead. "Egri! Guess who's with us this month." I came around the walkway, the bright fan-blades flashing behind grills in the high walls. I glanced to the side, waiting for her to catch up to me—so I could take her arm, I realized; which is what I would have done with any human or evelm from this particular locality. But polar Zetzor is not Velm's M-81. I slew the impulse. "Nea has something she wants to talk to you about."

As we came to the bottom of the ramp, Nea held out both hands, red foil, right; green, left. "Max, Shoshana . . ."

Shoshana stood up from the stool of the big console-size reader. "Nea? How have you been! What in the worlds are you here for? It's wonderful to see you. But—"

"Are your parents here?" Large Maxa rumbled affably from her perch. "It would be just like the lot of you to leap stars and not a word to anyone that you were arriving! You should have let us know—"

"It's just me, Max." Nea laughed. "And I almost had to break laws to get here. I'm officially enrolled as a student. But the real reason I've come is for advice."

"You came all the way from Zetzor, by yourself—for advice?" Shoshana's smile was disbelieving. "Really, the way you people flit from world to world—like gnats from one side of the Hyte to the other." She put her hand on Nea's epaulet. I saw Nea start to pull away, then remember she was not on Zetzor. (My social picture of the dark life in the canyon at 17? Endless horseplay of a distressing violence and stylization, laced with scabrously affectionate invectives, in which no two people ever touch. I'm diplomat enough to know it's a distortion, but it's a distortion of something there.) "I've visited fifty worlds by vaurine projection—" which is how most of us satisfy our tourist urge— "and two in vivo, when Egri took us to Kensitty. But," Shoshana declared, "I will *never* understand unlimited space-fare!"

"Neither do most of the shipping officials in the Zetzor north-quadrant spaceport. Otherwise I wouldn't be here." Nea stepped away from Shoshana, and looked up at the perch. "Egri, I thought maybe you could help me. I mean you've traveled from world to world and know the problems that occur between them. Thadeus thinks there's an opportunity to go to Nepiy as the Nepiy Focus Family. But it would mean . . ."

I went over and stood next to Shoshana, who leaned against the twelve-foot totem carving from some far north geosector (anchored three ways to the tolgoth planking by antique, black, flat-link chains), looked attentive, and did not listen as Nea retold with more detail and less clarity what she had outlined to me in the amphitheatre. The strange things about perfect erotic objects (when perfection is out to that many decimals): though you can remember dozens of details about them—a backlit ear clawed with rough hair, casting shadow on a pitted jaw; the wrinkle of a vein beneath thin skin lying over the ligaments fanning to pronounced toe knuckles; the wide lozenge of a thumbnail gnawed back from the callused crown, a knuckle below bright metal and brighter stone—still, you can never remember the woman; that is, you can never remember your sense of the woman as a self; at least not the way you can with any number of friends, acquaintances, or even some stranger, say, glimpsed frowning down at a gaming machine as you pass the door to a recreations lounge, maybe an outlet servicer logging her cheeses on the transport skid halted on a ramp from the lower level, or even some Web official with a mound of authorization stamps on the desk before, and a bank of check-out lights glittering behind, now half a galaxy away. Someone once pointed out to me that there are two kinds of memory (I don't mean short- and long-term, either): recognition memory and reconstruction memory. The second is what artists train; and most of us live off the first—though even if we're not artists we have enough of the second to get us through the normal run of imaginings. Well, your perfect erotic object remains only in recognition memory; and his absolute absence from reconstruction memory becomes the yearning that is, finally, desire. That socially surrounded absence, when you're young, masks a lot of things in the real world; when you're older and a few thousand sexual encounters have begun to clear what desire is about (or perhaps what really lies about desire) and you have begun to perceive desire's edges, its effect is not so much that of an obliterator any more as it is that of a distorting lens. If you can smile at what you see through, it's sometimes illuminating. That was the distortion I was experiencing now, so that when Nea suddenly exclaimed:

". . . but things happen on Nepiy that can't happen here! You can't imagine how different that world is from Zetzor!"

—what I saw was not the cities blasted into the shadowy walls of the canyons that worm the polar plates of Zetzor (its equatorial regions clotted with lichen jungles, fused deserts, and fuming bismuth swamps that make the -wrs of Velm seem like ancient carburetor leakings); what I envisioned was a scape of silicate sand, airs darkened to dim gold by dusts too hot to bear; and through kilometer after kilometer of umbrial dunes, the only irregularity beyond the grit rush was one shadow, barely human, stalking away. I imagined it; and thrilled to my imaginings—even as I realized that, like all our images of the alien, it comprised the simplest recombination of the familiar: the hotwinds that ravage for three months across Velm's own southern temperate zones transposed to Velm's own north-polar wastes.

"Well, you were right to be upset!" Shoshana announced at my side. "The Family/Sygn conflict is in the process of creating a schism throughout the entire galaxy, concerning just what exactly a woman *is*. And it may mean that instead of one universe with six thousand worlds in it, we will have a universe with one group of some thousands of worlds and another group of some thousands of others, and no connection between the two save memories of murder, starvation, and violence. And in a situation like that, no, you do not just simply decide to up and change sides! Even to become a . . . Focus unit!"

"Not just a Focus unit," Large Maxa said gently. "A Focus *Family*."

"It's the fame," Nea said, a green fist and a red fist tight against her hips. "Honestly, it is. A standard year ago, now, when we last visited a world called Ulus, we passed through a geosector called Ajegit and stopped at a city named Skesss. Among the white roads that wind the twelfth and thirteenth above-ground levels—Ajegit's bedrock is too hard to have underground stages as you do here—there was a major traffic artery, with shops and public art works, called Dyeth's Row, named after your seven-times-great grandmother. Thadeus made sure from GI; and we all went to see it."

"My dear," Large Maxa said, letting her green and glimmering head lean to the side, her gold eyelids sweeping across her onyx eyes, and some of her tongues a-twitter beneath the bony arch of her upper jaw, "there are half a dozen streets called Dyeth's Row scattered about the various urban complexes all over Velm. No doubt there are another fifty scattered about the cities of other worlds. Mother Dyeth toured with Vondramach for a while, both on this world and others. There was much pomp, much ceremony. Streets, parks, and concourses were named after various heroes in the Vondramach entourage. But that means nothing now. None of us have ever walked down more than one or two of them. Nor is there any reason why we should want to. And besides, to share a name with fifty or a hundred-fifty streets out of the hundred billion streets among a hundred million cities, most on worlds not ours, is not fame. What could it mean, to us or anyone?"

"It meant something to Thadeus. And Clearwater; and Eulalia too." Nea looked first at one of us, then at the other. Her skin was the ashy brown of a woman pigmented dark by heredity who has lived most of her life on a cold world at a pole turned eternally from its sun. "They very much *wanted* us to see it—that's why they took us there in the first place. They were proud for you, and proud for us that we knew you. . . . A Focus Family becomes a model unit for the women for an entire world. We would have streets and parks named for us . . . at least on Nepiy."

"It's to be expected—" Maxa boomed in her languid bass, though she had begun to flex the muscles that moved the spurs on the back of her hind claws; I wondered if Nea knew her well enough to recognize it for a kind of nervousness. (Though on most evelmi from the Fayne it indicates intense joy.) A second tongue took up "—on a world that received a touring entourage of Vondramach's a whole seven ripples ago. It means nothing today."

"Magma!" Nea declared, turning again. "It meant something to *me*, Max! Egri, Marq, you've traveled between worlds more than I have, unlimited fare or not. You mean to tell me that on this world or another you've never gone to visit a street just because it was named for the Dyeths?"

I haven't and was going to say so.

But Egri said: "Yes. I have."

"And didn't it mean something to you?" Nea looked like she might cry.

Egri kneaded a bony elbow with her knobby fingers. When she spoke, it was even slower than Max. "The point is, I think, that what it meant to me was very different from what it meant to Thadeus. Or to you."

Maxa gave that thunderous hiccup that passes for an evelm *humph!* "Just up and changing sides like this, it makes *me* think they've been part of the Family all along." She began to step around on the other little platforms that made up the rest of the perch, though her voice went on in its low, leisurely roar. "That kind of irresponsibility is a Family characteristic."

"Fiddle," Shoshana said. Her job$_2$ for the last year or so has been in an electronic instrument adjustment house. Fiddling, she tells us, is a very old term, whose origins no one is sure of, which means making small adjustments that are nevertheless absolutely necessary—though it seems to be connected somehow with some very ancient music. "Nea, I understand how upset you must be. And I'm even moved that you came all this way to talk about it. Simply because it's as serious as it is, we just can't make assumptions like that, Max. Zetzor, Ulus, Nepiy, all of them *are* very far away. We don't really know anything about them— and no," because Nea had raised one fist up to her shoulder, not in anger but in frustration. Still, Shoshana knew how easily Thants can take offense, even if it never lasts more than a month. "I'm not saying the tastes of any of your words suggest spoiled ingredients. I am simply saying that no meal yields up all its flavors at the first bite. Without contradicting a thing you've told us, I'm sure there must be more to it than that. We haven't talked to Thadeus. We haven't talked to Eulalia."

"Do you think I've been able to talk to them either? Not to mention Clearwater. I mean really *talk* to them? I know what they want, what they've said, and . . . *some* of the things they've done to get it. It makes me very frightened. Shoshana, Max, I don't know what to do!" Her last sentence was softer and shriller than the ones before. It's so easy to lose the nature of the distress when dealing with the crisis of people from another culture, much less another whole matrix of cultures—which is what a person from another world always is. "If Thadeus, Clearwater, and Eulalia do go off to Nepiy, what about the rest of us? Should we go with them, with some hope of sabotaging—"

"Certainly not," Egri said. "You'd be guilty of treason—and caught for it in the beat of a pearlbat's wing." Still squatting she put one foot down on the next inlaid platform, toes curling on the ornamental side.

"Or should we stay where we are, working on the Family's side to change their—"

Egri simply laughed, flexing the toes of both feet. "Soon you will have things too complicated for anyone to follow. No, let's try something more straightforward, more in touch with what you feel."

"But I don't *know* what I feel!" Nea declared. "I'm frightened! I'm confused. How am I to know what—"

"Are you hungry?" Egri asked. "Are you sad—"

"I don't . . ." and here Nea gave a little shudder, her fists and her lips held tightly. (I have been told that children, in the livable climes of Zetzor, are quickly taught not to cry: stoicism is a great virtue there and is expressed in all sorts of flamboyant ways.) "I don't . . ." she repeated. "I can't . . ."

Then, beside Mother Dyeth's silent personality column, light turned riotous in the entrance mirrors; mirrors swung in.

Bucephalus came lolloping inside, turned, and took the stance of an evelm dragon hunter many years older than she. On the other side of the door, Tinjo (who is a love, but also a bit of a coward) peered around the edge.

Small Maxa ran up to stand right by the jamb.

Bronze head, bronze feet, bronze hands, bronze torso bright with Iiriani outside: heaving up a brazen forearm, George Thant shoved Small Maxa across the chest back against the multiple hinges and strode through, going from bright to umber. "There! You *are* there! Nea Thant! Thant! Nea! Thant! . . ." (Have I explained how the folk of northern Zetzor use the order of your names to render crushing insults both to intimates and strangers? Oh, never mind.) "Treacherous pupa! You *are* claimed as a sister to me! But you are as a drop of yellow poison in the clear currents of our Family's love!"

EIGHT

Strangers and Visitors

"You have come here to betray your kin to the viper and the ant. You have disgraced your ancestors and your progeny. Your treachery has shamed me, hurt me, confused me, and I would weep tears of hot vinegar if I could!" (Stamp, stamp, stamp—a reference, I believe, to a curse contained in an oral epic from equatorial Zetzor which, for the last few decades, had been popular at the poles.) "You have squandered ice and soil, jeopardizing the entire custom of unlimited space fare, won for you by the work of your illustrious father, Thant Thadeus—" (You can also proffer resounding compliments that way too.) "—and your melodiously sung mother, Thant Eulalia. As you know, and that knowledge must be your shame, unlimited space fare *is* limited only to those uses which will broaden minds and enrich cultures. If one is caught abusing it, it can be rescinded at any moment!" (Stamp, stamp, stamp, stamp, stamp—five stamps, I think, was an allusion to some parodic use a Zetzorian academic poet of the south had made of that equatorial epic.) "You have besmirched two parents' joy at your birth and deepened the memory of pain your bodily mother, Thant Clearwater, still bears from her womb-work. Four siblings' shouts of laughter and cries of pleasure have stilled in a night of fire and chagrin. Oh, Nea—" (Stamp; which I guess was just George—) "What

203

did you call yourself *doing,* coming here like this? Now I am burdened with hauling you back. Thadeus commands it. Who knows what crazed notions you've left with our friends, the glaucomas and retinitises and cataracts with which you've infected their eyes so that whenever they gaze again in our direction, all their vision will be obscured by disease . . . !" George stalked back and forth, vituperating and stamping like some brass engine whose proper use no one can divine but which is nevertheless clearly malfunctioning.

Nea opened her mouth, then closed it and her eyes. She opened her eyes, her expression for a moment nearing rage—once she actually got out a "No . . . !" She closed her eyes again, touched two foil fingers to her dark forehead, and shivered.

". . . spawn of a sewage pump, descendant of a slime mold, all genetic congruences we share are discredited by your infamy and actions. How *could* you, female son of Thant! See how I wring my hands and wring my hands once more, till the flesh goes raw on my palms. I have searched swamp, dry-plain, and canyon for appropriate execrations, and have yet found none for the nuance of my distress . . ."

Shoshana and I glanced at each other. Years ago, along with V'vish, Kelso, and Alyxander, we had taken a vaurine-projection tour of Zetzor, basically to learn something of our friends' world. "Probably saw more of it than any of *us* ever will," was Thadeus's curt comment, on their next visit when we began to ask what we thought were polite questions. But while we were touring the ever-light south, we had gone to a theater in the well-touristed city of K and seen an evening of energetic satire in the public theater about the northern Zetzori. (Not that the southerners aren't strange.) One particular skit concerned a northern mother, from a Family enclave, going after a runaway child; it wasn't unlimited space-fare that was in jeopardy that time but some local county tax-rebate the youngster's presence in the mother's labor cooperative assured. Still, the gestures, phrases, even the stamps were practically the same. And there was George, from north Zetzor's 17, raving on and acting like a South Zetzorian parody of herself. It was funny and scary.

By now some of my other parents—Jayne (who is

human), Kal'k (who is evelm), Sel'v (evelm), Hirum (another human), and Hatti (human), and finally my sisters Alyxander and Black Lars (one human, one evelm; both IDs like me)—had come up on their various lifts to watch, quietly and wonderingly, the scene taking place in our west court vestibule.

"I do not know my actions," cried George, "yet what I have done and must do is lit by the reflections of starlight-gathering mirrors along the thousand-kilometer glacial fields." She marched back toward the door, then stalked forward again, stepped to the side (stamp, stamp), then back. "I do not know my feelings, yet the feelings I have already anent this matter, as well as the feelings I know are to come, wrack me as lava from Kromhatch Kone shatters frozen scalings collected on the south face. Oh, Nea—" She seized her sister's shoulder and pulled her toward the entrance— "let's go!"

The doorway, anticipating their exit, had not bothered to close. George dragged Nea stumbling out across the patio. Small Maxa, as the shimmering plates swung in, crouched in the doorway and began to cry.

Large Maxa swayed, platform by platform, down from her perch, her wings showing now and again their inner scarlet. First Jayne, then Black Lars, next Hirum moved to Small Maxa. The earlier shove from George she had taken fairly well. But she knew the Zetzori's aversion to contact. When George had grabbed Nea's shoulder, her reserves had broken. She squatted in the doorway and sobbed.

One, and another, we went to my crouching white sister, stooped to pat at (but not touch) the ivory fists bunched on her bony chest, to lick at (but not touch) her lightly veined ears, to rub at (but not touch) her knobby human back.

"Marq Dyeth . . . ?"

I stood, surprised.

At the top of the ramp, he had one hand on the rail. His call was oddly hoarse; also, oddly, hollowed by the height; and grossly accented.

He said: "Your students are here now . . . many of us."

And I knew somehow he had not come in to tell me that. Knowing it, I also knew he'd been standing there a while—though how much he'd seen of George's and Nea's altercation I didn't know.

"Yes," I said. "Thank you. Of course." I knew too his choosing to speak then was absolutely not what it would have been from me: the discreet throat clearing, the diplomatic cough, the reminder to people caught up in a private moment that they are, in fact, observed.

I cast apologetic looks about me. Only gold-clawed V'vish and bushy-haired Hirum caught them; they glanced at the stranger on the ramp, glanced back at me. I hurried across the vestibule and started up.

He stood just in front of the reflecting south court doors, not waiting, his long body burned a red-brown Iiriani could never match. As I reached the ramp's crest, he turned, and, with movements that (however awkwardly they nudged his wide shoulders, tilted his pelvic blades whose wings jutted above his raveling pants-waist) were completely familiar, he went through the swinging mirrors in the same motion with which, minutes ago, I had fled the polarized chamber.

As I neared the doors, the panels' silver gave me back, waving, only the thickset little male whose swagger is just a bit too much for any real elegance—but with the wreckage of a joy between short beard and heavy brows which, even seconds come to pieces, transformed what should have been the most familiar of faces: when the mirrors swung aside for me, I was not sure who walked out under the stone arch (he was gone . . . !), who walked down the steps, stepped wide of the grill, gamboled out onto the amphitheater skene, for I felt as though I were no longer who I had been.

In those few seconds, he'd vanished . . . ?

They were there—scattered up around the top ten tiers.

I looked around the empty seats far longer than I usually do. (He *could* have gotten back to the chamber . . . ?) Finally I said: "Good afternoon. I see most of you have gotten here. My name is Marq Dyeth. . . ." (Thinking: Why am I telling them? *He* knows.) "We'll be talking together about an hour, maybe two, possibly more, to orient you and answer your questions. But first why don't you all come down from your perches to the front rows here where we can make out each other's faces. Yes, that's

it. Come on, now. I won't urinate on you." (Suffice that
it's an evelmism and would take a page and a half to
explain fully. But they laughed, which was the important
thing; and began to gather up their readers, recorders,
miniscreens, and calculators.) "Just a second, I'll start the
moving stair. . . ." on which, among them, he did not
come down.

2.

I'm tempted to give you an account of the whole three-
hour orientation session$_2$ (they *do* go on), if only because I
know now that from his hiding place, he saw it all. I'm also
tempted to omit it entirely—as I want to omit from thought
all moments when he was not available to my sight, my
tongue, my hand. But the truth is it was a student orientation session$_2$ like any hundred others. There was the big-
shouldered, short-tongued algae farmer$_1$ from even further
south—an embarrassingly healthy creature who smiled at
everything and took down everything on a portable notator
that wept an endless curl of paper into her scaly lap.
Every minute or so she would wind it rapidly on another
little red plastic spool, tear it off, and push it into another
of the numberless pouches on her long vest. ("And do we
have any other algae farmers, $_1$, or $_2$, with us this morning
. . . ?" There were three, wouldn't you know: one from
Ly'el Complex a few dozen kilometers away; two others
from some geosector on the other side of this world.)
There were the four evelmi with steel-colored claws from
somewhere in the far north and shy of giving their profes-
sions$_2$ —where human/evelm relations are much less tran-
quil. They came and sat at the edge of the stage and were
quiet, diffident, and probably hugely suspicious. The largest one now and again turned to whisper something to her
smaller companions in a voice through which individual
words were indistinguishable but which nevertheless
sounded like a passing propeller platform; and I tried to
pretend it wasn't an interruption. There was the ebullient
little fifty-year-old med tech$_2$ (". . . this workshift, that is.
Last job$_2$ I had was in a wildlife preserve in the comb-
caves in the upper plateaus of the Veng'n'n Range, just
about—well, quite far east of here. I loved it. Might even

consider going back. But there's also a possibility of going
to work$_2$ in the bauxite mines out east—in accounting, of
course. Not actually *in* the mines. Even with GI, that's a
primary job$_1$ of course . . ." One suspected she'd been
retired from her own job$_1$, whatever it had been, for at
least ten years. "But it still sounds fascinating. Or then, I
could always go into . . .") One had come to study the
sculpture of Bybe't Kohimi (*That's* the name—I remember
now—of the artist who did the synapse-pillar's pedestal
and capital), of which Dyethshome happens to have the
largest collection on the two worlds where she worked.
Another had come to explore the documents in one of our
libraries on simulacrum technology as it segues into bioengineering. (Our libraries are both vasty and selective on
many subjects.) Another was here to learn more of the
early stage production techniques used in the folk theater
of Jae'l Bazerat, many of whose performances were first
presented in this very amphitheater just over a hundred
years ago. (Yes, extensive theater records are all on store
in one of our numerous basements.) By now most of the
affable, interested, and really rather bright group were
perching or sitting or squatting around the stage edge.
(Maybe five out of the two dozen had gotten stuck out in
the first row of seats.) I sat in the skene's center, suggesting to Ryla that she not try to see the Kyga-jewelry collection in the north court until after she had visited the G'har
gallery in the west court; or reassuring R'eb she needn't
worry about her various religious food prohibitions while
she was here; or dictating for the third time—just so Vagia
could make sure she'd gotten it down right—the access
number to activate the food choppers in the student kitchen
downstairs, since it had been accidentally misprinted in
the last brochure. Iiriani rolled like a flaring tread gear
behind high-colored glass, lighting us now deep orange,
now pale green, now a scalded yellow. But as I sat, naked
and cross-legged on the old planks, every few minutes I
would realize that, though he was not among their number, if he *had* retreated to some hiding place, he was still
watching me. And I would halt on a word, then rush on
among the coils of whatever explanation I was ensnared in,
while my ears and knees flushed redder than the free-
standing panes about the amphitheater of our rhetoric.

3.

When the session was over, I fled the skene for my room. But by the time I reached the unactivated entrance column, I suddenly found myself afraid of my open platform's sunset peace. Off I strode again, through underground halls, to search out Maxa and see her mines. Minutes later, when I heard her laughing in one of the lower galleries with Alyxander and Bu, I did not activate the drop-lift that would take me to them. Through bright corridors and across drear chambers I wandered into the dark, multi-columned hall we call the Old Library. Like the column by the vestibule entrance, these ornately topped and bottomed glimmerings (more Bybe't) were the personalities of other dead Dyeths. From the wallboard I took out (yet again) one of the tiny crystal volumes of Mother Dyeth's nine-volume memoirs that, in my rash adolescence, I'd promised myself I would someday read all through. A wonderful woman, my great[7]-grandmother had a dreadful prose style; but since so much of her life, not to mention Vondramach's, has been written about by people who didn't (including Vondramach), those memoirs are like the heaviest ore—laced with valuable yield, I'm sure; but the refinement techniques are all but beyond me. I sat at one of the large scarred tables, pushed open the cover to the dusty reader-screen, funneled the little text crystal (so different from books) between my fingers into the receptor dish, and for an hour stared at one page of limp, bitter bombast by a woman by report both salty and pithy.

I did not read, from one end to the other, another three sentences.

Suddenly I was up and out between the glimmering ghosts. He *was* in the polarized chamber. And there were ways to get there without going back through the amphitheater itself. (Why would you build one if there weren't?) What I wanted to avoid were the good-natured students still hanging around the stage. ("Oh, hey, Marq! We just wanted to ask you . . .") Well, there *were* ways. But I had to go to another library and look them up to make sure I had the various spells and incantations down. Dyethshome is a hive of mentally activatable intricacies scattered about five courts, and nobody knows them all.

Why hadn't I thought of this an hour ago?

I probably had.

But that many decimal places, not to mention the confusion of Nea, George, and their Thantish theatrics, had fouled my tongue and fingers till I'd lost all notion of recipe.

I rose beside him in a column of light.

4.

He sat on the cushioned bench along the chamber's rear, bare feet on the floor, elbows on his knees, bright and bald hands hanging down between. He stared at his toes for all the world as if he were about to pick one.

Out on the stage, three students sat and two stood, all laughing at a joke one of the algae-farmers$_2$ had just told. Off to the side in about row twelve, another student was bent over some mechanical gizmo, putting her in touch with a local orchestral performance, or a parent's admonitions to pay attention to what she ate during the length of her stay, or some other student who could only visit Dyethshome in vaurine projection and wanted an in vivo supplementary account.

"Rat Korga . . . ?" I said; and to say the name of your perfect erotic object is always to say it for the first time, even when it is the fiftieth repeated shriek and you are half blind with terror on the crags of a world so far away its night is virtually without stars. He looked up at me, and the eyes he wasn't born with were human and green. He frowned a little. The light about me from the entrance column dimmed. Then the frown seemed to crack away (as all changes of expression registered on his large-pored, pitted face). He smiled a little:

"Marq Dyeth . . . ?" Then, nervously and surprisingly, he stood.

He was *so* tall.

Iiriani was below the back wall of our glass-roofed chamber. But neither he, I, nor the chamber walls around us cast any shadow over the sloping seats—like those

creatures in the folk tales of a temperate geosector on
another world (I *can't* remember which, damn it!) who, by
such shadowlessness, signal mutually murderous intents.

His rough, unringed fingers came to touch my arm—
and stopped an inch off, as though he were I and I were
Maxa.

I said: "I'm sorry I waited so long to come."

"If you had come earlier—" His voice was rust rough
and mauled by accent— "I would not have been ready."

I guess that's those decimals.

I said: "Come with me," and stepped back onto the
limen plate. (If he *had* touched me, would I have fallen to
the ground . . . ?) He stepped forward onto the plate with
me. And his left nipple was centimeters above my right
eye. I wanted to lean my head back and lick it—not from
desire but from that idiocy always there to subvert desire
and render it ludicrous. Our human heat was a third
creature beveling between us.

We rose—or dropped—into the floor.

Did Korga think, the first time, that the halls and
underground corridors I led him through were more familiar to me than to him? (Home is a complicated place?
Well, Dyethshome is more complicated than most.) Some
near lightless passages we walked through; through some,
bright with intricate ceiling fixtures, we were carried along
by moving floors with ornate rails whose gilded newels
bore likenesses of great evelmi and humans forgotten for a
century, dead for two. In one such, as his arm almost
brushed mine, the milky wall glowed green. (The creamy
liquor of the local worm . . .) Small Maxa was running
along beside us. From time to time the white coins of her
fingertips, the small saucers of her knees pressed to the
other side of the pane, as if she could actually see us:
"Marq . . . ? Marq, where are you? Please, Marq, come
see my mine! You promised, Marq . . ." Behind her, in
the wall screen, I could see where she'd done a formidable
job of construction in one of our old playrooms. Korga
looked at me.

I smiled. "She wants to take up mining as her profes-
sion$_1$," I explained, and wondered whether he understood—or if I should tell him—how difficult her disability
might make that on some parts of our world. But we
turned into another corridor without a call-wall. And some-

how we were standing on the metal circle that would become the entrance to my room.

Korga said: "Marq Dyeth . . ." Both accent and injury kept me from knowing if it were exhortation or interrogation. And because, with either inflection, I hadn't the slightest idea what he meant, after a moment's silence, I said:

"This is my room. It's very far away. . . ."

When he said nothing, I activated the column.

5.

The Myaluths were profligate with Iiriani-set.

He followed me across the carpet. Blinding gold had wedged down between the hills. Morgre's park levels, ten kilometers off, were a tracing of girders. In the city, a few early lights, green and blue, battled for visibility. The hills were steel-colored; the sky was indigo and flame, the Hyte-wr, black and purple under its fumes' unraveling lace.

I walked to the desk, pushed aside things that clicked or just toppled, turned to face him, and sat.

The overhead lamp came on. One and another, the little spheres in the orrery swung their shadows across my hairy shoulder, down my snarled arms. (I hadn't activated the contraption, but sometimes it just starts up when I near it in certain moods.) He stopped by the bed, watching me.

I turned to look over the rail, beyond the tufted stones. Suddenly I got the strangest sensation that he was no longer behind me. I turned back.

He was. (It's that reconstruction memory . . .)

As I looked, his eyes came up and caught mine—still green.

They questioned a moment. Then he sat down, hands beside his hips on the mat. The way his high knees jackknifed—and he sort of bent forward now—he looked even taller than when he was standing. He brought his hands in. He opened his mouth, closed it again. Then he said, his voice even rougher than before: "Please . . . please, I need you to—"

I stood. "I will," I said, because I knew at least this

much about him. "You . . . you don't have to ask me, because I . . ."

It was brief, intense—satisfying? More dizzying, I think. On my bed, on the carpet, and on the bed again; there was a short time—or perhaps it was a long one— when we were quiet and very aware of one another. My feelings oscillated (and I could feel his feelings sometimes lagging behind mine, sometimes moving ahead) from warmth to misgiving to warmth.

We lay on the bed; and his hand on my chest was a stone outcrop on uneven giltgorse. His rough hair, with something reddish in it, was the hue of split tolgoth pith. Knees? Mine were much closer to my eyes than his. Stones? Crags? Hills at two distances. His cheek, near my face, was the slope of the Reya'j'as Plateau (north, in R-16), which had been peppered with meteors a million and a half years ago, and among whose craters, thousands of years gone, evelmi once gathered to perform mysteries whose significance even they have forgotten. My own breath against his neck came back to strike my face like a hotwind eroding the prehistorical escarpments of the oest to their characteristic roundness. The line between his arm and my chest was the crevice of some sunken -wr, the near bank, mine, heavy with growth, the far one, his, notably sparse.

I stayed a long time in that landscape, wondering what he would say when he next spoke, wondering what I should say if I spoke first, whether I should let him speak before me. I thought of: *Among the thousands of males I've bedded, at least a dozen times somebody has said to me, "You'll have to meet so-and-so. You'll just love him!" But this has got to be the strangest route I've ever traveled to end up sleeping with someone.* And didn't say it. I glanced at him instead; he shifted mountains, planes, -wr.

Green and ivory, his eyes blinked.

Then I asked: "What world are you . . . ?"

He looked down. "Mmmm . . . ?" It rumbled in the muscle and bone under my ear. "World? Where was I . . . ?"

My ear was on his arm. So I moved my head a little to hear better.

". . . I was remembering a black river. A great river. Under the ground, and lit by golden torches stapled to the rocks. Children in boats, rowing, were terrified because

the slimy mantichorion might surge up from the black
waters and upset their boat—not a real place." He chuckled. "It's in a . . . text. From my world . . . no, I don't
know if it's from my world or not. It may have been
brought there. Nothing important." He glanced down.
"You? Where are you, now . . . ?"

"Underground rivers," I said. "That sounds like someplace in the north of this world—where I'm afraid I haven't
spent too much time." I pushed up on an elbow. "Up
there, you know, sex between women of the same gender—
or of different species—is illegal. At least it used to be
until a hundred years or so ago. If it is now, frankly, I
don't know. My grandparents told me about it." I laughed
and put my head back to nuzzle his strong armpit. (Mine,
in this heat, with so much more hair, smelled so much
less. More genetic divergence within our world-sundered
species?) He said:

"On my world, sex between males was illegal until
you were twenty-seven, although it went on pretty constantly anyway. What was completely illegal on my world
was sex between a person your height and a person of
mine. For all genders."

I pushed up on my elbow again. "Whatever for?"

Sometime in the past minute, the light had dropped
below the refraction threshold of his artificial eyes. The
balls were glass-filled caves in which small machines spar-
kled. Korga smiled briefly around them, then looked up at
a star in the forking offshoots of a fire-cactus. The cactus
arms, knobby and black above us, hugged a star in its blue
patch. He raised his ringed hand to nick his middle fingernail three or four times on his bottom teeth. "It was a
law—a law that, today, I understand. Thanks to the Web.
But all I understood when I was a youngster, living off the
refuse of a city whose name I still cannot say properly
even in my own language, was that I wanted, and was not
allowed, to hold a little, hairy male to me whose head I
could look down at, to bend my face down to his when he
looked up, to rub my mouth and eyes in his hair when he
looked down." He looked at me, no smile now; and there
are worlds which have tales of demons with hollow eyes.
"I had chances to do it, or do things close enough to it."
He looked away. "But I have learned more about why my

world was the way it was in the time since it has been
gone than I ever knew while I lived on it."

"Rat, were you persecuted for your sexual predi—
. . . well, I mean—" (The first I was ever aware one *could*
be was on Senthy with Egri and Genya; there all sadomasochism was hunted out and punished with barbaric single-
mindedness; especially if concert was written out or clearly
specified by verbal contract, which their authorities considered the ultimate disease. It was Genya who, as we left
that moon in disgust, first pointed out to ten-year-old me
how, even as it was suppressed, sadomasochism there was
encouraged by every private park and public building
around the polar ocean we lived on: all were designed to
suggest some weapon or mangle in common use by the local
fisherwomen; all were invariably labeled with some written
plaque of prohibitions.) "I mean, were you ever legally—"

"Five or six times I was caught and reprimanded, or
put in a detention house."

Will sex between humans ever lose its endlessly repeated history? "Did it stop you from having sex?"

"For a week—perhaps even for a few months, the
first time." He moved a little, his whole body. "Finally, I
had no sex at all."

During my first three years as an ID, I thought my
job$_1$ was not to be surprised at the universe's human
variety. Later I realized that it was not to be surprised that
nonstop surprises would henceforth be my life.

"If you had asked me, on my world," Korga said,
"whether my five or six run-ins with our laws over sexual
infractions had anything to do with my choosing to give
sex up for what I thought would be the rest of my life, I
would have said no. I had had too many other run-ins for
too many other reasons so that the sexual ones seemed the
least of it. If you asked me here, however, lying with you
like this, I could not say for sure." His rough hand, with
its heavy jewels, moved an inch over his belly, then rested.
"One burden of all of this new knowledge is that old
certainties crumble beneath it. But this—" He watched
me with eyes it was hard to believe could see— "is the
first time I have lain down to make love with another
person since I was . . . nineteen standard years old."

I swung my feet off the mat and down to the rug and
looked back to where this male who was at least forty

standard years of age had not moved. "Oh, come on." No, he had not become anyone else, and yet— "I can't believe that anyone who is my . . ." Calling someone your perfect erotic object to his face seemed suddenly to express the perfection it stood for much too imperfectly. I took a breath. "How many times . . . eh, standing up since then?"

He shrugged. "Three . . . four. Once with a woman who stole me from my work station. Once before that and once after, with some others . . ."

"What about before . . . before you were nineteen?"

"A few hundred times—as compared to the few thousand you said."

"Oh." Our geosector has no particular prohibition about virginity; but I had just gotten a little insight into those worlds that have—the ones that forbid it totally. "It's still hard for me to believe."

"They told me," he said, "you had probably been to bed with several thousand males. They told me you went to bed with males the way I did when I was . . . before my anxiety was terminated. Only for you it was not illegal. They also told me that if I'd lived a more ordinary life on Rhyonon, I might have gone to bed with a comparable number of men—thousands, rather than the hundred or so I did—and I would probably feel very different about your going to bed with them than I do." Once more the empty eyes came back to me. "Don't you ever persecute people here for their sex?"

"Oh, no," I said. "I mean, I told you, a long time ago, in the north—"

"The language," he said. "That's what I mean."

I frowned.

"I lived on a much younger world, on which—they told me in the Web—we spoke a much older language. We had 'men' and 'women,' 'bitches' and 'dogs.' The men were all male and were called 'he' and the women were female and called 'she'—"

"I know the word 'man,'" I said. "It's an archaic term. Sometimes you'll read over it in some old piece or other."

"To take those distinctions away is a kind of . . ." He mused a moment— ". . . persecution."

"Perhaps to someone who's used to them . . ." I said. "We just have different—"

But he chuckled, briefly and for no more than three syllables. "On my world 'he' was what everyone, male or female, wanted to be . . . perhaps the males thought they were a little closer to it. On your world and, I have been told, on the vast majority of others, 'he' is what everyone, male and female, wants to have. Perhaps all of us are equally far away from that."

"You don't like that I've gone to bed with as many people as I have—or the way we talk about it?"

"I don't think about it."

"Mmm." I pondered. "You know, if you'd lived a more ordinary life on Rhyonon, you wouldn't *be* here. How do you feel about . . . me?"

He didn't smile. How long did it take me to understand he really did find things funny, but that humor for him—or for his world, I still don't know which—was simply the most private of emotions? He said: "They told me, and told me again, and told me yet again: I must remember that I am not on my world, I am on yours." The bedding whispered, shifted; he sat up beside me, where I was sitting, at the edge. His naked knees were above mine and wide apart. His eyelids smiled above me. "They also told me that when I don't know what to do, I should do what the person nearest me does—while I decide the questions I need to ask." He was quiet a moment; then he let out a long breath. "I never knew there was this much to know."

I started to ask what he meant. But he lay his ringed hand on my knee.

We looked at it.

The flesh was thick and dry. Through my thigh hair about them, I could feel wide palm and broad fingers, unsure of their own weight, now adding a little to it, now taking a little away. I thought: it feels more like warm stone than the bone-and-meat-filled hide it is. I reached out two fingers. My own hands have always struck me as very ordinary: the fairly small, somewhat fleshy hands of a fairly small, somewhat hairy fellow who only uses them for manual labor one job_2 out of three; and, wonderful as I've always found nail-biting in others, I've never been able to sustain the habit myself, so gave up trying long ago. I put my middle fingertip on wide copper set around both edges with green stone chips, some opaque, some glassy, the metal between geometrically embossed. The ring one further forward bunched his broad knuckle skin before it, wrinkled as a big knot or a small brain. Spreading my fingers wide, I touched my forefingertip to his forenail— side to side twice the width of my thumb. It emerged from beneath the cuticle bank, thickened against as much gnawing as the horn, went on the distance of the paler moon and that distance again, before the support structure broke down (I cannot say "was undermined" because all that could be had been, and then been bitten away); for this distance again, it clutched at the quick, its edges pitted so smally and myriadly it presented the regularity of the endlessly attacked border, marked by the dirt of an unknown task₃. The crown rose and curved away, twice the length of the nail itself, as it did on all his fingers, thrice, on thumb and little. As my fingertips moved on its upper surface, the heavy crown seemed of equal hardness—and clearly of greater endurance—with the horn. That surface bore the swirls and lines—fainter of course, and interrupted, and scarred—that, below, would let his finger print. I moved my hand, feeling the textures, copper, stone, nail, skin; and thought about the mechanics through which we locate beauty. By art, we can only do it through a disinterested precision which represses, while it mimes, all the interest that impels it. And we can only hope the difference between the repressed and the represented will read as intensity.

His hand was beautiful.

Korga said: "You see now: what my fingers hold is not only what my life has become since my world's death. You may find in their scars, if you look, all the poverty of the time before."

"Does that hurt?" I asked. "Does it worry you?"

"It hurts." He lifted his hand from under mine, put his arm around my shoulder; again I felt warm metal, cool flesh. "But one thing about what was done to me on my world: there are many worries—many kinds of worries—I do not have."

"The synapse-jamming?"

"Do you wonder what I would be like without it? It's not supposed to change who you are . . ."

"I hadn't," I said. "Yet." What I did wonder was what

worries a tyrant, priest, and poet, dead two hundred years, had carried with her after such an operation.

For a while, I felt one finger move on my shoulder, then another.

He said: "Your family—they are very angry."

I looked up at him, wondering what he could mean. "I know very little of families," I said.

"I had none," he said, "though I used to think of them a lot . . . when I was younger."

"I don't follow you," I said. "What family?"

He looked down, with the slight brief smile of puzzlement that was so like his slight brief smile of pleasure. "When I came in from the theater, your sibling—the one with the metallic yellow flesh—was angry at your black sister; finally she took her outside while the rest of you watched."

"George—my . . . ?" I looked up. "Nea . . . ?" I stood and I went to the chair on which his wrinkled pants were piled, here and there in the folds showing metal belt-links. "They're not even from our world. George and Nea are Thants. They're friends of Dyeth." But when it dawned on me, I laughed out loud. "You thought we were a family . . . ?" Then I smiled. "Suddenly some of the things you've been saying begin to make sense. No, the Dyeths are very much our own nurture stream—at least that's the translation of the northern evelmi's term for it. This particular nurture stream has been bubbling along for seven ripples now. There're only two older streams in the area—one at the tracer collective and one at the nematode farm. And I wouldn't be all that upset if ours went on for seventeen or twenty-seven more." There are so many small movements of response you expect from people when they listen to you—there the head nods slightly, here it raises a little, now the eyelids narrow. He, who, against me, forehead to foot, had responded so that, minutes ago, he had seemed an extension of myself, only sat, only watched. Though I was sure he listened as intently as anyone else could possibly listen (as intently as I knew I listened to him), still, before his still face, to believe it was all faith. "I was adopted by the Dyeths when I was a baby—from some infant exchange in the north; but most of my sisters come from even farther south. Small Maxa was semisomed from some neuroplasm that an evelm grandmother of mine,

N'yom, donated to a bioengineering experiment many many
years ago and that was just taken out of suspension about a
decade and a half back—though of course most of Maxa's
chromosome sequence was taken from humans. But in the
genetic sense she's part evelm. Still, there is no egg-and-
sperm relation between any of our parents and any of this
generation of children, nor between any of my sisters—
human or evelm—and each other." But certainly the Web
had told him this. Somewhere away from where words
gather before speaking, I vaguely saw us taking a walk
outside around the platform while we talked. And because
such images are closer to movement than words, I moved,
planning to speak. But he stood, with me, before words
came. And walked with me as I started to walk. (Thus faith
is rewarded.) "Rhyonon was a Family world, wasn't it?" As
we passed my workdesk, for a moment the lamp above it
gave his eyes back their whites and greens. And the de-
mon vanished into his pitted face. "At least someone told
me that it was about to fall over in that direction."

"The Sygn," he said. "They told me in the Web that
that's the side you and your stream . . . your world is on."

I said: "It's also supposed to be the side that Japril
and most of the Web are on . . . unless there's been some
new information that I'm not privy to." At the rail, I lifted
up the ornate triple hook from its hasp and swung out the
lacquered gate.

Korga nodded as we started down the wide plank
steps. "My world was just about to join with the Family
officially—when it was destroyed." Korga's toes and the
balls of his feet were so big they hung over the edge of
each step as he stepped down. His sole's thick rims were
rough and cracked, like a woman's gone barefoot twenty
years on sand. "And I did not even know there was a clash
between them or, really, the name of either side." As we
walked down, he kept very close to me. And the way
people much taller than you sometimes do, he rested one
hand on my shoulder.

That almost made me want to cry.

"Tell me about the Dyeths," he said, as we turned on
the clearing to walk beside the raised platform.

"Gylda Dyeth . . ." I said—recited really, as I would
have in any orientation session₂ had some student asked
me the same question; frequently when I want to cry, I

recite. "Gylda Dyeth migrated here to Velm, when she was nineteen, in a small shuttle of eight thousand colonists from a world called Klaven, which had recently become fearful of Cultural Fugue. It's a problem certain metal-ceramic-plastic-intensive worlds, with an economic variation displacement of more than point-seven-six, are prone to fall into . . ." I halted, thinking of Rhyonon.

There's a ten-day period right after hotwind season when I wouldn't let anyone—no matter how rough her feet—walk barefoot on fallen fire-cactus needles. Then the needles are bright red (and the cactus trunks smoke gray). But at this time of year they heap about in brown piles over the scrumbly soil (and the trunks are deep maroon). Those under our feet were almost as soft as the powder-soil discarded by the nematode strainers, or (more accurately) the sloughed scales over the floor of a seven-generation dragon cave.

His hand still on my shoulder, we turned to take the circuit of blunt prickles. "I've always imagined Gylda, when she got here, looking somewhat like Nea Thant does now—a tall, intense, black woman with somewhat yellowish eyes. She spent six years on Velm, first in the north at the other end of the world, and then here in the south. It was on a religious visit to our little moon, Arvin, where she met the woman who once wore your rings."

"Vondramach Okk . . ." He said the name with the uncertainty of a native evelm passing some polysyllabled human word from tongue to tongue, inserting all sorts of apostrophes. "Japril, Ynn, and Marta told me of Vondramach Okk."

"They hit it off pretty well. Gylda spent the next five years standard in Vondramach's services, doing jobs for her offworld that I like to imagine were somewhat similar to what I do today. Only my better judgment tells me that, given grandma's youthful accomplishments and Okk's mature needs, they were probably quite a bit nastier. Those five years took her all over the galaxy—sometimes with Vondramach, sometimes without. But as she had left Klaven, she finally left Vondramach's service and came back here to Velm. They parted on good terms. When she returned to this world, here to Morgre, Vondramach gave her—or had built for her—well, here it looks like we're outside it—"

"Dyethshome?"

I nodded.

We walked between tall cactus trunks. Brown needles brushed our shoulders. Thick shadows from the platform's central lamp barred the ground. Ahead, rocks broke away beneath netmoss. Arvin, the little moon that looks like a star, was up. Beneath it, the stream broiled through its crevice, searching for Whitefalls. "But there's nothing much more I can really say about it, other than that it's a stream where you are as welcome as I am, because each ripple, each wave and rill is held to the other by love. And I . . . well, guess I love you." I sighed.

We stepped wide of a small stone crevice onto netmoss. Last year's deader, darker tangle cushioned the coppery web of this year's. On the far rocks, banks of elephant lichen (trace of the Web's planoforming, common to so many worlds) raised their crinkly barks in the night-light.

Suddenly Korga's hand dropped from my shoulder. "That . . ." he said. "That's running water . . . ?"

"Yes. It joins with Whitefalls further along."

"It's the first I've ever seen." He squatted, staring.

I looked down at his back's curve, measured over vertebrae and ribs and planed one side with star- and Arvinlight, ghostly through cactus branches. He held his hand over waters ribbed with their own quivering rush. Momentarily stones and metal seemed suspensors holding those heavy fingers up.

He lowered them.

Water bubbled at his palm's edge, stilled between his knuckles. (His big toes broke the earth he squatted on.) He submerged his hand.

I asked: "Does the cold water do anything to the rings' functioning?"

He looked up. "Perhaps it gives me a kind of . . . But it's only the chill that would happen to anyone putting a hand in cold water." He stayed there almost a whole minute. "No."

When he stood, I said: "This way."

His hand wet and warm on my shoulder, we came on around the platform's fifth corner. As we started toward the stairs, I asked: "Rat, what do you feel about all this?" and wondered what his notion of "all this" was.

He said: "Relief, mostly. They told me you existed—I

had to wait most of a standard year, learning how to be a person who might walk, speak, and listen in your world."

"Relief . . ." I smiled. "Yes. I feel that too. They told me that you existed. And yet somehow my going on involved pretending you didn't."

"All around the relief—" Korga's wide heels hung from the back of each step as we climbed— "there is still anxiety. Yours, mostly. I sense it not as an emotional activity, but as a tenseness. Desire is still there; expectation is still there. A single orgasm in a single hour has not given me an answer."

Which made me gasp a little. "Yes, I feel that too. . . ." I pushed through the gate; he followed me. "And yet we're both—you and I—very different people."

"We are both in very different situations."

"We're both—" I started to say *from very different worlds*. "We are each likely to have very different feelings at what comes upon us as well. I know for myself—" I turned at the rail as he closed the gate behind him and stepped up to stand next to me: "I know I want to do wonderful things for you, because watching you, being near you, not to mention touching you or holding you, gives me so much pleasure. I suppose somewhere the rational part of me is wondering if perhaps the differences between us might not end up with my hurting over them, but . . ."

After a strangely long while he said (and he was halfway through his sentence before I realized it was an answer to mine): "You give me so much pleasure, why should I ever want to hurt you?"

Somehow I assumed, in the search for difference, we had found identical emotions. Somewhere across the rocks came the growing pedal-bass of a sand scooter.

I looked up to see if Korga was frowning at the sound. (He wasn't.) "Rat, I think someone is . . ." I leaned down on the rail, folding my arms and hunching my shoulders. Beside me Korga grasped the rail, arms straight, and didn't lean at all.

We looked across the clearing, beyond the night rocks, to distant Morgre's glimmer. Purple threads luminesced palely over the Hyte. At the horizon a few clouds streaked jet against starry blue.

First two scooters, then three more, bounced up over
the rock ridge. All but one had two riders.

6.

"Here it is! Look! Here!" one called.

Scooters swerved, slowed, hummed.

One and another they halted before the platform.

The woman who'd called out was our retired med-
tech$_2$. She got off the plastic and silver and treads and foils
that made up her shared mount. As others dismounted,
the scooters leaned over onto their stands. The med-tech$_2$
rubbed the silver filigree on her openwork head-protector
and turned to look across the dark stones, out at the
handful of glitter that was Morgre. "Yes, this is certainly
the view I visited in vaurine. The commentary said, now,
that, in the fourth generation of Dyeths, several of them
established their personal living rooms in this area." She
was reciting from a prospectus that she must have memo-
rized with the help of General Info.

"Do any of them still live here, Mima?" asked one of
the evelm students still seated with all six legs drawn up
on her swaying bike.

I nudged Korga's hand with my elbow and grinned as
he glanced at me.

"Let me see . . . It doesn't say anything about that in
my program," the med-tech$_2$, Mima, said. "But during the
Bazerat productions, some of the younger Dyeths—Genya,
Ari, or Maxa—would invite the performers and the techni-
cians up here to rehearse. Special pentagonal platforms
were built to facilitate the rehearsals." (Yes, mine/Ari's is
the only one left.) "Imagine, playmakers like Vhed'dik and
Cy'yja, or actors like Kand'ri, Sejer'hi, or Jae'l Bazerat
herself may have stood right here and declaimed the lines
of the Priest Passmar't, or the Worm Digger Avess, or the
Human Ambassador David." (Kand'ri's portrayal of the
human David, without make-up or holographic assistance,
is considered a high point in the illusionist art of the
highly illusive theater by evelmi and humans alike. Myself, though I'm impressed, I've always been more moved
by the evelm actors' clouds, rocks, winds, and oilslicks.
But these have a millennium of oestern equatorial tradi-

tion behind them.) "Any one of them," repeated the diminutive Mima, "might have stood right where I'm standing now!" Actually it was about two meters back, where Korga and I were leaning.

A tall woman I didn't recognize dismounted her scooter. She wore a black body mask, face to feet. One of the other human students turned to her and said:

"It was very nice of you to rent these scooters for us so we could come out and explore the landscape. It's left the taste of friendship in our mouths."

The tall woman said: "I am only too pleased to help the local students." Her voice had the faintly singsong quality of someone who had just learned the language through GI—a quality which, offworld, I hardly even noticed anymore, but which I had found myself listening constantly for in Rat's speech, only to find the gross deformation in both consonants and vowels that told of an awkwardly muscular attachment to a vanished language system I could not comprehend. "I am only sad," the woman went on, "that I have not yet met among your number the woman whose history particularly intrigues me. Well, as your study session goes on, perhaps one of you will introduce me. I intend to stay in Morgre for at least a week or so more. And I would like to spend as much time in your company as you would like to spend in mine." I wondered briefly if she were from one of the mining or manufacturing hegemonies further north.

Korga's and my shadows lay across the clearing among the shadows the students and their scooters cast in my platform's lamplight.

About a meter and a half away, right in front of the steps, one woman turned slowly in a full circle: "It's astonishing! We're here, all alone, with only history and the landscape."

As her eyes swept unseeing past ours, Korga looked at me, his features faintly unsettled on his deeply pocked face; I would soon learn that was as close to surprise as he got. "They don't see us . . . ?"

"Nor our platform. Nor do they hear us." I chuckled through a smile. "That's the chance you take, wandering the local countryside. You never know when you're chatting about your innermost feelings right under somebody's front porch."

"We're invisible to them," Korga said. "The way the chamber was. Back in the amphitheater."

I frowned. "Not exactly. In fact it's entirely different. The reason they can't see or hear us is because they're there, up in the hills, ten kilometers out from Morgre, and we're still in Dyethshome—which is just at the edge of Morgre complex itself." I pointed over the students' heads to the far city. "If it were a little lighter, you could make out the three stained-glass walls around the amphitheater . . . right about . . . there. Ten kilometers off. Which is where *we* are—right now."

Korga looked down at the students in front of us. He said in a perfectly normal voice: "The spiders who sent me here said that I must study such things while I am here at Dyethshome and learn to grow comfortable in such a technology." Most people when they speak in front of people who can't see them whisper.

"What a wonderful rise that looks like over there." One of the evelm, her steel-colored claws indistinct in the evening light, reared beside her scooter and pointed (with her longest tongue). "Let's go take a look at the view from there," she said (with one of her others), "and maybe we can catch the big moonrise."

"You're sure you're not ready to go back to town?" The algae-farmer$_2$ on the far scooter stuck out her own human tongue toward Morgre. (I've heard northerners say we southerners—human—who point like that just seem affected.) "I'll just take one of the scooters back by myself. You can all double up . . ."

"Oh, no!" declared the rather hefty evelm, stepping about on five of her six claws.

"Please come with us," said the tall masked human with the GI singsong.

And the evelm: "Please come. But then, of course . . ." Evelmi are a lot stronger physically than humans; and, in most of their societies, a lot more easygoing. The first is hereditary, the second cultural; and the interplay of both with humans from two profoundly different agricultural-intensive worlds has produced the tragedy of the north.

The big farmer$_2$ laughed. "All right, I'll go," and she flung her high-booted leg back over the scooter seat.

As the scooters swerved off toward another fine view of the star-lit Vyalou, I found myself thrown back through the many rides, night and day, I had taken over this landscape. "Rat," I said, "why don't you come with me—"

"I should go back to the other students now," he announced, almost as I spoke. His own thoughts had been turning among his own feelings, behind his still face.

"No, I don't mean now. Tomorrow. Come dragon hunting with me. Tomorrow morning. You want to become comfortable with our technology, and I can't think of any better way. Go back to the other students. I'll meet you in the student quarters just at—" I paused. "What month is it now?" (Those words, spoken or thought, are the signal for GI to play the time, day, week, month, and year across your consciousness by direct cerebral access: And it was ten o'clock of a balmy Yumber night, the seventeenth month of our seven-season year of twenty-five thirty-one-day cycles.) "Yes, just at sunrise. That's what we'll do. You go on now—" It was only because I was imagining seeing him again that I could dare tell him to go—and the telling was pain: something dull throbbed behind my knees. Above my testicles and between my shoulder blades, there seemed to be two pulleys, with a taut cable between, trying and failing to wind in opposite directions.

He looked at me, took a little step back. (His little step was the size of my normal one.) "Marq . . ." Korga's beardless and cratered face was lit sideways by the orange orrery light that I knew was shining down on my own, bearded and smooth. One after the other, his face did not achieve three expressions. His knee, suspended nearly a meter above his wide and horny foot, moved—bone under flesh. I watched the small, rough triangle of drier skin that humans, male and female, develop after age thirty-five a centimeter below the patella in a naturally selective response to some environmental condition vanished now a millennium.

He stood by the chair where his pants lay.

Suddenly he raised one hand to the other. Finger struggled with finger. One ring came off. He pulled off another three.

What did I feel? Numb terror. And what numbed finally sent the terror itself below perception's limen, so that all I saw was dim or brilliant stone, dull or bright metal, rough or wrinkled flesh occluded and occluded.

He dropped a handful of rings on his rumpled pants, pulled off the remaining three.

And put them down.

"Marq Dyeth . . . ?"

I wanted to tell him to go back to the others. I wanted to raise my hands to his wide shoulders. And while I wanted, his own hands came up to cage the sides of my head in his rough palms, his hard fingers. And I raised mine.

Both of us really naked for the first time, we made love.

Some three hours later, he put on his pants, his rings, his belt; and left.

NINE

From Breakfast to Morning

I pushed up the sarbdown sleeping mat—local shoots sewn
in an envelope (green) manufactured off in one of the more
abhorrent northern pits. Iirianilight, shattered by cactus
trunks, rouged the carpet, the desk drawer handles, the
bed legs. I thought: "Today I am going dragon hunting!"
—remembering when I'd first thought it, age seven, my
first hunt; and when I'd thought it, aged twelve and just
back from Senthy, my seventh; and why this hundred
twenty-sixth would be different— "We will hunt! We will
sing!"

I walked to the platform's west edge. Light fell between the thicker trunks. Hands apart, I grasped the rail
and looked over. A small, nine-shelf lizard perch was built
out from the platform base—the kind they use in the
eastern mountains. The palm-sized shelves, of redpith,
silver, and bone, were kollec-four—the pidgin term from
the forecasting process evelm hunters have used about five
thousand years now in our several climes. Kollec-four: four
finger-length lizards had, by now, availed themselves of
the ornate inlaid platforming. The little lizards are, evolutionarily speaking, close cousins to the great beasts we
would pursue—and rather more distant cousins to the
evelmi who first hunted them.

The hunters invoke complex divinations using the

perch: from the sex of the small beasts found on it at
sunrise, which platform they perch on, which direction
they face, old hunters will predict the plan of the day's
foray, each other's life-fate, and the governmental policies
of their tribes and federations. Fine points vary from area
to area. But what I knew was simply that when winged
neuter lizards squat on the upper silver or bone (cooler, of
course, than the dark pith lower down), it means spawning
is less than two nights off and all three sexes of the greater
dragon will be clustering around the nesting spas; if, however, little females crawl on the dark-colored lower platforms, male and neuter dragons aplenty will be flapping
and flopping over the feeding grounds—no, I'm not sure
why it works, though it's been explained to me enough
times.

Three of the lizards on the red platforms near the
bottom had the female gilded gill-ruff. The fourth, a wingless male, was climbing down from bone to wood, flickering pale tongues, stepping about on six single-spurred
feet: a day for the feeding grounds—which are more pic-
turesque than the spas anyway.

I turned to the metal plate bolted in the carpet's
corner that would become, at my will and silent incanta-
tion, the entrance column.

I walked to it.

I thought. Light rose. I fell into the foggy corridor.

I walked along tapestried halls, or ones with web-
hangings that had once decorated distant evelm cave
complex.

There are stairways up to the amphitheater.

I climbed one, came out a side kiosk looking over the
stage, and strolled out on the boards.

In the gray light, a warm breeze anticipated hotwinds.
Arms folded, I ambled before the stone steps at the stage-
back up to the west-court arch. I looked over the empty
seats fanning from me, to the freestanding walls of ornamental glass, their panes dull, now Iiriani was before
them. The kiosk down to the student quarters was behind
the bank of fountains at the stage's north edge. As I came
around the stone rim, I almost tripped over a mat stretched
out before the door.

"Oh, excuse me—!" She sprang up (the jyga-jewelry
student), blinking and remembering to smile. "Oh, hey,

Marq . . . !" Around her neck she wore the streamers that over the past few years I had seen from time to time in the streets of Morgre and that—for the past few days—I now knew came from Beresh. "You've come to take Korga hunting!" She sank back to her knees. "That's going to be wonderful for him. I wish we could all go with you . . . to watch him at the dragons. But . . ." She arched her gumridge.

I smiled back, confused: I hadn't *meant* to keep it secret . . .

"Oh, here! Let me move my bed so you can . . . we just thought it would be a good idea if someone slept out here in case anyone came in to see him who wasn't . . ." She shrugged scaly haunches. "Well, someone who wasn't supposed to." With the edge of the mat in both front claws, she dragged it a few feet back from the door, dropped it.

"Oh," I said. "Sure." Still smiling, still confused, I walked into the kiosk and down the spiral stair. The first chamber, with its stalactites and cool pools, was a replica of the antechamber of the cave of the P'ol'd of Q'ik'har, a great (evelm) Senator of the north, whose incredible complex, built eight hundred years ago, Shoshana says, has influenced architecture all over this world—human as much or more than evelm. As I came down beneath the dim dawn colors of the skylight, the inlaid steps widened; and I recalled, as I so frequently did in this hall, a conversation I once had with a famous v'ea'd (the 'd is the same root word as in P'ol'd and means something between professor emeritus, systems analyst, and black widow) from one of the seven hundred university-chains that wind from federation to federation over the surface of this world and through which the classical evelm education is disseminated. The v'ea'd had told me, as we strolled the nighttime crags of G'groth, below which smoked the Z'yz-wr: "That we evelmi can, with many of our tongues, reproduce sounds you humans will accept as language has probably generated as much evil as it has good between our species. The real affinity between us is that all our myriad cultures, and all yours, are founded on love of illusion. It is not that we both talk, but that we both talk endlessly of persons, places, things, and ideas that are not currently before us to taste. It is not that we both build home-caves, construct

travel-guiders that stretch for thousands of kilometers over
the land, lay out social grounds, or put together musical
compositions and complex combinations of food and flavored stone, but that we both build, construct, lay out,
and put together these things according to plans, visions,
imaginative schemes that, until we have realized them,
have no real existence." She flicked her wings, whose
lining was a dun and greenish bronze that had blacked in
the big moon's light. "In the north, Marq Dyeth, I have
been in raiding parties that have slaughtered you humans,
as humans have slaughtered my sisters, my university
colleagues, my male groomers and females whom I have
groomed. There is no peace between human and evelm. It
is only an illusion I am in love with as much as you, and it
is what allows us to walk and talk together here in the
south on this chill evening." As I went down, seeking
Korga, how many worlds, I wondered, how many ways of
life had suddenly made the transition to illusion, to mere
memory, to meaning without referent? I stepped from the
bottom step and looked over the underground lakes (and
though history had more or less absolved the P'ol'd, she
had been none too fond of those university chains by the
end of her reign) and started over the clay floor toward the
dormitory.

All the sleeping shells, ranged in two levels, had
facilities for domestic cassettes; anyone who brought hers
with her and put it into the playback would erect a fuzzy
black sphere around the blue plastic sleeping-pad holder,
her own environment within. Usually one could count on
eight or nine dark clouds.

There was only one, in the far corner, fuzzily private.

Usually less than half the students, up late talking
together, ended up falling out together here in the dormitory, since there were enough individual living rooms
further along the hall to accommodate many times the
usual student load. This morning on practically every shell
there was a student curled on green, yellow, or purple
matting. They were *all* here . . . !

Korga lay on his side in a shell near the center, one
frayed knee up, one out, unringed hand off the edge.

All six shells directly around his were empty.

As I started in among them, one of the students—the
one studying Bybe't Kohimi—raised her dark head and,

blinking, recognized me: "You've come to take her hunting?" She spoke softly. "It was wonderful when she came back here last night. We started talking with her. And she talked so simply . . . about her world, and what happened to it. Imagine!"

And the evelm student on the shell beside her rumbled in her sleep, "Imagine . . . When she came back . . . imagine . . ."

I gave her a smile nowhere near as surprised as I felt. I moved toward him among the shells. Someone turned on her pad. Another woke. I heard someone swing her legs from the shell to sit.

They were waking each other.

I reached his bunk—"Rat"—took hold of his thumb, and pulled. "Time to hunt dragons."

He opened his green eyes slowly.

The lids slid up the balls; that motion finished, his head rotated toward me; that motion done, he sat up on the shell's edge and dropped his feet over—you have to understand this was the first I'd ever seen a human wake like this. I recalled Japril's descriptions of his waking after his rescue and knew now what she'd meant.

"Hello, Marq Dyeth."

"Um . . . Rat," I said again. "It's time to go hunting."

Another student was up and standing beside the dark cloud around the cassetted shell, pressing the call button and calling softly: "Mima! . . . Mima! . . ."

As he stood, a muscle tightened on Korga's jaw, moving the dark skin with its small, beautiful wounds, the irregular motion completely at odds with his inhumanly smooth movements. At his waist, for about eight inches, his chain belt had left link marks, while the pants themselves were now inches below; the hair down on the great knob of his ankle lay flat to the bone on the outside and, I saw as the foot moved on the clay, spreading as he put his weight on it, still hazy at the other.

Another student in an upper shell looked down.

"Mima, she's gotten up. . . ."

As I walked with him out among the shells, I wondered at my own fascination at those places where sleep had inscribed his body at head, hip, and foot. I wondered too what had happened here before sleep. He had come as a student, yet I had never imagined his sharing their late talk, their brief or lingering affections. With no desire to keep our relation from them, I was still distinctly uncomfortable with what they might or might not have known. As soon as we reached the tiled pool, I whispered: "Rat, what did you tell them last night?"

He looked down at me. "I answered their questions." And his hand came down on my shoulder.

Which made me feel better. "What did they ask?"

We started up the steps.

He said (and I realized as he said it that what I had heard yesterday as roughness in his voice today seemed more like a resilient, a softened nap): "They asked my name, where I came from, what happened there; they asked why I came here, where I had gone with you, what we had done; they asked what we would do today."

"Oh." We neared the top door. "And you told them. . . ." From time to time I've bedded the odd student come to study, but till now better judgment had always made me put it off to the last few days of the session$_2$ when the class is winding up and plans are being made to go home—for everybody's peace of mind.

At the top of the kiosk, the student who'd decided to lie guard at the entrance squatted on her sleeping mat, hugging her middle knees with her forelegs and watching. "Good hunting. Good singing."

I nodded, smiled, and tried not to skirt too fast around the fountains.

On the stone steps up to the archway, Bucephalus and Black Lars (a step above) sat; and Alyxander (a step below) stood.

"Good morning, Rat," Black Lars muttered in her sisterly basso that with age had begun to pick up the same burr I identified with Large Maxa. "Good morning, Marq."

"We were wondering if you two wanted to come and breakfast with us before you went off to hunt." Alyxander fingered one of the small gray jewels clipped to her genital hair, which—as a human woman—was all she wore mornings. Her head hair was feathery, short, and for some reason wet. The breeze shivered it a little. She stood on the uneven stones, as the rose ruff on Black Lars' black neck shook to the same breeze.

"Of course, if you would prefer—" Black Lars switched tongues and voice timbre in the midst of the verb— "to remain and eat with the other students, we would understand."

Always reticent with strangers, Bucephalus only moved her long tail twice to the left and twice to the right as it lay on the stones—which, she'd told me some time in the last five years, was a sign of friendliness the neuter evelmi in an isolated mountain tribe in the far south used with one another, a language and custom that had all but baffled some of this world's leading ethnologists till very recently. I wondered if she thought this was communication.

"Eh . . . well, thanks." I wasn't sure if siblings *or* students were the breakfast companions Korga wanted.

Rat said: "I would like to come eat with you." He looked at me.

"Sure," I said. "Sounds fine." I mean they were trying to be nice.

"Did you sleep well?" Black Lars asked Rat as we started up the steps: she rose on her three downward legs as we reached them. Alyxander, on her human two, fell in beside me.

"We came in to say hello to the students last night," Black Lars explained, looking at me now, "just as Rat was coming back. She told us about what happened to her world, about coming here to see you, that you were going hunting—and the relationship between you. . . ."

"I *would* have told you," I said. "Only I didn't get a—" But Lars had turned back to gaze at Rat anyway.

Last to get up, Bucephalus only bounded after us when we were practically at the door.

We walked under the stone arch, the hanging green. In the shadowed mirrors I watched the five of us, Alyxander on two feet (the tallest), Bucephalus, on all tufted sixes (the shortest)—though she was also the longest—approach the doors.

Rat and I were dull in the plates, which, in this light, showed scars and old scratches. We moved forward, among my siblings' indistinct gestures, dim attentions, and shadowy concerns.

2.

"We don't usually divert the water through the fountain and spillway system inside the house," Shoshana explained, "unless we're having a formal party."

Alyxander had retired, with Bucephalus, about ten minutes ago, after presenting her food-gift and a polite minute of conversation. ("It's a shame we don't divert the water through the spillway system more often, but we only do that for a formal . . .") I was wondering what Rat made of the repetitions in conversations, in tastes: V'vish and Kelso, four minutes apart, had both brought small baskets of calla berries, which spoke of far too hasty planning. But Kelso, if I said anything to her, would simply protest: "You wouldn't want him to think we were *too* stuffy . . . ?"

Rat sat cross-legged on the leather cushion, his frayed knee brushing my bare one, while the dry sculptures leaning from the empty pool wrote across my memory the sprays and splashings complex meditations could activate—if I could recall the numbers, damn it! One after another of my parents presented herself with offerings of poached beetle flesh, fried cactus chokes, cheese, *more* calla berries, nectars, pickled lichen, or simple sucking stones.

Still, caught in some seven- or seventeen-hour ritual occasion on another world, I've often thought our informal breakfasts (which never last more than forty minutes) must be *the* optimum towards which all civilization tends.

This one lasted only twenty-five.

And seemed to go on six out of a seven-season year.

"Would you come look at my mines?" Small Maxa said with a slight incline of her head as she gingerly set down a tray of warm meat-patties.

"Yes." Rat stood up in a motion, his feet deep in the cushion.

Maxa blinked and looked confused, because there was no "of course," or smile, or phatic politeness.

She glanced about—suddenly she grinned, turned, and called, "Come on, then," and bounded off, with Rat striding after her over the sandy floor.

"Black Lars," I said, in whose room we had been

sitting for fifteen minutes now, with the sandstone walls to our left and the sky scribed with the towervines growing from the rocks to our right, "*what* in the world is going on? I mean, one brings people home to bed, and everyone is very nice. But why all this?"

"A fascinating human, a wonderful woman, don't you agree?" Black Lars dropped her head to the tray Maxa had just brought, wrapped two patties in two of her tongues, and held them up for me to choose.

I bent down and took one in my mouth, and nipped at her gently a few times with a motion considered horrifying in a number of evelm federations in the far north but which, here, in the south, is accepted as the best we four-limbed, two-jawed creatures can do. I sat back pensively and chewed: spiced shortpig. "Yes, he's fascinating. But I'm biased."

"Your Korga takes food from my mouth—"

"—and mine," I said.

"—like some barbarian from the equator." The bony ridge of her upper lip arched—a sign of humor here but, I could not help recalling, of distress only as far away as Beresh. She turned and licked at her gill-ruff with many tongues at once.

"He *is* from another world," I said.

"And that's what fascinates."

I frowned. "Black Lars, you've traveled to almost as many worlds as I have. We're both in the same profession₁. Why are—"

"I've traveled to half as many worlds as you have, Marq. I only work on worlds where, as on Velm, there are admixtures of both human and nonhuman societies—as you know. This is not the situation for you and your human sister, Alyx. And my jobs usually take three times as long as yours to perform, which is a thing we have discussed before."

"Oh, Black Lars—" I put both my hands below her aluminum-colored claws and squeezed the rough pads from which they extended. Her long spurs closed to the back of my hands. "In a moment we shall sound like squabbling northerners. And I know those squabbles, even here in the south, are real—"

"When we came into the student quarters last night," Lars said, "Korga told us of Rhyonon that had been de-

stroyed. A whole world: that's frightening, Marq. And Rat
Korga is the living sign of that fear, as well as the sign for
the possibility of surviving it. Rat told us the journey here
was to learn of our world. How wonderful that you lust so
completely for someone and someone so completely for
you. Because Rat *is* a fascinating, and frightening, woman.
But then, we are all fascinated by what terrifies. Go."
Before I could say anything, she loosed one claw, bent
forward, and put out her smallest tongue near my ear and
made it say: "Take Rat Korga dragon hunting. Then the
two of you come back to sup with me—an informal supper. Just us. Bring food if it would make Rat more comfortable. I love you, Marq."

"I love you, Black Lars." I turned to lick her tongue,
still humming from where it mimed vibrations mine could
only make in conjunction with voice box and oral cavity.

Maxa materialized in the lichen-hung entrance bower,
pushing aside flapping leaves of gray and purple.

Rat, hands at his sides, walked in behind her from the
limen. Maxa turned to grin at him.

Rat said: "I have never tasted anything like that before. Your mines are beautiful."

And Maxa, leering with pride, pressed pale fists to
her thighs.

Now Tinjo came in with an older woman (human) I
did not know and some bark pudding. The woman and
Lars recognized each other and started laughing about
something. And Tinjo kept on taking up Rat's hand and
saying things I guess she thought were poetic. But that's
Tinjo.

Jayne stepped out of the entrance practically as Tinjo,
with Maxa before and the woman after, went in.

A swaying evelmi followed her, someone I knew Jayne
spent much time with recently, but whose name I still was
not sure of. Both Jayne and her friend dropped lieg leaves
at the edge of the sand (which you do ritually if you're not
bringing food) and apologized that they both had to run.

And ran.

Immediately Sel'v and Large Maxa came in with a
shallow tray of spiced oil and commonplaces about the
weather around the Hyte. I said something about hunting.
Sel'v curled her tail through the sand and expanded her
green tufts. Max's wings fanned once as she settled, blowing sand against the wall.

The tray went on the sand that Black Lars smoothed under it with the midleg's brush.

One after another we bent our faces to touch our lips to glimmering yellow. After they had left, with ritual good wishes for the hunt, I glanced at Rat, to see his face still coated, cheekbones to dripping chin. I took up my napkin and laughed. (He hadn't touched his own.) "Wipe your face—like this—and the rest of the meal will be much more comfortable for you." I gave him mine to wipe with.

Hatti materialized in the luminous glow behind the leaves and came quickly through them, across the sand, green bark clutched in her hands. "I heard you were breaking your fast with us, Marq. And with your new friend, Rat Korga. Here are some tasteless nothings to cleanse the tongue since I am so late."

"A fallen shell is not only beautifully curved without and brilliantly colored within, it contours the currents flowing about it," I said and nodded.

And Korga, who had heard me repeat this traditional greeting eight times now in twenty minutes, repeated it himself for the seventh and, though it was completely inappropriate for anyone not in your own nurture stream, totally charmed another of my mothers.

"I grow some of the edible rhisomes indigenous to the north in the grounds around my room," Hatti explained. (Boiled, chopped, and mixed with alum they numb both human and evelm tongues.) She stepped down and opened the bark to show her breakfast offering. "A little of this, and you will be ready to hunt."

Black Lars turned her head to take the obligatory lick at the mud pool—obligatory, fortunately, only for the host.

Hatti (my mother the nematode geneticist$_1$) pressed her face into the chopped roots and raised it, with morsels sticking all over her mouth and chin.

Rat, who by now had learned, bent forward and licked off a few and then a few more. Hatti turned to me. I licked some from her cheek and then one from her nose. Hatti turned to Black Lars, who, with one tongue, left a spot of mud on Hatti's forehead and with another took off a few pieces of root.

Hatti sat back on sandy cushions. "You're very sure of yourself, Rat."

Alum tingled my tongue, obliterating the tastes of volatile oils and corrosive juices.

Rat just watched her.

She said: "You have firm lips." Standard end-of-breakfast talk, it happened to be true. "Soon I hope we will get a chance to converse for a length of time, free from the oils of hunger and the stones of flavor."

"Good," Korga said for the ninth time. "I want to talk to you too."

It was grossly impolite. Still, I'm sure all my mothers translated it: "I want to taste what lingers behind your lower lip," and made exceptions.

And Black Lars and I both—because we're really rather alike—mulled on the changes in this opening meal of the day that had occurred here in the Fayne-Vyalou to make it performable by (not to mention acceptable to) infiltrating humans.

Hatti held the leaves up before her face, turned, and hurried through green and purple.

Black Lars looked at us again, her broadest tongue extended now, cupping water that she had held in her mouth from the meal's start. One of her tongues beneath asked: "Would you like the final drink before setting off?"

Rat got up on his knees, leaned forward, and, one hand supporting the mottled flesh, sipped noisily.

"No thanks, love," I told her. "Got to dash. See you this evening." I pushed up from sweaty leather. "Rat, if we're going to get to the hunting grounds . . . ?"

"Good hunting," my sister said. "Good singing."

3.

We walked across green flags, over colored clays, between ivory cactuses, along clinking brown rollerways that carried us under overhead parks. "We'll have to stop off at the hunting union to get gear. You negotiated breakfast well. Here in the south, because we use such a range of feeding techniques—hands, implements, communal and individual feeding, or what have you—it can get pretty confusing for a human like you. Or me," I added; then felt awkward for adding it. "Anyway, it can get pretty confusing for humans. Or evelmi—" and felt more awkward. "I mean for anyone who's only used to one."

Korga said: "It was much like my home."

I looked up.

We were ambling across the blue stones of Water Alley.

"On my world," Korga said, "people wore hanging masks that dangled in pieces before their face. They were only supposed to turn the masks aside to eat or make love; or sometimes if they were working hard. On my world both love and food could get even messier than they do here."

I started to protest. But I'm diplomat enough to know that even on a single world one culture's variegated informality can be another's unholy mess. "You know," I said, "if you would be more comfortable, you could get such a mask for here. No one would mind—"

"On my world—" As we came under the shadow of a pylon supporting a section of overhead park, Korga's eyes lost silver for green— "I never wore one."

"Why not?"

"I think it was because—" We walked around the fountain base, dry as the Dyethshome spill— "I was always hungry . . ." He seemed to wonder at his answer. "Or because I was a rat." Perhaps I wondered and projected wonder into his rough voice.

By the pillar near the butcher's union door, copper hair, tanned hands—the redheaded apprentice stopped her headlong charge and clutched stone, staring, panting.

The gold-clawed apprentice behind her rumbled: "There. . . ."

The little human went: "Shhhh . . . !" as I glanced.

I smiled and was silently curious. Rat walked beside me, not looking. I looked; I waved.

The evelm apprentice reared on her hind fours and raised a gilded claw. "Hello, Marq Dyeth. Hello, Rat Korga."

Rat looked over now and raised his hand in acknowledgement.

Then a carping voice—Si-id on her morning inspection tour—called the two to come back in and get to work.

The human waved; the evelm arched her lip-ridge; and both were gone.

"You're becoming a well-known figure. I wonder if it was students, tattling? Or my siblings and parents, dropping little hints at various unions on their rounds of play, work, and survival?"

Rat nodded—and I wondered to which of my comments, on his world, nodding was the proper response. Rat's hair—dull brown with the red kiss in it human blood dries to—clawed at his ears, curled at his neck. "They told me this might happen."

"Back in the Web?"

"Yes. There."

We walked over cracked, dusty blue, and I thought: In anyone else that inflection would have to have meant, "There as well," implying she had been told it dozens of places before. But Rat's grasp of our language's music was so awkward, it was impossible to read the various subtexts that inscribed their co-messages on the flow of his breath, or among the stutters of his de- and re-voicings, rough melodies, and stops.

"Up this way," I said.

We mounted the narrow metal steps, the black finish pitted with past hotwinds. The support girders wove around.

We came out under Iiriani among broad blue and orange mural-fungi; their great sheets swayed above the gravel.

Rat blinked on mirror-bright balls.

"If we're going to walk across the city, it's nicer to do it up here in the park."

At the rail to this particular park (parks make a net above the entire complex, with, here and there, even broader parks a level up: we could see three of those from here, like giant tables whose webbed and re-webbed legs stamped down into the green and blue foliage that spread away on this one) only one woman sat on a curved bench, her scaly head bent over a reader which put out a fan of shadow up about her face. Two children were galloping about between a clump of cactuses further on, every once in a while one rearing back to spread dark wings, whereupon the other would fall to the ground, roll over, and kick all her legs, her low laughter reaching us like the roll of a gong.

"There're not many people out today," I observed. "But then, we're between shifts."

"Where are they all? Rat asked.

"At work$_2$, mostly." Squinting at him in the light, I realized his eyeballs must compensate for this overground brilliance; his lids were wide on their silver. "Some of them, I suspect, are in there—" I pointed to the moss-grown ridge of the run to our left, then pulled my tongue back in between tight teeth, which always tickles a little: "Did they tell you in the Web what that is?"

He looked at the mossy slope; about seven meters down, blobby bars erupted over the structure to form a free-form vent: "That is a run?"

I grinned. "That's right. Would you like to go in it?"

"Yes. I would."

I said: "This particular stretch is pretty tame by most standards. But it suits me. And the people who enjoy its style frequently come from quite a ways." I joined my hands behind me. "I've never really known if it was because it was so near that its particular offerings became my preferences, or whether I was just lucky enough to have my preferences fit neatly into what was available. But then, I have both parents and siblings who prefer city runs much further off."

"We climb in through there, don't we?" Korga said, pointing to the vent we were nearing.

First I frowned. Then I burst out laughing. "But there's a door right down there!" I put my hand up on his shoulder now. "The problem with General Information—" and then remembered he wasn't on GI— "I mean with information you get from someone who *got* it from GI—is that it's often ten years out of date—if not a hundred. Especially when it comes through the Web. If Morgre were a complex with only an evelm population, then of course we would enter by a vent—the one with the lower sill highest from the ground used to be the customary way. I think that's how they did it in Morgre up until about six years before I was born." I shrugged. "But cultures meld." I turned off the path and started for the entrance.

The door deliquesced.

Cool against my thigh, chest, and face, mist from the sill-trough blew back as I lifted my foot over the—"Hey, don't step in that!" I pushed up at Rat's shoulder—

His big foot came down with the heel a centimeter beyond the trough rim. He staggered around to face me, not looking surprised.

"You're supposed to step *over*. You yell at little kids for getting their feet wet in the door trough." I laughed. "Look . . ." as I stepped over.

The blue liquid, behind us now, began to foam; the foam rose, climbing at the jambs faster than in the middle; and darkening, and shutting out light as the door's semicrystals effloresced.

"Come on," I said. "It's all right."

Rat turned, his eyes gone empty glass; we started up the corridor.

"Oh, yes," I said—as Rat stepped wide of the irregularly shaped footpool with the bubbles shifting about on it—"you *are* supposed to step in that when you come in from outside."

And did.

So he went back and did too.

Tingling heels drying, we walked down the resilient woven flooring of the shadowy tunnel. Here and there along the arched ceiling or the curved wall, a meter-wide vent, or sometimes a three-meter-wide vent, let in light.

The abstract statues along both sides, no matter how many times I come in here (three, five, ten times a week since I was twelve—at least when I'm home), always look like people for the first few seconds, till your eyes adjust to the dimness—at which point you begin to make out the people, humans and evelmi, who stand or stroll among them: not many in this run, this time of day.

One I did recognize came over to me, didn't bother to sniff my feet (in case they do is why you step in the foot trough) and nuzzled my groin; I scratched behind his wide purplish gill-ruff (the male and neuter evelmi's most sensitive erogenous zone) and his great wings quivered a bit— and I walked on.

Korga looked at me with empty eyes.

I smiled. "You know, we've been going through this once a month at least since I've been coming here. I still don't know his name, and we've only had real sex maybe six times in all those years. Still, he comes over and greets me every time I come in. Or if I'm here when he comes in, I always greet him. Are there any statues that particularly intrigue you? If they're all too baffling, I'll just point out my favorites." I touched his arm. "It goes without saying, if you see anyone who attracts you more than the statuary, just go on over."

The hollow-eyed face looked down. "This is where you come for sex?"

"And sculpture." I nodded for him to follow me between two high vegetal shapes of plastic with a ring of taste plates at licking level. "At least for the day-to-day variety when you want to spend less than twenty minutes at it on your way somewhere else. The sculpture, at any rate, is a bit restricted. . . ." I nodded at the construction on our right: a female evelmi with claws of an impossible verdigrised bronze but, other than that, an uncannily lifelike reproduction. At the uncannily high level of reproduction, the artist had worked in a number of subtle contradictions: her turmeric-colored gill-ruff rustled as though she were perched on a mesa edge, moments before a hotwind. Her lowered head moved back and forth over a fraction of a degree as though she might bend to sniff the feet of anyone who passed in her run. The scales on her mid-haunches flexed slightly recalling the movements an hour after birthing (which only occurs months *after* hotwind time)—internal machines provided her with a dozen shadows of life, all from completely incompatible situations (at hotwind season, females do not usually come into all-male/neuter runs), the more shadowy for their bizarre dislocations—shadows that, as I watched, I wondered if Rat could even sense, much less feel the piece's dark and oppressive ironies. "Modern stuff. Very experimental," I said, and felt silly passing on these judgments that only brought home their arbitrariness. "Very unconventional." We wandered on until we came to the structure of black globes, pocked with crystal lenses, sending needle beams into the other black globes that, from floor

to ceiling, hung motionless in their suspensor field. "On
the surface of most worlds worth the name, there're
very few serious reminders that there are other worlds
about. When I got back from a diplomatic mission₁
three years ago, and dropped in here on my way home,
I was surprised to see what I assumed was a schema-
tic representation of one of the information nets in the
Web. Each of the worlds was represented as the same
size; the information itself is suggested by beams of
light . . . it all seemed too pointed not to be intentional."
I nodded sagely. "It's a giant model of microscopic luminous algae that you can find in the cover puddles floating
on the top of -wr's in the colder latitudes south and north.
At least that's what the artist told me when I looked
her up in the GI catalogue and called her to send my
compliments."

Mouth slightly opened, Rat raised his hollow eyes.
(The sculpted balls were black and opaque; light lanced
between them.) His eyeballs were black and clear. On
them, seen from the side, light lay out its web in a small
reflection.

"Excuse me." The hand on my shoulder, from weight
and heat and texture, was not his. I glanced back; so did
Korga. The other hand was on Korga's shoulder. The male
(human) said, mostly to me: "Could I interrupt you two
long enough to take your friend to my friend . . ." He
gestured with his tongue at a purple-black evelm, standing
a few meters down the run, foreclaws off the ground,
darting long and short tongues from his jaw, creating no
sound in anticipatory lust.

I said: "You must ask my friend."

Korga said to me: "Will you watch if I go? Please?"
And to the human: "Is it all right if Marq watches?"

The human, surprised, smiled and shrugged at once:
"Yes. Certainly. Of course." And to Korga: "You have
come from very far away, am I right?"

Korga glanced at me.

"But that's no matter." The human hand dropped
from my shoulder but remained on Korga's.

About ten meters up, there was a large ceiling vent
that let in its dozen trapezoids of light. I stood at the
shadow's edge, joined—before the three of them, Korga,

the human, and the evelm were through—by a dozen others, their cool scaled haunches and warm fleshed shoulders jostling mine.

"On my world, there were pictures—" Korga said, then interrupted himself. "Did you come?"

"Yes. . . . But you didn't."

"I was too excited."

"That can be a problem."

"Mostly by the human—but the other . . . you see on my world there were pictures," he repeated. "Of creatures, like that. Lizards. Dragons. Some had wings."

"The evelmi aren't dragons," I said. "And confusing an evelm with a dragon is rather like confusing a human with a chimpanzee."

"Chippa . . . ?" asked Korga.

"To be sure," I said. "There were probably no other primates besides humans on Rhyonon. Not that I've ever seen any in vivo myself. Still, dragons are what we're hunting, Rat. Evelmi—like you and me—are women. You don't know what goes on in the north of this world. A good deal of the trouble comes from certain humans getting rather confused about just such not-so-fine distinctions."

"But there were pictures," Korga said. "They were imaginary pictures. They weren't real. I used to look at them—sometimes for hours. They were beautiful. Some of them had wings. Some didn't."

"Females and neuters have wings. Males don't—generally. Of course that's true of evelmi, dragons, and half a dozen other trisaurian species on Velm."

"But I'd never seen one alive before. I never knew I could feel . . . lust with one!"

I laughed. "If I can, you can. And I have, many many times." We turned by a black, shaly structure, one of whose protuberances actually went up and out an overhead vent into Iirianilight. "That's Japril's decimal points at work again."

As we approached the wall, it collapsed into the trough. Handfuls of foam dissolved into clear blue between the ornate, tarnished jambs.

4.

An upper park lay shadow over us and the dark sand we came out on. Pole-lights laced their long reflections on the plastic blister rising among banks of maroon shrubs. (I looked for the light in his eyes—but his eyes were again white and green.) Some women—most human, most pregnant—came down the further path, carrying their heavy breasts and high bellies above the dim dyll clusters hanging at the tops of the squat rock cactuses that grew thigh high here out of the direct sun.

"The union we're going to is just down there," I told Rat. "Before we go down, would you like to see—" and some diplomatic sense (the same that had finally taught me to deal with Thants) decided me that ritual direction rather than ritual request would be less confusing: "I'd like to take a look at my old nursery. Come with me."

We walked across the clearing, between the shrubs, up to the carved wood rail around the plastic shell. "Look in." I leaned forward. "Go on. Look."

Beside me, Korga leaned among the narrow leaves and gazed through the plastic wall.

Each big as a big woman's two fists together—say Korga's—their infant fur, which would darken in a decade and fall off except for the leg pelts, now dull pearl, their belly scales metallic copper (some few out of them had silver stomachs), infant evelmi lay on their backs, kicking their six legs leisurely, licking and licking and licking their lips.

"There's another nursery just below it, where human children are taken care of before they start their official study groups," I told Korga. "Human and evelmi have such different life styles and rearing styles. Evelmi aren't ready for gestural language until four and verbal language till six. But it's still astonishing how much we've taken over from them. Not to mention what they've taken from us."

"Do they ever mix them together?" Korga asked. "All of the children, from both races?"

I watched Rat gaze at the evelm infants. Clawless fingers; pale fur that would become dark scales in maturity; what northerners called the "milk tongues" dominating their mouth movements—I guess because northern humans started it, the term is frequently considered offensive here in the south; but I always heard it in my stream, both from humans and evelmi, and I was ten before I learned to be circumspect about using it outside. "They all play together several hours a day." I glanced down at his big knuckles, his rings, his gnawed nails, remembering my time here. "More and more as we both get older."

Without looking up, Korga said: "Those women back there are watching us."

I didn't look up either. "Are they?" I tried to recall them, the humans in simulated purple scales; wondered if they would look away when I looked up. "Well, one of the more famous runs that females, neuters, and males use together lets out just down there. They're probably wondering if you're going to go in. Really, there must be quite a web of rumor forming about you. You've gotten quite popular in—well, it's under a day."

Korga's hand closed on my shoulder. He moved closer to me. "Should we go on, Marq?"

We walked along beside the pentagonal bases of the pole-lights, circling the big dome in which evelm infants so slowly grew. At the path side, we passed a meter-wide grill through which came the muffled screams, shouts, sobs, and laughter of the very loud human infants growing up below.

I glanced back at the women—who were, indeed, turning away; one gestured for another to look away.

"There's a drop-lift over there," I said. "The hunting union's a few levels down." We walked through different vegetations, none local and each from a vastly different latitude, each requiring careful and individual tending here in this alien clime by the night-shift gardeners$_2$, absent this morning. And because their foliage was all pale blue, I wondered if Korga took in any distinctions through his false eyes.

5.

Only a few other women were on the lift down with us, two in rather worn work tunics, one in a clean pink one with a spiffy new union insignia I couldn't quite make out because there was an anxious guy standing in front of her and swaying, naked—she must have been on a labor$_2$ sabbatical and leading the far more anxious life one does in such situations.

Through the gridded floor, I watched the cable loops drop faster than we did. At the next level, the irregular ropes and metal railing shifted, clanked, rose, and a very boisterous group of oldsters surged on, so that for half a minute we were caught up in the thunder of their converse, as this one jumped and waved her claws over the head of a friend to get the attention of a third, while that one, in her excitement, furled and unfurled great, red-lined wings.

Silence throbbed, a level after their departure.

We walked out below the thirty-meter pillars. Korga looked across the maroon and blue tiles stretching between them. In the distance a wall of mosaicked reliefs and light-shapes curved and recurved.

After a few more steps, Korga just stopped.

He looked some more.

"This is the second industrial level," I told him. "But it gets more ornate, the further down you go." The evelm influence. Humans seldom combine labor with anything *this* decorative.

Most of the unions on this level are entered from the top. Here and there over the floor, carved gates stood around entrance portals; workers$_2$ filed about. A few sleds, winged like dragons, with two or three women leaning at the rails, made their ways along farther transparent lanes. "We can walk," I told him, "or we can go up—" I pointed at a stairway to the overhead rollerways, fringed with ivory plants, indigenous to the hive caves one finds only in the north—"and ride."

Somewhere, wind rose a moment, then quieted. "Let's walk," Korga said, eyes still up and moving.

I began to walk.

His hand shifted on my shoulder; Korga walked with me.

As we came up over a blue, shaly outcrop, set each side with old statues that had belonged to some ancient labor co-op, here before the city was sunk, the sound of whirring treads cleared from the irregular underground winds.

"Hey there, you—"

I hadn't heard the tracer tank nearing us; I was surprised. I guess all the other attentions Korga had received today made me start to move off.

"Marq, how are you doing there?"

On the side of the big tracer's twin cabins' slant walls, with six handles both human and evelmi can hold, Santine hung and grinned and licked.

As the tank rolled up on its tri-treads, some of the youngsters craned over the mid-platform rail. Once Santine and I had worked$_2$ together in a fourth-level produce distributor union; and three years ago we had shared upstairs and downstairs living rooms, during a joint inner city labor$_2$ break—from which I had left on several diplomatic missions$_1$, then happily returned, days or weeks later, to the smell of excellent cooking. She waved a leg and a tongue, as the tank swept by, and called something into the grill—presumably she was telling the autodrive to halt.

The rumble became a whine.

The tread belts sagged, slowed, halted.

Santine grinned on. "I've been looking for you. We've found enough of *your* garbage—since you got back from Beresh, Marq. But you, my friend Korga, have had a very clean visit so far. Though I assume you were both at breakfast . . . ?" which, as a greeting, was informal, illegal, and highly complimentary.

It made me uncomfortable, nose to toes.

Korga waited, his hand still, still on my shoulder.

"Santine," I said. "How are you doing? And why are you doing it here?"

"I wanted to see you and your friend." She let herself swing out from the outrider by one set of claws. "I hoped you wouldn't mind."

"Korga," I said, "this is my old friend Santine. Santine, this is my new friend, Korga."

Santine leered happily. "And these—" She gestured toward the rail behind her— "are some of this season's most promising cadets. Korga, you're a student at Dyeth-shome now . . . ?"

Somewhere above me, Korga nodded.

"Well, if you want to transfer and come to the tracer cooperative, we would certainly be happy to consider you."

"What is the tracer cooperative?" Rat asked with characteristic bluntness.

Santine looked first unbelieving, then laughed. Some students looked at one another.

Santine, who after all has met other-worldlings before, said: "We . . . well, collect and dispose of the refuse that the women of Morgre leave behind them in the course of their material lives."

"They also record it," I said, glancing up at Rat; "they analyze it—that's how they knew about our breakfast—they make maps of it, which are carefully charted against the maps they made last week and last year, so that they generate both a synchronic and diachronic picture of just what material life in this urban complex is doing at any point in space and where it's been going between any points in time." Every sixteen-year-old evelm—and ten-year-old human—has to spend four months working and studying at the tracer cooperative, learning about the ecology of our urban complex, as well as learning the techniques of how to learn more about it. The ones with a feeling for it are invited to come back in fifteen—or ten—years as primary workers$_1$. "Santine and I met when I was a very young and she was a very old cadet there." The tracer cooperative is probably the single most prestigious institution about the city: "The tracers also form the primary advisory council for the domestic and industrial boroughs that govern our complex." I turned to Santine. "Have I about covered it? You know that Korga is from another world."

Santine's turn to be uncomfortable: "Our job$_1$, yes, is complex. We try to do well," she said, a bit inanely.

"I am complimented," Korga said, "that one of your profession$_1$ would want to meet me," which is the kind of treatment a tracer$_1$ like Santine expects.

Santine nodded her large scaly head and smiled her large scaly smile.

A cadet just behind her leaned over the rail and blurted: "But you don't have a world at all now—"

Another just behind: "Are you going to live on ours?"

"—here in the south?"

"—at Morgre?"

Korga looked at them.

Two more had stood up to see him. One, I noted, holding on to the upright rail at the cabin edge, looked as if she had just been, or was about to be, very upset—two or three tongues constantly licked her upper lip ridge; her rust-colored claws flexed on the upright pipe.

"I do not know yet," Korga said.

And for the first time I considered possible limits to his visit; beneath his hand, chills spilled my shoulder.

"Well, if you do decide to stay," Santine said, "in six days you have to register for one job_2 or another. I know it's a little unusual for the invitation to come like this, but then, you are a somewhat unusual visitor in a somewhat unusual situation, Rat Korga. If you would like, we would certainly be happy to consider you at the tracer collective. There are advantages to the job_2—but I'm sure young Dyeth can explain them to you."

"Thank you," Korga said, with that disconcerting calm; and said nothing else.

"That's very kind of you and your cooperative, Santine," I added; warm surprise overlay the chill. "It really is."

"Well, we'll let you go on." Santine knotted her claws and rapped on the grill. "Come on! Let's move!" She inclined her head toward us. "I'm sure you have other things to do than stand around yakking the morning away with a bunch of tracers with shit under their talons and their minds on Arvin," which is part of the ritual modesties necessary to survive when you are that high up in a culture that so prizes egalitarian ideals. "Good to see you, Marq."

A chatter of tightening treads; a whine; a rumble: the tracer tank rolled away Santine and the gawking students, till ribbed hangar doors folded back, and they grumbled into a flood of blue; I glimpsed the grapplers that would carry them to the interlevel where they collected the refuse for their field work.

"That's really something," I said to Korga. "It's funny, but I have no idea why this is happening. Still, everybody seems to know about you."

We came down the three rough steps in the rock to the tile level.

"On my world," Korga said (and I glanced up at his eyes, expecting to see them gone crystal, but there had been no change in the light: they were still a human white and green), "it was always assumed there was nothing about me to know. Here, everyone seems to know everything. I don't know—perhaps it is the GI they can't connect me with. But the feeling, Marq—" His hand slid forward on my shoulder, then back, and he moved a little closer to me with the next step— "is much the same."

The tile floor here was mostly yellow. Five rollerways met above us to the left in a formation we used to call a star-junction. . . . "Rat, when I was a kid, we used to call that . . . but then, I don't know whether its name has changed or—"

"Why are all those people waiting over there?" Rat asked.

The hunting-union entrance was surrounded by a gate topping a low wall of reliefs carved from blue-black stone.

Clustered around the entrance leading down into the union were two or three dozen people—some sat on portable mossmats that they had brought along. Most stood in little groups. On any other day I would have simply thought it was a bigger than usual hunting party collecting.

"Excuse me. But perhaps you know. Is the survivor here yet?"

Korga and I both turned. And I just knew Korga was about to say something honest and awful like: *I am the survivor and this is my friend*, or maybe, *Yes*.

"Over there," I pointed quickly. "That's the direction he's supposed to come from."

The three youngsters hurried off.

"Rat," I said. "What do you—?"

"Why are all those people waiting for us?"

"They're waiting for *you*," I said. "And I don't *know* why." I felt not only uncomfortable but awkward. "I guess we better just go on." I thought of back doors and service entrances—there was one to the hunting union, actually, on the abandoned canal system that you could get to by going about twenty-five meters down and through an archway humans had to duck for. . . . We started forward.

Something made me want to rush on. In the attempt to appear we weren't rushing, I felt I was hobbling in slow motion.

I don't know how many knew what we would look like, or how they knew.

I didn't hear anyone shout (or whisper), *That's them.*

I know that the first few women we passed were not looking at us, or if they were, were looking at us as they would look at anyone.

I know that the last ones all stood together, about a meter back from us on both sides, mostly smiling, a few gawking, evelm tongues a-twitter, human ones hidden behind teeth—smiling teeth, but teeth nevertheless.

Someone about three rows back called: "Have a good hunt!"

Someone on the other side said: "I was up on L'kr'l Slopes yesterday, and it was a pretty good gathering 'scape for—" till her friend nudged her.

Because they were smiling, I smiled too. And even felt good about it—though the good feeling wobbled upon a fulcrum of discomfort.

Korga looked around at them with a calm and unsettling expression about his green eyes, over his pocked jaw. The bright stones hung on his fingers.

I lifted the hook.

We pushed through the gate—

—and dropped through onto desert, set about with racks of grapples and radar-bows and portable blinds. Blue sky above us. About us a few union apprentices were carrying equipment here and there for even fewer clients. (I thought about whispering of my uneasiness. But the relief, surrounded by Korga's silence, was almost as paralytic as the discomfort itself.) Beyond gorse-scooters, sand lay to a horizon under a streaked sky. The Hyte's fumes twisted in an oestern colonnade.

Korga turned eyes, gone silver under Iiriani, about the union.

"A cassette," I told him. "Just like my room."

His hand relaxed on my shoulder as we stepped off

the entrance plate onto sand. When a clerk came up, Korga dropped his hand to his side.

"We want a tandem scooter for the day." My shoulder tingled. "I don't know if my friend here can handle a number-nineteen bow, though that looks like his size. It's his first time. He may feel more comfortable with a seventeen, or even a fifteen."

The clerk reared back and looked Korga up and down. "We have a few half-sizes in. Let me start her out with an eighteen."

I turned up my hands, dropped my head: "Do it."

The clerk hurried off between racked radar-bows. We ambled after her, among clerks and clients.

I don't know how the information followed us across the city; I don't know how it followed us into the union. But when the clerk came back around the end of the rack with the beautifully scrolled black and silver radar-bow, I knew she hadn't known before but that she knew now. "Would you . . ." She held the bow out by its damasked wind-vane. "Would you try this one, Rat Korga."

Korga took the cross-piece with one hand and with the other grasped the web of bowstrings—clearly he'd never held, or seen anybody hold, a radar-bow in his life.

"Here, just a second—" I grabbed the stock before the clerk did. She settled back, with faintly quivering wings. "Basically you handle it here—" I hefted the forestock— "and here." I grasped the arched shoulder brace.

Korga took the bow by stock and brace.

"That's right. Now hook that around your—don't let your shoulders hunch up!"

He didn't.

And *every* seven-year-old human, not to mention seventy-year-old one, who feels for the first time that unsteady weight down on her shoulders (it always seems heavier on one shoulder, but you can never be quite sure which one) tends to hunch up her shoulders for the first few hours, if not the first few days, of wear.

Korga got the stock, with its lateral indentation, under his arm; chest brace and alternate shoulder brace stamped their padded feet against his pectorals. Still, somehow their weights, with his own natural musculature working against them, seemed to pull him into the stance of a (human) hunter to the bow born—though one hand was down at the far end of the boomerang-shaped haft, where I've never seen *any*one hold it.

"This thing up here . . . ? That's to hold onto." I tapped the stained bone handle with my forefinger.

He slid his left hand up the brace.

"Wait! wait! wait—!" the clerk twittered with three tongues, one after the other. She reached forward, released the spring-clamp between the two bone pieces that made up the grip so that it separated to its greatest width.

Korga's bare, big-knuckled fingers clasped the expanded handle. "What's this?" Rat asked, looking down with metallic eyes at the cup quivering on three small chains just under his chin.

"Oh," the clerk said, "you put oil-soaked cactus bark, or various flavored pebbles in there, and lick them. While you're waiting for your quarry."

"You seem to have that pretty well," I told Korga. "Now just see if, still holding it like that, you can get into a crouching position—"

Korga squatted—which ended his natural hunter's stance. I steadied his shoulder and didn't laugh. "Not *too* bad. But try it more like this."

Diligently and dutifully, we three got Korga fairly comfortable among the vanes, scrolls, cords, sails, handles, grips, and braces of his bow. It seemed to fit. We went down two racks more to find me a size thirteen with an old-style selenium guidance system. (The new ones are supposed to be easier, but I've never gotten used to them. I'm offworld too much.) At various times two clerks and three clients looked around and between the racks to stare. At least three times I realized our clerk, even though she was fitting my bow, was a lot more interested in observing Korga than helping me. "We'll take a couple of daykits," I told her, as she looked back at me for the third time. "Really, that should do it."

"Do you want to take a portable blind with you?" she asked for the second time.

For the second time I explained. "We're only going to try the feeding grounds today, and since this is my friend's first time, I don't think we'll need one." (Blinds are good for the spawning grounds where the dragons can get a little feisty.) And for the second time the clerk arched her upper gum in faint surprise.

Any other day, I would have stayed around to ask about what the morning's kollec on the union perches had been, probably gotten into a conversation or two with some other prospective hunters, swapped two or three hunting tales and songs. But as we walked with our bows back among the racks of equipment, with this clerk staring and two clients ceasing their conversation as we came by, I just wanted to leave—and found myself angry and confused at Rat's even gait, which took the hunter-union's sandy ground no faster than the run's yielding floor.

I tried not to seem as if I were hurrying, and looked, I'm sure, like someone both hurried and confused. The clerk came with us to the scooter rack, stepped smartly around the back foils. "This one—?"

"Here, Rat. You sit there—you can hold on either to this strap, or put your hands on my waist if that's more comfortable."

The clerk lifted the large bow from him and joggled it down into the scooter's side braces, guiding its sails into the sail slots and pushing in the positioning ratchets.

My own bow went into the brace on the other side. I got my leg over, slid my bare butt back on the spongy seat, got my feet into the foot guides—which felt wrong. "Excuse me," I told the clerk, "do you have any human foot stirrups, to fit this one? These are still set up for evelmi."

The clerk dashed off, dashed back; the stirrups were changed in about forty seconds. Someone came to look; two others, already looking, walked away. I reached forward and pulled up the polarized sand shield.

Through the curving plastic, I looked out on—not sands, lichen, and the far horizon. (They, we know, are illusion. And the polarization cut them out.) The scooter was standing on a metal ramp, with more ramps either side of it. Ahead was an ornate arch in a stained enameled wall, its ornaments gritty with the dirt that collects on the real anywhere illusion reigns.

I glanced back at the clerk, who was stooping on the sand to strap our daykit to the back bar, the Velmian sky brilliant above her, behind her the orange plains and reddish mountains.

"All ready." She stood, stepped back.

"Just relax, Rat," I said. "Hold on, and when we turn, lean with it and don't worry." I looked forward at the shield—desert outside it, the enamel and metal of an urban traffic-way through it. With my heel I ignited the ignition.

We leaned forward, slid down the ramp—the union disappeared (Korga's hands were momentarily iron on my flanks); and the view without and within the shield matched.

We rumbled into the tunnel.

Left of us, behind the mesh fence, the transport rollerway carried stacks of cargo at twice our speed. Right of us, a few more scooters scooted through; and once a covered kar overtook us and moved up ahead to disappear in the tunnel lights' changing patterns.

I felt Korga move closer in behind me. Later I reflected on how well he took the curves—not like someone whose first scooter ride this was; and I've ridden with my share of those, evelmi and human. The tunnel curved and straightened around us. We curved. We straightened.

Through the air rush, I heard him speaking down at my ear: "Those radar-bows are confusing objects. They are strange weapons." And as we neared the tunnel's end and the true light of the desert opened over us, I realized suddenly Korga had no idea what, in a dragon hunt, we hunted.

TEN

A Dragon Hunt

More mica than sand.

With such an erosive climate, how does this land sustain so many edges? I'd asked the question as a child. General Information had let me over-lick several explanations, all of which centered about the geological forces underlying the markings and measurings of three-thousand-kilometer rock-plates floating and crashing (oh so slowly, over millions of years standard) above magma, as they tend to do on woman-sized worlds. To skim the mica sandshifts—these ten-centimeter ledges that worm the upper plateaus, over which silver falls in veils—was for me to traverse all the informative forces below that underwrite this landscape.

Down a cliff ragged with purple fungi, the Old Hunter moved by boulders, her daykit lashed between her wings with rags. Rags are human-made; our daykit was tied to the scooter's guide bar with the traditional yellow cord of fine braided cactus fiber. Cultural contamination? Cultural exchange? I've thought both over the years; I will think both again.

I halted the humming scooter, leaned it over, and got the triple stand stamped properly into the sand.

The sails on our bows wavered either side. The bowstrings buzzed notes too low for even dragons to hear. I kicked my foot out and swung my leg over the seat. The sand was still cool from the morning chill; kilometers away, a few twenty- and thirty-meter needle-rocks spoke of velmological happenstance.

Korga, all shoulders, knees, knuckles, and heels, dismounted, carefully awkward.

I grinned at him.

He gripped the handrail. Iiriani smoldered and exploded in his rings as he held it, dulled in his palm's callus as he released it.

"There's been good cliff-purchase as well as sage-signs for a couple of kilometers now," I told him. "We should find sizable dragons feeding." Microscopic and blue, sage is what dragons eat, and the cliffs, in the distance, rising broken, black, and yellow, are where they go to eat it. Korga stood beside the scooter, his broad hand on a bow sail, once more looking like a human hunter born in the brace and handles. "This is good hunting territory, Marq?"

"For what we want, we could probably hike a little further to the—"

Crunching over the heavy lichen at the road rim, the Old Hunter raised her dusty snout. She blinked her black eyes slowly, only tongue tips tasting in the dry air the dust that dulled her upper lipbone.

Korga turned to look, leaving his hand where it was. And what had been a brave stance, by the simple movement, again was comical. I saw the Old Hunter lick that awkwardness with her eyes and not change her expression.

That's why I loved her.

She extended one tongue: "You women are going hunting."

I nodded; and still wished she'd look away—or Korga would. "I guess so," and laughed, finally able not to care, with another memory of my own first hunt. "How's the catch been?"

Her head wagged a little. "Nothing so far. But there're dragons to sing of over oestwards." Her wings, without unfolding, hunched up on her back. She came up another few steps, claws too dusty to tell her origin, their points blunted by the sand she lived on.

She lifted her foreclaws a bit and raised her head, looking over our equipment. "Hello, young hunter." That was to Rat. "Where do you come from?"

Rat moved his hand a little down the sail. "Another world."

"Yes," the Old Hunter said. "I've heard of such among you humans. Is your world in the north?"

The young hunter in me jumped to explain. But the older one put her hand on my shoulder (where Korga's hand had so recently calmed me), and I watched.

"My world . . ." He paused, turned, and looked at our sun—his eyes momentarily blinded me. The afterimage, as I turned now, starred the landscape black. Rat pointed about thirty degrees above the horizon— "is there, about seventeen-point-three-four-two thousand light-years away." Sun in a red stone on his forefinger vied with the mirrored balls under his lids. I wondered if galactic orientation were also within those rings.

"That's where the tiny yellow dragon flies." Her lip ridge arched and other tongues came out to try the tastes we laid on the air. "The yellow dragon." Two indicator tongues came close together, miming 'tiny,' which Rat, I knew, would miss. "Your world. Yes. I taste your meaning, young hunter."

The tiny yellow dragon is an imaginary beast and part of a minor but famous and rather complicated local myth cycle; I watched Korga hear it and not understand.

"Your sweat leaves a strangely metallic taste on the air, young hunter," which, for the first few days after I came home from a mission, in some artificial offworld environment, strange evelmi are always saying about me too, though my friends ignore it. I pondered how short a time he'd been here.

"Well, while you are hunting dragons, I shall be hunting you. And maybe when we have finished our day, we can sing of our catch to one another." Her paws came down on the warm soil. "Remember, young hunter, as you aim through the sights and sails of your bow, I'll have you centered through my sights and sails."

I pulled down the release strap of my bow brace; the bow slid toward me and I caught it by the haft.

"You are Marq Dyeth."

I grinned, as pleased that she had recognized me this time as I had been the first time it had happened on my third hunt when I was a child. To evelmi most humans look pretty much alike. Those living with numbers of

humans develop their strategies for telling us apart; and
those who live for years in the same house with us have no
more difficulty distinguishing us than we—who live with
them—have distinguishing them. But the Old Hunter herself had once told me, years ago, that the only way she
could tell one human from another was by how she held
her bow. "Good luck to the two of you." Her spurs flexed
above the sand.

She turned away down the ridge.

Korga was looking for the release strap. "Marq, what
did she mean, she would be hunting us?"

I pulled the last sail out of the brace's sail slot. "She's
going back to her blind, where her bow and gear are
stored. And she's just letting us know that she's going to
be after us in exactly the same way we're going to be after
the dragons."

Korga stood. "Then she is our enemy." It wasn't fear;
but you could read fear into it. "We must avoid her,
Marq. Perhaps this is not a good day for us to hunt—"

"She's our best friend in this world," I told him. "The
Old Hunter, and hunters like her, are the reason that in
some of the southern geosectors, evelmi and humans can
live as one society. That's not the strap you want, Rat. Pull
the one below it."

Rat pulled.

The bow brace swung out.

The sails quivered, leaned—

"Catch hold of the haft!"

He did. And stood, the black-scored, light-absorbent
sail rising by one shoulder, the white reflectant one by the
other.

"Remember how you were holding the bow back at
the union? See if you can get it like that again—no, your
left hand a little further forward. There. That's more like
it."

2.

The Vyalou compresses immense variety into a landscape
that always looks, from any one position, comparatively
uniform.

We stepped over silver-shot sift-ribbons. On foot, we

wound the narrow paths between igneous boulders which
had cracked in two, the coal-black faces veined with yellow schist. We crossed a natural bridge over a dry gully
that had once been an underground river, left there by
early human colonists, whose roof had caved in. We paused
at a place where white blossoms the size of pinheads,
which you had to look at from less than a dozen centimeters to make out their individual petals, lay across the
sand, aping the north-polar frosts. We set our bows down
on their three-jointed feet; I made Korga put his ear to the
sand to hear the subvelmian thrum of waters crashing
some seven meters down—in a newer colonial waterway,
which an Old Hunter had assured me, in my fifteenth
year, would too lose its roof and dry, oh . . . within
three-quarters of a century.

"There, look—!"

Korga's head came up, sand and mica on his ear's
curve.

"—can you see her flying, toward the crag?"

He squinted silver into the sun. "Yes. . . ."

The dragon disappeared behind the stone.

". . . I saw her flying." He brushed sand and mica
from his cheek.

I got up and hoisted my bow. "Let's go on."

Korga hoisted his.

We trudged.

We crawled under a fallen sheet of elephant lichen
(ancient gift of the Web); it's dried crust lay over a gully so
close to the ground I wondered if we could get our bows
through.

We did.

We climbed a red-rock slope with its black and orange pittings.

The dawn wind was steady south. Once I looked back
to see, behind Rat, the Vyalou undulating away. The
nearer sand-sifts were dark lines, now and then pricked
with light.

"Around here and down . . ."

Rat caught up to me. I moved nearer to the ridge,
parked my bow beside me on the rock, and leaned over. I
heard Rat getting free of his own. Then his shoulder
brushed mine; his rough hand came down half on stone
and half on the back of mine.

Directly ahead, three beasts lazed and gentled on the air.

A wingless male was crawling down the rocks, going away.

Much higher up, another dragon, like a bit of sloughed tolgoth bark caught in a wind-swing, dove back and forth before Iiriani. As a child, when I'd first seen such configurations I'd always assumed the high beast was keeping guard for the others. Usually there'd be two or three males around—then I saw there *was* a second male, clawing around an outcrop of reddish stone to the right, talons making pink puffs as she scrabbled.

Two of the winged beasts planed toward one another and away.

The females' wings were wide as mechanical worm-strainers, half again the spread of their intelligent evolutionary cousins' and well over twice the area. Ethologists have described them, as I now whispered to Rat, as small herds of land-bound males, from two to ten, who roamed the rockier areas; and small flocks of females, from three to fifteen, who hover for a day or ten around them, before taking off to find another herd—while a lone neuter, almost half again the size of the females, flies high overhead, her singular flight patterns initiating intercourse among all three as she carries her load of nongenetic reproductive information. About seventy-five percent of the offspring are borne by the females, about twenty by the neuters, and five by the males. The male dragon birthing is violent, almost always injurious, and frequently fatal—it seems to be, evolutionarily speaking, on the way out. In the evelmi, only females and neuters carry—males sometimes have practically unnoticed abortions, though male births occasionally occur in folk tales and legends: it's probably projection, not racial memory, though there are adherents to that theory, too, in the north. "The fertilized zygote," I went on, "can end up lodging in either of the three sexes, though only the females and neuters seem biologically equipped with an efficient way to get the infant out of the body. Mostly what the muscles that control their wings really do is help in labor. People are still speculating on what environmental conditions nudged evolution in this direction sixty million years back when the pattern got established."

Rat pointed up at the highest flying beast. (Those immense hands could get dirtier quicker than anyone's I've ever known!) "That's the neuter . . . ?"

"I think . . ." and squinted, "that's probably a female. The neuters are usually much larger; and they fly so high you frequently can't see them at all. Though that *could* be a younger neuter, coming down for a while. . . ."

His hand came back to my shoulder again. We watched, as one female dropped to the soil and, with thrashing wings, beat up a gray-black cloud whose curling edges paled purple and shredded. She leapt away through her own dust, turning and cawing, as the males lumbered over, first one, then the other, pausing at the falling dirt, then one and the other nuzzling it.

"They're going to eat any micro-sage or mural-fungi she's turned up," I explained. "Good deal, huh? You want to take a few shots here, or look for a more active covey?"

He turned to me with silver eyes and that blank expression I would eventually learn to read as gentle laughter. "You tell me, Marq."

"Well, maybe we . . ." I gnawed on my back teeth. "But they're going to be here a while. Let's go on. If nothing better turns up, we can always come back."

Suddenly I was very aware of the heft of his hand, of the brush of his hip against my flank—he turned blazing eyes on me, his jawbone working behind pitted skin. So we stayed to make love, in our parked bows' angular shadows. He came twice, I, once, and we joked about it. Later, both our hands wet with his urine, we lifted our bows and carried them across the irregularly darkened sand he'd paused at to pour. I looked around for the Old Hunter, wondering if she had shot us already from some ledge, fissure, or cliff-niche. But neither her wing's dark sails nor her bow's bright ones were visible above rock or ridge.

We trudged on.

We found another covey.

We halted.

Rock rose to the oest. The ridge rolled up west. Over the remaining 215 degrees, sand and bramble fanned down from our crevice.

Dragons dove.

Dragons soared.

Three rose together, nipping at each other's lips, wings working, turning above and below each other. One huge one tore loose and rose and rose and rose, till she was an ash of night flickering on the day.

"*That's* a neuter."

"She *is* much higher than the other one was."

Dust at half a dozen places drifted around dragon wings.

"There're at least nineteen in the covey."

"Twenty-one," Rat said.

I nodded, wondering how he could count them that fast. Though it's something I had seen old hunters do. "The activity's good. The energy's high." I hauled up my bow, got the brace around my neck, the stock into my arm. "Do you see one you like?"

"You said," he said, "to pick one whose flight was beautiful."

I nodded: "Get your bow up." For a moment I really thought he was going to ask me: What is beautiful? "When you fire, try to think your own body into the same position as your quarry's. That'll make the transition less of a shock." I slid one hand forward on the brace, the other to the release.

More slowly, he lifted his.

"Got one all picked out?"

He looked at me with eyes gone normal in the shadow of the rock beside us. We squatted together.

Dragons worked in dust and sun out on the sand and above it.

He fired first—I heard the release *click*; his body jarred, as though some subvelmian troll had sledged up at the ground under his feet. Rat looked at me in blank astonishment.

"You missed, that's all." As V'vish and Max had explained to me on my first hunt, when I was seven, it's pointless to try to prepare someone for the effect of either a miss *or* a hit. I said: "Better aim a little more carefully. You probably don't want *that* to happen again."

He turned back to the flock.

I sighted through the cross hairs. "When you pull the release, make sure it gets to the second click," I told him. "That throws in the automatic tracker and raises your chance for a hit by a factor of six or seven."

At the same time as I realigned on a far female arching magnificently behind low dusts, I heard his bow, raised toward a flying form above mine, *click-click*. Then the black and silver creature cleared the haze and darted up through my sights. I pulled—*click-click*—and threw myself through myself—

—doubled in one sense, skewed in four others, my wings under-thundered gray sand in a dragon's eye. Breast bunchings lifted. At the down beat of spiny wings, small bones bellied: hollow bones thrilled; my eyes shook with sand. Handless, high, bouncing in air six sets of claws could puncture, fluting through bone, I searched dragons for his eyes in hers, flapped through dust looking for his in his. (Sand burned my heels as I leaned back, twisted in bow thongs.) Amazed and lazy on the lifting gale of some other dragon's wings, she soared. I sailed after, chasing him by chance. (It's the feeling you can control your dragon's body which is so strange, though it's only because you know so well all she knows so well.) Double all syntax, wondering what his movements hold; she held to the air before me, and I spired away, spying some male below in which I was less interested than my hormones were. She turned on the spoke of a breeze, and my spine's scales went quivery at the neuter beating above. Awareness in the splay and undulant vertebrae. The wing turned up in light like dust; lost in eyes with neither purple, rods, nor cones, the pattern of her dyed, and died on, my techtum. The more complex eyes of most velmian life see far more afterimages than we mammals: thus, we/they live under that different time her philosophers have storied. I saw her at a distance as a point-time event. I saw her up close as ten seconds' history made synchronous by its multiple shadows. Rat, written all over her (at least to my tongue), rose up, flapping wings, body bending. I arched my hips down for other males under my belly. My mouth was big enough for the whole of this landscape, through which tongue, over and after tongue, licked and lusted. I rose and watched high dragons rise. Why do dragons fly, I mean according to them? Dragons and their hunters know: the nerve endings concentrated in the flesh below the joint of wing and body is of the same order as those in the human genitals or the lining of the human ear: the stimulation of rushing air excites them—the sensation dying at precisely the rate (established by ages of evolution) to make the wings flap enough for lift-off. A permanent around-the-body high? Fly! I flew. Dust settling on one of my tongues made a fine mud speaking of silver salts and tolgoth pollen which other females had passed over. I rose, torn from the dust-bound males. My breast crawled, anticipating descent. Sex and hunger sweep round in the human body, through the day, failing and driving like unentailed tides, peaking together, or ranged in opposition: the drive that drags and pummels a dragon's body toward the behavior humans mistake for sex is almost three times as strong, far more pervasive, and concentrates in such different parts of the body—the pads of the middle set of claws, the flesh along the back culminating in two extraordinarily sensitive rings around the gills, the underside of the water-bearing tongue, and the upper side of the weakest taster—that humans, become dragon, sometimes cannot recognize it for hours. (Evelmi fare a little better, taking only minutes.) And there are two other drives that contour the actions of most trisaurian life, neither of them properly speaking hunger as humans know it. One is a yearning for a variety in tastes that can, if stifled, become true pain beating through the skull. The other is a gentle bodily urging toward certain kinds of motion. Together they can produce a behavior that looks, to a human, like a creature satisfying a ravenous appetite—only something, perhaps the darting about to different substances as avidly as a human would devour one, is off. But knowing the dragon's body from the inside is an adventure of a different order: in human women, hunger and desire, each sunk deep in the body, are always present, either as a full or an empty field. In the dragon the three drives, the one raging, the other two at sift and drift, in their various rhythms, are inconstant. Afterimages of Iiriani arched and lingered, paler and paler, as it went further down, mapped against my oscillate rise. I glimpsed the wider wings of the neuter above, and chills detonated my spine; my gills erupted rings of excitation, and I arched away, borne under the beat of other urges, to drop through the world built in my mouth, while Rat, at my shoulder, rose, her wings wild over, a racket on all, all over our

aural techta, the single sensory unit at cerebral surface
that, neurally congruent, women and dragons share—

"I was a dragon . . ." he said, voiceless enough for a
whisper. "I was a dragon? . . . I was a dragon! It was as if,
for a moment, for a year, I was a dragon myself. I didn't
stop standing here, but I . . ."

"The radar bow hooks on to a pretty complete map-
ping of the dragon's cerebral responses and, after a lot of
translation, plays it back on your own cerebral surface."

"Was it twenty minutes? An hour? I . . . I couldn't
tell how—"

"About seven seconds is the maximum it can hold.
Your shot was probably two and a half to three seconds.
That's about what a good beginner manages. But there's a
time disorientation factor."

"—how long I was a dragon. But I *was*!"

"Yes, you were." I glanced at the higher rocks behind
us, where the Old Hunter was removing her bow and
drawing in her wings, settling back below her rocky rim;
for the same seconds, she had been an alien male hunting
dragons on her own world.

"It's like reading," he said. "It's like reading a—!"

But I didn't understand and turned instead.

Korga turned to look where I looked.

I guess he saw her—and understood.

He raised his bright hand to hail her. Sunlight cut his
forearm where it cleared the shadow of the boulder I still
crouched by.

"Hey, Rat?" I stood. "Are you ready to sing of your
catch?"

His human eyes locked on mine, perplexed.

"Eventually, we'll actually run into the Old Hunter—or
maybe someone else."

"I waved to her. Why didn't she . . . ?"

"She probably just wasn't ready to sing about it yet.
When we do run into someone, they'll sing to us of the
quarry they've caught. We'll sing to them."

"The Old Hunter will sing about . . . being us?"

I nodded. "There're hundreds of traditional songforms
to cover the traditional forms of the experience. Those
from the last three hundred years that deal with evelmi

hunting humans—to be sung to human hunters—are among the most beautiful. But I'm biased. Anyway, you can deal with it any way you want. Amateur enthusiasm is always appreciated. And most hunters don't even attempt the traditional forms until after their seventh or eighth hunt." (Was I going to tell him that, precocious me, on my third I'd improvised a perfect single-voiced kahoud'di'i'mar, whose syllabic counts, sound repetitions, and alliteration patterns I will eventually set out for you? Vondramach Okk, on one of her visits here, became interested in some of our local song forms. She wrote a set in her private language, including a kahoud'di'i'mar, which is actually where I learned it. She also wrote about them in her journal—on the same page with her notes on possible assassination techniques for Secretary Argenia.) "If you'd be more comfortable with it, I'll teach you a short, traditional piece that will certainly do if we run into anyone." Three years ago, we'd taken some Thants on a dragon hunt. The catch had been superb, but the singing had been one of the traumatic confusions that can only happen between world-widened cultures. "It would only take me about three minutes to teach you a ditty that—"

His eyes turned to the naked ridge. "I would rather wait and hear you first. And perhaps the Old Hunter."

"Sure," I said, hoisting up my bow. "Sounds fine with me." The evelmi have high tolerance for the enthusiastic human amateur giving some local custom a go; in the north it's probably one reason for the trouble, just as here it is the reason for the peace. But that tolerance has taught me much of use for my profession[1].

Korga squatted to get his ringed hand under the haft, his bare one around the neck brace, and stood up with it.

We walked till we found another covey. And, with enthusiasm, I made two more shots—for there are a couple of songforms Vondramach never heard of that can be used to sing of multiple hits. Korga said he wanted to sit these shots out and simply observe me in my few seconds' contact—which is perfectly understandable, though because I've already done it, I also know is rather dull. If you look like anything at all during those few seconds, it's just mildly drunk.

* * *

Almost as soon as we turned from the natural blind of orange shales, two women cleared the ridge beside us, their braked bows glittering all about them under Iiriani. One was human, one evelm, both female; and both carried their bows with a surety that spoke an easy bowmanship greater than either Rat's or mine. One flexed her wings between the fiber cords that bound her daykit to her nape. Her companion, who had frizzy brown hair and freckles beside her nose, hung back a few steps, watching.

Momentarily I thought we would fall into that strained silence, resulting in meditation, that so frequently attends the encounter between strange hunters before song. Such silences may go on for half a day and baffle northern humans, who'd rather fall immediately into fighting than endure such protracted uncertainty. But above the ridge poked the broad and dust-darkened snout of the Old Hunter. "As I grow older," she said in her booming, burry voice, "more and more my task seems to be to introduce you one to another. Stand, forward Ollivet't."

The woman with the daykit bound between her wings bent to let her bow stamp the gravel and came forward on claws whose steely black put her racial origins from about the same area in the south as our big algae-farmer$_1$ back at Dyethshome.

"Ready yourself for song, Ollivet't."

The woman glanced at the Old Hunter, lifted first her left claw, then her right, and recited: "Thank you for permeating these dry healthful airs with the taste of my name."

The Old Hunter, her own kit still bound with soiled human rags, her gumbone stained and pitted, her face scales dull and ragged, came a few steps down the slope. "Stand forward, Marq Dyeth."

I set down my bow, stepped forward, then, in place lifted first my left foot, then my right. "Thank you for permeating these dry healthful airs with the taste of my name."

"Ready yourself for song, Marq Dyeth."

As the Old Hunter came down a few more steps, I looked at the woman across from me. Her facial scales, with only the light dust of a day's outing, held none of the damages of a life addicted to cerebral radar transfers in the wild; her gear was strapped with the traditional cord, rather than the cultural intrusion of fabric; her sharp claws spoke of much time spent in the better-tended, frequently refloored runs; and her proportional age was not far above mine.

We were all quiet for five, six, seven minutes. Knowing the difficulty humans can have with such pauses in communication, I wondered whether it was the synapse-jamming or simply life on Rhyonon that held Rat through the silence.

Ollivet't finally said: "I see, Old Hunter, you do not know my companion. Allow me then to usurp the tongue movements of the Introducer. Stand forth, Shalleme."

The human woman crouched expertly to shrug from her bow. Her finger- and toenails were painted gold, which meant she had been born far to the north, or wanted to be mistaken for someone who had been—though in the south fewer and fewer humans paint their nails each year, which, as long as the custom continues otherwheres, becomes a sign of origin in itself. She came forward quickly to stand by her companion, lifted one foot, then the other, so quickly and slightly one had to know the action to think it more than a flexing of her knees. She said, with a contralto richness that, in humans, still surprises me (though it shouldn't): "Thank you for permeating these dry, healthful airs with the taste of my name."

The Old Hunter said: "Ready yourself for song, Shalleme." After another wait of about three minutes, the Old Hunter went on: "I know this last young hunter, but I have not been privileged with the recitation of her name. Now I must choose between my right of relinquishing my privilege as Introducer, or my right of conferring a name on anyone who survives in my memory under the sign of the tiny yellow dragon." The Old Hunter came down the rest of the slope, moved over to Korga, bent her head to flick one of her tongues at his smaller toes (remember those foot troughs in the run), then ambled over to taste the dust on Ollivet't's midclaws, then stepped toward Shalleme's gilded feet but did not actually touch them, then came to me and licked first one of my testicles, then my knee, then walked back to Korga.

He watched her but (and I was thankful) did not say anything; and didn't put down his bow. I began to let Thantish memories leave me.

One tongue waved over one of Rat's feet, then over the other; two others darted out and retreated. The Old Hunter looked up, narrowing her eyes at Iiriani's glare. She took a few steps backward, up the slope, unfurling one wing, blackened on both sides with age, and folding it again, slowly. "I have chosen between my rights. I shall confer a name on you, youngest of hunters. I name you the Yellow Dragon's Daughter."

Korga carefully and awkwardly shrugged off his bow: first from his neck brace, then from behind his chest supports. Two legs ground in gravel—it teetered . . . but he steadied it, so that it didn't topple. For moments, he stayed crouched, looking at it as though the third leg might suddenly collapse.

Carefully, he stood.

Then he stepped forward.

He glanced at me, lifted his right foot, next his left. (I winced: it was the wrong order, but no grave matter.) His eyes, burning, moved from mine to the Old Hunter's, to Ollivet't's, to Shalleme's. "Thank you . . . for permeating these dry, healthful airs with the sound of . . . no, the taste of my name."

As he glanced at me again, I grinned at him. His pitted face absorbed it.

"Ready yourself for song, Yellow Dragon's Daughter."

The Old Hunter, with her six-legged gait, moved a few more steps back up the slope, shrugged her own bow off onto the sand (a perfect three-point landing, despite the incline), raised her foreclaws, expanded her gills, opened her mouth, and sang.

3.

It was a simple, beautiful, traditional song—I'd heard it fifteen or twenty times on various hunts ("I have come to carol my search for a quarry of the mind, only to encounter in the mind of another. . . ."); I was both moved and disappointed. There are flamboyant songs, sung with seven or more tongues at once, full of buzzings, clickings, and poppings, highly rhythmic, where one tongue actually slaps and vibrates against the others—songs designed almost exclusively to impress and excite humans, true. But if a human is untutored to the ways of dragon hunting, dragon singing, it never fails to convince her that she has encountered something truly beautiful, alien, and strange. They are vulgar songs; most hunters consider them somewhat cheap. Yet, oddly enough, because evelmi invented them for us, they make an astonishingly good bridge by which a human mind can move on toward an appreciation of true evelm singing. Then there are a number of songs that are complete appropriations of human musical pieces—evelmi have, after all, many tongues to sing with and can create an impressive range of sound with each—which, if only for the respect it shows directly for a human art, opens up the way for a mutual appreciation to grow. But the song the Old Hunter chose was of neither type. Its barking roughness, its single-voice drone, its limited tonal variety drifting about within a four-note range, required a thorough appreciation of the hunting song tradition, and in its most local form, in order to appreciate its rich beauties. And Rat possessed that appreciation no more than a Thant. But he listened, quietly if not attentively. By the end of it, the song's loveliness had touched me again, even if Korga could not really share it: its rendering was, finally, impersonal, meticulous, exquisite—which are all high compliments in this tradition.

When the song was finished, after the slow, final minutes of looser rhythmic improvisation on a single note, the two strangers smiled at the Old Hunter; so did I; Rat turned to me to see what he should do—a cloud passed from little Iiriani-prime, and, as he turned back, his eyes, which had the while gone human, blazed like mirrors. The human woman stared, blinked, frowned . . .

Nobody spoke though—it would have been unbearably out of place.

A minute later, Ollivet't began to sing, and I thought I recognized the stress repetition pattern; almost immediately Shalleme began to sing with her, a partially improvised duet, of a sort that I'd heard had become popular in the far oest. (Oest of what? It simply reflects the northern orientation of the humans on Velm.) The idea is that the single-tongued human adds her voice to the multiple voices available to the evelm, to increase the complexity rather than to compete, with only an impoverished instrument. As Ollivet't now brought two more, now three more of her tongues to the stressed and unstressed syllables, I marked the song of the dragon-flight's multiplicity, richness, and beauty, and marked how my world's culture had changed, under the impact of humanity, to make me, a human, part of it.

Their song completed, I silently smiled my approval. There are detailed commentaries enough to occupy a lot of human lifetimes and a good number of evelm ones on how the nuances of the performance may reflect (or pervert) the experience they represent. A year spent traveling along any of our world's university chains, and you will have been exposed to more such commentary than anyone should be expected to bear. Suffice it that I was impressed.

When I looked at Korga, he was standing with both hands joined before the groin of his pants, heavy human knuckles masking the jewels that extended his perception, his concentration, his comprehension. He was the only one of the five of us, I noticed, who wore clothing. Was it a sign of his alienness? Stripping myself of thought, I bent my head a moment, then began my song.

I don't know how well it went over. There is a tradition among the Dyeths, which dates back at least to Vrach Dyeth, Gilda's first adopted child, that humans should learn to sing as well as we can by our own standards in order to render our music. I took endless singing lessons— went around *breathing* all over everything—as a child, from human and evelm teachers, as have many, if not quite most, humans in the south. I have a pleasing voice, and a fair comprehension of the hunting song's fine points. I sang an old single-voiced form I thought would be appropriate: "Here when I hunt with a friend, phantasms of flight . . ." It alternates highly formal sections, on which I rather outdid myself, with improvisatory sections, that now seemed just lame—there *was* no way I could sing of what was unique for me about this hunt, at least not through any spontaneous outpour.

I finished. And the Old Hunter, as well as the pair of strange hunters, was smiling—the strangers more because of what my approach to song meant about me, and therefore about what one was likely to find in the world around here. After all, they were from a good ways away. I don't know what, if anything, they thought of it *as* song. But that, as Santine once said to me, is what you can never know and I can never tell you.

Only a little too quickly, Rat took a step forward. His eyes were closed. (I'd never heard anyone sing a hunting song with eyes closed.) When he opened his mouth, just a little at first, as if to taste the air, I was suddenly overcome with a cascade of anxieties. Did he even know what a song was? Only hours ago, he had completely misjudged hunting! In that inter-cultural presumption which may obliterate the intelligence of even the most experienced diplomat[1], had I simply presumed my total surround was his surround in a way which the first sound from him would make all too clear?

The first sound came. (Why didn't he open his eyes?) I have heard some evelmi say the untutored human voice is generally more pleasing to them in song than the trained one—even though they respect the training's intention. The rougher vibrations more resemble the multiplicity of sounds from multiple tongues. The speech impediment that blurred his accent leached all pitch from the note; but pitch is not the priority in hunting songs. That's why evelmian concepts of harmony, which are quite complex, are nevertheless so difficult for human ears. What I heard first, by whatever part of the ear meters and measures and counts despite all conscious intention, was . . . well, as clear as any pattern I'd heard that many times: dactyl, spondee, dactyl, trochee—the second beat of the spondee alliterating with the first beat of the second dactyl, and the alliterating sound repeated a third time on one or the other of the trochee's syllables. That, at any rate, is how Vondramach began her description of the form. Though Okk invented her own language, Okk scholars have been debating for years where she took her terms for prosody from. The only thing everyone agrees on is that they're not hers, and go back a ways. Spondee, double trochees (that rhyme), spondee, with the stressed syllable in the following anapest alliterating with the first syllable of the initial dactyl; then iamb. Now the first cesura: then dactyl (its first two syllables alliterating), trochees, second cesura; anapest, trochee . . . What was coming out of Rat's mouth was the form which had once taken me three months to master: Vondramach's version of a kahoud'di'i'mar. The words, however, were improvised and his own. I've writ-

ten them out for you once, though without their rough
melody: "Doubled in one sense, skewed in four others,
my wings under-thundered gray sand in a dragon's . . ." I
listened, searching for explanation. (". . . Rat, written all
over her, at least to my tongue, rose up, flapping wings,
body bending . . .") There's a fairly simple one, though
my mind had to scurry after it in the midst of my astonishment. On the high-silver soil and shale about, convoca-
tions of rock can act like reflecting antennae; and partial
overlay of his hunting experience into my memory or mine
into his was certainly possible if his bow shot or mine had
hit such a hidden silver mass at the proper angle. Partial
exchange? It had happened to me two or three times
before and hunter's tales are full of them. But such a
complete one? The only reason I could put together how
he could have lifted the whole songform from my mind to
fill it with his own roughly accented language was simply
that we had another example of Japril's decimals at work.
Through his recital, I watched Rat, then the Old Hunter.
She seemed pleased with her young hunter, the Yellow
Dragon's Daughter. Well, she had reason. But watching
her, hearing him, I realized that most of my fears for the
stranger loose in the alien land were unnecessary. Whether
he observed the proper information on his own, picked it
up by whatever method from me, or figured it out on his
fingers, whatever labor he laid to the task, the transition to
my home world seemed for him no more than the rushed
flights of gnats returning to the surface of some oil slick,
perturbed perhaps because of the shifts in its rainbow
colors, but still recognizing the basic scents they had left it
with when they had abandoned it in the morning. I looked
at the two women as Rat concluded his song. (After an
anacrusis, the initial spondee repeated, followed by the
four final dactyls, terminating with a long though unstressed syllable:) ". . . cerebral surface that, neurally congruent, women and dragons share—"

When Rat finished, the Old Hunter was already turning, already moving away—we Velmians on this side of the
Fayne-Vyalou are great on greetings but not much on
good-byes; and the Old Hunter had heard many songs,
would hear many more. A hasty departure was another of
her rights.

But both the women stayed; as I waited, curious, and

Rat waited for me to finish waiting, Ollivet't took a few steps forward. She said: "Nice singing," with one tongue out the side of her wide scaled mouth and her head cocked to one side.

"Yours too." Tell me how I knew they were tourists in our area; they weren't in reds. "Has the hunting been all you hoped?" Tell me *if* Korga knew.

"We've enjoyed it. Do you know the area well?"

"I've hunted in it on and off for twenty years."

The women looked at each other and made their respective racial signs for relieved amusement.

Shalleme stepped up beside her companion. "Perhaps then you know the way to Morgre complex? We've been hunting down along the whole length of the Fayne for six weeks now. But it's not too well marked around here."

"Certainly," I said. "None of the local hunters you ran into could help you? I've known the one who presided here for years. I'm sure she would have given you directions."

Ollivet't said, "I have not hunted in her territory for more than thirty. So I did not feel I knew her well enough to interrupt the proceedings."

I nodded. "I see. And there was no other Old Hunter that you encountered locally?"

"We ran into one," Ollivet't said. "She had wonderful songs, a great store and fund of lore—"

"But she hadn't the faintest idea where the urban complex was," Shalleme finished up. "Well, that's hunters for you. We were hoping we might follow someone in. Our scooters are only about a kilometer away. . . ."

I glanced at Rat: odd how I was slowly learning to read approval in his silver eyes, though they, of course, were what actually remained unchanged in the still face around them.

"Your song," he said, suddenly and surprisingly to the woman, "was wonderful."

Shalleme looked at his alien eyes with her human ones. "So was yours, Yellow Dragon's Daughter."

I said: "I don't see why we couldn't—"

ELEVEN

A Tale of Two Suppers

We'd come with one scooter and small daykits. They'd come down, they told us, with two; and daykit enough for weeks.

They went off to get them.

Rat leaned against our tandem. "Will they have trouble finding us?"

"The radar-bows." I joggled mine, so that it slid fully down into its holder. "They put out a homing beacon in case you get lost. Or in case someone else wants to find you."

Two scooters turned round a distant dune, both riders now crimson in tourist coveralls. Ollivet't hailed me with a red-draped wing over her bow sails.

"Come on." As I straddled the saddle, Rat pushed the brace closed around his own bow, and straddled behind me, hand on my shoulder, hand on my flank.

I stamped stirrups.

Moustache tickled back at my upper lip; beard flattened to my chin. The wind put her three cool paw-pads on my chest and knees.

We skimmed warm sand and mica.

2.

As you come in from the hunting grounds at daytime, Morgre looks very different from my room's nighttime view. Thin sculptures designating the old travel guide, from the pre-human days when neuter and female evelmi who could fly did a lot, leaned beside the human-built highway: pedestals and ten-meter clear display walls preserved by the evelm-human organizations who concern themselves with such. Bow-sail shadows shivered on pitted topping.

Overhead a propeller platform moved above clouds.

Right, humping above a shoulder of blue needles, tolgoth hid the -wr and its fumes. In the distance, Morgre was smudges behind girder-work, with a few towering stone supports walling its north end.

The webwork of feed-paths on our left stretched away to the child's red toys of the Myaluths, interrupted here by a weather tower, there by the verdigrised dome of one of the forty-thousand-cubic-meter water pumps that sucked the lower wet-sands dry, worked by a convocation of huge, flapping thermofoils taking power from Iiriani. At this range they looked like miniature radar-bows dancing beside the greeny globes, over the orange sand.

I don't recall when I noticed the half-dozen scooters zagging the narrow paths laid along the ancient runways. I first thought they were another hunting party—only no bows glinted and flopped on their racks.

I had been aware of them for five or six minutes when I realized, for all their swerving back and forth, how closely they paralleled us.

I thought of speaking over my shoulder to Rat. But air chattered by my ears. Then a moment of heat at my right cheek: Rat's mouth brushed it as he leaned close to shout: "They're following us, Marq . . ." which was neither about our northerners in reds behind us, I realized, nor the group of six. As I glanced back (his mouth still closing over my name), I saw, behind and beyond them another twenty—no, forty, or even fifty—scooters gliding along the sandy strips that lay like gold ribbons in an orange sandscape that would go copper at Iirianiset.

Negotiating the interwoven paths, lingering scooters joined the lead group. And I looked up—our scooter lurched a little—because the creatures laboring maybe a hundred meters above in the air were not small dragons, but some dozen evelm women.

The sky was streaked with the clouds we call fireneedles here and which, only fifty k's to the east, are called 'manshair: nobbly filaments of darkness like wires across Iiriani.

But do you know how rare it is to see evelmi fly?

They flocked.

Among the riders were more humans than one would have expected with a random gathering; almost forty percent.

Flyers and riders flocked nearer.

I looked back over Rat's arm at the two red figures following.

Ahead, three or five feed paths fed onto the highway— and a hundred meters further, three or five more.

Six, a dozen, twenty scooters splatted noise and shadow onto the road. Sound around us trebled. Bony faces passed, staring—too many without scales. (When humans mass in too great numbers on Velm, though I am one, I think of the dangerous north.) *Zub* and *zub zub zub* and *zub zub*, in the welter and rumble passing. Glancing right, I saw a dark face: her gum bluish, her black eyes narrowed in the wind, watching, her blue-black claws clamping her machine's guide bar. Then she dropped away among and behind others. Skimmers pulled ahead and fell behind. Their drafts slapped us like dragon wings.

I wanted to call out and could think of nothing to call. I mauled my guide bar with my hands and marveled Korga's hands did not maul me. We grumbled up on another sand-spilled junction. And, as the scooters had come, they went.

Scooters growled away along feed-paths, out across the plain.

We moved down the raw highway in our own quiet roar; I glanced aside to watch scooters dispersing over the sandy web, under the unsettling flights of the women.

On my left, sound increased. I shifted my shoulders under Rat's hands, and turned to see first Ollivet't's, then Shalleme's scooter pull abreast. Ollivet't said with three tongues at once, loud enough to cover it:

> "WHAT WAS THAT?"
> "WHAT WAS THAT?"
> "WHAT WAS THAT?"

I shouted, loud as I could (it doesn't compete): "I'LL TELL YOU LATER." Then as an afterthought: "YOU WOULDN'T BELIEVE ME IF I DID," and hoped Shalleme could read my lips. It's a talent many of us humans have been developing as a sort of racial compensation.

Their scooters fell behind, and I watched them to detect some reason in their passage—saw only their intentness at driving.

Morgre's stone walls—we were coming in at the Broidwey Tunnel—loomed, blotched high as the wingspread of a neuter dragon with the rock-algae that gives the stony Fayne (but not the Vyalou) its characteristic purple. We dove in.

3.

I'd never seen this many people in an industrial rotunda. Vaulted mosaics hung thirty meters above the covered catwalks, crane housings, and grapples. Guide patterns flickered and faded in clear flooring, dark as Korga's eyes, beneath myriad clawed and nailed feet. I pulled to a stop before a dozen parked scooters, beside the ambling crowds. Fifty meters away behind a wire-mesh wall, a roller ribbon hauled its load of cartons to rotundas further on.

Ollivet't and Shalleme pulled up beside me. The rotunda roared. More scooters echoed in behind us.

"What's happening?" Shalleme asked.

With wavering wings, Ollivet't pulled scaly claws free of her foot holders and came to four feet beside her machine, searching among the crowd. Turning to Shalleme, she showed the tongue configuration (one larger and two smaller) that means the unimportant questioning one could ignore.

Shalleme ignored it. "Is there something wrong?" she asked Rat—at least the question began at him. It finished at me, probably because he wasn't looking at her.

"No," I said, realizing I didn't know how to explain

that I suspected. "No, there's nothing wrong. At least I don't think—" Then I looked at Rat.

He was watching my foot—I'd been kicking at the stand to get it down.

Rat said: "No. No, there's nothing wrong."

Shalleme looked around again.

And Ollivet't's wings were moving.

I still hadn't gotten the stand down right.

"Marq?" Rat asked.

"What?" I got it.

"I think most of these people are here because I—"

"Skinura Marq!" The voice, at initial and final consonant, singsonged.

All ivory today, she strolled up through the gathered women. Most were facing away, the evelmi now and again rearing to see over those before them, the humans now and again jumping. She was tall, closer to Rat's height than mine. Her white body mask was shot with silver. I recognized her as the woman who had come up around my room with the students, as the white peeled away from her red skullcap, from her brown round face with its epicanthicked eyes, this time her amber irises filigreed with black. "Ah," she declared, "by my ancestors on Eurd, so it really is Skepta Marq. I do not need to inquire after the identity of your friend. I already know of Rat by legend and report." She turned to our hunting companions, as the body mask fell away from her lean neck. The gold bar with its ruby-tipped wires dropped on its chain across her sharp shoulders, down her long flat breasts. "But these . . .?"

Ollivet't said: "This is my companion, Shalleme Doru," with one tongue and, "I'm Ollivet't Doru," with another.

"Ah, it's Skalla Ollivet't and Skri Shalleme? Well, I'm delighted. But really—" The petals collapsed from her waist to suggest, below her breasts and belly, an oddly paneled skirt. She made the awkward bow of the very tall. "Enchanted. Now you must all come with me."

"There!" someone called.

I looked sharply around.

"Over there?" and, "I think it's . . ." echoed under the rotunda ceiling. But the surge of people moved somewhere to the right. Five hundred? Five thousand? When you are simply unused to crowds, it's difficult to evaluate their number. I only know that there were more people all around us than could fit in the Dyethshome amphitheater.

"Really," the tall woman said, "I think all you honorable Skryonchatyn should come with me. If they recognize you . . ." She inclined her head toward Rat.

"I don't under—" Ollivet't began with one tongue. "I mean," another continued, "we were only coming into the city here to—"

"All of you," the woman said. "You *must* agree with me, no? It would be safer."

"But what about the scooters?" Shalleme asked. "We were going to park them at the local hunting union before we—"

"You can see—or does it require a logical leap not usual in your culture? You cannot get anywhere near the union's port. If you like, we will leave you here to try—"

"Look," I said. "I'll disk the scooters, and you two can pick them up at Dyethshome later." I pushed a hand under the rough flap of our daykit and grubbed in twine, cloth, and small containers for the plastic-covered circles. I drew out a handful. "Here." I pressed the adhesive side of the green disks against the fork of our tandem, then turned to press two more against the forks of the other women's. "They'll be at Dyethshome in half an hour, waiting for you. It's very easy to find: the largest out-city co-op to the oest. Just ask for Whitefalls. Anyone can set you on the proper roller."

"Dyethshome," Shalleme said, turning to Ollivet't. "Wasn't that where Kessll and Via-pr'd went to study$_2$ about six or seven years back . . . ?"

In the dim light, Rat, his eyes flickering between green and clear, said: "Who are you?"

The tall woman, her hands at her side, her chin raising just a trifle, said: "My name is JoBonnot. Remember that name, Rat Korga. No one likes advice. I give you some anyway. Remember that name. Please." She glanced at me.

I turned from the foreigners, wondering what status accrued in that honorific-clotted home tongue to those free of all of them; and someone else shouted: "There! Just over there."

The black floor beneath us flared. Six inches down in the clear plastic, three-meter arrows suddenly mapped lapped paths about the rotunda. I realized as I looked around us that Rat, in a fuzzy glow of red, was the center of them all.

"Come with me!" JoBonnot barked. "Now they really *have* seen you!"

I began: "But where—?"

"We have supper with your sister tonight, Marq," Rat said, which, in the circumstances, seemed the oddest thing to remind me of.

But JoBonnot grinned at me with perfectly insistent delight. "Ah, yes. A message from your sister, the prudent and insightful Skern Black-lars," which was the way she pronounced it: not Black Lars, but Black-lars. "Her informal supper for the evening has been canceled. If you do not believe me, check the first time we reach a call station. Now come!"

I wasn't in mind to argue. "We'll go with you."

The women scattered near, all faces now, were—most of them—backing away. But between, I could see women running up.

I pushed Rat's elbow with one hand and slapped at the back of Ollivet't's mid-haunch with the other (comes from a local kids' game in which, by such slaps, you urge each other to run); JoBonnot shoved at Shalleme's arm with a gesture enough like mine to make the ID in me speculate briefly on the convergence of childhood games grown up worlds apart.

We hurried away from the scooters, the red glare, the convergent arrows.

"Our scooters," Shalleme said. "Are you sure they'll—" It takes a good three minutes for the identidisk to activate a local retrieval system, and I think she imagined the scooters immobilized by the crowd before they could begin their journey. Me too.

Some from behind were coming forward.

The red location light and bright guide arrows had stayed where they originally had come on—probably because this particular rotunda seldom received deliveries of moving cargo; tracking lights hadn't been installed here.

A few women looked at us as we hurried by. (JoBonnot: "No, *don't* run!") But most stared off at the red glow up from the floor between the three parked scooters.

We edged between some women who weren't watching us and some who were. Ten meters away, the wall of one of the block houses split on blue light. The slate door slid back. Blue flooded the floor. JoBonnot dashed through onto the meshed catwalk and turned to hand Rat, Shalleme,

Ollivet't, then myself among rising cables, descending hooks
and pulleys.

I looked back.

A few were coming toward the doorway. One dropped
to all sixes to run.

From Shalleme: "But where are we—"

JoBonnot said, "Your friend Skya Santine is waiting
for us in the interlevel," and did something so that the
door, much faster than it had opened, closed, shutting out
our pursuers. The railed lift we were standing on lowered.

Ollivet't reared to stare at the overhead machinery.

Shalleme leaned over the rail to gaze down.

"Marq?" from the shadows. "JoBonnot, did you find
them?"

I called: "Santine?"

The tracer's bulk came up. The lift shuddered, locked,
and Santine leaned from the tank's outrider. A bar light
came on beside her, glistening along her flank. "Hop
aboard. Well, it looks like you've brought a whole party."
Santine was alone. "This way."

Squatting to examine the rail catch, Shalleme pushed
something; the rail rose. She stood, looking at us to see if
she shouldn't have pushed it.

"Come on," Santine called again.

From JoBonnot: "Go, now." She herded us toward
the machine.

"Climb in!" Santine moved back from the forward
outrigger; JoBonnot pulled herself up.

We climbed on at mid-platform where cadets had
ridden that morning. A barlight on one side of the tunnel
went off; two on the other came on. Shalleme gave Ollivet't
a hand; she came, forefeet, middle, and rear, a furl of red
wing-lining showing beside her bright tourist vest.

Rat, in his roughened voice, asked: "Where are we
going?"

"Anywhere you like." Santine grinned. "The crowd
won't follow us here. We can get you back to Dyethshome
if you want. Or, if you'd prefer, you can visit with me in
my room on Dylleaf for a while—"

In her white skullcap, JoBonnot swung her head back
around the drive housing. "I would delay returning to
Dyethshome were I you. By now, that's where everybody
expects you to be. That is to say, you will be fairly trace-

able there, and not only by tracers. And for at least another hour or so, all the curious in Morgre will be trying to find you, now you've actually been spotted."

Ollivet't exchanged glances with Shalleme, who leaned against the corner of the rear housing, red-sleeved arms folded over the fringed edges of her tourist jumpsuit, open below her navel. She said: "We've reserved a visitor's room down in the Abakreg'gia—"

"—Perhaps you could take us there?" Ollivet't's black eyes gleamed. She glanced around at Shalleme. "Or take us somewhere from which we could *get* there?"

"We'll pick up our scooters at . . ." Shalleme stood up now and unfolded her arms— ". . . Dyethshome. We'll pick them up tomorrow."

Once more JoBonnot's head swung back around the tracer's cab: "My honorable Skyshottyn, would you welcome our group to your rooms in the Abakreg'gia, if by doing so you could render great aid to troubled women?"

Once more the foreign hunters exchanged looks. "Why should we refuse?" declared, or better declaimed, Ollivet't in a rumbling basso. "Come share our space a while. And perhaps you can explain some of this confusion."

"By all means, generous Skynosheani." JoBonnot swung back and out of sight.

The tracer tank lurched on its fat treads. Ollivet't and Santine immediately sat on their rear haunches.

Rat looked at both and squatted on the plates, ringed hand on the floor, swaying.

Shalleme took hold of the support-bar on the back cabin wall and stayed standing, watching now the tiles, now the girders, now the stone walls of the passing interlevel.

I put a steady hand on Santine's scaled neck and bent. "Where in the world did she learn to drive a tracer?" I whispered into the ridged auditory plate within the curved flaps of dark flesh just before her gill-ruff.

Santine stuck a smaller tongue out the corner of her mouth and said in the blurred boom that serves evelmi for a whisper: "Probably from the driver-instruction program I revised for our local GI service about fifteen years—" and another tongue, somewhere on the other side of her mouth, roared, "standard," and (as Rat and Ollivet't glanced over) went back to the whisperer, "ago now."

I scowled at Santine's left eye, which blinked at me. "What I mean, Santine, is where could she have come from?"

Santine turned her whole large face toward me. "Given the honorific system she uses, Marq, the chances are high she comes from Klabanuk . . . wouldn't you think?" Santine has never been offworld; but, prompted by her friendship with me, she's done a good deal of otherworldly exploration in vaurine. Years back most of her trips had been limited to worlds I'd worked₁ on, but she'd branched out since.

"Where's Klabanuk?"

A barlight on the left swooped its violet across plates and flesh and rails and scales. Santine swiveled her head to me again. "It's an open-run junction about twelve kilometers outside Hysy'oppi Complex—and Hysy'oppi, in case you've forgotten, is about fourteen hundred kilometers north, in G-19."

I frowned as another passing barlight lit our faces for each other. "Hysy'oppi is where you were born!" I said, and looked down at Santine's aluminum-colored claws which darkened to gun-metal as our tank lurched around another unlighted curve.

"With all your star stepping, I'd wondered if you'd remember."

I looked at the forward housing, somewhere to the side of which, and out of sight, the tall woman guided us along the bar lit dark. "Santine, what's the difference between a Skina and Skyochot?"

"I told you, Klabanuk was twelve kilometers away from where I was brought up; though I heard it enough when I was a child, I never bothered to learn the dialect."

We leaned around another corner; and the notion that this odd woman, whom I'd first seen almost a year and a galactic diameter away, hailed from only fourteen hundred kilometers to the west was enough to totally confuse. My mind leapt among explanations, from Santine's possible mendacity to the possibility JoBonnot herself was a free-agented professional₁ of a cunning to dwarf that of her erstwhile companion, Clym.

I looked at Rat, who still squatted beside Ollivet't, his bear hand over one knee, the other, on the plate, five fingers in a jeweled pentalon about which the rest of his tall weight swung as he watched slurred mosaics rush by in half-dark.

We lurched as lift grapples caught us. Shalleme, standing, and Korga, squatting, swayed. I nearly toppled as side grapples hooked into our flanks. There are some outlying interlevel drops that actually use black-chain over two hundred years old; but not this one. We lowered down the near vertical slope.

4.

Several centuries ago, a northern tribe developed a ceramic cooker, essentially a large clay pot, called, yes, a kollec, which is where the term used in lizard-perch divination comes from, by way of a metaphoric leap. You put water (or sometimes oil) in the kollec's bottom, and in on top of that you put a complicated seven-layer shelf with various perforations for rising steam, various ducts to conduct juices down from one layer to bypass another and shower over another still lower. Food on the different shelves cooks at different rates. Juices percolate to form a general gravy at the bottom. Individual essences are collected in draining cups at shelf edges on their respective levels. Elaborate meals can be prepared with a single kollec, and in a number of northern cities humans have all but taken it over for their own foods—omitting the inedible flavored stones and unchewable barks that still make up a large part of Velmian cookery but that we humans in the south are learning to appreciate if not actually enjoy.

The seven-level urban complexes, sunk all over the variegated surface of Velm, have been compared to kollecs in drama, song, poem, and philosophical meditation so often, all over this world, that it has somehow passed beyond cliché to become a sort of classical figure by which Velmian artists of all races signify (almost always in the antepenultimate act of the work) that the drama is to be read as aspiring to a certain ambition.

Abakreg'gia is under the base of the kollec, where the flames lick the bottom.

When Morgre was sunk in '43, ancient caves were uncovered, just as the workers reached the lowest point of the excavation, dating from perhaps a million and a quarter years prior to human arrival. (Could this have been the original Arvin? Yes, it could.) Work on the city was halted for three days; three days were devoted to detailed excavation, which was recorded in vaurine. Then the building of the city recommenced. Instead of filling the caves in, however, since they were at a depth below the official bottom of the city, they were turned into sub-city dwellings.

Five or six huge light globes hung like minor parodies of Iiriani in the sub-urban hollow. The small apartments had been refurnished just as closely to the primitive forms as the Velmian archeologists could reconstruct at the time; then necessary modern conveniences were added. Velmian tourists can enjoy them for weeks at a time, and humans who are not addicted to the light of a real sun can usually enjoy a few days in the falsely lit darkness. We walked along the upper apartment ring of g'gia-9. The nearest light, fifty meters off in the central auricle, laid our shadows over the fallen stones and obtruding boulders.

The amphitheater at Dyethshome was modeled on one in a federation about seven hundred kilometers west at K'l'kl'l, built perhaps four hundred years back. But I have always suspected that the amphitheater at K'l'kl'l was modeled—with how many intermediaries, no one knows—on the million-and-a-quarter-year-old one excavated right under Morgre, from a time when the Vyalou was radically lower.

We came around another rock outcrop.

"Here," Shalleme said, her eyes momentarily closed to consult the GI track guiding her.

The door was a curtain of flexible struts of immature tolgoth, which was the functional approximation the evelm archeologists could come up with to stick into the mysterious perforations along the upper lintel. The floor mat was old netmoss. The webbed wall hangings were based on "primitive" designs from the Judedd'ji excavations at the South Pole, so only half a million years out of date.

There were several modern stools.

There were two modern tables.

And modern means designed to be sat on (or at) by both humans and evelmi.

A holographic window showed a section of Fayne-Vyalou, rather like the one we had hunted in today, supposed to be rather like the landscape around here when all this was above ground.

Ollivet't turned and extended her broad undertongue, in which she had obviously carried water for a day or two now, from their home. With an overtongue, she said: "Welcome to our provisional habitat, all my friends, close, near and distant."

Shalleme bent to touch her tongue to the liquid puddling the mottled flesh; then Rat; then me; then Santine; and finally JoBonnot. With each of them I watched for individualizing motions and movements, but even though I could sense them, I cannot articulate what they were.

Shalleme went over to the wall cabinets to see what stones had been provided. (Rat moved to the side of the door, folded his arms, and stood for all the world as though waiting for instructions.) Ollivet't went about placing her heavy claws first on one rug-covered cushion pile, then another, to test for comfort, lumps, or sharp things left under wraps. Santine went to one Ollivet't had already plumped, tested it herself first with a forefoot, then a middle, then a hind, and curled down onto it, tail, tufts, and chin—then raised her chin a moment and purred appreciatively: "Marq, when was the last time you were here?"

I went to another cushioned pile Ollivet't had tested and sat down cross-legged. "Ten years ago at the least." I wondered if Rat would join me, but he stood, observing from black sockets.

"It's always been a strange place for me," Santine said affably. "With a whole seven layers of city hanging above you in the dark, sometimes women here will be hit with intense claustrophobia. Yet standing on the upper level of the apartment ring, looking over the broken tiers of the million-year-old amphitheater to the skene nearly two hundred meters down, the restored tiles glimmering, many also experience sudden vertigo. As a young woman, I recall coming here and going from one to the other in the space of seconds."

Shalleme had stretched out on her own cushion; and Ollivet't, who had finally found some flavor-stones, came back past her with several in her foreclaws. She went up to Rat and offered him one.

I guess he'd been on Velm long enough to learn that whenever you don't know what to do with something here, lick it. After looking at it for the length of three breaths, he raised the rock in both hands to his mouth to taste.

Ollivet't, now that some formal greeting had taken place, settled back a little without actually sitting, which you can do if you have six legs, and asked: "Who are you?"

From where she squatted, JoBonnot let out a sharp laugh. Her body mask had sealed to her neck again, forming a petular collar.

"I am Rat Korga, who survived the destruction of the world Rhyonon."

". . . destruction of a world?" Shalleme pushed herself up on one arm.

"How can a world be destroyed?" Ollivet't asked, selecting a stone for herself with one broad tongue, then going to offer Santine one.

Rat said: "Fire fell from the sky. Deserts melted to slag. Urban complexes, runs through the wild, and tribal federations were scorched away like flavors burned out of over-charred foods. Cultural Fugue, perhaps." (It was about here that I realized these were all borrowed metaphors.) "Perhaps worse. I alone can say that I was there."

"And that's why all these people are gathering, waiting." Santine regarded her rock while Ollivet't moved on to me, to JoBonnot, to Shalleme. "I would have come out to see you too, Rat, but as Marq's friend, I can see you even closer this way."

Shalleme, glancing at the rest of us who had come from such scattered spots over this one, asked, "What does it . . . *feel* like, to have lost an entire world?"

"Lonely." Rat raised his many-ringed hand to rub at his neck under his broad jaw. "But the loneliness comes from the question."

"The question, hey, Skoilla Rat?" JoBonnot, beside her cushion, rested only a white damasked glove on the webbed and re-webbed cover rug. "Tell a visitor to these alien climes what you mean."

" 'What is it like to lose a world?' is the first question everyone who meets me asks; so I am alone with my own feelings, sights, sounds, and experiences, which can only provide answer to the question: What is it like to be presented with a new one?"

I actually started to ask: What was the first thing I asked you, Rat . . . ? I turned on my cushion, lifted one hand from the rug—and was left with silence, in which I discovered I didn't remember the first question I'd asked him. And wondered if that meant Rat didn't remember either.

JoBonnot laughed. "It seems that everyone—at least everyone currently in Morgre—wants to know who this survivor is, how this survivor survived. Odd, don't you think?"

Ollivet't retired to her own cushion and sat, leaving Rat standing—like someone very used to standing, though. "But I am curious, too."

"You . . ." Rat paused— "create me with your eyes."

While we were all tasting the odd flavor the statement left us, JoBonnot laughed again. "Ah, that is like a poem—like the kinds of words your glorious Vondramach Okk would have put together in her odd and awkward language, yes, Skynia Marq? But I have come a long way to see you, Rat Korga, a very long way. I did not make you by pressing my eye or my tongue or my ear to you. So that is what is wrong with poetry. I think your glorious Vondramach must have known that, for she was a great saint too, yes? I honor her greatly: and I look at you and see exactly what you are, Rat Korga. I look at you and see the clear and cloudy intersections of what you must have been with what you may become. And that is what I have come here to see. And I am pleased with it."

Rat watched her with empty sockets.

Was it the singsong quality of her voice? Or was it just some diplomatic₁ sense? I said: "JoBonnot, you're not from this world, are you?"

She gave me a bright smile. "This world? This Velm, that circles the larger of the binary, Iiriani/Iiriani prime, swirling two moons about it as it goes? Oh, no. Certainly I could never be from this world." She shook her head. "Yes, that *is* a silly suggestion."

"Then why have you taken on the honorific system of . . ." I glanced at Santine— "the Klabanuk area, off in G-19?"

"Did it fool you, perhaps? For just a bit?" JoBonnot shook her head. "When we were together on the other side of the galaxy, I didn't even know whether you recognized it. On your part, very diplomatic, Skeol Marq. Very diplomatic. Really, it was the only recent program available to me on my own local GI series that concerned a region on your world anywhere near Morgre." She looked about the cave, let her eyes close, and drew in a lingering breath as if savoring the local actuality. "So I learned it—just another of the gambles one must take in my profession₁. There is no way to really know if I have won or lost. I fool you. I get a little time: to sit and talk with you. To watch you. To learn. And to teach. I hope I can teach as well as you, Marq Dyeth."

"Are you a free-agented professional₁?" I asked.

"Like my little friend, Clym, looking so much like you?" She laughed, glancing about at the others, while I wondered what they made of all this. "No. Clym is crazy. I am sane. You will find that I am profoundly sane."

"Where are you from?" Santine asked.

"I? Where do I come from?" JoBonnot shook her head. Collar petals flapped. "I thought you'd never ask. I am from a world where what you call night snaps about with lightning almost every day. I am from a world that sits on the edge of the Cultural Fugue and looks at you for aid and succor. Will you help us? Oh, I feel sure you would if you could. I am from a world where the Family and the Sygn contend to establish their incompatible versions of peace. I am from a world you may even know, Marq Dyeth—though worlds are big places and therefore you cannot know it as I do." She slapped her knees. "I am from Nepiy. Got unlimited space-fare, too—though I have to use it within limits. That's better than *some* people you know." In a couple of awkward motions, she stood, while the petals suddenly flapped up to close around her face so that one could see her lips moving behind the mouth grill, her lids blinking behind clear eyescreens. "Would you like to check on my accuracy in delivering your sister's message? Here, we've reached a call station. Between the Family and the Sygn, you know, there's a war on—though it is many worlds away. In such circumstances, with the fate of millions hanging in the balance—yes?—*I* certainly would never let such an opportunity pass to check it out. Oh, no, Skyle Marq, that is not any kind of good diplomacy."

I frowned, starting to wave away her hyperbolic suggestions; but some misgiving made me suddenly stand. "Excuse me," I said to Ollivet't and Shalleme. "May I use your photocall facilities? I'll recredit it."

"Certainly," said Shalleme.

I stepped to the side of the room, where the connections are better. I thought through the access code (my name repeated on three musical tones, followed by the ammoniated smell of cut tolgoth). "Black Lars?"

The blue fog of "hold."

Then Lars raised one claw toward her chest and said, "Marq, I'm so glad you called. Did you get my message?"

I grinned, very much relaxed. "I think so. A woman called JoBonnot told me you canceled our informal supper tonight? . . ."

Black Lars settled back and dropped her claw. "Oh, I'm so glad. I knew you were out-of-city-limits, and wasn't sure how to get in touch. We can expect you and Rat here in an hour?"

"An hour? I thought you said supper was canceled."

"Yes, the informal supper." Lars dropped her head to the side. "Didn't you get the whole message? We're having a formal supper instead. That's why I canceled mine. We begin in an hour."

"Formal?" I asked. "What on Velm for?"

She bent her lip ridge in laughter. "Nothing on Velm. On Zetzor." She reared up on her hind legs and folded four sets of claws together in a metallic knot before her stomach scales. "The Thants called up Max six hours ago, said they'd all just arrived. They made it clear they have something momentous to say, though nobody knows what. Everyone has been running around here as though firegnats had clustered under their vests." Suddenly she spread her left wing and beat it violently before her. "Well, the woman must not have remembered the whole message when she delivered it to you. I can see you looking confused. It's understandable, Marq. She's a foreigner from somewhere out near Hysy'oppi, and, though she's very nice, she doesn't know our local dialect terribly well. She was with the students this afternoon, and when I said I wanted to get to you, she volunteered to deliver a message. At any rate, our informal supper is canceled. And you must be back within an hour, because we're having a formal one in its place."

I started to say something, but her other wing now swept around before her.

"All right," I said. "I'll be there—we'll be there, Rat and me." I blinked.

And saw Santine and Ollivet't and Shalleme sitting about the cushions in the small talk that always quiets when somebody goes to the wall to call.

Rat still stood, still watched.

JoBonnot was squatting again, now that I had come out of my seconds of call-trance. She turned to me with fragments of her grin visible through the grill. "Well, you have begun learning to what extent you can trust me— trust me to distort information. Because everyone does. Very good, don't you think?" She grimaced. "Not very *much* distortion? But that is what this Family/Sygn conflict is all about. A few more times, and you will have an almost trustworthy model of what to expect of me. Very good? That's because I *am* so profoundly sane. I think eventually you, Skinu Marq, or maybe you, Skina Rat, will like that very much."

I looked around the room, at Santine, at Shalleme, and Ollivet't, and suddenly felt very apart from all three.

"No doubt you want to return to Dyethshome. With your good friend, Rat Korga. You are two in whom I am greatly interested, and I certainly offer my help. Oh, yes. The kinds of situations to which you returned at the hunting union will strew your path all the way to Dyethshome. And I have engineered even more restful, pleasing, and convenient ways to circumvent them than I did to get you here. Easy, pleasant, convenient, oh yes? Come with me."

Perhaps it was her association with little crazy Clym, or just the general confusion that seemed to inform everything.

Did I start for the door, or for hollow-eyed Rat beside it? (Yet someone who is all that was ever desired is as much escape as home; and his eyes that were not there met mine.) I saw Santine start. I knew Doru and Doru were confused. I pushed through the spokes hanging at the door and knew Rat followed me. I heard JoBonnot call: "So quickly you go? Without me?"

But I was already hurrying outside where seven city levels weighed over me and a topple down a million and a quarter years (nonstandard) of archeology hung below; as we rushed along the apartment ring toward the exit rollerwalk, Rat closing behind me, I was overwhelmed by how much, future and past, distorted all present vision.

TWELVE

Return to Dyethshome

"Do you want to go through the run?" I stopped at frilly dyll.

Rat squeezed my shoulder. "Yes. Is it shorter?"

I glanced up between girders. Park lights blotted the dimmer stars. "No. But sometimes you just feel better when you come out the other end."

We weren't *in* the park, but in a fourth level industrial sector cassetted to look like one. And when we stepped through the mossy siding over the blue trough, we came not through the irregularly glazed ceramic walls of the upper level runs, but through metal ribs that joined at the peak of the vaulted hall.

The foot pool before the door was half-covered with some organic slough. I didn't step in it and didn't remind Rat to. A rollerway moved sluggishly. I stepped on it, drifted forward of Rat, who a moment later, caught up, looking around at the ceiling vault, at the tall, intricate, and unremarkable sculptures to our left. A section of ceiling lights had gone out, so the most remarkable thing about the pieces carried back at their evenly disordered distances (prescribed by city ordinance) was the shadow between them.

Ahead, a voyeurlight glowed between two larger statues. As we drifted up, we saw two males, both evelmi, the smaller covering the larger, claws loose and legs tight about the flanks of the other, haunches, three pair, hunching and hunching. Both wore patches of simulated blue scales over their normal black and green. Both wore the double half-scaled cloaks, one at each shoulder, that most women—whatever their race, whatever their sex—have long forgotten began as a human attempt to imitate the great wings of the neuters.

Rat turned to watch them, scratching his chest with naked nubs, then sliding that hand down his belly.

"Rat, did you have runs . . . places like this, on Rhyonon?"

"Yes." Another work of art, in darkness, passed. "But they were not—well, all over the way they are here. And they were illegal. But we had them. The ones just for males like me—and you—were always shut down when the authorities found them, because the people who used them were too young. The ones for men and women stayed around much longer."

I chuckled. "Here, each neighborhood is required to have at least three different kinds. But the runs were here before humans came. They're an integral part of most Velmian cultures. We just moved right into them, at least in the south."

Rat asked: "And this is just for males here? Very tall, or very short ones. Like me? And you?"

I frowned. "This one has the same makeup as the one we were in before. The style is a little different, though."

"But no females," Rat said. "No very tall woman, like the one who took us to the caves. They don't come here?"

"There's nothing to keep anyone from dropping in to take a look," I said. "And we all do. But I believe there actually are some ordinances about forced participation in sexual acts in any run. By and large the character of a run isn't so much a matter of edict as expediency. As far as height's concerned, well . . ." I shrugged. "This one happens to be one we can feel at home in and also happens to take us toward—"

She must have been resting in a cushioned alcove beside the rollerway. She uncoiled, all in green scales, and sprang to the walk.

Rat—I felt it in his grip—flinched.

No, she was only a little taller than I was; but already I was seeing things in Rat's terms.

As darkened statues gave way to lit ones, she came toward Rat with a strange expression on her human face. (She *was* a female; I hadn't been sure.) "You're . . ." she began. "You're . . . really him. The survivor? I've called dozens of people, getting descriptions, composite and speculative portraits. I went everywhere I thought you might be. I knew you couldn't have been where the crowds were gathering. But I also knew you had gone through a park level run out near Whitefalls this morning. I took a chance on a similar run, here, waiting for hours on the possibility—" She stopped, brought her gloved hand back to the opening cut away around her pubis. "I've been mistaken three times already . . . I mean, you *are* the—"

I actually started a diplomatic evasion, hesitating only over my confusion as to whether it would work or not, when Rat's hand dropped from my shoulder. "I am Rat Korga, the survivor."

"You . . . *really* are?"

I dropped my hand from Rat's.

She came a few steps up the walk.

We passed some people strolling in the opposite direction.

"May I touch you? Please! You've survived a world—" and to both sides she turned her eyes momentarily, as lights swept back beside us, dark as Rat's in half-light, before she stepped forward.

Rat stepped forward too.

"Please, I want to touch you—or you to touch me. That would be better—" She seemed suddenly to remember herself. "With your friend, if you like."

"I don't want to have sex with a female," Rat said. "Now. Here. We came into this run because, on our way, we might find men—males. Here."

"But you—" She stepped closer. "I thought perhaps you'd be—you would understand. Because of what you've survived. I need you to . . ."

Rat put both his hands, ringed and unringed, on the dark-haired woman's shoulders. As we passed more lights, his eyes went from clear green to clear. "Leave this run. Please. I think you should leave this run. It would be better if you left this run." (I actually found myself smil-

ing: One after another, Rat was running through all our
polite forms of requesting someone to leave.) "I feel that
you should leave—"

"Oh, but I—" She blinked, uncertainly. The colored
insignia on the patch of shoulder scales told of a job_2 at a
major distillation house, which left her job_1 open.

"Please leave this run," Rat said. "You don't belong
here."

She seemed to pull her wide shoulders in from under
his hands. She raised one wrist up toward her mouth.
"But I need . . ." Then, with the beating eyes and intricate expression of someone who has learned some desperate necessity will not be met, she stepped back. Then,
anger. Her noise was more evelmian hiss than human
growl. She turned and walked off between some five women
(all males or neuters, all but one evelmi) who had stepped
up to watch.

Rat turned to me. "Did I speak improperly, Marq?"

One watcher reared on hind legs. "I'm glad you said
it. It's something we all feel." I wondered if we were going
to have to hear something about human women being
more likely to show up where they're not wanted than
evelm. A commonplace of the south, it still makes me
uncomfortable.

But there was only the soft boom: "Most of us are too
polite."

The others laughed in a pulsing admixture of racial
laughters. And the shortest one of them walked up and
began to lick Rat's face—the human, wouldn't you know.
Rat turned away; his hand, back on my shoulder, urged
me on with a motion recalling the one I'd started him with
on our way to the g'gia.

We walked on up the walk.

We walked off it, between statues, where now were
three, now twelve, now two, some entwined with one
another, some watching, now a hand, not his, lingering
somewhere on his body or mine. Once we moved through
maybe twenty, most in sexual contact with one another. In
such groups, running, we were too close for personal
recognition. Eyes, neither black nor silver, moved near,
moved away, while others moved in to replace them, the
many bodies centimeters away moving together, apart, in
the warmth, a moment of cool as contact broke, then

warmth again, to hold, to handle, and, even though we
only moved through, as supportive as if we'd stayed.

2.

A dozen women wandered Water Alley, younger ones
sprinting. As we came off the stairway, I saw gold claws
lock the column across at the butcher's union, and the face
of the little redhead, peering over the other apprentice's
scaled shoulder. Then they were off inside.

"Come on, Rat."

We started across cracked blue, when Si'id rushed
out between the two kids. "Marq Dyeth . . ." Her tone
was conspiratorial, her arms heavy and hairy, and I recalled, from some drunken encounter years ago, her telling me that when she was in the bath and the water
washed back toward her neck, all those hairs curved around
to look like scales: "Excuse me, Marq. . . ." She was in
front of us, so we had to stop. "I'm so pleased to meet
your friend. I cannot say, with my poor single tongue, the
honor it is. Really—" One hand on my arm, she guided
me around, perhaps to avoid the people. Rat stepped
around with me. "I have hungered all day for this honor—"
A sudden grin. "But you saw, I had stationed my young
ones out to wait for you—like hunters spying for the
passing of dragons, yes? But then, it's clear, the whole of
Morgre has developed an appetite for our fine friend." She
held a breath, making fists of both reddened hands; then
she said: "You survived!" A fist went high as Rat's elbow.
"You survived—what that must have required from you!
What it must have meant for you. And what it means to
us—" She bent forward. "What it means for any creature
with a sense of her own life as a closed limited system. We
are all famished for a taste of that survival, Rat Korga. . . ."
Si'id pulled her lower lip into her mouth for a moment.
Suddenly she stepped back to paw among robes and aprons.
"It would be such an honor if you'd let us satisfy that
appetite. I know your friend, Dyeth—" She nodded to me
while she peered in one pouch, then thrust her artificially
clawed hand in another— "would urge you to accept."
From a left pocket she finally pulled a sampling knife.
Multiple steels glistened from brass bladespines. Rubber-

ized clamp and stained bone handle both looked well worn. "There's very little pain involved. Marq can assure you of that, if you're unfamiliar with the custom. But if you would give some of your flesh to appease our hunger . . ." She reached forward with the knife toward Rat's shoulder.

"Will I be killed now?" Rat asked.

"No, but—*Look*, Si'id!" I took her wrist. "You can't just run out and slice off a piece of meat to start a cloning culture just like—Hey!" Because Si'id had taken Rat's arm in one hand. "Come on, why don't you let Rat come back some other day so that—"

"But it would be such a triumph!" Si'id pushed the blades and clamps against Rat's shoulder.

Rat didn't flinch because, well, that's just the way Rat was. "A triumph for the union." Si'id squeezed the sampler's trigger.

I was surprised, confused, and angry. I started to pull Rat away. But a microscopic needle, sunk to the bone marrow to gather generating cellular material, can hurt if wiggled. The three surface blades bit in to collect dermal enzymes and to hold the needle steady while it was digging.

Si'id released the trigger. Somewhere from within Rat's shoulder a microneedle withdrew. The blades came away from the flesh, leaving three little reddish lines, one of which spilled one, and another, then a third scarlet drop down Rat's arm.

"Oh, thank you!" Si'id exclaimed. "Yes, a beautiful sample. We will savor the complexities of your flesh for years to come, and it will lend its subtleties to myriad complex meals. Marq Dyeth?" Si'id turned to me. "Your new friend is a joy and an honor to Whitefalls. To Morgre. To our Fayne-Vyalou. To our world!"

I started to say something ugly, but five or six women had stopped to watch; and two others were coming over. I took Rat's arm, starting to speak and feeling him start with me so that speech was unnecessary.

"Felicitations!" Si'id called out after us. "What a wondrous pedigree this will begin. Wonderful!"

I said: "Come *on*, Rat."

"You have honored our union with a gift to the taste of our whole populace!"

"Are you all right?" I asked.

As we walked, he reached across to rub his shoulder. "I don't understand."

"Oh, soon they'll have that little piece of you growing up on their shelf behind a big coppermesh screen." I'd always thought of mine as a pretty civilized world—at least my section of it. But when your local butcher₁ comes up and just helps herself to some of your perfect erotic object's most intimate genetic material—! "Come on, Rat, let's get back to Dyethshome. We'll be there in a minute."

3.

When we came off the rollerwalk, through the wall of high, yellow cactus, many, many women—many more than had been in the industrial rotunda—crowded the wide pathway, or stood before the steps, or squatted on the high rocks around, obscuring green flags, stone pools, and layered mirror portals.

"Marq Dyeth—?"

It was (ex-medical technologist₂) Mima.

"Marq Dyeth, this way." She licked air for us to come over. We hurried to her. "This way!" As the three of us trotted behind the crowd, Mima explained: "We've got students all along here, waiting for you. We, at least, know what you look like. Most of those around here don't—yet. How did . . . you like your dragon hunt, Rat Korga?"

And Korga, striding by me, admitted in his rough voice: "It was the most thrilling thing I have done." As we sidestepped a clump of women, two of whom reared to watch him, he added, "Ever."

Mima smiled in a way that suddenly made me like her a lot. "We're going to take you in through the entrance into the North Court."

I knew it was there, but I don't believe I'd ever used it. But that's Dyethshome. From behind a cactus whose nobby stalks were streaked beige, our algae-farmer₂ looked out and gestured as we reached her. "This way. This way. . . ." Clearly she was enjoying herself.

The clay that Rat and I ended up on was brown, with yellow to one side and to the other green. Mima and the farmer crowded us onto it (some women turned to glance at us), and one or the other of them thought something.

We fell into the ground.

—and were hurrying through a hallway whose straight ribs met overhead at a completely unfamiliar angle.

"Here . . ." from the algae-farmer$_2$. "At least I think it's here." The embossed metal plate bore designs I had perhaps last seen before I went to Senthy. But when you live in an institution with over fifteen kilometers of connecting hallways, ten of which are almost never used . . .

The North Hall is tall.

Stained-glass portals let in light six meters up its west wall. Among the thirty-foot columns about its terraced floor, the memory of an assassination two centuries past still chills.

We wandered across gray flooring that glowed red about our feet, no doubt through the same technology that had lit guide arrows in the industrial rotunda. As we walked, the light gleaming off Rat's blocky ankle turned purple; that about Mima's, blue; about mine, green; the farmer's heliotrope. (A ball here begins all bloody and ends all rainbow.) We moved toward the steps up to the bright blades of the door.

"Rat," the algae-farmer$_2$ said suddenly, "the woman who wore those rings you have on *murdered* someone in this room!" with the same delighted grin with which the students had been negotiating the general excitement.

My head jerked around—too little to be seen? But the account seemed so anemic, so reduced, that I felt, here, in my home, I had been jerked out of my own world. One risks that, living in an historical artifact, inhabited by its students. We mounted into mirrors that began to swing, their backings pitted, their surfaces stained yellow as human urine.

I had never felt this hall the heart of my home. (Vacant, avoided, disused.) Despite all ancient reason, it had become completely marginal. But a student's word, as it displaced me from my own image of its history, by the same movement, replaced this abandoned hall in some eccentric centrality that only struck me as we left it.

4.

Water rilled, divided at the shallow carvings, closed over them, chattering, and rippled up the tall ones to the brown and green water line. Blue and white water spumed along the spill, to swirl the ramp foot across the hall before it fountained and fell, foaming.

Kal'k said: ". . . and I thought Vol'd, Abrak'd, and Vo'd'ard'd, since they were in Morgre; Jayne spoke with them this morning. . . ."

Hirum said: ". . . then, of course, I asked Vizakar, Mammam'm, and Clent from the farm, who should be here soon. . . ."

Shoshana asked: ". . . is Santine available? Oh, I know it's late. But she's been so considerate in formal emergencies. . . ."

Sel'v said: ". . . can't always count on tracer representatives every time we throw together a snack. But we have Menek coming. She's likely to bring someone impressive. . . ."

Max, with Egri at her purple mid-haunches, came over the small bridge. "Well, Rat Korga, as my child's companion, you will certainly be one of the most honored of our visitors."

Hatti asked: "How many of the students have accepted?"

Black Lars answered: "All of them."

"Oh. Well, I suppose it'll be all right. It *is* because of you." Rearing, Sel'v expanded a protective wing about Rat's shoulder. "That's astonishing. . . . Students don't usually like formal occasions. *All* of them?"

Black Lars nodded her black head.

Tinjo came up slowly, leaving wet footprints on the stone. The waters roared around us. "Why are all those people out front? Are we going to invite them in?"

"I was thinking of it," Large Maxa said.

"Of *course* not!" Egri declared. "They're here to see Rat. We can't just put a guest on display like that. We'll no more invite them in than we'll send Rat out."

Just then the reservoir behind the hall's south wall filled. The fluted lips overflowed. Ten meters of sculptural mosaics became a green and white cascade. "Well, to your food, your food!" Hatti admonished. "To your—"

Sel'v suddenly expanded both wings and reared. "Oh, dear. We've got a photocall."

Everyone looked at each other. At a formal supper, when a guest calls to cancel, everyone already there must be present. I whispered to Hirum: "You know Rat isn't connected up for direct neural access. . . ."

Max said: "As it should be," and extended a number of tongues beside the one she'd spoken with. (Have you ever wondered why, just before a group call, everyone drops her eyes?)

We dropped our eyes.

And on all sixes Santine looked up at us, with that side motion of the head one had come to associate with her over two decades: "Got home," she declared with one tongue; "Got your invitation," with another. "How kind. I'll tell you, just so there won't be any untoward encounters: I'm bringing a woman, Marq. She's quite strange and from another world. I assume it makes her a positive addition to our number this evening. That's the sweet. The sour is she's awkwardly eager to come. It could just as easily be her presence turns out negative. Since I know this is in honor of your offworld friends, I don't want you to have any unpleasant surprises. Worlds can be small places. I imagine universes don't *have* to be much bigger. We'll be there in half an hour." She vanished.

We looked up.

I turned toward Egri to mention JoBonnot. But Hatti was repeating: "To your food, then. At least that's all it is. They're coming. To your food . . ." And anyway Egri, with Max beside her, had already started across the court.

"Come on, Rat," I said. "Let's cook!" We hurried along raised gray paths between freeform statuary jutting in white waters.

5.

Fell in light, wandered in shadow, rose in light . . .

I walked across the carpet to my desk. "You don't have to do anything. Just relax."

I glanced back to see Rat drop to the orange nap,

cross-legged, inches from one of the six clawed feet. I squatted by the desk, hooked my fingers under the lowest lip, and swung out the food drawer. In the silvery plastic trays, meat lay on the right, with roots and leaf vegetables to the left. The pink haze of the bactereostatic field shimmered about the glass plates in the corners. "Would it bother you if JoBonnot showed up here for dinner?" I pulled out an upper cutlery drawer and pawed through delicate blades.

"No." Ringed and unringed fingers lay on one another, not meshed. "Not here."

"Good." I pressed the green plates on the drawer edge. Nap retracted into the carpet, leaving a clean, blue surface on which to sit and prepare. "Are there any formal dishes you particularly enjoy?"

"I know the names of some," Rat said. "They told me about them in the Web. But not what they taste like."

"To be sure," I said. "That's the Web: tell you the names of famous local concoctions, show you pictures, give you some insight into how they're made, or even instruction in traditional ways to eat them—only they don't bother to let you taste, which, after all, is what food is about, no? What in the world can the Thants want now? *I'm* making Hunters' Beacon," which is what I make half the time for formal dinners anyway. I swung the large slicer from its niche. "Rat, would you look under the bed—"

"—for the food form? Yes." Which surprised me. But that *is* the Web. The part of their job they do, they do well. Rat swiveled around, lay back, and wedged himself half under my bed; I heard metal and wood clack and clank. He came out with it: lots of pith and metal dowels bound together with bark cord (and two replacement bonds of ragrope). "I will get the base dish too."

"Yes . . ." *of course*, I started to say. "Please."

Rat swung himself back under the bed; and swung out again, gazing not quite quizzically at a dish made more or less of the carved and polished pelvis of a beast who—happily—does not live in this latitude. I watched while he got the central pole into the metal socket in the dish's center, saying instructions to myself, but not out loud, because his actions were simply, for me, too fascinating to break the silence.

He looked up.

The sky had gone a blue deep enough to strike his eyes glass.

From some remembered diagram, from some Web outprint on "culinary customs of the Fayne-Vyalou, southern Velm," Rat arranged the racks, then set the dish carefully on the rug. He ran his crystal eyes up the meter high struts.

I started the slicer.

Hunters' Beacon: a paper-thin ribbon of raw meat, five inches wide and cut so that it folds out to several meters, draped, folded, and looped about the rods of the foodform, sprinkled with powders, pieces of root, spices, minerals, acids, and oils, each of which flavors or ferments different portions of it differently, some of which chemically cooks portions of it to various degrees, many of which color its parts to different hues.

I stood up.

Rat stood up beside me.

"How does it look?" I put the oil and acid decanters back on the desk, which hummed, beeped, and swallowed them.

"Like the picture they showed me."

"Let's hope it fits through the door."

"Does it usually?"

"Always." Formal dishes by tradition should take no more than twenty minutes to prepare, though some of my older parents have been known to lavish an extra three or four. Nobody begrudges them.

Rat asked: "Can I carry it?"

When someone has taken the time to learn your customs, you tend to be both surprised and pleased in a proportion that, itself, both surprises and pleases.

"Sure." Rat's and mine: an exchange thousands of years old between humans, contoured by Velmian life to its particular slant, pitch, meaning. That most formal of exchanges, informed by what we felt for each other, lost all formality. "Thanks."

6.

Hunters' Beacon? Cactus curls, hot and cold pulps and piths, rainbow foam, of course calla berries (plunged in boiling broth to split their pale skins for evening), lichen chokes marinated in Beetlesblood (the name of a wine imported from the north), racks of worm—pickled, poached, or pounded flat and fluted—vine strips shaved with the curlings dipped in sundry flavored oils . . .

"The Thants are here!" Bucephalus lolloped between Rat and me toward where her own offering for the evening— tall sparoria leaves, rolled and shredded at the tenderer ends, surrounded by crocks of spiced yogurts—stood on the spidery previewing table.

Large Maxa and Sel'v came in through the small doors. Max unfurled her wings and beat them. The waters stilled around the crystal clutch.

Large Maxa announced: "Who comes to visit this run with a history of monotony in saltiness, bitterness, sweetness, sourness, . . . ?" Humans have five basic flavors that become smell without perceptual hitch. Evelmi have twelve basic tastes and no nasal-based olfactory sense—though they can detect, with some tongues, even a molecule or two lingering on the air. Rat, beside me, moved his lips to ghost the nineteen words covering the basic twelve Large Maxa intoned.

Sel'v announced: "Come from a federation rich as our own, yet whose flavors present themselves in different order, noon to noon: Alsrod, Nea, Fibermich, George, Eulalia, Clearwater, and Thadeus, touching tongues and feet to the stream of Thant, flowing toward the stream of Dyeth, contouring the currents like shell whorls."

Then, around the central mirrors, the two-story-high wall mural began to bubble. Floor fans blew away fumes as one mural, then the mural beneath it, cleared. Pictorial layer after pictorial layer melted off.

Ahead, first Small Maxa, then V'vish, then Shoshana's friend (with Shoshana beside her, a hand on her haunch) picked up their offerings from the previewer and began to walk about the hall, while Sel'v and Maxa repeated the invocation.

The last mural bubbled, reticulated, ran, and dripped away from darkness.

Through swinging doors by the dim crystal column, not waiting for the ragged meltings to be sucked into the floor grate, the colorful privacy cloud that hid Thadeus Thant came up, stopping now and starting.

". . . a history of monotony in saltiness, bitterness . . ."

Behind was one of gray metal. It paused at the diminishing threshold. Then whoever was inside the cloud stepped over. And I remembered the aluminum circles that had hung about Alsrod, now in flight about (certainly) her. Beside them, jewels. Jewels swarmed and glittered about someone as certainly Eulalia—since she was the only Thant who wore them.

". . . present themselves in different order . . ."

Rat picked up the Hunters' Beacon from the preview table. The dish against his stomach, his great hands either side on the bone handles, we walked out into the room. With the meter-high rack before him, on and about which the food hung, I wondered at his view through, and walked beside him among others holding their racks and skewers and dangling hooks of food.

". . . who comes to visit this run with a history . . ."

From the dark patio a glittering cloud came forward. I assumed the swarm of green foil was Nea—and the black glitter just behind her to the right was Fibermich, because the other cloud off to the left, a storm cloud (billowing mists, rushing droplets flickering within, pearling the humid gray or looping through three-quarters of a rainbow) must have been Clearwater.

"Odd," I said to Rat. "Thadeus usually wears some sort of privacy apparatus, but this is the first time the others have." Among Vizakar, Clent, Vol'd, walking in from the terrace to follow the guests of honor, I saw, coming over the cleared limen, George Thant, her veined arms brazen and folded, her temples veined and scowling. As our circuit brought us near, I started to speak, but saw, at the same time, just beside her, Santine.

Anticipating ominous Jo, I flinched. But the tall woman who came up with Santine was not the one we'd left her with in the g'gia. "Marq Dyeth." She extended both hands.

"Japril," I said. "Honestly, you are not whom I expected to see here." I took them, squeezed them.

"But I am here." She wore some seven formal body jewels of a somber gray and stunning quality that is the way the Web does things. "Actually." Her sunburst of office hung above her right shoulder, its rays rotating slowly, like another body jewel, too bright and too gaudy—which is also the Web.

"You know Rat of course." I turned to George, who had stopped, still glowering, two steps off. "And this is Thant—"

As I spoke, George's metallic skin began to shiver, to shatter, and brass flecks swirled out and about, obscuring her like fire gnats at Iirianiset by the Hyte. In a rising chitter of flake clicking flake, she strode away.

"What was that?" Japril asked with the amiability of the interworld traveler used to the vagaries of interworld manners, where neither insult nor compliment should be assumed unless you have it in writing.

"George Thant," I explained, "one of the evening's guests of honor."

"Ah," said Santine, who had just turned on three legs from talk with someone else (which she finished up with another tongue while she said to us): "So I *have* brought you an old friend after all. Universes *are* small, no matter how big worlds are. Marq, how are your aging parents? But I shall see in a moment."

"Santine," I said, "you've met my friend, Rat Korga."

At which Santine reared up on two legs. "Rat Korga!" she cried, just as if this were a first meeting—which is the way of formal affairs. "What wonderful flavors must be deployed about that Hunters' Beacon. You look ancient! May I take a turn with you around the hall as you display your friend's offering and we leave these two to talk?"

"Yes," Rat said.

At which Santine went back down on all sixes, frowned a moment, then raised her forelegs. "You are exceptional! Direct, clear, a unique flavor around which all complexities clarify! I marvel. Come." Santine put a foreclaw under the dish's bottom, to relieve him of a kilogram or two of its seven or eight kilograms' weight, and began to walk away, perfectly in step so as not to upset the food—a skill it takes a good six weeks' practice to achieve, sometime back at age thirteen or fourteen, or twenty-three or twenty-four, depending on whether you're a six-limbed or four-limbed creature. For a moment I watched them and loved my world. "Japril," I said, turning back, "why are you here?"

"Didn't Rat tell you I was coming? He knew, you know. Ynn and Marta are waiting outside. But we thought it would be better if only one of us showed up in vivo. Though Ynn is just wild about your place here. I practically had to restrain her. We didn't know anything about the party, other than that it was for some offworlders. We don't know anything about their allegiances and we don't care. But if they're from one of those worlds with select unlimited space travel, such folk can get awfully paranoid if too many high-ranking Web officials just happen to be on the welcoming committee. I've seen it happen before, and we aren't here to make problems."

I laughed. "I'm afraid you've got it. They do have unlimited space-fare on their own world. Actually, we're wondering why *they*'re here. Two of them showed up . . . yesterday, I guess it was. And now the entire stream has come torrenting down on us."

"Ah," said Japril and touched my arm with a complicitous sigh that, from past years, I knew meant little.

"Was Rat *supposed* to tell me you were coming?" I paused. "But then, I didn't ask him."

Japril sighed. "I see you've learned a lot about our tall friend in twenty-nine hours—I dare say Rat's learned a lot about you too. Shall we take a turn around the hall?"

"Yes," I said.

She looked at me a moment, then laughed. "Well, it's good to see you both, again and together. Come."

We moved through the hall, passing relatives, friends, Thants conspicuous in their clouds.

"All those people outside. Your guests of honor this evening must be quite something."

"The Thants? Oh, they come to visit perhaps twice a year. Usually only a dozen or so people come to watch—mostly those intending to take a vaurine tour of some other world who want to see what an offworlder looks like—in vivo."

"There're certainly more than a dozen or so people out there now. When we came up, Ynn said there were seven hundred eighty-four, with another hundred-seven coming."

Only the Web. "They're here for Rat."

Japril raised an eyebrow. "All eight hundred ninety-one?" The question had a falling inflection.

"As far as I can tell."

Japril looked down at her hands. We passed between modest and ornate fare. "You know we advised him to discourage any public announcement of his arrival."

"There wasn't any announcement," I said. "As far as I can tell, it's all through word of mouth."

"Rumor?" Japril's long, efficient face fixed itself between dislike and worry. "Not good. But then, we've come here for a party—you're *sure* it's word of mouth?"

I shrugged. "Yeah."

"Well, then," Japril took my arm again. " 'These flavors have been arranged for your guests of honor and we must sample.' " A line from *the* most famous opera composed in our hemisphere during the past fifty years, which Japril quoted courtesy GI. I was charmed. "Come," she said. "Introduce me."

I looked up to do it. ". . . All the Thants are still in privacy apparatuses." Thadeus will sometimes drift in in a cloud; but though I've always realized Eulalia's trailing jewels could gather round her and close out vision, I wondered now that I'd never seen her use it. "This is formal. So we just have to wait."

As we walked, I looked about and realized others wondered too. Perhaps half our guests had met the Thants on other occasions. Now Abrak'd or Mammam'm would glance toward the hovering metallic green or parti-colored swirls; they and the other guests were intrigued as well. Perhaps the Thants were indulging some obscure holiday custom. Perhaps it was simply a random gesture they themselves never envisioned might cause concern. Or perhaps it was an aesthetic decision calculated to elicit respect and pleasure. And yet I could not avoid thinking that it had something to do with yesterday's encounter on our green porches.

Egri came up beside us, carrying a candelabrum (called a krutchk't) stuck about with seared and pickled kharba leaves. "Ah, an officer of the Web, and no doubt a friend of my child's."

"Egri, this is Japril," I said. "I've mentioned you both to one another, I'm sure. Egri used to be an ID before she retired$_1$."

"How pleasant to have you join us," said Egri. "Tell me, are you familiar enough with our customs to feel comfortable taking my food offering about for a bit while I confer with the youngster?"

"I only know what GI has been able to teach me,"

Japril answered. But I could tell she was pleased to be asked.

"Then honor us." Smiling, Egri presented the three-handled foodform to Japril, who silently debated which two handles to hold it by—while GI gave her no help.

"Those two . . ." I whispered. "If you would honor our stream . . . ?"

Japril took the form, beaming, and walked off with the adorned krutchk't among the guests.

"Watch a moment," Egri whispered to me.

Japril walked four steps forward and, with a circular movement of her head, turned sharply left and started again.

I smiled. Apparently GI had given her some old, formal display pattern-paths to walk, of a kind I'd last seen at a formal dinner up in Farkit when I was twenty. In Morgre, they more or less went out by the time I was ten. But like the body-jewels, they would impress our guests who recognized the old custom—which would not be Thants; or Rat.

"Let's get Lars and Alyx," Egri said. "I'm not exactly sure what's going on."

When I looked where Egri was looking, I saw three of the privacy clouds: Clearwater's little storm, Eulalia's jeweled nebula, and Nea's flickering green foil. As I watched, Alsrod's aluminum refulgence and Thadeus's multi-metal moved toward them: George's bronze flitter moved away.

"You said to join you," Alyxander said.

"And here," Black Lars said with one tongue; and with another, "we are. What *is* going on?"

"I don't know," Egri said, while I realized she had called together all of us in the stream who were ID's.

"Why the diplomatic conference?" Alyxander said.

"Shoshana and V'vish are worrying about how to start serving while the Thants are still sequestered."

"Are the Thants saying something to us?" Black Lars asked.

"Well, they're certainly not saying it very clearly."

"That's why I thought we'd better take over as interpreters," Egri said. "It's considered highly impolite on Zetzor to communicate with someone who's sequestered herself in a cloud at the beginning of an evening. And on Velm, you *don't* start a formal dinner without telling peo-

ple personally that you're going to. I'm taking Thadeus
and George. Lars, you take Eulalia and Fibermich. Marq,
you take Clearwater and Alsrod. And Alyx, you take Nea
and keep an eye open to see if any of us needs back-up."

"Now just *what* are we supposed to tell them?" I
asked.

"Apologize for intruding, and say that dinner is served."

"Gotcha," Alyxander said.

And we all turned, dispersing.

Thunder on the left. I looked to see, through guests
and stream members still treading their display measures
(an old-fashioned phrase that doesn't really mean anything, left over from when Japril's display steps were the
rage), some with food and some without, the storm flickering and abroil.

I approached it as the gray and light-shot privacy
cloud halted its movement; someone within had stopped
to watch me.

I wondered whether I should use the praiseful form of
address ("Thant Clearwater") or merely the formal—opted
for that: "Clearwater Thant: I am presuming both on your
presence and your patience, I know. Still, I would ask that
you forgive me and accept our announcement that dinner
will be momentarily served and to prepare to receive your
placement."

Thunder rumbled.

A brief flicker.

The cloud darkened.

"There are some rudenesses that are simply unavoid-
able, am I right?" Accompanying Clearwater's voice was
the sound, from within, of rain.

"I'm afraid so."

Rain is not a natural phenomenon at this latitude on
Velm.

"I have heard what you have to say." The thunder
was very different from an evelm whisper. "Still, that does
not make it any the less rude."

I paused, then lowered my head—an evelm making
the polite gesture before tasting a great sculpture; and
because a similar gesture was a remark of respect among
humans on Zetzor—turned, and walked away to look for
Alsrod.

Looking, I saw Black Lars had already reached her

second goal, Fibermich's cloud, shiny, black. The cloud's glitter reflected on the scales about her flat, black eyes. "Thant! Fibermich! Thant!" one tongue began and went on chanting, "Thant! Fibermich! Thant! Thant! Fibermich! Thant! Thant! Fibermich! . . ." The first continued, and another took up: "No doubt you wonder why I address you in such an insulting form. But since I know that to violate the signs of privacy is in itself an insult, I feel that anything else would be an equivocation. It saddens me that I do not understand your motivations. Nevertheless,

{dinner is served."
{". . . Thant! Dinner is served!"

I guess, as I said, it's the way you make some people feel at home.

I walked on and, between Vol'd and Vo'd'ard'd, saw Egri talking to Thadeus and knew that she had used the superlative-polite, "Thant Thadeus," that she had taken the longest time with her communication, and that she had probably produced results equal to if not better than Lars's, Alyx's, or mine. She had trained us all. She had inculcated into us that each be sensitive to her own diplomatic style. She had been brought up in a Sygn monastery in the north, however much she rebelled against it, and she used to tell us: There is only one right thing to say in any crisis situation, as there is only one trunk to a cyhnk; yet there are more ways to say it than there are branches leading away from the trunk to the bright and scattered gems of truth. When we were older, she announced: If you can list for me everything wrong with that very seductive and profoundly wrong-headed statement, you are ready to deal with diplomacy$_1$ as the art, rather than as the science, that it is.

The click of aluminum disk on disk: "Marq Dyeth?" Her voice, a child's I'd almost forgotten, undercut the metallic sussurus: "The greatest rudeness on my home world—in our particular geosector of it, at any rate, among the particular people we associate with, from our particular range of acquaintances in 17—is to act in such a way as to compel rudeness from others."

I turned to her. "Sometimes," I said, "such unkindnesses are necessary. But it is still kind of you to explain the custom to me."

"Yes," Alsrod said from inside swirling aluminum. "I

suppose it is. But it is such a complicated concept that I was afraid without an explanation you wouldn't understand what we were doing at all—this being another world and everything." Momentarily I looked for the bald young woman I could not see in the chattering metal. "Alsrod, you are kind."

"No, I'm not," she said. "But our gesture, which we have put so much thought into preparing, would be absurd if you could not follow its intent because of cultural differences. I said to Clearwater, and Eulalia, both: I said, there're geosectors on our *own* world where what we are doing would not be understood. How can we hope for comprehension on a world sixty-eight thousand light-years away? But nobody listens to me."

I smiled, hoping she could see it from inside. "Will you forgive me if I counter your kindness with another small rudeness? Dinner will be shortly served."

Alsrod sighed. "I knew it was going to be something like that. Food, eating, meals, they're just not going to be as flexible on your world as they are on ours. I told them that too. But they never hear."

The cloud chattered its brittle commentary to our odd, yet oddly typical, interworld converse. "I think you've given me more of an entrance to the hive-cave complexities of all of this than any of us have had till now."

"I hope so," Alsrod said. "I said it was too confusing to deal with like this. We should just come out and *say* what we mean—that's what I said. 'Well, we are,' is what Eulalia said back. 'At least in a way that anyone with a grain of either civilization or sense should understand.' And *I* said—but then, I'm the youngest, and nobody ever . . . only you don't even know what *that* means! I got connected up with your local General Info this time; and *it* says that because of the age differentials that automatically exist between your two major races, the age-based hierarchies that obtain in most human cultures throughout the universe don't apply here."

I wasn't sure what *that* meant. But just then Japril, from her round of food display, came hurrying up with Egri's krutchk't. "Marq, is anything wrong? I've gone through the formal steps *twice* complete, and GI said that anything more than two or three steps beyond a single cycle usually heralded some major problem . . . ?"

"Frankly, I still don't know if the problem's major or not. Japril, this is Thant Alsrod, there inside her privacy cloud. Alsrod, though once more I risk rudeness, this is my longtime acquaintance from the Web, Japril—"

"*Oh!*" declared Alsrod. Or that's what I think she declared. It was more a squeal. Chitter became clatter: flying disks flew faster. Somewhere within it, Alsrod turned and hurried it away.

"*What* world did you say your friends are from?" Japril asked. "A fascinating cultural pattern!"

"Really, I *don't* know quite what this is about. But we'll be serving soon, I'm sure." I took the krutchk't's third handle to add my help. "Come with me while I find Egri and the others."

We started, in step, across the floor.

Black Lars walked away from a green cloud. She raised her head as she neared us. "Well, I've done my bit—"

V'vish rushed up, pushed at my hip, booming: "7a-12c—that's right over *there!*" I glanced at the ceiling, with its silver grid, let go of the krutchk't, and moved off to take place without finishing my sentence. I didn't even glance to see if Japril understood where she was to go. ("You! 3a-44r. Hurry!") But if General Info had given her the classical display pattern, it had most certainly imparted the import of serving placement coordinates. As Shoshana and V'vish bustled about the hall, both tapping the people present and calling out their placement positions beneath the carefully marked silver ceiling pattern— V'vish's multiple tongues booming louder and louder, Shoshana's human voice becoming shriller and shriller—I looked for Rat.

And saw him.

He gazed up—no, he was not connected with local GI, but his Web instructors had been. They'd surely told him such things. (You wanted to know how Vondramach managed to assassinate Secretary Argenia in the north court two hundred years ago? She whispered her the wrong serving coordinates for dinner.) Still holding the Hunters' Beacon rack, abandoned by Santine who had gone off to take her own place, Rat— "There, Santine: 72r-4c, quick, quick, quick!"—moved a little to the left, a little to the right, aware of the importance of his position.

Under me the floor thumped.

By Rat, flame shot high as his shoulder, then retreated while the grilling plates on their thin chains plum-
meted down beside him, to be caught by the four
spear-headed spikes that jabbed up from the floor.

The tiles in front of me had folded up two small trap
doors. Twin eyebolts snapped out, just as the two hooked
cables swung down from the ceiling and—ch'chank'nk—
caught. (I've been at one formal dinner, thankfully not
here, where a cable missed and flew on to tear into the leg
of a woman standing just one serving position behind me.)
Refuse trays, on supports and wheels, came clattering
down, hit the stops just at hip level. To my left someone
gasped. I looked. A student had been splashed a little
when the rinsing fountain jetted up beside her as the
deflecting vanes, on their various pulleys, clamps, and
cables, slung down from the ceiling into the freshet. But
by now the whole hall was a roar of chains and running
ropes, rumbling wheels, fluttering flame, riffling waters. I
looked off at Rat again, through stationary and swinging
haul-lines, through ranks of lowering shelves and rising
implements on thin, hydraulic stems. The charred walls of
the old-style furnace had come chank-changing up on three
sides of the flame beside him. And off by the student the
base of the fountain had closed around the protruding
nozzle to restrain the splashings. Trays flew, thrown and
caught by mechanical grapples. Pulleys dropped from the
ceiling and swung out to pull taut the slack cables hung
with serving implements. I saw Japril, food aloft, face
triumphant, and, thanks to GI, undaunted. I didn't see
any more Thant clouds, which probably meant they'd turned
them off. "On my world," an acquantance light years away
once told me after visiting mine in vaurine, "we eat with a
knife, perhaps an enamel spoon, and two sticks of wood
manipulated in the hand to pick up smaller morsels. On
your world—at least at formal affairs—you use the whole
dining hall!"

One or two people, now the more dangerous equipment was in place, had begun to step about. Were Rat
from the north, I would have been mildly embarrassed for
our provincial impetuosity.

I waited—like the students, who, here and there
among the other guests, craned and gawked—until the
first spit, a rod about two meters long, traveled by on one

of the overhead cables that had lowered from the ceiling. I tapped it lightly to set it swinging and started off, three steps beside it, and then headed for Rat.

Another spit came by, this one already set with food, a few leaves hooked on the small barbs, dressed with aromatic oil. I grasped it and lifted it down from the cable, turning it to the other end. Wanting to reach Rat, I stepped around a high display case that, still empty, had just risen from the floor. Around it from the other side lumbered ancient Abrak'd; and manners, after all, are manners. "A pleasure to see you at dinner. You are so old."

"You will be old soon, too. Oh, yes, Marq Dyeth, isn't it? You *are* aging nicely."

I extended the spit, and Abrak'd nipped off the dressed leaves, purring approval. I continued on, looking for a cable now to hang the empty hook over. The rinsing fountain? I stopped beside it and plunged the hook into one of the bubbling basins, turned it about, shook it, and decided I might as well set it again. To the right was a free display stand, hung with shaved and crackled skate-belly. Little knives and ornate scissors still swung from their chains. I took some snips of brittle gold and fixed some to the spit barbs—

"There you are!" Another spit-end waved in my face. And another. "There, Marq!"

Before me on the ends of damasked tines: from Bucephalus some worm roe (my favorite), from Tinjo some calla berries (which I could have done without). I bit from one; I bit from the other. "Don't you two think you should be spreading yourselves out? Mmm," which was because I liked the roe. "You're looking older every day, Bu."

"And I suppose I'm looking younger," Tinjo said, acting human, acting sly. I frowned.

Both of them laughed and turned to the three-tiered rinsing fountain.

"Come on, come on." I hooked my spit on the overhead chain; it moved off, swinging. Stepping up between them, I slapped the back of Bu's scaled neck and roughed the curls over Tinjo's human head. "We've got guests now. Spread out and use different rinsing fountains, will you?"

Both turned to me with the same look of amused

consternation on their so different faces, registering with
such different signs a look I would like to have believed
was universal between siblings in any social grouping even
resembling a stream—but which I know is not. Bu projected a tongue: "You can hardly get near Rat. I love you,
Marq," marking her both as an alien and my sister.

I grinned.

Tinjo giggled.

Bu rose on her hind claws and lolloped away, carrying her spit high. In the other direction, off marched
Tinjo.

I went on between shelves, racks, carts, cabinets, and
guests. I passed by the ornate stand on which Japril had
parked Egri's krutchk't before going off to circulate, and
took down a passing spit still unset, hooked its twisted
tines with seared lichen, and turned toward where I thought
Rat might be.

A meter or so from the furnace, some seven or eight
guests clustered. Her long-handled fork set with something that needed a few moments' fire, Shoshana thrust
the spit through the grill, while flames licked from tiny
triangular openings at the fluted corners.

As I came up, she withdrew the spit and examined
the gray dough, touched here and there with gold, sizzling
against the metal. "Your friend, given her age, is almost
too popular." Shoshana smiled. "I shall feed Rat this and
go see about some others." She turned to extend the long
spit over the shoulders of the gathered guests.

In their corner, I saw Rat, turning with eyes now
green, now silver, to nibble from a bit of blue leaf on one
guest's long fork, now from the worm meat at the end of
another, now from the cactus curls at the end of still
another, while still another and another joined them. I
watched, amid the roar of complimentary chatter, as he
turned to bite here, to bite there. A confection of hot
cheese and grated nuts, as it came away in his teeth,
strung down his chin, so that he tried first to toss back his
head to get it in his mouth, then to lick it in; failing, he
seemed to forget it and turned to bite at something covered with toasted crumbs, half of which fell as he bit, so
that his long face, chewing and biting and moving, looked
not like a woman's, evelm or human, but like a sick
dragon's or an acned ape's.

One guest, Vizakar or Clent, left. Two others, Vol'd and Mammam'm, came up to extend spits set with the evening delicacies over backs and shoulders.

As Rat turned here and there to bite and bite, his eyes—green, glass, silver, green—caught mine. The muscle in his cratered jaw bunched and bunched. One shoulder moved. He raised an arm. Holding his own spit in his ringed hand, he held it out toward me. The tines were set with some salad such as I'd fed Abrak'd. I bit into leaves, richly sour and peppery, and looked down the foreshortened rod leading to his fist's knotted and jeweled knuckles: knuckles, gnawed fingers, knobs of bone, knots of muscle, wrist, forearm, biceps, shoulder. He grazed on what they fed him, trying to keep looking at me with an expression not a smile but on which I could have certainly written one.

I thought to extend my own spit. But Rat's arms were longer than mine.

I couldn't have reached him.

While I chewed, somehow in my distraction, his tine hit my gum. Trying not to show it because it was an accident, I drew back at the pain, behind the others feeding him.

He could have fended their clogged attention.

If he had been used to our formal affairs, he could have parried this fork or that with some light comment or general protest. But as I watched, trying not to bring my hand to my sore mouth (he still held out his spit to me), I was struck with a moment's vision where, through his stranger's clumsiness and my fellows' eagerness, these most formal and age-old gestures were rendered as absurd-looking as if I were experiencing them for the first time in some society organized about principles and prohibitions unknown.

I nodded to him uncertainly, trying to chew and take cognizance of the flavors in my mouth. (Was that blood . . . ?) I stepped back, nodded again . . .

He put down his arm, went on eating, went on watching. More guests came, extending food and compliments.

Bucephalus had been right.

You couldn't get near him.

I tried to smile, though my face may have remained as blank as his.

Then I turned, hurrying off among high racks, low furnaces, falling and flopping fountains.

Japril had stopped by a stand on which rested my bone dish with its wooden dowels draped with the meaty multi-flavored ribbon, from which she was cutting a small section with one of the new food shears Shoshana had gotten for the party, then fixing it to the bobbed tines with what were, incidentally, our stream's oldest set of tongs, and, all in all, thanks to GI, looking far more comfortable with my local customs than I felt. She turned as I neared and, replacing tongs and knives on the hooks at the stand's edge, extended the spit toward me. "It's wonderful to see how clear are the marks of your aging since I saw you last."

"Five minutes?" I asked.

There's a certain kind of intellectual irony that GI is not set up to deal with. Japril frowned.

"But of course," I said. "You mean from last year." With my teeth I tore, tastefully, at the rare meat on the end of her spit. "Thank you, that *is* good, if I do say so."

She looked around for a rinsing fountain. One ear was lit from her hovering sunburst. Her face still bore what I assumed was distress from my flippancy. But as I fell in beside her, she said: "Marq, tell me again about all those people gathered outside Dyethshome."

I chewed. "I don't know quite what you want to hear."

We wandered by another furnace, ducked beneath more dangling spits.

"They're *all* here for Rat?"

"As far as I can tell."

"Marta just called in to say that the rumor among the crowd is that your offworld guests have come here across light-years of night to meet him too."

I frowned. "I suppose that's possible. But I doubt it. Still, we don't know why *they're* here, really. Yet. But what I think far more likely is just that our friends outside, since they've all come to gawk at Rat, haven't really considered that anyone might want to drop by for any other reason."

"Dropping by when folks are doing it on this scale—" Japril stepped up to a fountain basin whose rim was set with luminous gray stones—"becomes another rather fuzzy-

edged phenomenon." The stones were almost identical to
the ones she was wearing—and though I'd seen that particular fountain hundreds of times before, I'd just never
made the connection.

"Pardon?"

"Sorry. I was just talking to Ynn." She plunged the
spit, and swiveled it, making foam along the brim. "She
says that in the last half hour the arrivals have gone from
just under a thousand to over nine thousand people outside; they're backed up for almost a kilometer. About two
thousand have arrived in the last ten minutes alone—"

"Nine *thousand?*"

"Another two thousand are expected within the next
few minutes." She raised the spit's business end and shook
down droplets on the water. "I have to go hang this up
somewhere and set food on another free one, now, don't
I?"

"Oh," I said. "Of course," remembering the spit,
already set, I held. Protocol forbade me to offer it to
someone who had just fed me. And Japril was wandering
off anyway, no doubt having been reminded by GI how
unnecessary formal leave-taking was in formal situations.

I turned from the basin, saw a cable full of empty
spits go by on my right, saw Santine brandishing a set one
off on my left. Where, I wondered, had the Thants gotten
to—and came around between three of the hall's rough
stone columns, with a net-hanging between them almost
too old and worn to discern any of the pale colors of its
intricate knots.

The privacy clouds—except Thadeus's—were gone.

They had gathered near a large, three-winged furnace. And even through Thadeus's multichrome glitter, I
could see the human figure, the back curved almost to a
hump, the shoulders and knees extraordinarily thin, the
hair wild, the eyes all shadowed within the careening
flicker.

They held no forks, though a cable carrying dozens of
them jerked and jangled just beside them.

Thin, white, curly-haired, Small Maxa was the only
person I saw near them. She carried a spit at her side. At
the bottom of the single step, she moved along, observing
with a combination of awe at offworlders and the ease
which comes from knowing that, however alien, they were

only human—an awe and an ease I fancied a younger me
had possessed; and which I thought, in her first visit, I'd
read in Alsrod.

Maxa paused, then extended her spit, set with some
meaty dyll nut sections, toward Eulalia, whose jewels had
settled low at her shins, bobbling. Eulalia was talking with
Fibermich. It seemed she didn't notice Maxa's gesture,
though Maxa's dyll hung less than ten centimeters from
her mouth. She didn't turn away. She didn't acknowledge
it. She went on talking.

It produced the oddest sensation in me.

After a few moments, Maxa took a step back and
leaned forward to bring her tines to the same distance
from Fibermich's lips.

I frowned. Lifting my own spit, I walked to Maxa. I
started to say something jocular, but Maxa's expression, as
she leaned to present her offering, was pained. Had she
been any other sibling, parent, or friend, I would have put
my arm around her. But because she was Maxa, all I could
do was what she did.

I extended my spit toward Eulalia, my offering hanging centimeters away from the dyll.

". . . civilized around here, but of course it's the
furthest thing from it, really. Are they human? Yes, but
they've been reduced to beasts. . . ."

I wasn't really listening to Fibermich's response to
her mother. But the sudden discomfort, and perhaps a
memory of Rat, glutted with more offerings than a human
(though not an evelm) might swallow, made me think that,
somehow, if I tried another Thant, it all might be recti-
fied. I stepped to the side, to move my spit from Eulalia to
Clearwater; at the same moment I saw, from the corner of
my eye, Santine approach with a spit hung with some of
Shoshana's pickled worm.

". . . reduced to animals who copulate with animals,
call animals their sisters and mothers. . . ."

". . . so old," which was Santine. "All of you, so
marvelously old." Somewhere between Maxa and myself,
she brought forward her own spit in her foreclaw, her dark
and scaly head, with its luminous gill-ruff, heavy with
tongues poised for witty compliments. "Really, you, I, all
of us are looking perfectly ancient. . . ."

". . . not as if they don't acknowledge it themselves.

Our way is older, purer, human. And animal as they are and act, they know it. . . ."

I'm not sure where social discomfort interfaces with social panic. Perhaps some sign of distress in Santine—or Vol'd, who had followed her, or Mammam'm, who, I saw as I moved around the gathered Thants, had apparently been standing just behind them, her own unrecognized spit extending only centimeters behind Nea's right ear, still as a hunter poised for the shot—produced a paralytic astonishment at this incomprehensibility. It made me step even further around and actually thrust my spit into the glittering confusion of Thadeus's cloud.

". . . reminds me of the stories of our shepherds up at the equator. Those little furry creatures they drive about the slopes? Well, you know the jokes about the male shepherds and their favorite fur-balls in the pack . . ."

Sudden as some contrivance governed by a timer, precise laughter exploded from all six Thants. I looked from one to the other. Before Alsrod, who was speaking, another delectably set spit hung.

". . . but our equatorial herders at least have the decency to be ashamed of their indiscretions. . . ."

I followed the spit down to the dull claws of my mother Sel'v (the traveling composer[1]), who, now that she'd joined us, straining forward with food, let go the faintest sigh of confusion. I saw her gum ridges start to arch, then go taut.

". . . eat and procreate, eat and—but one can't even say that. Not only the males with the females, but the males do it with males, the females do it with females, within the race, across the races—and what are we to make of neuters—as if they had not even reached the elementary stage of culture, however ignorant, where a family takes its appropriate course. . . ."

There were at least ten, now, circling them, spits extended, straining toward faces and mouths that refused any converse other than among themselves. There was another fusillade of precise hilarity. We circled, waiting for them to taste, refuse, disdain, even insult. But all they did was ignore. I moved aside from V'vish and bumped shoulders with Shoshana. Both leaned forward among the others that had gathered, unable to retreat in the paralysis of breached protocol.

". . . so old . . ."

". . . so old . . ."

". . . aging beautifully, really, truly . . ."

". . . marvelously old . . ."

Ritual compliments, from worried tongues, at all volumes and timbres, threatened to drown whatever the Thants recited among themselves.

". . . to call them animals, you know—the humans among them, that is—suggests an innocence that, frankly, they don't warrant. . . ."

". . . criminal then . . ."

". . . a disease is not innocent, and this equation of unnatural crime with innocence is, in itself, a disease, which can only be cured by the most primitive means: quarantine, fire, prayer. . . ."

Somehow the whole dinner had become polarized between Rat, who would accept anything offered and—since manners demanded one not feed the same person twice—the Thants, who, accepting nothing, had become a dam against which all must eventually break. The circle around the Thants thickened, with siblings and guests. Now Alyxander, lower lip between her teeth, extended cactus curls. Now Black Lars lifted her midclaws again and again in anxiety, with a foreclaw extending her spitted sarb-bulb one more centimeter than politeness would tolerate toward George's bronze lips.

". . . their own bad smell, where they sniff it out in those elongated troughs of depravity that run through the land, where the females are allowed to be as licentious as the males. . . ."

We are slaves of custom. No one knows that better than an ID, who is no less a slave than anyone else. My shoulder ached from holding out my arm. I moved my leaves now to Nea, now to Alsrod, now to Fibermich, now to Clearwater, trying to think of something to do. I had the vaguest notion that if I listened to what they were saying, I might understand what they were doing. But though I heard their words accurately enough, I understood nothing. Because each notion I arrived at was arrived at in desperation, it crumpled on desperate contradictions. A memory of Rat—I suddenly felt the first impulse to forsake custom, throw down my spit, and return to him. What halted me, I think, was that I now saw, among those trying to donate some food or flavor or nourishment to our guests, Egri. She did not appear upset. She held her offering out with the perfect self-assurance that, somehow, good manners—if only the others would perhaps cease a moment—must prevail. And watching her, my mother and mentor, she seemed the most preposterous of us all.

I would run to Rat—

And Rat's hand took my arm. I jerked around to see. The hand—bare—moved up to my shoulder. He glanced at me, ordinary-eyed, then looked back at the Thants. His ringed hand, on the long handle of his spit, was about six inches off the place where decades of claws and fingers had worn the rough-out leather handle smooth. With no lean in it at all, his presentation stance was as absurdly awkward as his early moments with a radar bow. I glanced at Egri again. Somehow her self-confidence and grace, coupled with his clumsiness and ignorance, put parentheses around the whole range of painful unknowing, so that again, here in my own home, I felt as alien as I ever had at any distant revel, cultures and light-years away.

"Marq, this is terrible! What are they doing . . . !" which was Japril at my shoulder, her new spit again extended. "What do you think they're—"

Which is when the shadows and winds from Large Maxa's wings beat up beside and behind me. "Marq—?"

I turned.

Max caught my shoulders in her claws. "Marq, please, you must—"

"What—?"

"Just come. No, this is beyond all—" and tugged me, as if I were some six-legged pup, across the floor, so that I did drop my spit. "Max, what . . . ?" I honestly thought she was talking about the Thants.

THIRTEEN

Formalities

Once, I got in a look back. At least half our visitors were circling our oblivious guests of honor, awkward and unacknowledged offerings hanging on the ends of their long forks. The other half seemed to be standing about behind them, bewildered among the fountains and furnaces or under the cables, chains, and dangling instruments that had been summoned from floor and ceiling.

Rat came behind me. Japril dashed up after him.

"Outside," Max explained. "The crowds! We have to *do* something!"

Kelso, V'vish, Hatti, and Jayne were waiting for us. Japril and Rat came too.

"People will be crushed," Max went on. "They're already pressed up against the walls!"

"Shall we open the doors?" Jayne demanded. "Perhaps that will take some of the pressure off and let the ones in front get free."

"But if the ones in back think we've opened Dyethshome to the public," Large Maxa bellowed, "there'll be a surge forward—"

Somehow, with the private catastrophe of the Thants, we had all but lost connection to that tall, barefooted human beside me, in the rough cloth pants chained low about his hips, the thick fingers of one hand heavy with jewels, the jaw cratered with old wounds below his green, unstable eyes, about whom this public catastrophe centered.

We moved toward the confusion of mirrors, as though by looking at the fragmented conglomerate of our own reflections we might see through to a way of ending the confusion outside.

"The crowd is still growing, Marq," Japril whispered. "I just got a call from Marta, and Ynn said . . ."

Then there was no hand on my shoulder, which made me look off. Korga was walking toward the transparent column by the door. He squatted before Bybe't's irregular black casting, the pedestal of leaves, rocks, and wings breaking about geometric uncertainties and topologic singularities, to gaze up where meters of misted crystal rose to the capital's folds and spikes—

Suddenly the glass glowed.

Within, bubbles of light.

Bubbles fell and rose.

Rat now stood to gaze. Light lay on the floor about him, quivered on his rings, deviled his shadow's edge behind him.

Kal'k started forward. I pushed past Hatti to overtake her, hearing behind:

"What did—?"

"Did Rat turn it—?"

"How—?"

As I came up, the speaker, in the mouth of a gaping dust-skate at shin level, asked:

"Who are you?"

I had never heard my seven-times great-grandmother's voice, but I had read enough descriptions of its velvet body, its scrap-silver nap.

"You wear the rings of Vondramach Okk, and . . ." In the pause, I thought perhaps Gylda Dyeth's synapse casting had failed. But light coursed on within the irregular transparency: "And there are people gathered outside in numbers I have only seen the likes of during a visit from Vondramach herself. Who are you? What do you want here? Why have you wakened me?"

I reached Rat's side, reached up to hold Rat's high, hard shoulder.

"I am Korga, the porter, Rat. And I come from—"

"Rat," I whispered, "how did you turn that on?"

"—Rhyonon. But that world is now destroyed."

I said: "Rat, you're not connected up for neural access. How did you activate that?" Then suddenly I thought to ask: "Mother Dyeth, what will we do about all those people outside? They're going to hurt themselves, if many of them haven't already."

"And they're here to see *this* one?" my seven-times great-grandmother demanded.

"As far as we can tell." (Japril moved up beside me.) "That's certainly what it looks like."

"It happens with certain guests of honor." Somewhere an elderly woman sighed with resigned ire. "I assume, from what I see about me, that this is a formal supper and this Rat is our guest . . . ?"

"This is a formal supper," I said. "But Rat's not the guest of honor, Mother Dyeth; only a visitor."

"Mmmmm," she said, which is a sound I've heard many humans make, but none who were born here on Velm. "Last time I saw folk gathered outside that way for someone who wore those rings but wasn't the guest of honor, well . . . we had an unpleasantness in the north court that I hope, by now, has been forgotten. But I doubt it. So, they're here to see this one. Have you shown this Rat fellow to them?"

"No," I said. "We haven't."

"They're not going to go away until you do," Mother Dyeth said. "That's what we always did when hundreds gathered outside to see Vondramach."

"This is thousands, Mother Dyeth," Japril said, surprising me. "Do you think Rat Korga's presence should be publicly announced?"

"Hundreds? Thousands? What woman has any concept of the difference between them! But I know that if those good people don't know for sure Rat Korga is here, rumor must be doing its damnedest."

"How do we show them?" I asked. "Should we just open the doors and let people in? There're already too many for the amphitheater to hold. I don't think—"

"Do it the way we did it. Activate the walls. That shouldn't be beyond you."

"The walls . . . ?" One of my mothers, Kelso I think, asked behind me.

"The multichrome walls. That's what they're there

for. It's the trouble with this heap, you know. There're so many things it can do, nobody can keep track of them from one year to the next."

"We'll have to look it up in the library," I said. "I'm not really sure even what you mean—"

"She means using the projection facilities in the free-standing walls," which was little Mima, med-tech$_2$ and student of ancient folk theater. "When the audience overflowed the amphitheater, and they wanted to project the performances to those gathered around the house, they used the multichrome walls."

"Oh," I said. There're lots of things that have happened around this place in the last couple of centuries I've just never known about.

"The last time they were used was well over a hundred years ago," Mima explained, "just before the Bazaret Troupe disbanded."

"We still have to go to the library to check the access codes. Nobody's going to know them after this many—"

"I do," Mima said.

Maybe that's why everyone needs students.

"Japril," I said, turning the other way, "you said something about public announcements?"

Japril looked very unhappy. "You don't really have much choice. Marta says that from her position the situation looks bad and Ynn says that, from where she is, it looks even worse."

"Rat, do you mind if—" but realized with him the question was irrelevant. "Mima?"

"Come this way." She started across the floor toward the ramp. "To the amphitheater. That's where you project from."

"Come on, Rat."

We went over small bridges. Alsrod Thant came running up, jangling aluminum disks on chains. "Marq, what's going on? I—" Clearwater and Eulalia were behind her. Whatever the reasons for their outrageous behavior, they had apparently dissolved before curiosity. I wanted to say something, but Rat, Mima, and about six other women (I think Tinjo, I think Santine, among both parents and students) rushed up the ramp with us toward a lot of mirrors.

Our images bloomed about us and fell away. As we came out from the stone arch and down the steps, somebody turned on the lights. The night sky blackened and lost stars. The high walls stood around. "Are you sure you know how to work the—"

"Oh, yes," Mima said. "You just stand on the stage, you and Rat—just the way you did when you gave us our orientation session. Only with Rat. One moment—" She thought some access code over; along the stage edge tiny traps opened up to reveal black ceramic elements that I vaguely remembered having seen in pictures as a child, but (one) had never known what they were and (two) had just assumed they'd been removed.

Empty seats rose round us in the dark to the walls themselves.

"You just go out there to stage center. Marq, maybe you could introduce Rat. Like Bazaret introducing the show."

"Huh?" I said. "Oh, yeah. Sure." Well, isn't that part of a diplomat's job? "We'll just stand . . ." I took Rat's arm— "over here?"

"The very spot from which Kand'ri herself delivered the Ambassador David's famous seventh-act soliloquy. Oh, this is exciting!" Mima stepped to the side of the stage. "You would like to see your audience, wouldn't you? Bazaret didn't. But Sejer'hi and Kand'ri wouldn't perform if they couldn't. They said that's what made it *folk* theater, you see?"

"I guess so." I glanced up at Rat, but his eyes, hollowed in the darkness, looked out on the empty seats.

"Good," Mima said. "Because that's the only way I know how to do it."

"You'd better hurry," Japril said, from where she and the others had gathered behind the fountain. "Marta says more are coming. And Ynn—"

"All right." Mima closed her eyes.

The sensation was exactly like that ambiguous up-down fall through a limen plate.

A cloud-streaked night. I looked about. A dark rectangular plate stood behind us to the left. Another stood to the right. In front of us, or rather in front and below, there were detailed shapes, and small lights among them—and we must have been visible on the freestanding multichrome walls above Dyethshome; hopefully, the crowds moving up had now stopped their forward surge and possibly were even allowing the ones in the front to move backwards a little. And I realized what Rat and I were gazing down over: the upper park levels of Morgre, their rails crowded with women, then women behind them, and behind them more, standing by the pole lights, gazing towards Dyethshome. I glanced down. Below the dark domes just at my feet (the court roofs), figures crowded the forecourt. On the rollerway up between the cactus, figures milled and pushed and jostled. I gazed down at it all from some two hundred meters; above the roofs of our cooperative, the city before us was an astonishing playroom toy.

"Excuse me," I said. My voice sounded boomy and distorted. "I am Marq Dyeth, and this is Rat Korga, the survivor whom you have all gathered to see—no, please. Move backwards, not forwards. Those of you out around Water Alley, *please* move back. You are endangering the lives of those nearer Dyethshome. You can all see from where you are. Please, don't move forward any more. This is a matter of life. If those of you there and there—" I pointed— "can all move back ten steps . . ."

I saw it happen; and also realized how large our image must have appeared because I saw how small their motions were.

"Good. Still, if those there and there can move back, say, fifteen more steps."

They did it. "Thank you. You must start to move people away from the grounds of Dyethshome. There is still room up in the upper park level, and the view is probably better from there anyway." Here and there what had been a clear forward motion began to swirl, and then reverse. "Thank you. Again, I want to introduce to you . . ." I started to say, *my friend*, but thought better: "Rat Korga, the survivor of Rhyonon, who has come to visit our world, our city."

I glanced up at Rat beside me. "Rat, will you . . . uh, say something to the women here at Morgre?"

He seemed so real beside me, gazing. I wondered if he recognized what he looked at, or the change of scale that accompanied it, or indeed if it mattered. "I am Rat Korga. As my friend, Marq Dyeth, said." The accent that in a day I had almost grown used to, now that I knew thousands heard it, seemed as intrusive as when I'd heard his first words. "Thank you. That is all I can say to you. I have no world, now; and its destruction hurt me in many ways. Thank you for letting me visit yours."

I looked about again, as Korga seemed to have said what he had to say. "May we ask you," I said, "to return to your living rooms. Rat Korga has been with us a day, and has already walked in our streets, moved through our runs within the city, hunted dragons on the sands outside it. But by this disruption of your own lives, by gathering to see Rat here, you only disrupt his and ours as well. I know as you go about our city, from center to rim to center, many of you will pass him and will extend the same courtesy to him you have extended to visitors in our clime for centuries now. Many visitors have stayed to call this, our world, home. . . ." I looked at Rat and wondered what I was trying to say, wondered why my single tongue stumbled now saying it. "The complex of flavors that awaits each of us is unique, interrupted only by sleep and ended only with death." It's a hopeless cliché, and where it came from, to spring out of my mouth just then, I later wondered for hours. "Return to the flavors of your lives and let us again take up ours. You've come to see Rat Korga, and you have. Please go, now, so that we may go on. Good night."

As I glanced at Rat again, with his wide shoulders and hollow eyes, I saw he had raised his bare, big hand to those who stared up at us, with neither distress nor humor on his long, pitted face.

2.

Out between low hills was the smaller more distant toy. ". . . I have no world, now; and its destruction hurt me in many ways. Thank you for letting me visit yours." Above the courts' five domes, projected on the freestanding walls, a tall doll and a short doll stood together. ". . . the complex of flavors that awaits each of us is unique, interrupted only by sleep and ended only with . . ." The comscreen, sticking above my desk's clutter, concluded the replay Mima had thoughtfully made.

Rat sat on my bed. "Why did we come here?"

I walked across the orange carpet to the desk. "Formal suppers always have intermissions, where everybody retires for a while. There're waiting-rooms for the guests to use. With all the confusion, Max and Shoshana thought this might be a good time to have it." I glanced at the small, planetary spheres about the suspended lamp globe. They began to circle, each with its swarm of tiny moons.

"I'm still hungry," Rat said. "I didn't eat much."

"No one ever really does at formal affairs. You just put in a lot of work doing it. But there'll be the pickings once it's all finished. Late-night snacks after these things are not to be believed." I came around the desk and leaned my hip on it. Behind Rat, fire cactus bent thick branches in a warm gust. Falling needles ticked the rail. "This has been quite an evening. I still don't know what the Thants were on about. All those things they were saying—those idiotic statements—they made me feel as if I were living on some world out of history where all that we do here was against the law!"

Rat said: "No, they didn't."

I frowned.

"They didn't make you feel that way. That's the way they made me feel."

"I don't understand what you mean."

"You didn't grow up on such a world. You didn't spend your childhood and make your transition to maturity on a world where bestiality and homosexuality were legally proscribed. So you do not possess the fund of those feelings to draw on. I do."

"But they spoke to me as much as . . ." I felt confused and angry again.

"They come from such a world," Rat said, looking down at his lap. "Otherwise, it would never have occurred to them to say such things."

". . . but the north," I said. "In the north of this world, at least up till comparatively recently, bestiality . . . as you call it, was illegal."

"Before I came here, they told me as much about the north of your world as they did about the south." Rat's eyes, in the lamp light, moved now to human, now to hollow (and the all-black eyes of the evelmi, in such light, frequently look hollow). "Is the north your world?"

"More than it is yours."

"I have no world, Marq Dyeth."

I stepped toward him in what I thought was anger—
and suddenly reeled within the combative flavors of desire. I shook my head, to see that he, standing, had
stepped toward me. And knew that the desire we felt
would not be consummated now. And at the same time I
watched all sensations in me that were not desire fade on
my tongue (metaphors of taste are so inadequate to describe what in reality is an appetite!) so that I was finally
licked all round by it, till I almost fell, and would not
because he did not fall.

More fire-needles dropped. A breeze (and we were
only millimeters apart) took the physical warmth from
between us that would have done for contact.

"Rat Korga?"

It was Japril's voice on the comscreen, and I was the
one who stepped suddenly back. (It was his hand, halted
under its jeweled weight, that reached forward—and, possibly because of that weight, did not quite touch me.)

"Marq, I'd like to see Rat. I'm in the south court. It's
important. . . ."

I didn't speak.

But seconds later, Rat turned and walked to the metal
plate in the corner of my rug.

"Rat's on his way, Japril."

I sat down at the desk, while Japril's face dissolved to
abstract colors. I wasn't breathing hard; but I seemed
aware of every alveolus as it filled with air to froth the
bloody rush. My heart was not beating more strongly; but
the slippage of muscle fiber against muscle fiber seemed to
create a friction I could feel.

"Marq Dyeth!"

I sat, terribly conscious of the juncture of foot and
rug, buttock and bench.

"Hey—Marq?"

I looked up, where George Thant materialized in the
column, bronze, transparent, swaying in the view-light
where, moments before, Rat had been.

"Don't answer me, if you want. I don't care—" Her
words were slurred. I wondered what she'd eaten or drunk
so much of as to half-drug herself. "Marq, let me in—!"

I thought through the entrance code out of habit, the

way the first notes of a melody—George's demand—produce
the concluding ones without real effort. She staggered
forward, then caught her balance. "So. This is where you
run off to, hey?"

"George," I said. "Look, I'm not sure what you and
your folks are doing. But a lot's been going on here that—"

"Well, we're sure what you've been doing—you *and*
your folks." She shook a big metallic finger at me; then the
gesture lost focus, and she reached up to rub her bald,
bronze head. Looking about through brazen lids, she took
a few more steps. "Here, I've finally made it into one of
your lizard-lover's inner sanctums."

And Rat was right. As an insult it only seemed odd.

"Now what do I find? That your world's just the same
as mine!" She looked around again. "This is no different
from my room, a sun and a world and sixty-eight thousand
light-years away. Not a puff of difference." She came up to
the desk. "Did you know that? There, in the cells of 17,
cut into our canyon walls—you call yours Dyethshome, we
call ours Thantspace—my living room is *just* like yours.
Here—" In a crisp motion belying whatever drug her
staggering had mimed, she grasped my desk edge, pulled
out the small control drawer from under the lip, and
reached inside. "I'll show you!"

"George," I said, "what are you—?"

George twisted things inside, knocked others with
her knuckles, flattened still more under her polished palm.

"George, *what* in the—?"

Stars and clouds went out.

The hills, with Morgre between, vanished. George
laughed. Fire cactus faded. Somewhere the stream ceased
to plash. Bed and desk and rail and carpet disappeared.

Three meters by three meters, my living room's wall
plates had once been sprayed, probably back in Ari's time,
with a translucent green gum that had now worn off the
center of the floor, showing tarnished blotches. Where the
metal bolt-heads were deeply inset, some of the coating
had pulled loose, though after a century it still accom-
plished its major job: to keep any random chemical reaction in the walls' surface from adding some upsetting order
to the image the plates could be excited to project.

George, no longer bronze and not quite as tall, stood
by the control post that slanted up, off center, in the

pentagonal floor. "Same technology. Same everything. . . .
Not a bit different from mine."

I uncrossed my legs, feeling warm metal uncomfortable under my buttocks, and started to stand—even three
years ago I could still get up from a cross-legged position
on the floor in a single motion. But now I had to push
myself up to my knees, roll around a little, and then get
one foot under me, shove, and then another. "George," I
said. "You are rude beyond bearing—which is no news.
But this takes all!"

George was looking at her arm, thinner than it had
been. Above her elbow was a small sore. "That's not
supposed to be there," she said. "At least not now. Oh,
this is crazy . . . !"

Projection lenses lost their glow and retracted into
the ceiling. Two metal doors clicked closed over them.
(Three others did not, which meant some of the backup
circuits were no longer working. But the room was
overdetermined by a factor of seven, which meant *maybe*
my great-great-great-granddaughter might have to have
one or two repairs done before she moved in.) "I don't
know . . ." George shook her head, where, without the
projection, there was at least three weeks' growth of hair.
"But—well, I guess . . ." She looked at the green, irregularly shaped walls. "No, it's *not* that much like mine,
really. Mine's cubical—and the realspace must be half
again the size of this. I bet some sociometrician could
make a good argument that's why I have my personality
and you have yours." Teeth together, lips pulled back, she
rubbed one thick thumb over that sore. "Shit . . ."

"Get out of here," I said. "I don't know what you
think you're doing, but at this point I don't *want* to know!"

"You don't?" George looked up, glowering. "Nea tells
you that we're trying to take over the position of Focus
Unit on Nepiy; you report our takeover to the Web; we
come to confront you and receive your accusation directly—
tonight the place is crawling with Web officials! Now you
claim you 'don't *know*' what we're doing'? *I* said no, that's
not the Dyeth's style. But Thadeus said: 'You just watch!
We'll go there, try to make an honorable showing. Will
they say a thing? They'll have the odd Web officer just
standing around, as if they just happened to be invited for
some other purpose entirely. Chances are, they won't

even have told her yet. They'll tell her after we go. They
think that's stylish.' Well, we're leaving your stylish, deca-
dent, beastly little world. And when we leave, we're going
to Nepiy. And we're going to take it over. And neither you
nor the Web can stop us.'

"George," I said. "I've been a little confused up till
now. But you've just taken that confusion into another
realm entirely. What *are* you talking about?"

But George was fingering her sore again. "The medical program gave me a point-three chance that it was
bacterial and a one-point-six chance that it was viral, both
of which go up by a factor of two-point-eight if it lasts
more than four days. It's going to be four days tomorrow. I
don't want to be sick. I was sick last year, for two whole
weeks, and it was the scariest thing that ever happened to
me. Oh, shit . . ."

"George," I said.

"Well, Thadeus is right." She looked up. "I said, 'no.'
Alsrod said, 'no.' And Alsrod is pretty smart, and I always
listen to what she's got to say. But Thadeus has the experience and knows what to expect. Ordering experience is
what a Family's all about, you know? And we're a Family,
now. But don't worry: we have our own ways of getting
what we want, spiders or no spiders. That's why we can go
to Nepiy and still be who we are. We take our history with
us." She looked around, frowning. "Though this has been
the most unpleasant experience of *my* life—imagine, you,
betraying us to the spiders! But what could you expect
from you lizard-loving perverts!"

"Betrayed you to—?"

George pulled her brown hand from the control post's
control plate—and grew large and bronze, while the green
walls grew distances and stars and night and hills and
railings and carpet and desk. She removed her hand from
the drawer; and slid it closed. I sat down in the chair that,
behind my desk, had once more molded to my shape.

As I moved my bare feet over the rug's orange nap,
bronze George stepped back onto the limen plate, laughing.

Light rose around her. George and her laughter faded.

More fire-needles fell.

All I could think was: Would hotwind season arrive
early this year?

I know how much of my world—its streets, its hills,

its runs, its rains, the halls, the heat, the sky, the stars, the stream itself—is and is not illusion. But for a moment, as I sat by my desk, still lost in the disruption from George's invasion, I felt foreign as a creature from one of those primitive geosectors on some world where all reproductive media are safely contained in clearly visible frames; who, for the first time, confronts a modern society where all is what we once called—to use a word that in one ancient human language or another referred to vision but here on Velm had shifted to denote taste—spectacle.

Then, beyond the rail, a rustle of leaves, needles, wings.

"Marq . . ."

I looked up from the wrinkled covers on my bed.

"Marq?"

I blinked at the railing around my room. The shapes and objects beyond it came into night focus.

"Marq . . . !"

A dark forehead's wide scales beneath gorgeous gills: Sel'v walked up over fallen needles toward my platform. I saw her face above the floor boards and below the lower rail-rung. The line of light moved down her neck, and I saw Small Maxa, thin and white, beside her. Sel'v's wings sculled on the dark, and Maxa scooted ahead to the platform edge. "Go on, go on, go on . . ." Sel'v said with several tongues. Then my mother leaped, momentarily to perch on the rail, beating up tape and clutter to balance. Then down to the carpet, glancing back. "Hurry up, now, dear. Tell Marq what you told me."

For a moment Maxa stood, grasping her thin elbow with the knuckly fingers of her other hand. Then she grasped the platform edge, vaulted up and hunkered under the railing to stand at our mother's hinder haunch, blinking creamy eyes.

I frowned. "What is it?"

"Marq . . ." Maxa's hair was a rough, white cloud. "Marq, Rat's gone."

My fist, among dice and tape, opened on the desk's varnished pith. "What?"

"Rat," she said. "Rat left. With that woman, the one from the Web."

"With Japril," I said. "Yes, I . . ."

Maxa looked up at Sel'v and a jaw muscle bunched.

Sel'v lifted her foreclaws, swung her head from side to side, and said: "Go on, dear. Tell Marq everything."

"Rat Korga, your new friend," Maxa said, "the survivor of Rhyonon . . ." Her voice was so low she only seemed to talk with half the tongue she had. "Rat was leaving with that Web woman. I met them outside on the terrace. The dark erased his eyes, Marq. I asked them where they were going—you know, Rat went with me to look at my mines this morning in the playroom."

"Yes, of course," I said. "What did they say?"

"Rat didn't say anything," Maxa said. "Only looked at me. And because of that look, I came to tell you."

"Sel'v?" I stood up. "Maxa—this whole day has been full of people telling me things I don't seem to be able to understand."

"Tell Marq what she said," Sel'v prompted, "what the spider said."

"What *did* Japril say?"

"She said they were leaving this world forever. She said they were leaving Velm. She said that this world would not do for Rat. She said that she was sorry. And she said that I should relate this to you. But it was because of Rat's look, Marq, that I—"

I don't remember lunging across the carpet. I don't remember grasping her shoulders. I know she screamed. And I know it was not because she felt my hands on her flesh—it was only another photocall. We were not near enough to the wall for the connection to be that good. Still, the notion that I might even mime such a violation brought her to writhing sobs.

She turned her white hair aside, now left, now right. "Oh, Marq! Marq . . . !"

Crying, she looked up at me. Spittle on her chin had streaked the dust from the mine-clays that always grayed her face. There were tears on her cheek. Beside us, Sel'v had risen to her hind feet, to claw the air with four claws, her wings unfurled, making their own hurricane about my dwelling with her own distress.

"Marq . . . !"
"Marq . . . !"
"Marq . . . !"

I pushed myself away and lurched, unsteady as George, for the limen plate.

3.

Dark enough to strike the Rat's eyes' glass.

A dozen women still stood or squatted, on two feet, four, or six, about the colored clays before the terrace. A few waited by the pool (I recognized the two hunting scooters, parked by the black and silver wall, showing no trace of the thousands that had milled around them only an hour ago), the same number now who might have gathered to see guests arrive and depart at any formal supper.

But because, with Rat, I had watched the crowds begin dispersing when we had hovered above them on the freestanding multichromes, I had somehow carried through that dispersal, in my mind, to completion:

The remaining women surprised me.

Had they watched, with Small Maxa, Rat and Japril leave?

Angered, I turned to reenter Dyethshome, and saw my face break up on a hundred mirrors.

At the column, Large Maxa stood, her foreclaws against the crystal, her midclaws just off the floor, her wings loose about her on the floor in folds of scarlet and dark green. She played one tongue and another on the glass surface, entranced with this one sculpture which, for so long now, we had all but ignored. I started to go past. My mother's aesthetic interest seemed the most experienced and useless of things, and I wanted to be away from it.

But, bubbling, light still lived and rose inside it.

I frowned, looked back, turned back.

Without ceasing her appreciation of the sculptural marvel, Large Maxa looked at me with eyes whose blackness recalled his: she must have seen, with hers, even in her half-hypnotized state, my despair. She turned her great head to continue her examination of the column and to cut short, as one can only with members of one's own stream, the necessity for greeting.

"Mother Dyeth . . . ?" I said

"Mmm," said the pillar's brassy contralto. (Large Maxa's wings rippled on the floor, but that was the only notice she gave of the vibrations that inscribed themselves across her study and pleasure.) "I've been playing through the research channels in the library. Someone was thoughtful enough to connect me up to those permanently when I was built. So: you're one of my seven-times great-grand-offspring. Marq Dyeth, it's nice to know you."

I couldn't very well interrupt Maxa to ask; no doubt we were interrupting her enough by my childish curiosity in this synaptic image of my human forebear. "Mother Dyeth," I said, "where is everybody?"

"Gone home, back to their respective rooms, their respective worlds. From what I gather, this hasn't been the most successful of parties."

"The Thants . . . ?"

"Your offworld guests of honor?" Her voice, by silence, projected the disapproval that a human face would sign by a slight lowering and an evelm face by a slight raising. (Large Maxa's head, still licking, still without looking, raised; and I wondered what my grandmother made of my mother who tasted and tasted her gleaming flank.) "No, they were the *first* to leave. They're not very friendly. I like you, boy. From what I overheard, you love the tall human with the rings. Yes? You remind me of me—and of my children. Are you old enough to remember my boy, Vrach? Vrach, with a lover, Orgik Korm, took this stream on into its second ripple, you know. I must say, the place looked very different back then. Not better, mind you. Just different."

"I've heard of them," I said. "But they died a hundred, a hundred-fifty years ago, grandmother."

"Of course." There was laughter, ending in a sigh. (Max's wings whispered.) "I'm tired now. Do me a favor there, Marq. Turn me off."

"Mother Dyeth," I said, "I'm sorry. I don't know how."

I read a human frown in that absent voice.

"Don't know *how*? Oh, well." The sign that came next revised that frown's meaning: "Well. Well, well."

"How did Rat turn you on?"

She was a book, she was a text, she was a set of signs, some present, some absent but implied, and many just forgotten, to be interpreted like the interminable crystals I had been trying to read since adolescence. She was a hermeneutic enterprise I could not bear, who mocked me

by the miming of a desire stronger than mine to withdraw
from the encounter. "No, don't go yet, Marq."

"Perhaps," I said, "I can go look up the access
numbers—"

"It's not necessary."

"You know, Mother Dyeth—" It seemed the diplomatic thing to say—"I'm reading your memoirs. Really,
I've thought about you on and off all my life."

"On and off," she said. "On and off. When I was
alive, there were lots of worlds with switches that you
actually had to *do* something to in order to activate. I
guess they're being phased out—at least here."

I started to say something. Then I frowned. "How *did*
Rat turn you on?"

"I was constructed," Mother Dyeth confided, "so that
anyone who wore those rings could activate or deactivate
me."

"Some information the rings contain?" I asked. "The
rings of Vondramach?"

"No," she said. "Actually, no."

"Is it information you can give me? Can you tell me
how?"

"Yes."

"Go on, then."

The voice became breathy, boomy, and I wondered if
the synapse caster had erred, though the voice's intention
was clear. From an evelm tongue it would have been a
whisper, though it filled the whole dim waterless court.
(Someone—Egri? Maxa?—had turned off the spill.) "Look
down at the pedestal just about level with the thickest part
of your calf. You will see there some metal leaves. Just
below them and to the left, you will find a small, black
button." I heard the sound of a deep and resigned breath.
"Take your finger, and *press* it."

There were the dyll leaves, sculpted centuries ago by
Bybe't. I stooped. Under them, in the shadow of Large
Maxa's loose wing, was a small black protuberance. In
thirty-six years, child and adult, I'd never seen it.

Mechanical switches *are* less common than in my
seven-times great-grandmother's day. Still, I wondered
which finger I should use. There are cultures where,
depending on what you want to accomplish, it matters.
Finally, however, with a forefinger, I jabbed.

Above the fluted pedestal, light died.

There was only the sound of delicate wet tongues peeling and peeling from glass.

It might as well have been silence; and unlike the silences that had interrupted the voice till now, no new words would come to enclose it, and thus inform it with meaning.

I stood, as Maxa moved further around the column, to taste other irregularities in the darkened crystal, dragging brilliant wings.

Walking back across the small bridges above dry carvings, I saw Egri come up the spiral stair, among the silver stars of *Mu*-3. She looked about. But the dining apparatus had all been retracted into floors and ceilings. She walked to the perch and climbed, tiredly, from one inlaid shelf to the other, finally to sit, one leg up and one hanging, blinking about the court. I walked up the ramp.

I had seen those mirrors so many times I missed my multiplication as I came out under guanoed stone to step down stone steps.

The amphitheater lights were still on.

"Sklenu Marq . . . ?"

Cross-legged at the center of the skene, JoBonnot turned herself around on red-gloved hands to look up at me.

"Ah, yes. So. You are a fool, poor Squellem Dyeth."

"JoBonnot—" I stepped over the grill— "where are they?"

About the amphitheater, students sat here and there, whispering to one another, walking about in the aisles, oblivious to everything and anything that might have been going on on that bright stage.

"In fact—" JoBonnot leaned her masked head to the side— "as far as your GI can tell me, there are no words in the four major language groups that humans and evelmi share in this world to designate precisely the kind of fool you are."

"JoBonnot," I said, "Rat Korga is gone. He's not on . . . on Velm any more. On my world."

"Look up," she said. "Look at the real stars in the real sky that you can't see from here because the damned lights are too bright and because there are three freestanding multichrome walls around this amphitheater that block out anything interesting."

I frowned. "Where has Japril . . .?"

She laughed. "Oh, what a marvelous and charming fool you are, my most undiplomatic Marq Dyeth! It starts on Zetzor and ends at my home, Nepiy. *My* world, Marq Dyeth. Where they are soon to be something close to kings. Oh, Skena Marq, as we gaze up at your own world's sky, tonight, *do* you know what it is that you don't see there? Do you know what sweeps invisible across it, even as I speak?"

"What?"

"A fleet of three-hundred-sixty thousand Xlv ships, circling, circling, circling this world, your world, Velm, in orbits ranging from nineteen minutes to point-oh-two hours in duration. That's very fast. No, don't worry. They won't do anything. I have more information about this than you. They're watching. Watching you. Ah, I am receiving a report now . . . yes, some of them have started to leave already. The Web shuttle, flown by three cunning spiders, has just lifted above them, you see, and is laboring out between your two tiny moons." She snorted a little, behind the white and red striped plastic covering. The sound came clearly through the grill at her mouth. "Myself, I'm quite terrified, sitting here, on your world, knowing what I know about Korga, the Xlv, you, Rhyonon, Velm. . . . Really, you are the most disrupting and random of factors in a very complex equation, Marq Dyeth. I am terrified, yes. But I am also profoundly sane. What such sanity as I have gains me is a good sense of what terrors to trust and what terrors to fight, even to death. Have you figured out, yet, that I can help you, Skene Marq?"

"Can you help me find Rat Korga?"

She turned to look up among the amphitheater seats, while students did not look at us, did not stop whispering and walking. Above the ninetieth ring, among the shadowy statuary, I fancied I saw a short, heavyset male. And in the moment I thought I saw, I was sure she was waiting for the tall woman in the red and white body-mask before me.

"You have a job$_1$ to do, Marq Dyeth. Go back to your room and prepare to do it." In a single motion she stood, turned, and was at the skene edge, from which she leaped down. She clambered up over seats, now stepping on a cushion, now on the stone between. I read her motion as a headlong rush toward the distant figure who, later, I decided was just some sort of shadow, a projection of my own anxieties, my own terror for my threatened world. After all, he looked too much like me.

At the twent-first row, she disappeared.

So had the mysterious male.

I started to call out, but a vast paralysis seized me that any attempt to break made that muscle—foot or tongue or hand or heel—cramp with pain. The theater around me swam and cleared and swam again as I blinked away the waters in my eyes. My cheek became a spill.

All the little traps about the stage edge were closed.

And JoBonnot had vanished into the polarized chamber.

I dragged in some loud, raucous breath; and didn't fall.

Only one student—the evelm algae-farmer[1]—even looked up.

EPILOGUE

Morning

Night passed; another night followed; and another. I don't remember when, among them, I first realized that I had no memory of the morning after his departure. The morning before? How could I forget rolling from my sleeping mat on my six-legged bed, the expectation of the hunt, the lizard perch, the trip to the student quarters and his seamless waking. Yet the morning after is as blank as the other is vivid. Time articulated itself over nights, days, evenings—and, yes, more mornings. But as, among them now, I began to move, to $work_2$, to function, to $work_1$, I found myself dwelling on that dawn absence in memory's continuity, caused certainly by the intensity of loss, the absolute vanishing of the possible. Recollection, which custom edits as it sediments, is a notorious trickster. Yet what's sedimented here is forgetfulness itself. I suppose if I were going to dwell on an absence, it would be easier to ponder what, by a slip of attention, I missed than what, through an imponderable clash of chance, I had lost. Some midnight, some noon, on my world or another or halfway through the dark between, I would try again to recall that subsequent waking, those first thoughts on the first day without him, but as soon as I would press my mind against the edgeless dislocation that marked the nothingness between that night's half-sleep and a loggy waking, an ex-

hausting frustration would couple with, finally, some kind
of willful inattention and slip my mind to alternate dawns.
For while we search out one fugitive reflection, another
can snag the disengaged and free-spinning engine of effort;
and I would end up reviewing, say, this most rehearsed of
recollections. From another world and neither the most
vivid nor the earliest, it is still among my most tenacious
memories. I was perhaps ten. I don't know which world it
was, but it must have been one on which we'd stopped en
route to Senthy.

Night:

A trip across an open field, on my back, in some
flapping container, while shadows loomed hundreds of
meters into the air around. Wind tugged at the scarred
translucent covering, and I realized at one point that I was
being borne by beast, not machine. I know I drifted off to
sleep. And I know now that while I slept I could as easily
have been carried a thousand light years as a thousand
kilometers.

I woke.

Gauze hung around me; light poured through an octagonal opening in a slanting wall. I pushed up on the
sleeping pad, scrambled through the gauze, did not go
through several dark openings lower down, but clambered
through the bright one. Air. Sky. Something smooth under my hands; something rough under my feet; and the
pithy taste of an atmosphere not mine.

I stood up outside.

The pale blue near the horizon became much darker
overhead, which later I would learn meant a world with an
artificial atmosphere held down by force.

A sandy horizon, gray, flat: here and there black rocks
broke it. Here and there dark machines labored on it.

I don't remember if the gravity was slightly more or
slightly less than I was used to.

But I knew some things about my location. The thrumming down below the metal plates I stood on had something to do with large pumps and a small water supply.
Inside the great, shaggy fences off to the left were beasts
similar to the ones that had borne my carrier before. But
the isolation of these facts suggests things I'd either been
told or figured for myself. They do not sit among a galaxy
of facts as do data acquired from General Information. I

sidestepped down . . . a rut? A gully? The crease in the
loose soil, its bottom filled with pebbles, could have been
the result of either attention or erosion.

With round black rocks set among flat tan ones, a
stone wall rose to a mossy overhang at about eye-level. My
ten-year-old toes and fingers would find easy purchase in
those crevices. I was human. It never occurred to me *not*
to climb it.

As I put one bare foot on the sandy stone, above the
wall I suddenly saw a brownish stalk, on the end of which
were five or six transparent globes, packed and backed
with dim foil, each of them folded within dark membranes, which closed and opened, now over one, now over
another, so that—I suddenly realized—I was gazing at an
alien gazing at an alien gaze.

Yes, the reality struck me in that complex a set of
terms.

The eyestalk retreated.

Pebble hit pebble on the other side; I heard a scrab-
bling, then movement away.

I wasn't scared; I didn't feel confused. The encounter
halted me, and I stood—halted—staring above the mossy
rocks for a while. Then I climbed again.

Elbows fixed on the gritty stone, I leaned over. On
the dirt below, the regular squiggles certainly looked like
tracks, but not from a creature with feet as I knew them.

They angled from the wall, stopped for a meter, then
took up for another two, stopped . . . if they took up
again, they were lost in the rock-pocked sands.

Had it squirmed away?

Had it leapt?

I felt around with one foot to continue my climb.

"Marq—?"

I glanced behind me in the windless air that (later) I
would connect with large open expanses on a newly
planoformed world.

"Marq, *please* come down from there!"

I don't know whether it was Hatti or Sel'v who called.

"Really, dear, you *don't* know where you are, and
while I'm sure nothing's here that can hurt you, still, until
Genya gets here, I wish you'd come back to the compound. It's very early."

In the trip to foggy, gardened and oceaned Senthy,

somehow that interim world never got a name. Often, though, I have thought that this, my first unfettered experience of alien life, had far more to do with my choosing my particular profession₁ than all the force of Genya, Egri, or my older sisters together.

But why, I wonder, when I tell you of that morning memory, does this one come to interrupt? (The more we come to rely on GI, the more our daily consciousness becomes subservient to memory's wanderings; and day begins with morning.) A dozen or so had gathered in the ship's viewing chamber. The transparent canopy was most of a half-sphere that went down to the meter-high black wall. Only a dozen of us, from among the thousands on the ship, had contracted to go without anti-anxiety drugs for a day and had been taking, instead, for the last three hours, the capsules that actually had to be swallowed with long draughts of water from special collapsible containers.

"Shortly we will deopaque—" which is a solecism in Arachnia too— "the viewing canopy, and you will be able to look directly on what is, to date, the largest known object in the galaxy: the central red giant of the Aurigae system. We are at a distance of just slightly under thirty light-minutes from the stellar surface. Its mass is approximately two hundred thousand times that of a standard G-type star, such as Sol. Its diameter, were it in the center of the Sol system—" this, you can tell, was a Family ship— "would engulf Mercury, Venus, Earth, Mars, the asteroid belt, Saturn, Jupiter, and extend halfway to Uranus." (It's always strange to hear aloud information that you've just received, minutes back, through GI—that extended déjà vu of the ear.) "When we transpare the viewing canopy, the sky will be dark blue; that is because we are well within Aurigae's atmosphere—an atmosphere which, at this distance, is hundreds of times thinner even than Mars's, but which, because it extends for practically half a light-year, has a diffraction ability to rival your home worlds'. We will use the viewing chamber's simulation facilities to imitate a rotation of the ship, so that the stellar disk of Aurigae will appear to rise to your left, cross the sky, then set on your right."

Blessedly, as the dome began to clear, there was no music.

Oddly, I *didn't* think "sky" before that purple dis-

tance. (It wasn't really blue.) Indeed, I thought only that
something a little more than near-vacuum extended before
me half a light-year.

It was luminous purple. There were a few stars visible
in it. From GI, I knew that there were other stars among
the thirty or so that made up the Aurigae system, at least
three of which were almost half as big as Aurigae itself.

They were all moving to the right.

Then, left, a line of red. (And some music did start:
diatonic, full of trumpets, half a millennium old, no doubt
a Family import from Old Earth itself.) It was curved, yes.
But it looked like a wall, not a sun. The wall was mottled
red and black and brown, and moved up over the viewing
bubble. "Aurigae's surface temperature is no more than
650 degrees Celsius. Its composition is mostly helium. Its
average density is substantially less than that of water, but
is substantially more than that of gaseous hydrogen at one
standard gravity. It has been estimated that had Aurigae
been only two percent denser, it would have collapsed
into a black hole at least a billion and a half years ago. Less
than point-oh-seven percent of the stars in our galaxy are
in the narrow margin of mass required to become such
super-giants. Ordinarily, red giants, of course, are a tenth
the diameter and fairly common. Of these super-giants,
Aurigae was discovered from Earth and almost immediately estimated as the largest stellar object in the universe
(though its actual mass and size, until the advent of space
travel, were underestimated by several decimal orders of
magnitude); it is still, as far as we know, the largest,
though there have been, to date, ninety-three other giant
stars, still expanding, that within another two billion years
will be substantially larger than Aurigae today. By that
time, Aurigae itself will have begun to contract. The darker
areas that you see in swirls over the stellar surface are
mammoth tidal areas where the surface temperature of the
star has fallen as low as 450 degrees. At the surface of
Aurigae, emitted light would not be enough to produce
the bright display we are currently seeing, if internal
temperatures, many thousands of times greater, did not
cause what is sometimes known as the photon-cascade
effect, which only occurs in gravitic fields more than six
hundred times Earth standard, and which, unknown until
three hundred years ago, is responsible for both pulsars

and quasars, phenomena that once mystified early Earth astronomers, and caused the original underestimation of Aurigae's size." By now the deep red, glimmering field had risen to cover half the bubble. The curvature was visible, but you had to look back and forth to see the expanse of it. "The smallest of those mottled dark spots which you can see in the glow are large enough to absorb the planet Jupiter without visible disturbance—indeed, if Jupiter were at the stellar surface, it would take up a space one-one-hundredth as many seconds of an arc as your own little fingernail when looked at at arm's length." For moments, wider and higher than my own vision, red and black Aurigae was all I saw. Then—how many hypnotic minutes later—to the left, the slightest purple atmosphere, scimitaring the glimmer. "We will halt the simulated rotation of the ship with the stellar disk set to a minimum of thirty-four percent of the viewing canopy, as you saw it in the vaurine brochure. You will have another hour to observe it, before we once again opaque the chamber and request that you return to your sleeping cells. Again, let us remind you that no further drugs need be taken to return you to semi-somnolence. They will be administered automatically through the air."

The motion stopped.

The music died.

One and another of us, we looked at each other, then up at the swollen star. Over half the women on the ship, as I recall, were not human—but I don't recall which species they were. One—who was—looked at me with a small, cramped laugh: "It *is* large!"

My own laugh was probably no less cramped.

We were the first two to rise from our benches. For about fifteen minutes we walked to this side of the chamber, then that side, looking up at the purple, whose diffraction indeed was like no planetary atmosphere I've ever been in, now out and down and around at the star into which Iiriani, not to mention Iiriani-prime, might both have fallen without a noticeable splatter.

One and another, people began to leave.

Eventually I was left with only one other woman. She had a small steel-mesh disk among the fleshy folds of reddish skin (darker than Aurigae) which, just as I realized it was a human-speech translation device, began to talk:

"Were you at all offended that they gave you the analogic information in Solar Systemic terms, human?"

I smiled. "Myself, I'm much more comfortable on Sygn-style ships than on Family ones—true. But I suppose I just took it as a somewhat chauvinistic habit left over from the dawn of space travel. GI converts it into whatever terms you're most familiar with, anyway."

"An intriguing strategy," the bland and inhumanly self-assured voice addressed me while fold on fold thrilled and rippled. "I spent six years on Old Earth—at least a planet *called* Earth. I was at North China University."

I did *not* make the standard comment I would have on my own world about universities being a wonderful way to travel. "University life always seemed a fine way to age."

"Ah, yes. One does seem to age there. Talk of Solarcentric chauvinism is frequently a good opening conversational gambit for humans of a certain Familiar orientation, I find."

"Is it?" My world was a Sygn world; but then she was not human. "It seems somehow strange to me to talk of Solarcentricism before something like that." I gestured toward the great sun.

"How true," returned the measured, featureless voice. "I would chuckle in amused agreement, but the laughter switches of my translator have been malfunctioning for the past six hours. You understand."

"Certainly," I said. And somehow felt much more comfortable. "Now, myself, I've never been to an Earth."

"And here I would laugh with surprise if I could!" the alien exclaimed. "How provincial of me, to assume, just because you are human . . ."

"Oh, I'm sure there is a flavor about all my movements and manners that gives you a taste of my origins."

"Flavor? Ah, yes. Myself, I have twelve different faculties that you would call senses. But the ones you humans call sight, taste, and smell are not among them. Oh, you have no idea how much difficulty that gave me on your planet—your racial origin planet, that is. (If, indeed, it was!) At your university. Eventually though, through trial and error, I was able to develop quite a complex algorithm for translation purposes. I'm very proud of it, really. It's never failed me yet. *Your* binocular vision, I

know, can actually perceive directly the spherical solidity
of that great globe. I can't, not at this distance."

I looked out at the sun again. Yes, the parallax of my
minuscule eyes was enough to register its stupendous
curvature. "As a matter of fact I can. It does curve away.
Tell me, which sense are you perceiving it with?"

"I? How polite of you! It's a kind of aural rendition
that requires the light to be translated into ultrasound
waves. Indeed, it sounds like one of my own home world's
dawns, only much vaster, harmonious, resonant."

I looked up at the purplish immensity that was all
space for half a light-year, but which, from here, seemed
smaller than the star that filled it. "It does remind me of a
strange and alien morning."

"In the light of such a sun, one would think it should
always be noon. Yet morning is certainly the way it strikes
me. Do you agree?"

I nodded, wondering at the vagaries of translation.
"To me," I said, "it seems at once both bitter and sweet; it
speaks to me of concatenations of tastes as eccentric as
mace, vinegared lichen, and powdered alum served three
hours after sunset at the very moment when the musicians
cease to play—it casts me out of myself, then hurls me
back like a suddenly encountered odor from childhood
that, as I name it, I only then realize I have mistaken for
some other, and I am forced to contemplate all the possibilities that, in their shadings and subtleties, must be as
varied as the red and black variegations on that star itself,
and thus I am struck with the notion of something so large
it might as well be infinite, so old it might as well be
eternal."

"Precisely," said that steel translator's voice for this
creature who possibly possessed none of her own. She
started to drift along the rail, rippling. "That is precisely
the way it sounds to me. I could not have put it better,"
leaving me to wonder what, precisely, precision was on
the other side of that steel disk. That she and I had both
found something matutinal to contemplate, for whatever
our vastly different reasons, in that huge fire, seemed the
most stupendous of cosmic accidents and was, finally, where
all real wonder lay.

*   *   *

To arrive at dawn on a world where you have departed
nighttime (or daytime—no matter) from some spot on that
same world is to enter a welter of possibilities. I recall my
departure from the moonlit shore and, an hour later, my
arrival at the morning Flame Fields of Rhys-s'kelton where,
beyond the great ceramic baffles, the flickering light dark-
ens the sky into a parody of night, even when their tiny
sun had lifted above the broken horizon. As I walked along
the covered arches that wormed through the air from one
governmental institution to the next, I looked down over
the rail, through the clear wall at the lavid fissures a
hundred meters below, hot with copper and rose. But
every dawn-time flicker over the artfully bland facades I
could read as a sign whose meaning had been given me by
my previous nights, days, evenings on the world itself,
signs I knew, even if I had hopelessly mislocated them on
this particular fragment of it, signs that would adjust and
rearrange as the day and days went on: a situation that
allowed morning to be a beginning by anchoring it to a
succession of days and nights—an arrival inscribed all over
by an obsessive security that a person who has lived on a
single world can never really know, because she has never
been without it.

But have you ever arrived *on* a world at dawn?

The ship orbits, usually for an hour or three, before
landing. As one watches in the binocs (that the better
ships provide to tape over your eyes) you can see the
world, this one orange and green with hydrocarbon soups,
that one blue and white with oxidized hydrogen broths,
another grit gray, still another dust brown, but all, whatever their dominant color, scythed away, as one circles,
with night.

If your mind turns in such aubadinal directions, you
become intensely aware how arbitrary a concept dawn is.

First of all, it is all choice: to arrive on a world in the
morning is a decision completely at the whim of those
conscious priorities that run from pragmatics to aesthetics.
Power and desire are both given voice, each allowed their
necessary pages in the decisionary print-out.

The tumble—where they tell you *not* to look—feels,
most of it, not like the soar through space, but rather like
a jarring, an inadvertent jiggling, that would shake up
some container in an earthquake, lodged at a mine's bottom.

And on the vast majority of worlds, when you emerge from that ill-bounded structure, the ship, you are (more or less) underground.

Sets of identification crystals spun in invisible reading fields between tall, worn elements; a moving roadway, which I realized to my astonishment from the hum underfoot, was propelled by *mechanical* rollers; and I emerged from a round kiosk in what at first looked like some horizon-to-horizon rippling mirror: water, but it was rare that I had seen so much of it at once. Only a few centimeters deep, I was later told. And here and there lay the purple and green algae-patches harvested over the grand-paddy with those tall cranes, most, at this hour, immobile across the silver flats. To my left the sky was dark. To my right, red washed through the overcast. On a meter-wide ridge of wet gravel ribboning away, some women in heavy boots, bulbous gloves, and tarnished metallic suits crunched up. Most of them looked at me—one or two smiled, as if in acknowledgment of my offworld dress. (Save my slippers, I was naked.) They came by me into the kiosk, which fed into a local transport as well as the ten-kilometer shuttle from the spacefield. Were they coming from a work shift? Were they going to one? To arrive on a world at dawn, despite GI's preliminary scatter of information, is to read the whole roster of signs you are used to for morning over the expanse of what you see, and at the same time see those meanings start to transpare as one begins to see the possibilities—a world of possibilities—clear behind them.

To leave one spot on a world at dawn when your destination is another spot on that same world is to be assured coherent passage ahead into day or back into night. The aerial city of Datchog consists of fifty-five giant condenapts hung between towering pylons rising six hundred meters above the mist-filled canyons. The inhabitants still talk of the collapse of '37, when one of the huge structures tore loose from its moorings to fall against furze-blotched rock, killing more than a hundred-fifty thousand. At such heights, dawn arrives before it does on the misty crags below. I waited on the great mirrored terraces for my flyer, an inverted image foot to foot with me, where, on another surface, I would have merely stood at the base of some elongated right shadow. From time to time I would go to the rail and gaze down at the shadow-pearled

rocks which had not yet vaulted into day, till vertigo drove
me away and I retreated to the cushioned area on which
rested those of us waiting to shuttle a fifth of a world
away—to a desert cut through by a famous river of liquid
galenium beneath whose shore in a room not unlike my
own lived a solitary hermit-philosopher, musician, and
crafter of miniature star-maps. Her work would allow me
to complete this particular mission$_1$. Travel engenders a
certain anxiety, no matter what assurances overlay it. Yet
in that part of the mind where signs both of anxiety and of
surety lodge their conceptual referents, the coherence of
the world to which travel is limited allows whatever anxiety or anticipations you have to *have* direction, to keep
course and discourse, to be.

But leaving a *world* at dawn? A job$_1$ about to begin
breaks up into little jobs$_2$, which, as they are finished,
cohere into a job$_1$ completed. My green-windowed con-
veyor lurched through sub-city caverns along old tracks.
Outside the purple light strips set into the wet rock suddenly glowed a soft, vivid red, lighting the backs of my
knuckles where I held the support bar—the sign, on that
part of the world, for morning. The tattoos on my hands,
which, on almost all parts of that world, one had to wear
simply to maintain decorum, would dissolve and vanish
with the first round of preparatory drugs I would take at
the space port, GI had assured me back on my arrival.
This job$_1$ had taken me to half a dozen spots among the
most populous sectors of the planet, that only seemed one
to me because of the three-quarters-standard gravity: hot
desert inns with great plastic windows looking out over
gray sands and up at a sky never lighter than star-pricked
indigo; dry ice canyons, roofed with hundred-year-old ribbed
and riveted plates, where day and night were at the whim
of the controller illuminating the greater and lesser blue
and yellow globes floating above; modern, freeform architectural compounds set on semi-airless rock, cassetted to
look and feel and sound and smell like the blue-veined,
dim, and somewhat ammonia-laden atmosphere that, apparently, the last batch of human colonists, fifty years
before, had called home.

As my conveyance turned down the dim, craggy h'Hol
Karvern, the light went from dawn red to daytime white
(morning was a great deal shorter in some parts of this

world than in others). As we passed the stainless steel gridwork rising over the rock face, which I had heard praised in six different geosectors of this world, I considered, still awash in morning thoughts, though the leisurely day about me had begun, my coming departure. Alone, borne in metal, plastic, and ceramic, toward the spaceport, I realized that in the brief months I had stayed here, I had made friends whose insights into my psychology had altered my life: whose sudden and affectionate advances had moved, in that society far more liberal than any I'd ever known, into a comradely sexuality that had first frightened me and then freed me to deal far more realistically with that of my own world's rooms and runs. I had read tractati written here of a complexity to reorganize my whole view of woman's place in an expanding universe, eaten meals of a simplicity that had made me learn things about my human tongue that, on Velm, I might never have discovered. And why do I tell you about leaving it, and not the life-changing simplicities that were the world itself? Because that morning departure, fifteen or seventeen years ago, is all, really, I can name of it. The rest is only its synopsized results. Since its cities and its people had no names (only its streets and geosectors bore labels), in a year's time or less I could not even recall the *number* of that world!

To leave one part of a world in order to visit another is to indulge in a transformation of signs, their appearances, their meanings, that, however violent, still, because of the coherence of the transformative system itself, partakes of a logic, a purely geographical order, if not the more entailed connections lent by ecological or social factors: here they do it one way, there they do it another—with no doubt as to the identity of the antecedents of both "its." But to leave a world, and to leave it at dawn, thus delaying all possibility of what one might learn in a day, is to experience precisely the problematics of that identity at its most intense: to see that identity shatter, fragment, and to realize that its solidity was always an illusion, and that infinite spaces between those referential shards are more opaque to direct human apprehension than all the star-flooded vacuum. "To leave a world, you have to forget so much of it," is the truism, if not the cliché, constant among the workers of the Web, or indeed, among any other world-bounding profession₁. To leave a world at dawn, however, is to know how much you can want to remember; and to realize how much, because of the cultural and conceptual grid a world casts over our experience of it, we are victims to that truth against all will, once we tear loose from it into night.

"The dawn of space travel. . . ." Has that phrase already been loosed in these pages? (Certainly anyone familiar with any of the numerous histories of the Web will likely have encountered, somewhere or other, the equally common apothegm: "The dawn of space travel is the dawn of woman.") To look at any such generalization closely, however, is to ensnare oneself in endless confusion: woman, space travel, morning—none are simple concepts; none have simple histories. And put in any combination, their complexities multiply. The dawn of space travel, for example, appears as a phrase in a number of old Earth texts dating from well before humans even reached their own moon, which makes it a bit problematic deciding just what it was supposed to refer to. Later commentators, of course, used the phrase to refer exclusively to humanity's interplanetary ventures within its own solar system, so that dawn, in that particular metaphor, is associated with precisely that fount of solarcentricism my alien acquaintance mentioned in the light of Aurigae. Still later commentators used it to mean the first hundred-fifty years standard of interstellar travel. At any rate, in the light of the suns of six-thousand-plus worlds, "dawn" becomes (another) rather fuzzy-edged phenomenon. Add to this the extreme locality of the use of morning/dawn as a metaphor for commencement/birth, and the whole notion crumbles. Indeed, on those sections of those worlds where morning is a metaphor for beginnings, or is associated with creativity—as it is throughout the oestern half of the Fayne-Vyalou (the Fayne half) which is, on my world, my home—someone like myself is usually and quickly comfortable. Not that other meanings of other phenomena are similarly consistent, but such a metaphor is a point of contact from which consistency can be constructed. Even on those parts of those worlds where morning is traditionally a metaphor for death, termination, and destruction—such as Veyed on equatorial Pyrel, where, due to tidal forces in the magma just under the surface, the tremendous quakes that crack the gray-brown rock are almost always a morning occurrence ("The high towers come down at dawn . . ." begins a Veyedishke epic song-cycle that still makes me weep) —the simple inversion provides the logical correspondence point among the further complexities by which the culture manifests its conceptual systems. Yet when any set of signs is loosed from a world, it always surprises how much their form and significance may change. (In a sense, keeping clear the sense of the changing tastes throughout those changes is the ID's prime job$_1$.) Words, the Web, woman, world—all of these have their nebulous position in a cloud of shifting meanings.

But are you ever more aware of the shifts, the displacements, the uncertainties that, together, make up what we call meanings, than you are when you are on no world, but rather half-asleep on some freighter or shuttle between them, or relaxing on some station circling above dim scimitars of dawn and evening, the bright and black alternates of day and night on the planetary disk below, while you search for some morning lost light-years away?

Through half-conscious dozing, I became aware of yellow fading slowly to green, while hearing the first three digits of my home-mail routing number recited in my sister Alyxander's voice, followed by the sudden stench of burnt plastic—

I sat up in the dark, while restraining straps pulled gently at my knees and shoulders. My call number had rung and, only half thinking, I'd answered.

I was wondering where I should go, but there was a faint bong: and off in the dimness, a woman looked up from her desk.

"Marq Dyeth." She didn't smile.

After a moment I said: "Japril." Could I say that she was not whom I was expecting to see?

"Marq," she said, "I'm sorry. But our experiment didn't work. Marta, Ynn, and I conferred, and we all agreed: it was just too dangerous. That's why we took Rat away. She had to go, Marq. If there'd been any way to let the two of you—"

"What?" I said. "What? What? What? What—?" There was the length of a breath or three between each. The third cracked shrilly. And two of them were whispered so quietly my lips didn't even brush sound. Japril waited out them all. Yet each felt as stupid in my mouth as the whole cascade of flustered interrogation would have read without pacing, dynamics, or inflection, as all I'd nearly managed to forget in my search for a forgotten morning now raged back. "*Why*—?"

"You saw how your city reacted, Marq. Cultural Fugue was only . . . who knows how far away. You've seen the response from his merely leaving and returning to the place over one day."

"Japril," I said, with the articulation born of a despair that was too total to be experienced as such, "a world is a big place. And a city is a *very* small one—"

"I'm sorry. We can't have the two of you there," she said. "We can't have the two of you together yet."

"What . . . ?" It stuttered in my mind, unanswerable.

"How do you feel?"

Which seemed the most preposterous and idiotic of questions she might have asked then. "I don't feel anything—or rather, I feel as if some giant claw has come down and ripped away all feeling . . ." Trickling into the wound was the little spill of language, already tuned to that surprising degree of articulation that had nothing to do with him, me. I looked at my shadowed hands. "I'm in a kind of shock. I suppose I'm too numb to notice particular symptoms." I looked up at her. "It's like the switches in my head that allow the proper emotions to come through to let me function have been shorted closed or else jammed and smashed that way, so that I believe I *can* function, yes, but without nuance or color to what I perceive or do. From time to time I suppose women look at me and flick one tongue or another as if trying to figure out whether I'm really there or not. And I think perhaps they're right to doubt. Japril—" I moved suddenly forward in my restraining web.

She jumped a little.

"—you know that even for an ordinary, human, homosexual male, my sexual map is somewhat unusual. In general youth and fine features have never been particularly attractive to me. And what in most is a genital focus, in me seems to be divided between hands, genitals, certain facial features, feet—"

"It was bitten nails and pockmarks, if I recall—"

"Bitten nails in humans and strong claws in evelmi," I

said. "Pitted human skin and a particular dark shade of evelm scales—they go together, somehow. In me. But Japril, do you know what any of that *means*? I mean, can *you* know anything about my home, my world, the universe in which I live? It's a beautiful universe, Japril, wondrous and the more exciting because no one has written plays and poems and built sculptures to indicate the structure of desire I negotiate every day as I move about in it. It's a universe where hands and faces are all luminous, all attractive, all open for infinite contemplation, not only the ones that are sexual and obsessive but the ones that are ordinary and even ugly, because they still belong to the categories where the possibility of the sexual lies. It's a universe where what is built, what is written, what has been made, makes hands hold the beauty they do; and what is thought, or felt, or wondered over is marvelous because someone has clutched their hands, or held them very still, or merely moved them slightly during the thinking or feeling of it— Oh, no: don't think I find all bitten nails attractive and all unbitten ones without interest. I have half a dozen categories within each of these groupings, now for the shape of the thumb's first joint, now for the fullness or stubbiness of the little finger, now by width or narrowness of knuckle, now by the thickness of cuticle, among which, in my journeys from one to the other, desire—or repulsion—may surprise me at any turn. And yet the revealed line between quick and crown remains the border on one side of which, far more than the other, desire lies. But I say I have categories of hand, of nail, of finger? I have ways of categorizing whole geosectors: this one or the other on this world or that. I know on the hot area of Ice-Mond IX, where social decorum insists all women wear light, white gloves in public, the habit of nail-biting turns out to be much more pervasive in both females and males than in the Fodrath Sector of Clinamen 14, where, if you ask some woman who does indulge the habit, she will tell you, laughing, of a parent making her sit on her hands as a child whenever she raised her fingers to her mouth. You see, besides the coordinates the Web lays out for us, I have my own map of the universe, where (though I only visited it for a day) Trynid is privileged because near its northern pole all the human children have retractable metal claws grafted into their fingertips on both hands, while only twenty kilometers to the south, where the custom of enclawing has not been taken up, nearly three out of five by my count of both adults and children gnaw on their own. Oh, I speculate on causes, run through correlations—but what I'm talking about, Japril, is information, some of it logical, some of it mythical, some of it in error, and much of it, yes, no doubt merely wrong or right. But it's information beautiful yet useless to anyone but me, or someone like me, information with an appetite at its base as all information has, yet information to confound the Web and not to be found in any of its informative archives."

"Mmmm," Japril said. "I wouldn't doubt it."

"My universe, Japril, is marked by the tips of claws and fingers at every point, touched by them everywhere, you might say—and could *only* say it of mine, but not, at least in the same way, of some handful of worlds where breasts or buttocks or baskets were the marked monuments to lust. Fingertips organize my movement through any crowd, become points of frustration when, say, a thumb is hidden in a fist by a passing human or a claw is submerged in a foot-trough the moment I happen to glance over at an evelm, where a chin was turned out of the light, or shadows lay too thickly over some great woman lumbering by on all sixes. Hands and claws told for me endless stories of the origins and labors of the women who bear them; but more important, they made tales unnecessary because each could inscribe its own present lyric by any one of a myriad gestures made before me. Oh yes, beauty passed me going up on any number of lifts, as I was going down; yes, I wondered why I could not know the bearers of them all. But everyone I knew, everyone I know, even you, Japril, I could identify if, say, I only saw a finger. A small universe to live in? Oh, no! It extended between stars and other worlds, wherever there were humans and a good many aliens besides. It's a rare universe, Japril, a rich universe, an extraordinarily generous universe in its pleasures and sadnesses and passing ecstasies to dazzle; and a walk down any human or evelm street was as wonderful as a trip to the night's rim and back—walks and trips that have now lined how many light-years with as much pleasure as I had learned to read in the running of my own city. I used to think, Japril, that were I ever to

excrete some text on my life the way, say, my seven-times
great-grandmother did in her memoirs—oh, nothing so
diffuse, I hope—still, the pleasure, the joy, the value for
others would be the revelation of all my world's marvels
and corners and hues of horn and chitin, all that make it
private, rich, terrible, and familiar—"

"Sounds obsessive," Japril said. "How did you ever
manage to get any work done?"

"The question for me, Japril," I said, "is how any of
the rest of you ever found *energy* to work in your gray,
gray universe. But I suppose your universe is finally no
grayer than mine, controlled and mapped by whatever
gives it reasonable form to you. Perhaps the greatest generosity of my universe is that in so much it's congruent
with the worlds of others, which I suppose is finally just
one with the generosity of my evelm parents, who thought
my unique position among humans quite charming and
were proud of it, and my human parents, who from time
to time worried if, as distinct from more usually sexually
oriented males, gay or straight, I might not encounter
some social difficulty, say, of the same sort as I might have
had in some societies had I been a nail-biter myself. But
both spoke, both agreed on who I was, that I was a ripple
that shored their stream, so that their universe, with all its
idiosyncratic wonder, unique to my eyes, has still, always,
seemed a part of mine—at least it was until you thrust *him*
into my world—this male who, by all rights, should not
even be alive; who, as far as I can tell, is hardly prepared
to live, but whose knuckles and nails and mouth and knees
and jaw and genitals and the ridges of his shoulders, the
horn of his foot, the hollow above his clavicle, the width of
his thumb, and the ligament lining behind his knee, and a
certain roughness to his voice resolve all the dispersed
yearnings that have mauled me, happy, through my universe—so pleased at its variety of satisfactions and fruitful
distress—within the integrity of a single body.

"And now you've taken him away. . . ." I took a breath.
"Desire isn't appeased by its object, Japril, only irritated
into something more than desire that can join with the
stars to inform the chaotic heavens with sense. To remove
the agent of such astonishment after it's been dropped,
like some heavy, hot isotope into an already smoldering
and ancient pile . . . ? What you've done is strike all

amazement and logic from the set, Japril! You've stolen—
you've practically destroyed—my home. The soiled hand
of a working woman, whether it ends in evelm horn or
human, means nothing now. Reticulations of scale or pit?
Fingers can't point to anything anymore. And without
such indications—oh, I still walk where I walked, look
where I looked, but where I saw what once seemed wonderful, I see so little now—I *feel* so little. And the little I
feel mocks all I know there is to be felt. I'll masturbate,
and not enjoy it. I'll couple in the runs and feel no pleasure and, even less, no community when this one whispers, 'Thank you,' or that one presses my arm afterwards
with some gesture habit has made me read as caring. And
as for individual sexual relations, *they* are inconceivable.
You see—"

She looked startled again; and I'd felt my voice tense.

"You've blotted the rich form of desire from my life
and left me only some vaguely eccentric behaviors that
have grown up to integrate so much pleasure into the
mundane world around me. What text could I write now?
It's as though I cannot even *remember* what I once desired! All I can look for now, when I have the energy, is
lost desire itself—and I look for it by clearly inadequate
means. At best such an account as I might write would
read like the life of anyone else, with, now and again, a
bizarre and interruptive incident, largely mysterious and
completely mystified—at least that's what it has become
without the day-to-day, moment-to-moment web of wanting that you have unstrung from about my universe. Without it, all falls apart, Japril. In a single gesture you've
turned me into the most ordinary of human creatures and
at once left me an obsessive, pleasureless eccentric, trapped
in a set of habits which no longer have reason because
they no longer lead to reward. And if I had enough self-
confidence, in the midst of this bland continual chaos into
which you've shunted me, for hate, I should hate you. But
I don't have it."

"It's a silly thing to say, I know," Japril said, nervously. "But you love Rat Korga, don't you? And Rat
loves—"

"Love . . . ?"

She blinked.

"A silly thing? To say? Japril, it's idiotic! I was only

with him for the single turn of a world between its suns—a third of which time I slept. And in the time I was awake, I wasn't in any state near level-headed or responsible enough to negotiate the rapids of desire at the confluence level of love. In love? How could I know? But given the situation, is it so much to have wanted time enough to find out?"

"It wasn't so much. But sometimes what's little in local terms overwhelms in the larger view—" Suddenly she reached over to slip something out of one of her sleeve pockets—was it a small gold bar, with knobs at both ends?

"Japril—" I took another breath, and realized that my chest hurt in the straps around me. "What, what, *what* do you want from me? What now—?"

"I wanted to—to see you. To talk to you. But—I'm sorry, Marq." She stood up from her desk. "Good morning."

And she—and the desk—vanished, leaving me in the confused dimness of my harness, my drugs, my ignorance. Where, among all the six thousand and their many moons, might she have been that she could end our interview with, "Good morning"? A *good* morning? A bad morning? A morning whose badness is organized by everyone's expectations of good? A night without edges or end, where one can only throw memory back onto the round, simple surfaces of worlds, whose meager rotations create the temporal interruptions, morning and night, to which we fix the cyclic expectations of renewal, commencement, ending, beginning.

Good morning?

Nowhere, I suppose, does the metaphor crumble as spectacularly as it does on Klyvos, about which I had heard for several years before a job$_1$ took me there. Klyvos keeps a single face towards its sun and is therefore surrounded by an unmoving band of half-light: really, whether you call it dawn or evening, you still distort the part it plays in this world's conceptual pattern. In that unchanging shadow-band, storms constantly crash and flicker over uneven orange hills at the equator, or over black fissured ice-fields in the north, or along green glaciers to the south. Its dozen native races, though none has ever reached true technological competency, would travel there, nevertheless, from both night side and day side, now to conduct violent intertribal rituals, now to hold genocidal intratribal war. Klyvos is a world of thousands on thousands of sub-

language groups, mostly native, but—now humans have
been there for three hundred years—many human ones as
well. Almost all, however, contain some cognate of "chyani,"
which is their oldest root for that eternal circle of morning.
And in one culture after another, it serves as a metaphor
for chaos, for violence leading to no end, for Cultural
Fugue itself—not so much destruction ending in death,
but rather the perpetual and unremitting destruction of
both nature and intelligence run wild and without focus,
where anything so trivial and natural as either death or
birth is irrelevant.

To turn from the Klyvotic dawn—immobile, divisive,
chaotic—allows the question with which we began—"What
is morning?" —to be asked with a greater order of purity,
if not intensity.

And the final image I am left with—though it does not
really *answer* the question any more than does the rest of
this divagation—is from that odd hour, on a colony ship
plying between stars, taking me from job_1 to job_1, either
bringing me light-years closer to home or moving me
light-years further away; I can no longer recall which:

A bell through humming haze. A shoulder shrug, a
flexed foot, the pressure of lid squeezed to lid identified
for me sleep's end. And the bell, again or for the first
time, I was unsure.

I turned in my webbing, and the ribbons, in response
to chemical changes in my skin, began to fall away. Strung
up in webs, each thirty-five centimeters from the next,
two thousand humans hung in drugged sleep. The woman
diagonal to me had her hand thrust through her net to the
forearm at an odd angle.

As I pulled myself out of mine, I took her arm and
tugged it—once I'd woken up and found my own arm
caught that way: *my* shoulder and upper arm were pained
and stiff for three days.

She turned a little in her hanging; her arm pulled
back inside her net and folded itself around under her
breasts.

I floated free of my hangings to move among the
sleeping colonists in the vast hangar, run through with
glimmering threads of light.

I pulled myself among the dozing passengers toward the long, bright split in the black plastic wall. I pushed through into the striped corridor.

The bell again.

And the orange strip-light just behind the handrail I was holding turned blue, which, on the great colonizing vessels that have, finally, taken me on over half of my assignments₁, is how *they* signal for "morning." The change in the light registered clearly enough to make me realize I was still drugged. I reached for the next handhold, unsteady either for the first time or, more likely, free enough of the quickly decomposing drugs to realize I *was* unsteady— and a memory of the woman's arm I had straightened suddenly clouded. Had I really done it, or was it a half-waking dream about a ship-waking years before when my own arm had been cramped, and memory and anticipation and waking to no pain all had involved themselves to produce the waking, drugged dream?

I pulled myself along the railing, along the corridor, curving away through weightlessness. Once I stopped for six, seven, eight breaths.

A faint click came from a speaker plate just beyond the white plastic padding and before the black padding took up again: "Marq Dyeth, please continue your morning exercise circuit. Please continue, Marq Dyeth."

As I pulled myself on through the blue glow, my attention would snag, now on the design patterned into the support posts on the hand-rail I grasped, now on the hall's converging curves ahead, now on the movement of a muscle at the back of my own shoulder which I would feel shifting on the underside of my own skin while I reached for the next hold. Now and again any or all of these sensations appeared to contain detailed locations for all knowledge about the play of the infinite universe along whose tiny segment I hauled myself; and the dazzle of its totality threatened to halt me in fatigued wonder.

"Marq Dyeth, please . . ."

I hauled on. The timed drugs had released me from deep-suspension coma long enough for these bodily exercises to prepare me, after a much lighter sleep, for a proper waking. (I would depart, on a shuttle, a world away from any of the other colonists.) I was by the slit again.

The entire circuit, I knew, was just over three hundred meters. Though individual hand-hauls had seemed to take hours, I felt as though I had completed the entire round in less than a minute.

Exhausted, I let myself drift back through the slit, into the huge cool chamber of hanging sleepers.

My own webbing floated near. I grabbed it, pulled myself up against it, felt the smooth ribbons against my face, grappled at them with my toes. I got one foot, kicking and kicking, inside. I felt myself slide within.

"Marq Dyeth, please fold your arms around in front of you so that you do not get caught in a damaging sleep position."

Indeed, one hand had caught for a moment in the net. I pulled it free. As I slid it around under my other arm and under my naked male breasts, I felt myself fall away into the next stage of consciousness—although, really, I knew no more of what it was than I had of the stage before I awoke, still I knew that morning, whatever it was, was over.

When I woke again, it would be day.